PENGUIN CLASSICS

THREE ELIZABETHAN
DOMESTIC TRAGEDIES

Keith Sturgess has been Lecturer in English Literature at the Universities of Khartoum and Lancaster. At present he is Director of the Nuffield Theatre Studio, Lancaster and Head of the Department of Theatre Studies. He has also edited *Three Plays* by John Ford for Penguins and is currently publishing a book on Jacobean Private Theatre.

Three Elizabethan Domestic Tragedies

EDITED WITH AN INTRODUCTION
BY KEITH STURGESS

Anon
ARDEN OF FAVERSHAM

Anon
A YORKSHIRE TRAGEDY

Thomas Heywood
A WOMAN KILLED
WITH KINDNESS

PENGUIN BOOKS

Penguin Books Ltd, Harmondsworth, Middlesex, England
Viking Penguin Inc., 40 West 23rd Street, New York, New York 10010, U.S.A.
Penguin Books Australia Ltd, Ringwood, Victoria, Australia
Penguin Books Canada Ltd, 2801 John Street, Markham, Ontario, Canada L3R 1B4
Penguin Books (N.Z.) Ltd, 182–190 Wairau Road, Auckland 10, New Zealand

First published in Penguin Books 1969
Reissued in Penguin Classics 1985

Printed and bound in Great Britain by
Cox & Wyman Ltd, Reading
Typeset in Monotype Bembo

Contents

Acknowledgements

I am grateful to Miss K. M. Lea and Mr G. R. Proudfoot for reading and commenting on the Introduction; to Mr M. P. Jackson for allowing me to read his highly informative B.Litt. thesis, 'Material for an Edition of *Arden of Faversham*' (Oxford); and to my wife for typing, proof-reading and acting as midwife.

K. S.

Introduction

Some time let gorgeous Tragedy
In scepter'd pall come sweeping by,
Presenting Thebes, or Pelops' line,
Or the tale of Troy divine,
Or what (though rare) of later age
Ennobled hath the buskined stage.

MILTON's diffidence about his country's achievements in tragedy probably had more to do with style and treatment than with subject-matter. Among the Elizabethans, Tragedy had mostly continued to bear the 'scepter'd pall', its characters were princely and its actions heroic. But a small, well-defined group of tragedies marked themselves off from the critically conventional by attempting to portray the unheroic crimes and passions of ordinary life. These were the domestic tragedies, in their purest form murder plays, of which half a dozen or so survive. In the eighteenth century they helped to inspire a new interest in bourgeois tragedy, the fashion for which was carried to France and Germany, merging with the growing realism of European narrative art. In many ways these Elizabethan experiments anticipate our twentieth-century 'kitchen-sink' drama.

There were probably many domestic tragedies which have simply not survived. One of them, for example, was *The Lamentable Tragedy of the Page of Plymouth*, a collaborative work by Jonson and Dekker, payment for which is recorded in the diary of a famous man of theatre business, Philip Henslowe.* Those which have survived are

---

*H. H. Adams, in Appendix A of *English Domestic or Homiletic Tragedy, 1575–1642*, New York, 1943, lists over twenty lost plays whose titles suggest they were domestic tragedies.

the ones reprinted here together with three or four others:
the anonymous *A Warning for Fair Women* (published
1599); *Two Lamentable Tragedies* (published 1601, possibly
by a mysterious Yarrington who may merely have been
the play's scribe); *The English Traveller* (published 1633,
Heywood's second attempt at a domestic tragedy which
is not a murder play); and perhaps Dekker, Ford and
Rowley's *The Witch of Edmonton* (published 1658, written
a generation earlier). George Wilkins's tragicomedy, *The
Miseries of Enforced Marriage* (published 1607) is an interesting near relation of *A Yorkshire Tragedy*.

Of these plays, only Heywood's two tragedies have
fictional plots. The others are all dramatizations of actual,
historical events, in each case a sensational murder; and
the plays themselves are anxious to emphasize their non-
fictional nature. Their title-pages speak of their 'truth',
by which they mean not imaginative truth but literal
truth – truth to life, not truth to Life. The personification
of Tragedy near the end of *A Warning for Fair Women*
claims 'Now of truth I sing' and later refers to 'true and
home-born tragedy'. The events were real and they concerned English people. And in each case the murder
stories had received characteristic, journalistic treatment
outside the plays themselves. The events behind *Arden of
Faversham*, the murder in 1551 of Thomas Arden of
Faversham by his wife and her accomplices, are recounted
in detailed fashion by the play's source, Holinshed's
Chronicles (which gave Shakespeare the plot for a more
heroic murder play, *Macbeth*); it is reported briefly in
Stowe's *Chronicle*; and there is extant a ballad on the
same theme, 'The Complaint and Lamentation of Mrs
Arden of Faversham of Kent', which is probably based on
the play. The crime of *A Warning for Fair Women*, again
the murder of a husband by his wife and her accomplice,
is reported in a pamphlet of 1573, *A Brief Discourse*; in a

ballad, 'The Woeful Lamentation of Mrs Anne Saunders';
and in Antony Munday's collection called *A View of
Sundry Examples* (1580), which recounts twenty such
murders. *A Yorkshire Tragedy*'s real-life story reached a
Jacobean reading and play-going public in two pamphlets,
a ballad and two plays; besides being recorded in Stowe's
Chronicle.

Apart, then, from Heywood's two domestic tragedies,
these plays are in the first instance journalistic in flavour,
even if not always purveying entirely up-to-date matter.
They have a sort of documentary authenticity. And in at
least some cases, the plays were serving the strict journalistic purpose of conveying fresh news material. *A Yorkshire Tragedy* shows this particularly well. Its villain/hero's
murder of two of his children occurred in April 1605. In
June appeared a pamphlet recounting the crime and ending with the fact of the murderer's being in prison. In
August he was executed. At some stage the play was
created directly out of the pamphlet and like the pamphlet
it ends on a note of indecision, with justice not having
been meted out to the prisoner and with the wife resolv-
ing to do all she can to save her husband from execution.
It is reasonable to infer that the play was written and
staged before the end of the story was known, that is,
within three months of the actual murders. The play was
retailing sensational news of the moment, and the performing company, the King's Men, was cashing in on the
topical interest in the crime. Nothing could be more
different from the noble intentions of high tragedy or the
durability of serious art. The loss of many of these plays
is undoubtedly linked with their journalistic function.

However, as with the popular press of today, the writers
of domestic tragedies based on real-life events saw nothing
inconsistent in titillating the audience with sensational
stories on one hand, and providing overt moral instruc-

tion based on those stories on the other. These plays, in fact, properly belong with the popular kind of didactic material known as 'warning' literature. In the sixteenth century, the idea of the Tragedy of Fortune, exhibiting an arbitrary change for the worse in man's material position to demonstrate the vanity of human wishes, was being replaced by the more moral notion of the tragedy which exhibits God's retributive justice on the vicious and unwary. The 'warning' literature served up practical examples of just this, deriving authority from the real or assumed authenticity of its narrative material. Hence the plethora of murder pamphlets and collections of crime stories such as Munday's, with its significant title: *A View of Sundry Examples*. Observe and do otherwise, the writer said, at the same time as an unacknowledged voice said, observe and enjoy. In the 'warning' literature writers happily combined the triple intention of reporting, moralizing and titillating, and produced a wealth of sub-literature of considerable interest to the literary specialist and the social historian.

The tone of the opening lines of the pamphlet on which *A Yorkshire Tragedy* is based exactly conveys this complex impulse:

There hath happened of late within the county of York, not far from Wakefield, a murder so detestable that were it not it desires record for example sake, humanity could wish it rather utterly forgot, than any Christian heart should tremble with the remembrance of it.

The writer of this might easily earn for himself a job with a popular newspaper of today. He begins by emphasizing the topicality of his story – 'There hath happened of late'; slips in a little factual detail to establish authenticity – 'not far from Wakefield'; quickly adopts the note of righteous indignation which is the excuse for the piece – 'a murder so detestable'; openly expresses the didactic function of the exercise – 'it requires record for example sake' (i.e. this is a piece of 'warning' literature); and ends by dropping effectively emotive words to fill the reader with a glow of moral superiority – 'humanity' and 'any Christian heart'. And all this is designed to whet the interest.

This complexity of intention permeates the texture of the whole pamphlet which is patently intended for the bourgeois reader and calculated to appeal to that reader's taste. The domestic tragedies as a group are allied to this 'warning' literature and are a sub-section of it. *A Warning for Fair Women* in a curious way manages to separate the different intentions by presenting news-report and sensationalism by one technique and the moral message by another. News-report and sensationalism are presented through realistic portrayal of character and action; the moral message by allegory. The play moves abruptly from realism to allegory and back again. The title, of course, emphasizes its oneness with the other 'warning' literature.

The blurb on the title-page of *Arden of Faversham* outlines the intended moral effect of witnessing or reading this kind of play:

The Lamentable and true tragedy of M. Arden of Faversham of Kent. Who was most wickedly murdered by the means of his disloyal and wanton wife. . . . Wherein is showed the great malice and dissimulation of a wicked woman, the unsatiable desire of filthy lust and the shameful end of all murderers.

This brings out the lesson, points to the general application behind the particular circumstances, and finally alludes to the inevitability of punishment for the wicked. The punishment, implicitly, is guaranteed by the Christian scheme of things. In the course of the play, the theme of the influence of divine providence over the action becomes pronounced. Alice, Arden's wife, and her maid, Susan, try to destroy the evidence of their crime by washing Arden's blood from the floor:

SUSAN: The blood cleaveth to the ground and will not out.
ALICE: But with my nails I'll scrape away the blood. –
    The more I strive the more the blood appears.
SUSAN: What's the reason, mistress; can you tell?
ALICE: Because I blush not at my husband's death.

(xiv, 261–5)

As the murderers carry Arden's corpse into the field there is a sudden snow-fall which stops when they return and thus discloses their tracks and leads to their discovery. Alice recognizes the moral universe she lives in, she confesses, is repentant and begs forgiveness (assuming, incidentally, that she will go to Heaven). And thus she makes what is known as 'a scaffold speech', a characteristic moment in the domestic tragedy when the hero/villain undergoes a Christian repentance and thus himself underlines the simple ethos of the play. The ballads referred to earlier in connexion with *A Warning for Fair Women* and *Arden of Faversham* both take the form of the erring wife's lamentation and are a sort of 'scaffold speech'.

The marked religious awareness of these plays and their ethical pattern of sin, discovery, punishment and expectation of divine mercy has led to their being associated directly with the Morality play, the medieval, allegorical drama which itself developed out of the church sermon.* But the close dependency of the plays on their sources demonstrates that the playwrights were using those sources as they might use stories from the Italian *novelle* or the English chronicles. These plots were then inevitably shaped to conform to an ethical pattern of 'warning'

*See Adams, *passim*.

literature in general – often already present in the source material itself. To derive the domestic tragedy from the Morality play is to miss its journalistic aspect. And with regard to formal technique, the Morality play and murder play are utterly dissimilar, the former embodying moral and truth in allegory and personification (i.e. through deliberate generalization), the latter embodying moral truth in a representation of actual events (i.e. through realism).

Heywood's plays, *A Woman Killed with Kindness* and *The English Traveller*, are not journalistic, but in their sympathetic depiction of unheroic crimes in a middle-class English setting they clearly must be labelled domestic tragedies. Not relying on authentic story material and ignoring the sensationalism of bloody murder, the tragedy of his plays lies in the disruption of family unity itself, and especially in the breaking of marital bonds through infidelity. Marriage itself is his theme, both in these plays and elsewhere in his work.* Towards the end of the Jacobean period other playwrights wrote tragedies with citizen protagonists and with an evident interest in domestic relations – notably Ford and Middleton. And Webster's *The Duchess of Malfi* has perhaps some of the most poignant dramatic writing about domesticity in the whole period. But all the major dramatists outside Heywood sought the freedom of a foreign setting to give distance and colour to their tragic vision.

Although *Arden of Faversham* and *A Yorkshire Tragedy* have been attributed to Shakespeare, he does not seem to have turned his hand to the domestic tragedy either in the limited sense of the murder play or in the Heywoodian sense. All Shakespeare's tragedies depend for their intensity in part on a sense of disruption in family relationships.

*See M. Grivelet, *Thomas Heywood et le Drame Domestique Elizabethain*, Paris, 1957.

In *Hamlet* and *Lear* the loves of son for father, mother for son, daughter for father, are an intrinsic part of the play's meaning; but this aspect is always set off against an awareness of political and even cosmic disruption. Lear as father divides his possessions among his daughters; as king he divides his kingdom. In *Macbeth*, the hero's tyranny is only part of a dramatic pattern which includes his family relationship with Duncan and with Lady Macbeth. It is *Othello*, of the major tragedies, which most clearly focuses attention on the domestic situation, necessarily because of its emphasis on the private issues of jealousy and infidelity. This tragedy about a handkerchief has the least cosmic grandeur and the least sense of universal significance of all the major tragedies. But even here Shakespeare has taken care not to portray the common man. In the first scene in which he appears Othello claims his 'life and being / From men of royal siege [= rank]'. And the Cyprus locale is at the farthest remove from the home-born settings of orthodox domestic tragedy.*

A domestic tragedy, then, is a play with a sad end which seriously depicts crime and punishment in the lives of ordinary men, often dwelling on the disruption of normal family relationships. It is set in London or the provinces, and it teaches a simple moral lesson. This lesson is brought home to the audience by the authenticity, real or assumed, of the plot material. At its most extreme, the direct, moral effect of such a play is described by Hamlet:

> I've heard that guilty creatures at a play
> Have, by the very cunning of the scene,
> Been so struck to the soul, that presently
> They have proclaimed their malefactions.

*For the view that '*Othello* is eminently a domestic tragedy' see G. W. Knight's chapter on the play in *The Wheel of Fire*, Methuen, 1949.

Just such a proclamation is recorded by Heywood in his *Apology for Actors* where he claims that plays have discovered murders:

We will prove it by a domestic and home-born truth which within these few years happened. At Lin, in Norfolk, the then Earl of Sussex players acting the old History of Feyer Francis, and presenting a woman who, insatiately doting on a young gentleman, (the more securely to enjoy his affection) mischievously and secretly murdered her husband, whose ghost haunted her; and, at divers times, in her most solitary and private contemplations, in most horrid and fanciful shapes, appeared and stood before her. As this was acted, a towns-woman (till then of good estimation and report) finding her conscience (at this presentment) extremely troubled, suddenly screeched and cried out, 'Oh! my husband, my husband! I see the ghost of my husband fiercely threatening and menacing me!'

It transpired that the woman had murdered her husband seven years previously. The 'Feyer Francis' play evidently had a plot rather like that of *Arden of Faversham* and *A Warning for Fair Women*.

The Elizabethan theatre seems, retrospectively, to have been the inevitable provenance for this entirely new dramatic form, a form without warrant in classical or renaissance dramatic theory. It was inevitable because the theatre was popular, not aristocratic (at least in its youth); and unlike the practice in France or Spain there was a significant gap between it and the theoretical critic. The theorist had little influence over the emerging dramatic forms.

Critical writing about drama in England, as in other European countries, was dominated by a sense of class distinction. Traditionally, tragedy drew its events, characters and diction from the courts and palaces of the great. Originally owing to its derivation in Greece from religious ceremonies in honour of Dionysus, tragedy took its plot material from the legends about gods and heroes. Though Aristotle perhaps does not make a class distinction in describing his requirements for a tragic hero, renaissance commentators read into him an absolute demand for aristocratic birth. Only the courts of princes could furnish the splendid deeds and magnificent crimes consonant with the dignity and passion of tragedy. The common man, for his part, was a figure of fun or an object of social comment as far as the dramatist was concerned; his proper place was comedy. Sir Philip Sidney pursues a typical line in his *Defence of Poesy* when he declares that aristocracy and commoners should not mix in drama or the result would be the bastard form, tragicomedy.

Intuitively responding to its audience's interests and values, ignorant or scornful of theory, the Elizabethan theatre produced domestic tragedy, but did so with a ready awareness that it was doing something utterly unconventional. Most of these plays, in prologue or epilogue, apologize for their bareness of theme or style, deriving authority, where possible, from the authenticity of their material. Heywood, unable to claim literal truth, makes a typical apology in his Prologue to *The English Traveller*, forswearing the extravagant embellishment of the heroic play:

> A strange play you are like to have, for know
> We use no drum, nor trumpet, nor dumb show;
> No combat, marriage, not so much today
> As song, dance, masque to bombast out a play.

Heywood is to try 'if once bare lines will bear it'. Compare this with the similar disclaimers in the Prologue to *A Woman Killed with Kindness* and the Epilogue to *Arden of Faversham*, 'this naked tragedy / Wherein no filed points are foisted in'. Most fascinating of all in this respect is the Induction of *A Warning for Fair Women* (a play in the style of *Arden of Faversham*) where fun is poked at the more extravagant forms of Senecan tragedy.

It is difficult to estimate the popularity of the domestic tragedy on the Elizabethan stage, but it is undeniable that in its narrowest form of the murder play it had disappeared from the boards long before the closing of the theatres in 1642. The exotic form of tragicomedy, popularized by Beaumont and Fletcher, the arrival of the upper-class theatre and the general turning towards more sophisticated sensations than those offered by home-born drama all contributed towards the disappearance of the domestic tragedy. And after the closure, the aristocratic theatre of the Restoration with its penchant for the heroic play could hardly have been more different from the context in which domestic drama flourished in the last decade of the sixteenth century and the first of the seventeenth. It was not, in fact, till the second quarter of the eighteenth century that social and theatrical conditions were again right for the re-emergence of a home-born, bourgeois tragedy; and significantly the writers of it turned to the Elizabethan efforts in the genre for patterns and plots. All three plays reprinted here were rewritten in the eighteenth century: Aaron Hill re-created *A Yorkshire Tragedy* as *The Fatal Extravagance* (published 1726 under the name of J. Mitchell) which was a leader in the new fashion; George Lillo adapted *Arden of Faversham* (published posthumously in 1762); and Benjamin Victor turned *A Woman Killed with Kindness* into *The Fatal Error* (never acted, published 1776).

A comparison of these reworkings with their originals demonstrates forcefully the fact that a new sensibility, that of a new age, had gone into their making. In Lillo's *Arden*, Alice has been married to Arden against her will, having loved Mosby in her youth; Mosby's plan to kill Arden is repellent to her; she fails to kill her husband in

his bed and in her remorse is reconciled to him; at his
murder she tries to defend him and his death drives her
mad. This is an obvious sentimentalization of the Elizabethan Alice who single-mindedly and callously pursues
her husband's death; and there is a similar change of spirit
towards sentimentality in the other adaptations. Far from
being guilty of adultery, Victor's Anne Frankford, who
has become Lady Frankford, is ravished by Wendoll (now
Cranmore) and only conceals the deed from her husband
for the sake of the children. In these eighteenth-century
adaptations we are in a world of optimism in which Fate,
not character, creates the tragic situation, man being in-
nately good. But the Elizabethan domestic tragedies
face evil squarely, allowing their sense of it to be alle-
viated only by a belief in the possibility of Christian
redemption. Only the ends of the Elizabethan domestic
tragedies are likely to appear sentimental to a modern
audience.*

Despite this change of sensibility from one age to
another, there is nevertheless a direct link via Hill's
Fatal Extravagance between the Elizabethan domestic
tragedy, its eighteenth-century counterparts, and the
export of the genre to France and Germany. Lillo's most
famous play in this kind, *The London Merchant*, was
translated into French in 1748 and formed the basis of
Lessing's *Miss Sara Sampson*. So that in part, the Elizabethan domestic tragedy is linked with the emergence in
the eighteenth century of a bourgeois drama which itself
made possible the arrival of Ibsen and the 'problem' play
in the nineteenth century.

The important characteristic linking these phases of
European drama across three centuries is the serious depic-

* The relationship of eighteenth-century domestic tragedy to its
Elizabethan counterpart is examined by E. Bernbaum, *The Drama
of Sensibility*, Gloucester, Mass., 1915, pp. 33–7.

tion of the common man in a faithfully realized domestic and social ambience. The Elizabethan exponents of the domestic tragedy were little concerned to reflect critically on the society which they depicted (though this is not entirely true of Heywood); but with due decorum they were led by their subject-matter to present the social and domestic setting realistically. It is this strain of realism, permeating style and presentation, which is the most immediate source of these plays' aesthetic pleasure for a modern audience. We shall not find in them an illumination of man's struggle against the cosmic forces which seek to overwhelm him; nor shall we find an affirmation of the greatness of man in adversity. On the contrary, human nature in these plays is frail, aspirations are sordid, and passions are self-destructive. And this raises the larger, critical question: Can drama which attempts a sort of realism be tragedy at all? Might not 'domestic tragedy' be a contradiction in terms? In these plays we see the Elizabethans doing what Hamlet encouraged but what seldom was done, the holding of a mirror up to nature. And the reflection is surprisingly modern-looking, except that the modern tragic hero is forced to go on living; life is his penance, not death.

*

The influence *Arden of Faversham* had on *A Warning for Fair Women* suggests that if not the first of these plays it was an important early example. Thomas Arden, the title-character of the play, was one of the chief citizens of the town of Faversham in Kent and in 1548 he served as the town's mayor. He was involved in the business of the distribution of confiscated church property, had himself acquired the grant of some of the land of Faversham Abbey, and had been given the lucrative post of Commissioner of the Customs of the port of Faversham. On 15

February 1551 he was murdered by his wife Alice, Mosby her lover, and their accomplices. The murderers were quickly apprehended and executed, and the events aroused considerable interest in London. The story of the murder was recorded briefly in the Wardmote Book of Faversham and at greater length (with some details different) in the 1577 edition of Holinshed's *Chronicles* (reprinted as Appendix A). From these accounts one gets a circumstantial picture of a sordid, domestic affair of marital infidelity, murder, social pretension and acquisitiveness.

Arden of Faversham first appeared in print, anonymously, in 1592. The play is patently based on Holinshed's account, following it in detail and on occasion echoing it verbally. It must therefore have been written between 1577 and 1592, and no more precise dating has been possible on internal grounds except that the relative sophistication of the play suggests a date nearer the end than the beginning of that period. The authorship question remains similarly unresolved. The play has been ascribed to the three most important playwrights on the London scene at the time of the play's printing – Kyd, Marlowe and Shakespeare. Kyd's extant output is so small that stylistic comparison between it and *Arden* is nearly impossible, and his editor, F. S. Boas, suggests that the closely parallel passages in *Arden* and *The Spanish Tragedy* prove not a common authorship for the two plays but an imitation of one by the other. Certainly, the realistic vein of *Arden* is at the farthest possible remove from the Senecan rhetoric of *The Spanish Tragedy*. The case for Marlowe also largely rests on parallel passages, this time in *Arden* and *Edward II*; and it is true that some of the verse of *Arden* has, in its manner and quality, a Marlovian ring. The ascription to Shakespeare was made in 1770 by a Faversham man, Edward Jacob, who edited the play. An earlier suggestion of Shakespeare's authorship was noted by W. W. Greg who showed a probable misprinting in a play catalogue of 1656 which, if corrected, ascribes *Arden* to Shakespeare.* But the catalogue postdates the play by over half a century and is certainly wrong in other ascriptions it makes. The best internal evidence for Shakespeare's authorship is the realistic characterization of the play, quite unlike that of *The Spanish Tragedy* or of most of Marlowe's work. Collaboration by two or all three of these playwrights has also been suggested, and what undoubtedly causes the anxiety to find a major author for the play is its intrinsic merit and maturity at a time when Elizabethan dramatic form was still a thing of experiment and trial and error.

The play does what it intends to with a remarkable sureness of touch. Its poise can be gauged from the subtle changes it makes in Holinshed's account. Holinshed or his reporter tells the story without flourish and with an almost complete absence of the sort of intrusive, moral exhortation which characterizes the murder pamphlets. What gave the story its particular interest was not the mere fact of the murder of husband by wife, but the number of attempts necessary before the murder was successfully achieved. A killing in passion was one thing, but the cold-blooded contrivings and plottings that went into the killing of Arden were another. And so the episodic and cumulative nature of the narrative material is not accidental to the story's shape but essential to it. This episodic shape the play retains; but it departs from its source in a number of ways in the interests of creating a play rather than a dramatized narrative. It invents the figure of Franklin, Arden's honest friend, who functions in various ways – as an *alter ego* for Arden enabling him to externalize his emotions and anxieties without too much reliance being placed on the soliloquy; as a choric figure,

*'Shakespeare and *Arden of Feversham*', *Review of English Studies*. xxi, 1945, pp. 134–6.

interpreting situations for the audience; and as an excuse
for Arden to leave home and stay some time in London.
Several episodes in the play are independent of the source,
usually making precise what is left vague in Holinshed.
For example, the half-comic, half-chilling scenes with the
Ferryman in the mist (scenes xi and xii) in which Arden
unwittingly avoids ambush, replace Holinshed's: 'Now
Black Will stirred in the morning betimes, but he missed
the way and tarried in a wrong place. . . . By reason that
Black Will lost his way, Master Arden escaped yet once
again.' In the same way, the failure of Black Will to kill
Arden at St Paul's (scene iii) is given added dramatic point
by the episode, independent of Holinshed, of the apprentice and his stall. The subplot of Michael and the Painter's
rivalry for the affections of Susan is again the playwright's
invention and ironically burlesques the triangular relationship of Arden, Mosby and Alice in the main plot.
Susan, in a neat piece of dramatic economy, is a conflation
of two characters in Holinshed, Mosby's (widowed) sister
and a rarely mentioned maid in Arden's house. The play
introduces Shakebag much earlier than Holinshed, thus
gaining in dramatic economy (one introduction does for
both of the ruffians) and allowing the early establishment
of that serio-comic double act by which the playwright
creates a ready means for varying the mood of the play.
Only one added detail indicates an unease in the playwright over the parochial nature of his narrative material
– that of the poisoned crucifix (never used) which suggests
a hankering after sophisticated Italianate villainy in contrast to the unsubtle brutality of Black Will and his crony
(i, 608–35, and x, 83–7). Apart from this last, the changes
are all in the interest of making firm the play's structure
and outline.

Moreover, the playwright has also seen the advantages
of modifying the characterization of his source. In Holin-

shed, Arden cuts a more despicable figure than he does in
the play. He winks at his wife's adultery in order to protect his business interests (see p. 291) and he is a physical
coward, refusing to fight with Mosby on more than one
occasion. Conversely, the play blackens the character of
Mosby who in Holinshed recoils in disgust from the last,
cowardly plan to murder Arden (see p. 296). Nor does
Holinshed's account lay so much emphasis on Mosby's
wavering loyalties towards Alice. And so the moral oppo-
sition of the main male characters and their relationship
with Alice has been delicately but firmly refashioned. But
the ennobling of Arden's character in the play is only
partial. In his business dealings the play emphasizes his
callousness and unscrupulousness by the confrontation of
Dick Reede and Arden (scene xiii) created out of a post-
script in Holinshed. Reede's curse on Arden makes Arden's
death both inevitable and deserved; and the dialogue points
up Arden's lust for gain at the expense of others in a way
that is meant to recall the earlier dialogue on the same theme
between Greene and Alice (i, 450–82). Neither Greene nor
Reede is a rogue, and their murderous desperation makes
a moral point about Arden.

The play, then, follows its source unslavishly, and it
makes room for three sorts of realism, that of character
portrayal, that of the presentation of a social milieu, and
that of atmospheric use of local detail. The character
portrayal is the play's outstanding feature. The characters
are presented not as types or moral symbols but as indivi-
duals. The realism is psychological, and we are allowed
insight into the flux of feelings and intentions that moti-
vate sharply differentiated characters. The relationship of
Alice and Mosby is analysed dispassionately and acutely,
in a way that transcends the immediate, ethical intentions
of a Morality play. The playwright who created, for
example, scene viii, the quarrel scene, could never have

written the unsubtle, didactic recipe on the title-page of
the play (quoted earlier). This scene is not in Holinshed
and it is the playwright's skilful way of maintaining
interest in Alice and Mosby while the narrative interest
of the play lies elsewhere. In it, Mosby's petty-mindedness
and shallowness are played off against the towering
passions of Alice. Alice's love is entirely irrational and
undeserved, and it is to the playwright's credit that he
makes no attempt to explain it away. She is the most
forceful character in the play and has been variously
described as the play's soul, as a bourgeois Clytemnestra
and as a female Faust. She tears the prayerbook as a sign
of her allegiance to the religion which controls her life,
her love for Mosby, and this is one of the many touches
which go to establishing her as a tragic heroine of some
stature. The mutual recriminations between her and her
lover in the last scene are the last sure touch of a percep-
tively presented relationship. To find something parallel
in kind and scope one has to go to *Hedda Gabler*.

The handling of Arden himself is less sure. The playwright demands our sympathy for him over the infidelity
of his wife, creating in the opening of the play a mood of
sick despair on Arden's part which is re-emphasized in
the dialogue at the beginning of scene iv and Franklin's
soliloquy which follows:

> Ah, what a hell is fretful jealousy!
> What pity-moving words, what deep-fetch'd sighs,
> What grievous groans and overlading woes
> Accompanies this gentle gentleman.   (iv, 40–3)

But our attitudes are less firmly directed over the issue of
Arden's dispossessing others, poorer than himself, of their
land and livelihood. He denies Reede's charges in scene
xiii, and Franklin, the honest broker in the play, wholly
accepts the justice of his friend's position (ll. 57–8). But at

the beginning of the scene the presentation of Reede is sympathetic and the sailor with him delivers an epigrammatic summary of Arden's character which has an authoritative air:

> His conscience is too liberal and he too niggardly
> To part with anything may do thee good   (xiii, 2-3)

Only a subtle reading of the play at a tangent to the text can demonstrate that Arden's gloom, which he attributes to his wife's infidelity, is in part the expression of guilt of a conscience not at all liberal. The playwright has failed to harmonize within the play the different attitudes towards Arden and therefore the play's own attitude remains unclear.

Franklin remains undeveloped but an astonishing feature of *Arden* is the success with which all the minor characters have been humanized, not left as ciphers or dramatic functions. The sense of struggle in Michael, the conflict between his love for Susan and his loyalty towards his master, made complex by his fear of the murderers, is an obvious instance of this. At iv, 59-87, the struggle is externalized in a full-blown soliloquy. And elsewhere in the play the dramatic liveliness of wholly minor characters bears witness to a constant concern to present the illusion of life. This is, in fact, very much an actor's play, and in this spread of dramatic liveliness there is further argument for Shakespeare's authorship, though hardly a powerful one.

The realism of the presentation of a social milieu includes a sense of community in the provincial town and port, conveyed by the fear of gossip, of 'narrow-prying neighbours' who 'blab' and the visiting of neighbours in the last scene. More importantly it involves a sense of social status and social aspiration in the main characters of the play, an important element in the characters' psychological make-up. It is not just his wife's infidelity which sickens Arden in the first scene, it is the base origins of his wife's lover: 'to dote on such a one as he / Is monstrous and intolerable'. Arden is a man of position and wealth, himself newly prosperous but of citizen rank. Mosby is a botcher or tailor by trade seeking to raise his status by cunning and flattery and via a stewardship. The first meeting in the play between the two is dominated by their awareness of social status. To Arden, Mosby is 'villain', 'groom', 'goodman botcher', a 'velvet drudge, / A cheating steward, and a base-minded peasant'. Arden's disarming of Mosby is a symbolic way of reducing him to his proper social rank:

> So, sirrah, you may not wear a sword;
> The statute makes against artificers;
> I warrant that I do. Now use your bodkin,
> Your Spanish needle, and your pressing iron,
> For this shall go with me.   (i, 310–14)

Earlier in the scene, ll. 198–204, Alice has already made the same point against Mosby and in the quarrel scene she echoes Arden's scorn:

> Even in my forehead is thy name engraven,
> A mean artificer, that low-born name.   (viii, 76–7)

Thus the social picture is an important part of the play's texture, and all the characters play a part in a well-defined social structure, including Black Will and Shakebag, who, far from being mere stage villains, are a typical feature of the Tudor social pattern. The masterless men who drifted back from the wars in France via Boulogne and earned a dishonest penny on the road were a constant menace to travellers.*

* See R. Chapman, 'Arden of Feversham: Its Interest Today', English, xi, 1956, pp. 15–17, for a fuller discussion of the social aspect of the play.

This social documentation merges with the third sort of realism, the attention to local detail which has encouraged some critics to assume that the author was a Faversham man and others to assume he was a Londoner. Michael's reference to the neighbouring village of Bolton at i, 173, is just such a detail, and Black Will's piece of self-aggrandizement at xiv, 13–30, with its detailed account of a London protection racket, beautifully evokes the raw side of life in the capital. The Jack Fitten passage of ii, 36–81, which provides the excuse for Bradshaw's journey and subsequent return with the letter, is a sustained example of this feeling for local detail. Independent of the source, the episode presents the story of Fitten and the stolen plate with such circumstantial detail that the crime may well have been one of local notoriety. Certainly, two of the details owe nothing to imagination: Lord Cheiny – or at least Sir Thomas Cheiny who was Lord Warden of the Cinque Ports (see Holinshed, p. 295) – and Sir Antony Cooke were real personages of local repute. The realism of local detail, whether imagined or not, enhances the authenticity of the dramatized story.

Despite this realism of detail, of social picture and of characterization, the play aims at a larger significance in two ways – in its poetry and in its awareness of forces for good and evil outside the little world of man. The poetry of the play creates moments which seem larger than their context. The nimble dialogue is counterpointed with large, set-piece speeches like that of Arden describing his dream (vi, 6–31); and richness and intensity are added to the impassioned moments by the use of figurative language and rhythm, for example in the quarrel scene, viii. Furthermore, with Shakespearean generosity the playwright has lavished poetry on the minor characters as well as the major ones. Michael expresses his inner struggle through metaphor (iii, 193–211); and Shakebag heralds

night (v, 1–8) with felicitous language that anticipates
that of the First Murderer awaiting Banquo and Fleance in
Macbeth (III, iii). In respect of its poetry *Arden* is quite
unlike *A Yorkshire Tragedy* or *A Woman Killed with Kindness*. Only the author of *Arden* has ornamented his domestic drama with references to the classical myths.

In the play behind the play in which the larger moral
forces are deployed against each other, *Arden of Faversham*
achieves in a minor way something of the poise of a more
illustrious play, *King Lear*, in which

> As flies to wanton boys, are we to the gods:
> They kill us for their sport

is balanced by

> The gods are just, and of our pleasant vices
> Make instruments to plague us.

Arden does not make authoritative, general statements
of that sort but works towards the same 'meaning'
through detail of character and situation. Fate seems to
drive the characters on to destroy themselves. In the opening scene Alice succumbs to the blandishments of Mosby
against her better self:

> So list the sailor to the mermaid's song;
> So looks the traveller to the basilisk.
> I am content for to be reconcil'd,
> And that I know will be mine overthrow.
>
> (i, 213–16)

In a different mood Black Will boasts to Michael that he
is the instrument of destiny:

> I am the very man,
> Mark'd in my birth-hour by the destinies,
> To give an end to Arden's life on earth.
>
> (iii, 160–62)

Arden's dream and the haunting scenes in the mist contribute to the feeling in the play of ineluctable forces controlling the actions of the characters. The actions themselves are of people living in an amoral universe. They continually bind themselves by the solemn act of swearing to the wrong course of action, and major and minor characters alike pursue their desires with a single-mindedness which involves the dismissal of moral scruples and religious sanction. Alice can say:

> Love is a god, and marriage is but words,
> And therefore Mosby's title is the best.
> Tush! whether it be or no he shall be mine,
> In spite of him, of Hymen, and of rites.   (i, 101–4)

And less than a hundred lines later her philosophy is echoed by her servant, Michael, who says of Susan:

> I'll make her more worth than twenty painters can,
> For I will rid mine elder brother away,
> And then the farm of Bolton is mine own.
> Who would not venture upon house and land,
> When he may have it for a right-down blow?*
>
> (i, 171–5)

In an amoral universe there is no answer to Michael's question, but the play also presents the other side of the coin. There is a growing sense throughout the play of Providence, and the amorality of the characters is replaced by an awareness of a moral scheme which includes retribution. The would-be murderers begin to see Arden's continual escapes as evidence of God's intervention (ix, 143 and xiv, 31–2); and Reede's curse, calling for a miracle to punish Arden's unjust treatment of him, appears to mark Arden's last chance to set right a life dominated

* Compare Clarke's similar sentiments at i, 267–72.

by the egoistic pursuit of wealth (he, like Alice, has his own demon). The providential nature of the last moments of the play is marked. The difficulty of washing away the blood, the snow-storm and the bleeding corpse act successively to jolt Alice into an awareness of a moral universe she has forsworn. And in this way the play imposes a sense of Providence on that of Fate. In this lies the poise of the play.

In the final analysis, the play's tragic impact is blurred by the double interest of the play – in Arden's falling foul of a moral universe and in Alice's parallel culpability. Some commentators have seen Arden as the centre of the play, some have seen Alice. The playwright's fidelity to Holinshed and to the 'simple truth' which should be 'gracious enough' prevented that final shaping of his material which would have created a single focus.

*

The journalistic aspect of *A Yorkshire Tragedy* has already been stressed. The play was one of several attempts to convey to the Jacobean theatre-going and reading public the story of Walter Calverley, head of a well-known Yorkshire family. On the 23 April 1605 he had killed two of his three children and injured his wife, and had been apprehended while trying to reach the third child who was at nurse some miles off. Refusing to plead, he was executed on 5 August by the method called *la peine forte et dure* or pressing to death. Two plays, two pamphlets and a ballad on Calverley's story reached the press in the next three years, though one pamphlet and the ballad seem not to have survived.

The extant pamphlet, the anonymous *Two Unnatural Murders*, tells the Calverley story in its first half and in its second recounts a similar matter involving a Mistress Browne who murdered her husband. The Calverley

narrative, reprinted as Appendix B,* begins with Calverley's betrothal to the daughter of his neighbour and tells
how he was forced by his guardian to marry his guardian's
niece. This aspect of the story has been shown to be his-
torically untrue,† but it was this aspect that most interested
George Wilkins, the author of the other play on the
Calverley theme, *The Miseries of Enforced Marriage*, published 1607. Wilkins's play is a sociological treatise on the
subject of its title; the hero of the play, Scarborrow
(= Calverley), ill-treats his family and treads a prodigal
path because of the enforced marriage. The relationship
of this play with *A Yorkshire Tragedy* is enigmatic and
will be discussed shortly.

The relationship of *A Yorkshire Tragedy* and *Two Unnatural Murders* is perfectly clear, the play being directly
dependent on the pamphlet not only for episodes and
details of the story but in its phrasing and vocabulary.
Except in its first scene, the play has turned third-person
narrative into dialogue with slavish fidelity, often merely
versifying the original. (I give no example as the reader
can quickly make comparisons.)

In spite, however, of this slavish fidelity, the author of
A Yorkshire Tragedy has made proper and necessary use of
dramatic conventions and techniques to transmute the
narrative into drama. Just such a convention is the
'lament', the set-piece speech of lamentation which is a
widespread feature of Elizabethan drama and which at its
most characteristic makes use of a series of accepted
formulas and rhetorical figures.‡ There are four laments

*Together with what purports to be Calverley's deposition
before the magistrates which carries a different motive for the
tragic deeds.

†Baldwin Maxwell, *Studies in the Shakespeare Apocrypha*, New
York, 1956, pp. 157–64.

‡For a discussion of the 'lament', see W. Clemen, *English
Tragedy before Shakespeare*, Methuen, 1961.

in the play, the Wife's soliloquy with which scene ii opens (ll. 1–24); another soliloquy by the Wife at the end of scene iii (ll. 81–97); the Husband's soliloquy in scene iv which is the climactic moment in the play (ll. 55–93); and the Husband's speeches of lamentation and repentance in the last scene as he mourns over his dead children and injured wife. These 'laments' raise the emotional tone of the play, heighten the characterization and make articulate the usually unvoiced anxieties and sorrows of the characters' inner selves (though in the interests of moral exposition, not of realistic character portrayal as such). Compare, for example, the fluent grief of the last scene with the pamphlet's description of Calverley seeing his dead children: 'He was melted into water and had not power to take any farewell of them but only in tears.' The pamphlet is true to life, the play to drama.

The beginning of scene iii represents another dramatic convention, that of the reporting speech to replace direct representation. Here, in the business of the Wife's visit to the uncle, the playwright is coping with the problem of two simultaneous actions. Any clumsiness involved in the device – the servant clearly knows what is being carefully described to him – is offset by certain advantages. There is, to begin with, a gain in economy and pace, the author having dispensed with the introduction of a new scene and of a new major character. Then there is the gain in intensity through the play's action being restricted to the house until after the murders. And finally, the reported visit allows a fierce irony to be achieved by the juxtaposition of the Husband's brutal threats at the end of scene ii and the Wife's new-found optimism in the reporting speech which opens scene iii. The speech is not in itself dramatic but it is part of a strikingly dramatic episode in the play. The hasty onrush of the tragic events produced by such a technique is one source of the play's power overall.

The most significant change made by the play, however, is one not involving dramatic form. The title-page
of *Two Unnatural Murders* presents a woodcut of the
murder scene: Calverley inappropriately wields a club,
the wife and two children lie prostrate, and a dog slinks
away in the background. But most interestingly, on the
left side of the picture is a devil-figure surveying the
events. Surprisingly, the narrative itself makes no mention of demoniac possession of Calverley, though this is
a recurrent motif in other 'warning' literature. The
theory of demoniac possession, besides being good theo-
logy and ethics, was also good psychology; it explained
fits, neuroses and implacable evil with the same satisfying
swiftness. The playwright has incorporated the idea carefully and consistently so that it becomes a theme of the
play and an explanation of the Husband's behaviour. The
idea is hinted at twice in scene ii (ll. 38 and 143) and
it is taken up by the servant of scene iii (ll. 24–7). The
'lusty' servant of scene v gives added force to the idea in
his struggle with the Husband (ll. 37 and 43) and finds no
other explanation than demoniac possession for the Husband's strength (ll. 57–62 and 84–5). In the last scene the
Husband himself recognizes the fact of his possession
and vividly describes his freeing from it:

> Now glides the devil from me,
> Departs at every joint, heaves up my nails.
> Oh, catch him new torments that were ne'er invented;
> Bind him one thousand more, you blessed angels,
> In that pit bottomless; let him not rise
> To make man act unnatural tragedies.　　　(viii, 18–23)

These many references, all independent of the source
pamphlet, have a considerable, iterative force in such a
short play. In a work from which he borrowed a couplet,
Nashe's *Pierce Penniless*, the author of *A Yorkshire Tragedy*

would have read, in the long discourse on demonology, of the second kind of devils employed by Lucifer:

These know how to dissociate the love of brethren, and to break wedlock bands with such violence, that they may not be united, and are predominant in many other domestical mutinies.

And this is what the play is about, and this is why the long-suffering Wife can accept her husband at the end of the play; he has been untrue to his real self. In this respect, *A Yorkshire Tragedy* is a more conventional play than *Arden of Faversham*.

A Yorkshire Tragedy, then, does not look for a socio-logical explanation of Calverley's ruinous course. The idea of the enforced marriage and the breaking of a pre-vious contract are not themes of the play, the forsaken mistress motif appearing only allusively in the first scene. This scene stands apart from the rest of the play in four respects: it is not based verbally on the pamphlet; its characters are named; its low comedy is not single-mindedly concerned with the play's plot; and it suggests details of the story contradicted by or unconnected with the rest of the play. No bridge is made between the scene and those following, and the forsaken mistress is never again mentioned. Without the pamphlet we might sus-pect, as did eighteenth-century commentators, that the 'young mistress' of scene i is the Wife of the play, and that the Husband has contracted a bigamous marriage in London as reported by Sam. Clearly the scene implies that the Husband's marriage and prodigal course are tak-ing place in London and this is contradicted at ii, 116–19, and viii, 1, where we are made aware of the provincial setting. Whatever function the scene is intended to serve, it is reasonable to assume it was a late addition and formed no part of the original plan of the play. The Wife's opening speech of scene ii adequately does the job of exposition. It seems doubtful whether one should include scene i in a modern revival of the play.

One explanation for this scene is contained in an attractive theory concerned with the relationship between *A Yorkshire Tragedy* and Wilkins's play on the Calverley theme, *The Miseries of Enforced Marriage*. *The Miseries* is a tragicomedy. A tragic climax, in which Scarborrow murders his wife and children, is headed off at the last moment by the arrival of the news that Scarborrow has inherited a fortune from his guardian. Husband and wife are reconciled and all ends happily. It seems likely that an early version of the play ended tragically. *The Stationers' Register* describes the play as a tragedy, and G. H. Blayney has plausibly demonstrated that a hasty revision to replace the tragic end with a comic one has left glimpses of the original end showing through.*

Early commentators, assuming a revision of the end of the play, saw in *A Yorkshire Tragedy* the discarded, tragic end itself. They could derive support for this from the enigmatic head-title of the quartos, *All's One, or, One of the Four Plays in One*, claiming that in *The Miseries* are discernible the other three story motifs making up this four-part play. And they could also derive support from that curious scene i which could, with some changes, be fitted into an early place in *The Miseries* where Wilkins treats at length the 'forsaken mistress' part of the story. But the theory does not work. Blayney shows that the early version of *The Miseries*, though a tragedy, could never have accommodated *A Yorkshire Tragedy* as its end. Further, the shorter play does not look like the lopped-off end of another play. It is self-contained, proceeding from its expository beginning in scene ii (I assume scene i to be

*'Wilkins's Revisions in *The Miseries*', *Journal of English and Germanic Philology* LVI, 1957, pp. 23–41.

a late addition) to its conclusion without loose end or unexplained detail, and its dependency on the source pamphlet reinforces the impression. Though no other dramatic presentation of this kind survives, we must assume that the play was exhibited with three others of a similar length and presumably on a similar theme.*

A discussion of the play's authorship necessarily follows an account of its making. It might be said that the fidelity with which the play follows its source and the unfussy ease with which it turns this source into drama precludes the possibility of a personal idiom or viewpoint appearing. Because of its remarkable genesis *A Yorkshire Tragedy* has an anonymity of style which would make author-hunting otiose were it not for the fact that the first and second quartos and the *Stationers' Register* all ascribe the play to Shakespeare. Its omission from the first collected edition of Shakespeare, the First Folio of 1623, is powerful external evidence against the ascription, and most critics agree that few lines of the play suggest the poetry and power of the playwright who at that time was fashioning *Macbeth* and *Lear*. Revision by Shakespeare is possible and some of the prose of the play, especially the Husband's soliloquy in scene iv, is extremely vigorous and expressive; but the publisher who made this ascription, Thomas Pavier, was demonstrably dishonest elsewhere in his dealings and was probably using Shakespeare's name as a selling point.

Only two other ascriptions have been seriously made, George Wilkins and Thomas Heywood, author of *A Woman Killed with Kindness*. Wilkins, as has been explained, is associated with the dramatization of the Cal-

---

Two Lamentable Tragedies, which alternates two stories scene by scene, is another odd dramatic structure which draws attention to the fact that 'domestic tragedy' is a description of content, not a precise formula.

verley story and the theory that *The Miseries* originally included *A Yorkshire Tragedy* would lead to the conclusion that Wilkins wrote the shorter play. A. M. Clark★ accepted the theory but claimed *A Yorkshire Tragedy* for Heywood, asserting that the original, four-part play was a collaborative effort of Wilkins and Heywood, Heywood's contribution being the piece eventually discarded as *A Yorkshire Tragedy*. The argument for Heywood rests, most inconclusively, on stylistic grounds. Although *A Yorkshire Tragedy* never belonged to *The Miseries*, Wilkins's claim to the play seems to me to be the strongest.† There is some stylistic evidence for his authorship and we know he was connected with the dramatization of the Calverley story. It is possible that he hastily turned the first half of *Two Unnatural Murders* into *A Yorkshire Tragedy* in 1605, and at greater leisure made a freer, full-length play out of the same narrative material, which was published as *The Miseries* before *A Yorkshire Tragedy* got into print. But it is probably more sensible, and it is certainly easier, to see *A Yorkshire Tragedy* as a product of its circumstances rather than to try to identify a particular author for it.

It is as a product of circumstances that it is paradoxically able to convey something to the modern reader (and occasionally to the modern audience). Hasty and rough-hewn as it is, it frequently employs an emphatic terseness of speech which shows up brightly by the side of its stock, pedestrian verse. Its spareness and momentum give it a dramatic forcefulness which complements its un-

★A. M. Clark, *Thomas Heywood: Playwright and Miscellanist*, 1931, Appendix V.

†Baldwin Maxwell, in *Studies in the Shakespeare Apocrypha*, New York, 1956, pp. 193 f., argues against Wilkins's authorship on the grounds that *A Yorkshire Tragedy* shows dramatic qualities beyond the capability of Wilkins.

ostentatious documentary of events. Its lack of rich characterization and of poetic structure contribute to a bleakness of effect which is the play's most striking feature.

*

Little is known of the life of Thomas Heywood, author of *A Woman Killed with Kindness*. Born in 1573 or 1574 and probably a student at Cambridge, he devoted his long working life from about 1596 till his death in 1650 to the profession of letters and especially to the commercial theatre. He wrote mainly for the Earl of Worcester's (later Queen Anne's) company and, a frequent collaborator, could make the astonishing reference in the Address to the Reader in *The English Traveller* (published 1633) to the 'two hundred and twenty [plays] in which I have had either an entire hand or at least the main finger'. He professed to be uninterested in publishing his plays and only twenty or so survive, but these fully demonstrate the scope and vigour of his dramatic work as he tailored his output to meet the new fashions and moods during a career spanning the reigns of three monarchs. The author of chronicle plays, plays based on classical legend and myth, romantic adventure plays and realistic comedies in the vein of Middleton and Jonson, he is best known as the dramatist of domestic life, a conscious originator in the depiction of conjugal relationships treated seriously and even tragically. The best known of his non-dramatic works is *An Apology for Actors*, published in 1612 but probably written some years earlier. In it he demonstrates the respect with which he regards his chosen profession. The playhouse, he claims, provides the populace with moral edification and historical instruction; it cheers the tired and the melancholic; it refines the English tongue; and – a typical piece of patriotism – it is an ornament to the city, capable of impressing foreigners.

References in Henslowe's *Diary* allow a fairly exact dating of Heywood's masterpiece, *A Woman Killed with Kindness*. In February and March of 1603 Henslowe recorded payments to Heywood for the play itself and to a tailor for the provision of costumes for it. Heywood received the regular fee of six pounds, while the costumes – for Anne Frankford in the last scenes of the play – characteristically cost rather more. The *Diary* also shows that *A Woman Killed with Kindness* was only the last of a whole series of dramatic enterprises undertaken by Heywood in a matter of months. The play was a considerable success and was printed in 1607, the first publication with Heywood's name on the title-page. It was reprinted in 1617, and perhaps once more previous to this as the 1617 title-page refers to that reprint as the third edition.

A Woman Killed with Kindness is a double-plot play, a form that Heywood was fond of using, particularly, as here, with the main plot and sub-plot only tenuously linked. After the first scene of the play the actions proceed independently of each other to the end (though the main characters from both plots are summoned for the climax of the main plot in the last scene). The materials for the sub-plot, the Mountford/Acton story, come originally from a Sienese novella by Illicini which found its way via Bandello and Belleforest into two English versions, by William Painter and Geoffrey Fenton. Heywood probably knew it in Painter's rendering, in a collection of stories, often plundered by Elizabethan dramatists, called *The Palace of Pleasure*, 1566.

Illicini's novella is a *Romeo and Juliet* story with a happy ending. The Montanine and Salimbene families engage in a long blood-feud after an incident arising out of a boar hunt. The feud ruins the Montanines and prevents Anselmo Salimbene, of the second generation, from declaring his love for Angelica, a member of the Montanine family and sister of the last-surviving male of that family, Charles. Anselmo pays Charles's prison fine when he is gaoled on a trumped-up charge. Charles attempts to repay Anselmo by offering him Angelica but the courteous Anselmo takes her as his wife. Heywood naturalized the story, giving it a Yorkshire setting and English characters, changing the boar hunt to a hawking match, and, most important, reducing the quarrel and love story to one generation. Consequently, Mountford and Acton do not have the innocence of Charles and Anselmo. Mountford is guilty of a rash anger which results in killing and he has something to expiate; Acton takes an active part in the fight, is insulting and vindictive towards his fallen enemy, and tries, as a final blow, to seduce his enemy's virtuous sister. Only the force of sudden and unexpected love brings about the reconciliation. The power of love to overcome a disunity in the order of things is the burden of Illicini's novel; the power of love to refine the moral sensibility of the individual conscience is the burden of Heywood's version. However, the sub-plot is strictly subordinate to the main plot. Its characters are less interesting and its end is sentimental. Its importance lies in its relationship with the Frankford story.

Various narratives in *The Palace of Pleasure* have been suggested as Heywood's source for his main plot but none of them fits in sufficient detail. Neither does a story by Greene, also suggested as the source, which at least has the merit of being English in setting and tone.* For Heywood's main plot is thoroughly English in atmosphere, so much so that at least one commentator assumed that it was based, like other domestic tragedies, on an actual, contemporary event. It seems likely that Heywood put

* See W. F. McNeir, 'Heywood's sources for the Main Plot of *A Woman Killed with Kindness*', *Studies in the English Renaissance Drama*, Louisiana 1962, pp. 189–211.

together hints and details from various stories to create his plot, and it is one of Heywood's contributions to the domestic tragedy that he depended on his own moral vision and dramatic skill to gain acceptance for his play rather than on a journalistic interest in the events portrayed.

His other departure from the *Arden* type of domestic tragedy lies in the deliberately unbloody and unsensational ending. No one and nothing in the play condones Anne Frankford's adultery; but her husband, eschewing violence and thus allowing his wife the opportunity for repentance and forgiveness in Heaven's and his eyes, gives evidence of a sensibility which finds revenge brutal and the vindication of personal honour irrelevant. And Heywood clearly recognizes the originality of what he is doing. Acton, Anne's brother, stands for the orthodox position on revenge for adultery when at the beginning of the last scene he says:

> My brother Frankford show'd too mild a spirit
> In the revenge of such a loathed crime;
> Less than he did no man of spirit could do.
> I am so far from blaming his revenge
> That I commend it. Had it been my case
> Their souls at once had from their breasts been freed;
> Death to such deeds of shame is the due meed.
>
> (V, iv, 16–22)

This is exactly the spirit of the world of the Italian novella; it is the motive that animates Othello in another play about infidelity. Later in the same scene Acton himself has learnt the lesson of compassion and can admit the moral efficacy of Frankford's treatment of Anne:

> Brother, had you with threats and usage bad
> Punish'd her sin, the grief of her offence
> Had not with such true sorrow touch'd her heart.
>
> (V, iv, 133–5)

In a general way, the sub-plot, with its sudden violence, its changes of fortune, and its improbable strainings of honour contrasts sharply with the sobriety and simple humanity of the main plot. The Sienese world of blood-feud is only partly accommodated to its Yorkshire setting, and Mountford's outrageous decision to repay Acton's kindness to him with the only thing he has at his disposal, his sister's honour, draws from Acton himself the ejaculation:

> Was ever known in any former age
> Such honourable wrested courtesy?
>
> (V, i, 120–21)

The convention of sudden love with which the sub-plot cuts its Gordian knot is appropriately romantic.

However, the sub-plot illuminates the main plot in a more detailed way than the simple one of contrast of tone. The two plots, with their symmetrically organized trios of main characters, invite a continuous effort of cross-reference from the audience. It was orthodox to regret the romantic sub-plot as mere padding until Miss F. L. Townsend★ demonstrated in a sympathetic way the thematic intertwining of the two plots as they examine the concepts of honour and virtue. Peter Ure† took Miss Townsend's case further by analysing the strange paradox of the play, implicit in the title and worked out in the action of both plots, of the 'surcharge of kindness'. Mountford is prepared to sacrifice his sister's virtue to repay his enemy's kindness and thus redeem his own honour; Anne must find a way of repaying Frankford's kindness and thus punish herself for a sin Frankford has

★'The artistry of Thomas Heywood's Double Plot', *Philological Quarterly*, xxv, 1946, pp. 97–119.

†'Marriage and the Domestic Drama in Heywood and Ford', *English Studies*, xxxii, 1951, pp. 200–66.

let go unpunished. Acton's marriage to Susan at the end of the sub-plot is a further act of magnanimity, parallel to Frankford's giving back to Anne the names of wife and mother at the end of the main plot.

The symmetry of the three leading characters of each story and the contrasted movements of those stories, from harmony to discord in the main plot and the reverse in the sub-plot, betray the formal care with which Heywood has constructed the play. But the contrasting character relationships in the two parts break down the obvious pattern, creating instead a complex series of connexions which define and present Heywood's moral themes. Often, particular aspects are emphasized by juxtaposition: Frankford's generosity to Wendoll in II, i is followed by Shafton's hypocritical generosity of II, ii; Anne's loss of virtue and honour is exposed to a censorious world in IV, iv and contrasted with Susan's resolve in the next scene to retain her own virtue and honour by suicide (the form of Anne's self-inflicted punishment). But in a general way the thematic concerns of the two plots can be seen to be one. The two plots bear the same sort of thematic connexion as the main plot and Gloucester sub-plot of *Lear*.

It is through this process of parallel and contrast that Heywood makes his moral point. Nothing could be more different from *Arden*, with its linear plot which is almost no plot and its examination of moral issues as lived by the characters. Heywood's is a more deliberate and self-conscious art, and his characterization will appear wooden to readers and theatre audiences brought up on Shakespeare. There is not in Heywood the psychological power of characterization which endows characters with the illusion of a life outside their dramatic context. Hardin Craig in *The Enchanted Glass* has shown that the characters are constructed according to a conventional theory of faculty psychology rather than according to direct observation of people. In the important seduction scene, II, iii, the struggle within both Wendoll and Anne is a vying for domination by passion over reason. Wendoll's soliloquy is the longest speech in the play and Heywood evidently attaches much importance to it. Anne's fall – to the disappointment of many critics – is much briefer as she succumbs to the wiles of Wendoll's attack, an attack based on the tactics of courtly love, desiring pity not reciprocation of passion. Anne is the type of the frail woman, soft and impressionable, without the moral fibre to resist Wendoll's appeal to her mercy. She does not love him; she simply loses her sense of moral direction:

> What shall I say?
> My soul is wand'ring and hath lost her way.
> Oh Master Wendoll, oh!   (II, iii, 150–52)

However, this conventional characterization does not lead to lack of moral vigour in the play. Rather, it enforces the moral definitions worked out by parallel and contrast, and it allows the play to take the unblurred shape of a moral fable.

Furthermore, the schematic characterization in no way affects the sort of dramatic vigour that is the hallmark of the professional dramatist working in close touch with the theatre. Arthur Brown* has stressed the fact that Heywood possessed two essentially theatrical skills which it is possible to miss in the reading: speed and timing. Heywood knew how to tell a story in dramatic form, and he paid attention to the visual aspect of his plays, concentrating attention in his stage directions on a character's mood as shown in his appearance: *Enter Master Frankford in a study; Enter Wendoll melancholy; Enter Sir Charles in*

---

* 'Thomas Heywood's Dramatic Art', *Essays on Shakespeare and Elizabethan Drama in Honor of Hardin Craig*, ed. Richard Hosley, Routledge, 1963, pp. 327–39.

prison, with irons, his feet bare, his garments all ragged and torn; Enter Anne in her smock, night gown, and night attire. Each entry is a speaking picture, stylized and unsubtle, but economically establishing a mood or focusing the audience's attention in a particular way.

And with this interest in dramatic eloquence as opposed to literary eloquence goes Heywood's talent for creating scenes of theatrical excitement. The high points of the main plot in this regard are the card game of III, ii and the discovery of IV, iv. The card game is a masterpiece of sustained metaphor as the fact and proof of Anne's infidelity are conveyed to Frankford through the unerring choice by each character of the meaningful pun. The pairing of Wendoll and Anne against Frankford is an image of the larger truth; and whether we read the scene in a Freudian way – Anne's guilt dictating her punning – or see it simply as a stylized representation of the real situation, it remains a theatrically brilliant scene. The discovery scene calls from Heywood the most dramatically effective verse of the play. Tension is aroused by Frankford's gradual penetration of his own house (he has become an outsider) and by his hesitation to go through with an action that is hateful to him. Any suggestions of the melodramatic are tapped off by Nicholas's flippant asides and matter-of-factness. The poignancy of Frankford's speech immediately after he has seen the lovers together (ll. 50–64) saves him from appearing inhumanly judicial later in the scene. His concise utterance of one of the constant themes of European literature – 'that it were possible / To undo things done, to call back yesterday' – is utterly moving. It is with tact that Heywood allows him to pursue Wendoll with a sword and betray his humanity. The Maid, preventing him from gaining revenge, is the angel's hand staying him from a bloody sacrifice (ll. 66–7). This makes an economic transition to the judge-like dispenser of moral and divine justice of the second half of the scene because we are being shown Frankford as man and as Christian; and the two roles, the play shows, are compatible. The brief entry of the children defines for Anne and the audience the domestic sanctity which Anne has violated. In this scene character, dialogue and action merge in a meaningful experience which is theatrical rather than literary. It is in the incident and the scene, full of symbolic power, that Heywood's poetry lies.

And it is essentially the poetry of domesticity. It has been said that the house is a character in the play. It is certainly true that the servants are more important in this play than as mere fetchers and carriers. Apart from the narrative importance of Nicholas and the constant counterpointing of his sober good sense with the passion and fancy of his social betters (even in the last scene), the servants as a group symbolize normality and security in the household and are meaningfully presented for this purpose in many scenes: II, i and iii; III, ii; IV, iii and iv; and V, iii and iv. The two scenes they have entirely to themselves, I, ii, and IV, iii, are effectively contrasted, the first celebrating the marriage with its promise of harmony, the second demonstrating by crude innuendo the depths to which the marriage has been dragged. And domesticity successfully invades the actions of the main characters who are continually shown going to or coming from meals. In III, ii, immediately before the significant moment when Nicholas tells Frankford of Anne's adultery, we get the characteristic entry for Frankford: ' Enter Frankford as it were brushing the crumbs from his clothes with a napkin, and newly risen from supper'. It is through the domestic pursuit of card-playing that Frankford tests the charge for himself.

The authentic domestic atmosphere is a means to an end, because it is the decorous context for the high seriousness with which Heywood treats the theme of conjugal relations. So too is the verse of the play, which is at its best when it is terse and transparent. Heywood does not aim at the sublime resonance of high tragedy, not even at the climax of the play when man and wife are reunited in a marriage which is more important than, indeed is made possible by, death:

FRANKFORD: My wife, the mother of my pretty babes,
  Both those lost names I do restore thee back,
  And with this kiss I wed thee once again.
  Though thou art wounded in thy honour'd name,
  And with that grief upon thy deathbed liest,
  Honest in heart, upon my soul, thou diest.
ANNE: Pardon'd on earth, soul, thou in Heaven art free.
  Once more thy wife, dies thus embracing thee.

                                        (V, iv, 114–22)

Perhaps Eliot was right in claiming that Heywood's tragedy is the drama of common life and therefore not, in the highest sense, tragedy at all; 'there is no supernatural music from behind the wings . . . he is eminent in the pathetic, rather than the tragic'.* But Heywood was creating a new idiom to express an area of human experience hitherto almost neglected in literature. It was the eighteenth-century novel which fully developed that idiom.

University of Lancaster   KEITH STURGESS

* *Elizabethan Essays*, Faber, 1963, p. 116.

A Note on Staging

ELIZABETHAN plays were written for an unrealistic style of presentation as regards the *mise en scène*. To begin with, the absence of a realistic background or other localizing feature in the Elizabethan theatre permitted the convention of continuous staging. A character might remain on stage but the locale would change, this change being noticed only in the dialogue. Consequently, a scene division concerned only a change of personnel on stage, not a change of place. This allowed two advantages: a greater fluidity of action than the naturalistic theatre can achieve; and the lack of a need to imagine a precise locale for each scene if a precise locale were unnecessary. Thus, the actor – his gestures and words – was the focus of attention for the audience.

The labelling of each scene with a locale by later editors works better in heroic tragedies than in domestic ones. The palace or court's mixture of public and private rooms provides endless locales for the anonymous scene which the playwright has not localized in the dialogue. But fluidity of action in the domestic tragedy makes the labelling of many scenes hazardous. No single locale, for example, can cope with the first scene of *Arden of Faversham* or the second of *A Yorkshire Tragedy*. The immensely long first scene of *Arden* – one scene because the stage is never empty – shifts its locale from Arden's house at the beginning, to the Painter's, and back again to Arden's. And the breakfasting of Arden makes it impossible to imagine the sort of staging characteristic of Roman comedy – an open air setting in front of two or three houses. In the second scene of *A Yorkshire Tragedy* the opening domestic strife of husband and wife demands an interior locale, but the Husband's chance meeting with the three gentlemen and then the single gentleman demands an exterior one. The Husband carries his own scene around with him.

Many other episodes in the three plays show a change of place within the scene. Twice in *A Woman Killed with Kindness*, IV, iv, and V, iv, we get characters passing from outside to inside a house without leaving the stage. Scene v of *A Yorkshire Tragedy* has been three scenes in all editions after and including Malone's, the divisions after ll. 154 and 161. Malone labelled the middle one of the three thus formed, 'Court before the House'. But the quartos do not give an exit and re-entry for the Husband after l. 154, merely the significant stage direction; 'The Master meets him'. The injured wife and dead children are visible throughout the scene. Scene ix of *Arden* involves travelling within the scene on a large scale. The opening sees Black Will and Shakebag in their ambush positions on Rainham Down and they never leave the stage till the end of the scene. Arden's party enters, Michael exits, and Arden and Franklin are to be imagined travelling towards Rainham Down, the telling of the appropriate tale of the guilty wife beguiling the time. As they draw near the ruffians, Lord Cheiny's entry prevents the murder.

The characters in this scene are, of course, on foot, and this represents another convention of Elizabethan staging. The references to Michael's horse at the beginning of the scene and to Lord Cheiny's at l. 117 suggest to the audience that the journey is in fact a horseback one. Similar moments occur in the other plays. At the beginning of IV, iv, of *A Woman Killed with Kindness* we learn that Frankford and Nicholas have just tied their horses to a tree; and at the beginning of V, iii, Anne has just left her coach: 'Bid my coach stay. Why should I ride in state

. . . ?' In *A Yorkshire Tragedy*, scene vi opens with the stage direction: '*Enter Husband as being thrown off his horse, and falls*' and the Husband then addresses the off-stage horse as it escapes. As with the changes of locale, the play-wright depends, in this convention of journeying, on the audience's not requiring a realistic representation of action.

Two of the three plays illustrate a third important convention of Elizabethan staging – the bedroom scene. The sudden appearance of a bed on-stage, already occupied, is frequent in Elizabethan plays. There are three methods by which this may have been achieved – the simple thrusting-out of the bed through curtains at the rear (and this is known to have happened on occasion); the discovery by the drawing of curtains of a bed situated on the inner-stage; or the use of a previously positioned bed with curtains of its own. The idea that the Elizabethan theatre necessarily had a sizeable inner-stage seems to have lost favour in recent years. The crucial scenes in this regard are the last scene of *A Woman Killed with Kindness* and the murder scene, scene iv, of *A Yorkshire Tragedy*. In the former, the visitors to Anne's house learn from the servants of Anne's ill-health and then the stage direction reads, '*Enter Anne in her bed*'. In *A Yorkshire Tragedy*, scene v opens with the stage direction: '*Enter a maid with a child in her arms, the mother by her asleep*'. For the latter I have assumed a discovery and interpolated '*is discovered*' before '*by*'. It is interesting that when the Wife evidently goes to sleep or contemplates doing so at the end of scene iii she is given no exit by the quartos. The use of an inner-stage would solve these problems of staging, but only a modern sense of propriety, unshared by the Elizabethans, would make such a thing necessary.*

* I discount the extended use of an upper-stage (situated over the hypothetical inner-stage) which E. K. Chambers, *The Eliza-*

bethan Stage, iii, 115, suggested for scene v. In no one's reconstruction of the Globe would actions at floor-level on an upper-stage be visible to a large part of the audience. In _Arden of Faversham_, an inner-stage would be useful, though not absolutely necessary, for the staging of the murder scene, scene xiv. The inner-stage would represent the counting-house where Black Will and Shakebag hide and in which Arden's body is at first deposited.

A Note on Texts

I HAVE modernized spelling and punctuation, retaining quarto '-'d' in preterites and past participles in the verse alone. Short, explanatory notes are given in footnotes, longer ones and textual variants are given in the Additional Notes. I have not recorded changes – many in the case of *A Yorkshire Tragedy* – from the lineation of the quartos. Additions to the stage directions of the quartos are given in square brackets.

Arden of Faversham was printed in quarto in 1592, 1599 and 1633; *A Yorkshire Tragedy* in 1608 and 1619; and *A Woman Killed with Kindness* in 1607 and 1617, though there was probably a lost quarto between these. I have consulted copies of all these quartos, using the first edition in each case as copy text. I am grateful to the Bodleian Library, Corpus Christi College, Oxford, and the British Museum for their permission to use their first editions respectively of *Arden of Faversham*, *A Yorkshire Tragedy* and *A Woman Killed with Kindness*.

Other editions of *Arden of Faversham* I have consulted are: C. F. Tucker Brooke, *The Shakespeare Apocrypha*, 1908, and A. K. McIlwraith, *Five Elizabethan Tragedies*, 1938. I have seen almost all editions of *A Yorkshire Tragedy*, the most important of which are E. Malone, *Supplement to Johnson's Shakespeare*, 1780, and Tucker Brooke. Editions of *A Woman Killed with Kindness* I have seen are: Pearson, *Heywood's Dramatic Works*, 1874; W. A. Neilson, *The Chief Elizabethan Dramatists*, 1911; K. L. Bates, *A Woman Killed with Kindness* and *The Fair Maid of the West*, 1917; Baskervill, Heltzel and Nethercot, *Elizabethan and Stuart Plays*, 1934; R. W. Van Fossen, *A*

Woman Killed with Kindness, 1959.* In a few cases I have accepted emendations by other editors recorded though not accepted by the above editions. I have not recorded the first appearance of each new reading.

None of the quartos is divided into acts and scenes. I see no evidence for the five-act structure accorded to *Arden of Faversham* since Tyrrell, while, on the other hand, the five-act structure of *A Woman Killed with Kindness*, not allowed by Van Fossen, seems to me to be clearly marked. In the latter case I have followed the act division of Neilson and Bates. All editions since Malone have divided *A Yorkshire Tragedy* into ten scenes, and one edition, that of A. F. Hopkinson, 1891, into three acts. I have divided the play into eight scenes.

Arden of Faversham appears to be a faithful printing of a 'bad' or reported text; *A Yorkshire Tragedy* is a faithful printing of a good, though hastily written text (it is extremely rough rhythmically, many passages being half-way between prose and verse). *A Woman Killed with Kindness* appears to be a fair printing of a good text though Heywood's handwriting was notoriously bad and I have emended freely.† I allow the 'second' quarto of Heywood's play (1617) less authority than does Van Fossen.

*This edition usefully reprints, with omissions, the source of the sub-plot.

†Speech prefixes appear to have caused particular problems.

Facsimile title page of the first edition of
Arden of Faversham

THE
LAMENTA=
BLE AND TRVE TRA-
GEDIE OF M. AR-
DEN OF FEVERSHAM
IN KENT.

Who was most wickedlye murdered, by
the meanes of his disloyall and wanton
wyfe, who for the loue she bare to one
Mosbie, hyred two desperat ruf-
fins Blackwill and Shakbag,
to kill him.

Wherin is shewed the great mal-
lice and discimulation of a wicked woman, the vnsatiable desire of filthie lust
and the shamefull end of all
murderers.

Imprinted at London for Edward
White, dwelling at the lyttle North
dore of Paules Church at
the signe of the
Gun, 1592.
*

Dramatis Personae

ARDEN
FRANKLIN, *his friend*
MOSBY
CLARKE, *a painter*
BRADSHAW, *a goldsmith*
ADAM FOWLE, *landlord of the Flower-de-Luce*
MICHAEL, *Arden's servant*
GREENE
RICHARD REEDE
A SAILOR, *his friend*
BLACK WILL ⎱ *murderers*
SHAKEBAG ⎰
A PRENTICE
A FERRYMAN
LORD CHEINY, *and his* SERVANTS
MAYOR OF FAVERSHAM, *and the* WATCH
ALICE, *Arden's wife*
SUSAN, *Mosby's sister and Alice's servingmaid*

Enter ARDEN *and* FRANKLIN

FRANKLIN: Arden, cheer up thy spirits and droop no
      more.
  My gracious Lord the Duke of Somerset
  Hath freely given to thee and to thy heirs,
  By letters patents from his majesty,
  All the lands of the Abbey of Faversham.
  Here are the deeds sealed and subscribed
  With his name and the king's.
  Read them, and leave this melancholy mood.
ARDEN: Franklin, thy love prolongs my weary life.
  And but for thee how odious were this life   10
  That shows me nothing but torments my soul,
  And those foul objects that offend mine eyes;
  Which makes me wish that for this veil of Heaven
  The earth hung over my head and covered me.
  Love letters pass'd twixt Mosby and my wife,
  And they have privy meetings in the town.
  Nay, on his finger did I espy a ring
  Which at our marriage day the priest put on.
  Can any grief be half so great as this?
FRANKLIN: Comfort thyself, sweet friend; it is not 20
      strange
  That women will be false and wavering.
ARDEN: Ay, but to dote on such a one as he
  Is monstrous, Franklin, and intolerable.
FRANKLIN: Why, what is he?
ARDEN: A botcher, and no better at the first;

11 *shows* grants (for my use).
13 *for* in place of. *veil of Heaven* i.e. the sky.
25 *botcher* tailor who does repairs. *at the first* in his origins.

Who by base brokage getting some small stock,
Crept into service of a nobleman,
And by his servile flattery and fawning
Is now become the steward of his house,
30   And bravely jets it in his silken gown.
FRANKLIN: No nobleman will count'nance such a
            peasant!
ARDEN: Yes, the Lord Clifford, he that loves not me.
But through his favour let not him grow proud,
For were he by the Lord Protector back'd,
He should not make me to be pointed at.
I am by birth a gentleman of blood,
And that injurious ribald that attempts
To violate my dear wife's chastity –
For dear I hold her love, as dear as Heaven –
40   Shall on the bed which he thinks to defile
See his dissevered joints and sinews torn,
Whilst on the planchers pants his weary body,
Smear'd in the channels of his lustful blood.
FRANKLIN: Be patient, gentle friend, and learn of me
To ease thy grief and save her chastity.
Entreat her fair; sweet words are fittest engines
To raze the flint walls of a woman's breast.
In any case, be not too jeal[i]ous,
Nor make no question of her love to thee;
50   But as securely, presently take horse,
And lie with me at London all this term;

26 *base brokage* pimping.
30 *bravely* in fine array. *jets it* swaggers.
33 *his* Lord Clifford's. *him* Mosby.   36 *blood* noble blood.
37 *injurious* insulting. *ribald* 1 base fellow; 2 wanton.
42 *planchers* planks (i.e. the floor).
46 *entreat* treat. *engines* mechanical contrivances (engines of war).
48 *jeal[i]ous* trisyllabic (cf. 'outragious', l. 53).
50 *as securely* trustingly. *presently* at once.
51 *lie* lodge. *term* period of session of courts of law.

For women when they may will not,
But being kept back, straight grow outragious.

ARDEN: Though this abhors from reason, yet I'll try it,
And call her forth, and presently take leave.
How, Alice!

Here enters ALICE.

ALICE: Husband, what mean you to get up so early?
Summer nights are short, and yet you rise ere day.
Had I been 'wake you had not risen so soon.

ARDEN: Sweet love, thou know'st that we two, Ovid-   60
like,
Have often chid the morning when it 'gan to peep,
And often wish'd that dark Night's purblind steeds
Would pull her by the purple mantle back
And cast her in the ocean to her love.
But this night, sweet Alice, thou hast kill'd my heart;
I heard thee call on Mosby in thy sleep.

ALICE: 'Tis like I was asleep when I nam'd him,
For being awake he comes not in my thoughts.

ARDEN: Ay, but you started up, and suddenly
Instead of him caught me about the neck.   70

ALICE: Instead of him? Why, who was there but you?
And where but one is how can I mistake?

FRANKLIN: Arden, leave to urge her over-far.

ARDEN: Nay, love, there is no credit in a dream.
Let it suffice I know thou lovest me well.

ALICE: Now I remember whereupon it came.
Had we no talk of Mosby yesternight?

FRANKLIN: Mistress Alice, I heard you name him once
or twice.

ALICE: And thereof came it, and therefore blame not me.

54 *abhors from* is at variance with.
62 *purblind* quite blind.
73 *leave to* cease.
76 *whereupon it came* how it came about.

80 ARDEN: I know it did, and therefore let it pass.
    I must to London, sweet Alice, presently.
    ALICE: But tell me, do you mean to stay there long?
    ARDEN: No longer there till my affairs be done.
    FRANKLIN: He will not stay above a month at most.
    ALICE: A month? Ay me! Sweet Arden, come again
    Within a day or two or else I die.
    ARDEN: I cannot long be from thee, gentle Alice.
    Whilst Michael fetch our horses from the field
    Franklin and I will down unto the quay,
90 For I have certain goods there to unload.
    Meanwhile prepare our breakfast, gentle Alice,
    For yet ere noon we'll take horse and away.
        Exeunt ARDEN *and* FRANKLIN.
    ALICE: Ere noon he means to take horse and away.
    Sweet news is this. Oh, that some airy spirit
    Would, in the shape and likeness of a horse,
    Gallop with Arden across the ocean
    And throw him from his back into the waves.
    Sweet Mosby is the man that hath my heart,
    And he usurps it, having nought but this,
100 That I am tied to him by marriage.
    Love is a god, and marriage is but words,
    And therefore Mosby's title is the best.
    Tush! whether it be or no he shall be mine,
    In spite of him, of Hymen, and of rites.
        Here enters ADAM *of the Flower-de-Luce.*
    And here comes Adam of the Flower-de-Luce.
    I hope he brings me tidings of my love.
    How now, Adam, what is the news with you?
    Be not afraid, my husband is now from home.
    ADAM: He whom you wot of, Mosby, Mistress Alice,

99 *he* Arden.
104 *Hymen* god of marriage.
109 *wot* know.

Is come to town and sends you word by me   110
In any case you may not visit him.

ALICE: Not visit him?

ADAM: No, nor take no knowledge of his being here.

ALICE: But tell me, is he angry or displeased?

ADAM: Should seem so, for he is wondrous sad.

ALICE: Were he as mad as raving Hercules
    I'll see him. Ay, and were thy house of force,
    These hands of mine should raze it to the ground,
    Unless that thou wouldst bring me to my love.

ADAM: Nay, and you be so impatient I'll be gone.   120

ALICE: Stay, Adam, stay; thou wert wont to be my
        friend.
    Ask Mosby how I have incurred his wrath;
    Bear him from me these pair of silver dice
    With which we play'd for kisses many a time,
    And when I lost I won and so did he –
    Such winning and such losing Jove send me!
    And bid him, if his love do not decline,
    Come this morning but along my door,
    And as a stranger but salute me there.
    This may he do without suspect or fear.   130

ADAM: I'll tell him what you say, and so farewell.
    Exit ADAM.

ALICE: Do, and one day I'll make amends for all.
    I know he loves me well but dares not come
    Because my husband is so jeal[i]ous,
    And these my narrow-prying neighbours blab,
    Hinder our meetings when we would confer.
    But if I live that block shall be removed,
    And Mosby, thou that comes to me by stealth,
    Shalt neither fear the biting speech of men

117 *of force* fortified.
120 *and* if.
137 *block* 1 obstruction; 2 hard-hearted person.

140   Nor Arden's looks. As surely shall he die
    As I abhor him and love only thee.
       Here enters MICHAEL.
    How now, Michael, whither are you going?

MICHAEL: To fetch my master's nag. I hope you'll think
    on me.

ALICE: Ay, but Michael, see you keep your oath,
    And be as secret as you are resolute.

MICHAEL: I'll see he shall not live above a week.

ALICE: On that condition, Michael, here is my hand:
    None shall have Mosby's sister but thyself.

MICHAEL: I understand the painter here hard by
150   Hath made report that he and Sue is sure.

ALICE: There's no such matter, Michael; believe it not.

MICHAEL: But he hath sent a dagger sticking in a heart,
    With a verse or two stolen from a painted cloth,
    The which I hear the wench keeps in her chest.
    Well let her keep it; I shall find a fellow
    That can both write and read and make rhyme too,
    And if I do – well, I say no more:
    I'll send from London such a taunting letter
    As she shall eat the heart he sent with salt,
160   And fling the dagger at the painter's head.

ALICE: What needs all this? I say that Susan's thine.

MICHAEL: Why then I say that I will kill my master,
    Or anything that you will have me do.

ALICE: But Michael, see you do it cunningly.

MICHAEL: Why, say I should be took, I'll ne'er confess
    That you know anything, and Susan being a maid
    May beg me from the gallows of the sheriff.

ALICE: Trust not to that, Michael.

MICHAEL: You cannot tell me, I have seen it, I.
170   But mistress, tell her whether I live or die,

150 *sure* betrothed.
153 *stolen* plagiarized. *painted cloth* common sort of room hanging.

I'll make her more worth than twenty painters can,
For I will rid mine elder brother away,
And then the farm of Bolton is mine own.
Who would not venture upon house and land,
When he may have it for a right-down blow?
   Here enters MOSBY.

ALICE: Yonder comes Mosby. Michael, get thee gone,
And let not him nor any know thy drifts.
   Exit MICHAEL.
Mosby, my love!

MOSBY: Away, I say, and talk not to me now.

ALICE: A word or two, sweet heart, and then I will.   180
'Tis yet but early days, thou needest not fear.

MOSBY: Where is your husband?

ALICE: 'Tis now high water, and he is at the quay.

MOSBY: There let him be; henceforward know me not.

ALICE: Is this the end of all thy solemn oaths?
Is this the fruit thy reconcilement buds?
Have I for this given thee so many favours,
Incurr'd my husband's hate, and, out alas!
Made shipwreck of mine honour for thy sake?
And dost thou say 'henceforward know me not'?   190
Remember when I lock'd thee in my closet,
What were thy words and mine? Did we not both
Decree to murder Arden in the night?
The heavens can witness, and the world can tell,
Before I saw that falsehood look of thine,
'Fore I was tangled with thy 'ticing speech,
Arden to me was dearer than my soul –
And shall be still. Base peasant, get thee gone,

172 *rid . . . away* get rid of.
175 *right-down* downright.
177 *drifts* plottings.
181 *early days* early in the day.
191 *closet* private chamber.

And boast not of thy conquest over me,
200   Gotten by witchcraft and mere sorcery.
For what hast thou to countenance my love,
Being descended of a noble house,
And match'd already with a gentleman
Whose servant thou may'st be? And so farewell.

MOSBY: Ungentle and unkind Alice, now I see
That which I ever fear'd and find too true:
A woman's love is as the lightning flame,
Which even in bursting forth consumes itself.
To try thy constancy have I been strange.
210   Would I had never tried but lived in hope.

ALICE: What needs thou try me whom thou never
           found false?

MOSBY: Yet pardon me for love is jeal[i]ous.

ALICE: So list the sailor to the mermaid's song;
So looks the traveller to the basilisk.
I am content for to be reconcil'd,
And that I know will be mine overthrow.

MOSBY: Thine overthrow? First let the world dissolve.

ALICE: Nay, Mosby, let me still enjoy thy love,
And happen what will, I am resolute.
220   My saving husband hoards up bags of gold
To make our children rich, and now is he
Gone to unload the goods that shall be thine,
And he and Franklin will to London straight.

MOSBY: To London, Alice? If thou'lt be rul'd by me,
We'll make him sure enough 'fore coming there.

ALICE: Ah, would we could!

MOSBY: I happen'd on a painter yesternight,
The only cunning man of Christendom,

200 *mere* absolute.
201 *countenance* be in keeping with.   209 *strange* distant.
225 *make . . . enough* destroy him. *'fore* before.
228 *only* most.

For he can temper poison with his oil
That whoso looks upon the work he draws   230
Shall, with the beams that issue from his sight,
Suck venom to his breast and slay himself.
Sweet Alice, he shall draw thy counterfeit,
That Arden may by gazing on it perish.

ALICE: Ay, but Mosby, that is dangerous,
For thou, or I, or any other else,
Coming into the chamber where it hangs, may die.

MOSBY: Ay, but we'll have it covered with a cloth
And hung up in the study for himself.

ALICE: It may not be, for when the picture's drawn   240
Arden I know will come and show it me.

MOSBY: Fear not, we'll have that shall serve the turn.
This is the painter's house. I'll call him forth.

ALICE: But Mosby, I'll have no such picture, I.

MOSBY: I pray thee leave it to my discretion.
How, Clarke!
        Here enters CLARKE.
Oh, you are an honest man of your word, you serv'd
        me well.

CLARKE: Why sir, I'll do it for you at any time,
Provided as you have given your word
I may have Susan Mosby to my wife.   250
For as sharp-witted poets, whose sweet verse
Make heavenly gods break off their nectar draughts
And lay their ears down to the lowly earth,
Use humble promise to their sacred Muse,
So we that are the poets' favourites
Must have a love. Ay, Love is the painter's Muse,
That makes him frame a speaking countenance,
A weeping eye that witnesses heart's grief.
Then tell me, Master Mosby, shall I have her?

ALICE: 'Tis pity but he should; he'll use her well.   260

233 *counterfeit* portrait.   260 *but* unless.

MOSBY: Clarke, here's my hand; my sister shall be
  thine.

CLARKE: Then brother, to requite this courtesy,
 You shall command my life, my skill and all.

ALICE: Ah, that thou could'st be secret!

MOSBY: Fear him not; leave; I have talk'd sufficient.

CLARKE: You know not me that ask such questions.
 Let it suffice, I know you love him well
 And fain would have your husband made away;
 Wherein, trust me, you show a noble mind,
270 That rather than you'll live with him you hate,
 You'll venture life, and die with him you love.
 The like will I do for my Susan's sake.

ALICE: Yet nothing could enforce me to the deed
 But Mosby's love. Might I without control
 Enjoy thee still, then Arden should not die;
 But seeing I cannot, therefore let him die.

MOSBY: Enough, sweet Alice, thy kind words makes me
  melt.
 [*To* CLARKE] Your trick of poisoned pictures we dis-
  like;
 Some other poison would do better far.

280 ALICE: Ay, such as might be put into his broth,
 And yet in taste not to be found at all.

CLARKE: I know your mind, and here I have it for you.
 Put but a dram of this into his drink,
 Or any kind of broth that he shall eat,
 And he shall die within an hour after.

ALICE: As I am a gentlewoman, Clarke, next day
 Thou and Susan shall be married.

MOSBY: And I'll make her dowry more than I'll talk of,
  Clarke.

CLARKE: Yonder's your husband. Mosby, I'll be gone.
  Here enters ARDEN *and* FRANKLIN [*and* MICHAEL].

274 *control* restraint.

ALICE: In good time, see where my husband comes.   290
  Master Mosby, ask him the question yourself.
    Exit CLARKE.
MOSBY: Master Arden, being at London yesternight,
  The Abbey lands whereof you are now possess'd
  Were offered me on some occasion
  By Greene, one of Sir Antony Ager's men.
  I pray you, sir, tell me, are not the lands yours?
  Hath any other interest herein?
ARDEN: Mosby, that question we'll decide anon.
  Alice, make ready my breakfast; I must hence.
    Exit ALICE.
  As for the lands, Mosby, they are mine,   300
  By letters patents from his majesty.
  But I must have a mandate for my wife;
  They say you seek to rob me of her love.
  Villain, what makes thou in her company?
  She's no companion for so base a groom.
MOSBY: Arden, I thought not on her, I came to thee;
  But rather than I pocket up this wrong –
FRANKLIN: What will you do, sir?
MOSBY: Revenge it on the proudest of you both.
    Then ARDEN *draws forth* MOSBY'S *sword.*
ARDEN: So, sirrah, you may not wear a sword;   310
  The statute makes against artificers;
  I warrant that I do. Now use your bodkin,
  Your Spanish needle, and your pressing iron,
  For this shall go with me. And mark my words,
  You goodman botcher, 'tis to you I speak:

290 *In good time* at the right moment.
305 *groom* fellow.
307 *pocket up* take without showing resentment.
311 *makes . . . artificers* provides against the wearing of swords by
handicraftsmen.
312 *warrant* have warrant for.

The next time that I take thee near my house,
Instead of legs, I'll make thee crawl on stumps.
MOSBY: Ah Master Arden, you have injur'd me;
I do appeal to God and to the world.
320 FRANKLIN: Why, canst thou deny thou wert a botcher
once?
MOSBY: Measure me what I am not what I was.
ARDEN: Why, what art thou now but a velvet drudge,
A cheating steward, and a base-minded peasant?
MOSBY: Arden, now thou hast belch'd and vomited
The rancorous venom of thy mis-swol'n heart
Hear me but speak. As I intend to live
With God and his elected saints in Heaven,
I never meant more to solicit her,
And that she knows and all the world shall see.
330 I loved her once; sweet Arden pardon me.
I could not choose, her beauty fired my heart.
But time hath quench'd these over-raging coals;
And Arden, though I now frequent thy house,
'Tis for my sister's sake, her waiting-maid,
And not for hers. Mayest thou enjoy her long;
Hell-fire and wrathful vengeance light on me
If I dishonour her or injure thee.
ARDEN: Mosby, with these thy protestations
The deadly hatred of my heart is appeased,
340 And thou and I'll be friends if this prove true.
As for the base terms I gave thee late,
Forget them, Mosby; I had cause to speak
When all the knights and gentlemen of Kent
Make common table-talk of her and thee.
MOSBY: Who lives that is not touch'd with slanderous
tongues?
FRANKLIN: Then Mosby, to eschew the speech of
men,

322 *velvet drudge* menial in velvet livery.

Upon whose general bruit all honour hangs,
Forbear his house.

ARDEN: Forbear it? Nay, rather frequent it more;
The world shall see that I distrust her not.   350
To warn him on the sudden from my house
Were to confirm the rumour that is grown.

MOSBY: By my faith, sir, you say true.
And therefore will I sojourn here awhile,
Until our enemies have talk'd their fill.
And then I hope they'll cease and at last confess
How causeless they have injur'd her and me.

ARDEN: And I will lie at London all this term
To let them see how light I weigh their words.
        Here enters ALICE.

ALICE: Husband, sit down, your breakfast will be cold.   360

ARDEN: Come, Master Mosby, will you sit with us?

MOSBY: I cannot eat, but I'll sit for company.

ARDEN: Sirrah Michael, see our horse be ready.
        [*Exit* MICHAEL *and re-enter.*]

ALICE: Husband, why pause ye, why eat you not?

ARDEN: I am not well; there's something in this broth
That is not wholesome. Didst thou make it, Alice?

ALICE: I did, and that's the cause it likes not you.
        Then she throws down the broth on the ground.
There's nothing that I do can please your taste.
You were best to say I would have poisoned you.
I cannot speak or cast aside my eye   370
But he imagines I have stept awry.
Here's he that you cast in my teeth so oft;
Now will I be convinced or purge myself.
I charge thee speak to this mistrustful man,
Thou that wouldst see me hang, thou, Mosby, thou.

347 *bruit* report.
367 *likes* pleases.
373 *convinced* proved guilty.

What favour hast thou had more than a kiss
At coming or departing from the town?

MOSBY: You wrong yourself and me, to cast these
doubts;
Your loving husband is not jeal[i]ous.

380 ARDEN: Why, gentle Mistress Alice, cannot I be ill
But you'll accuse yourself?
Franklin, thou hast a box of mithridate;
I'll take a little to prevent the worst.

FRANKLIN: Do so, and let us presently take horse.
My life for yours, ye shall do well enough.

ALICE: Give me a spoon; I'll eat of it myself.
Would it were full of poison to the brim!
Then should my cares and troubles have an end.
Was ever silly woman so tormented?

390 ARDEN: Be patient, sweet love, I mistrust not thee.

ALICE: God will revenge it, Arden, if thou dost,
For never woman lov'd her husband better
Than I do thee.

ARDEN: I know it, sweet Alice; cease to complain,
Lest that in tears I answer thee again.

FRANKLIN: Come, leave this dallying and let us away.

ALICE: Forbear to wound me with that bitter word.
Arden shall go to London in my arms.

ARDEN: Loth am I to depart, yet I must go.

400 ALICE: Wilt thou to London then, and leave me here?
Ah, if thou love me gentle Arden, stay.
Yet if thy business be of great import
Go if thou wilt; I'll bear it as I may.
But write from London to me every week,
Nay, every day, and stay no longer there
Than thou must needs, lest that I die for sorrow.

382 *mithridate* medicine regarded as a universal antidote against
poisons and infectious diseases. See note.
389 *silly* defenceless.

ARDEN: I'll write unto thee every other tide,
And so farewell, sweet Alice, till we meet next.
ALICE: Farewell, husband, seeing you'll have it so.
And Master Franklin, seeing you take him hence,   410
In hope you'll hasten him home I'll give you this.
And then she kisseth him.
FRANKLIN: And if he stay, the fault shall not be mine.
Mosby, farewell, and see you keep your oath.
MOSBY: I hope he is not jealous of me now.
ARDEN: No, Mosby, no. Hereafter think of me
As of your dearest friend. And so farewell.
Exeunt ARDEN, FRANKLIN *and* MICHAEL.
ALICE: I am glad he is gone; he was about to stay,
But did you mark me then how I brake off?
MOSBY: Ay, Alice, and it was cunningly performed.
But what a villain is this painter Clarke!   420
ALICE: Was it not a goodly poison that he gave!
Why, he's as well now as he was before.
It should have been some fine confection
That might have given the broth some dainty taste.
This powder was too gross and populous.
MOSBY: But had he eaten but three spoonfuls more
Then had he died and our love continued.
ALICE: Why, so it shall, Mosby, albeit he live.
MOSBY: It is unpossible, for I have sworn
Never hereafter to solicit thee,   430
Or whilst he lives once more importune thee.
ALICE: Thou shalt not need; I will importune thee.
What, shall an oath make thee forsake my love?
As if I have not sworne as much myself,
And given my hand unto him in the church!
Tush, Mosby, oaths are words, and words is wind,
And wind is mutable. Then I conclude,
'Tis childishness to stand upon an oath.

425 *gross and populous* coarse and crude (in flavour).

MOSBY: Well proved, Mistress Alice, yet by your leave
440   I'll keep mine unbroken whilst he lives.
ALICE: Ay, do, and spare not. His time is but short,
    For if thou beest as resolute as I,
    We'll have him murdered as he walks the streets.
    In London many alehouse ruffians keep,
    Which, as I hear, will murder men for gold.
    They shall be soundly fee'd to pay him home.
        Here enters GREENE.
MOSBY: Alice, what's he that comes yonder; knowest
        thou him?
ALICE: Mosby, be gone; I hope 'tis one that comes
    To put in practice our intended drifts. *Exit* MOSBY.
450 GREENE: Mistress Arden, you are well met.
    I am sorry that your husband is from home,
    Whenas my purposed journey was to him.
    Yet all my labour is not spent in vain,
    For I suppose that you can full discourse,
    And flat resolve me of the thing I seek.
ALICE: What is it, Master Greene? If that I may
    Or can, with safety, I will answer you.
GREENE: I heard your husband hath the grant of late,
    Confirmed by letters patents from the king,
460   Of all the lands of the Abbey of Faversham,
    Generally intitled, so that all former grants
    Are cut off, whereof I myself had one;
    But now my interest by that is void.
    This is all, Mistress Arden, is it true nor no?
ALICE: True, Master Greene, the lands are his in state,

444 *keep* lodge.
446 *pay him home* kill him.
452 *Whenas* since.
455 *flat resolve* completely satisfy.
461 *intitled* deeded.   462 *cut off* superseded.
465 *in state* by legal ownership.

And whatsoever leases were before
Are void for term of Master Arden's life.
He hath the grant under the Chancery seal.
GREENE: Pardon me, Mistress Arden, I must speak,
For I am touch'd. Your husband doth me wrong   470
To wring me from the little land I have.
My living is my life; only that
Resteth remainder of my portion.
Desire of wealth is endless in his mind
And he is greedy-gaping still for gain.
Nor cares he though young gentlemen do beg,
So he may scrape and hoard up in his pouch.
But seeing he hath taken my lands, I'll value life
As careless as he is careful for to get;
And tell him this from me: I'll be revenged,   480
And so as he shall wish the Abbey lands
Had rested still within their former state.
ALICE: Alas, poor gentleman, I pity you,
And woe is me that any man should want.
God knows, 'tis not my fault. But wonder not
Though he be hard to others when to me –
Ah, Master Greene, God knows how I am us'd.
GREENE: Why, Mistress Arden, can the crabbed churl
Use you unkindly? Respects he not your birth,
Your honourable friends, nor what you brought?   490
Why, all Kent knows your parentage and what you are.
ALICE: Ah, Master Greene, be it spoken in secret here,
I never live good day with him alone.
When he is at home, then have I froward looks,

467 *term* period.
470 *touch'd* wounded (metaphorically).
475 *still* ever.   477 *so* provided that.
479 *get* acquire (wealth, etc.).   488 *crabbed* ill-tempered.
490 *nor . . . brought* i.e. in way of dowry.
494 *froward* ill-tempered.

Hard words and blows, to mend the match withall.
And though I might content as good a man,
Yet doth he keep in every corner trulls,
And weary with his trugs at home,
Then rides he straight to London; there, forsooth,
500 He revels it among such filthy ones
As counsels him to make away his wife.
Thus live I daily in continual fear,
In sorrow, so despairing of redress
As every day I wish with hearty prayer
That he or I were taken forth the world.

GREENE: Now trust me, Mistress Alice, it grieveth me
So fair a creature should be so abused.
Why, who would have thought the civil sir so sullen,
He looks so smoothly. Now, fie upon him, churl!
510 And if he live a day he lives too long.
But frolic, woman, I shall be the man
Shall set you free from all this discontent.
And if the churl deny my interest
And will not yield my lease into my hand,
I'll pay him home, whatever hap to me.

ALICE: But speak you as you think?

GREENE: Ay, God's my witness, I mean plain dealing,
For I had rather die than lose my land.

ALICE: Then Master Greene, be counselled by me:
520 Endanger not yourself for such a churl,
But hire some cutter for to cut him short,
And here's ten pound to wager them withal.
When he is dead you shall have twenty more,

495 *mend the match* make up the marriage bargain.
497, 8 *trulls, trugs* wenches, harlots.
509 *smoothly* courteous.
513 *interest* legal right to possession.
521 *cutter* cut-throat.
522 *wager* pay (as wages).

And the lands whereof my husband is possess'd
Shall be intitled as they were before.

GREENE: Will you keep promise with me?

ALICE: Or count me false and perjur'd whilst I live.

GREENE: Then here's my hand, I'll have him so
dispatch'd.
I'll up to London straight; I'll thither post,
And never rest till I have compass'd it.　　　　530
Till then farewell.

ALICE: Good fortune follow all your forward thoughts.
Exit GREENE.
And whosoever doth attempt the deed,
A happy hand I wish, and so farewell.
All this goes well. Mosby, I long for thee
To let thee know all that I have contrived.
Here enters MOSBY *and* CLARKE.

MOSBY: How now, Alice, what's the news?

ALICE: Such as will content thee well, sweet heart.

MOSBY: Well, let them pass awhile, and tell me, Alice,
How have you dealt and tempered with my sister?　　　540
What, will she have my neighbour Clarke or no?

ALICE: What, Master Mosby? let him woo himself.
Think you that maids look not for fair words?
Go to her, Clarke, she's all alone within;
Michael, my man, is clean out of her books.

CLARKE: I thank you, Mistress Arden, I will in,
And if fair Susan and I can make a gree,
You shall command me to the uttermost
As far as either goods or life may stretch. *Exit* CLARKE.

MOSBY: Now, Alice, let's hear thy news.　　　　550

ALICE: They be so good that I must laugh for joy
Before I can begin to tell my tale.

539 *them* i.e. the news (plural concept).
540 *tempered with* worked upon.
547 *gree* agreement.

MOSBY: Let's hear, then, that I may laugh for company.

ALICE: This morning Master Greene, Dick Greene I
           mean,
From whom my husband had the Abbey land,
Came hither railing for to know the truth,
Whether my husband had the lands by grant.
I told him all, whereat he storm'd amain,
And swore he would cry quittance with the churl,
560   And if he did deny his interest
Stab him whatsoever did befall himself.
Whenas I saw his choler thus to rise
I whetted on the gentleman with words;
And to conclude, Mosby, at last we grew
To composition for my husband's death.
I gave him ten pound to hire knaves
By some device to make away the churl.
When he is dead he should have twenty more
And repossess his former lands again.
570   On this we 'greed and he is ridden straight
To London to bring his death about.

MOSBY: But call you this good news?

ALICE: Ay, sweet heart, be they not?

MOSBY: 'Twere cheerful news to hear the churl were
           dead,
But trust me, Alice, I take it passing ill
You would be so forgetful of our state,
To make recount of it to every groom.
What! to acquaint each stranger with our drifts,
Chiefly in case of murder! Why, 'tis the way

558 *amain* mightily.
559 *cry . . .with* get even with.
562 *Whenas* when.
563 *whetted on* incited.
565 *composition for* agreement over.
575 *passing* extremely.

To make it open unto Arden's self,   580
And bring thyself and me to ruin both.
Forewarn'd, forearm'd: who threats his enemy
Lends him a sword to guard himself withal.

ALICE: I did it for the best.

MOSBY: Well, seeing 'tis done, cheer'ly let it pass.
You know this Greene. Is he not religious?
A man, I guess, of great devotion.

ALICE: He is.

MOSBY: Then, sweet Alice, let it pass. I have a drift
Will quiet all, whatever is amiss.   590

        Here enters CLARKE *and* SUSAN.

ALICE: How now, Clarke, have you found me false?
Did I not plead the matter hard for you?

CLARKE: You did.

MOSBY: And what? Will't be a match?

CLARKE: A match, i'faith sir! Ay, the day is mine.
The painter lays his colours to the life,
His pencil draws no shadows in his love;
Susan is mine.

ALICE: You make her blush.

MOSBY: What, sister, is it Clarke must be the man?   600

SUSAN: It resteth in your grant. Some words are past,
And haply we be grown unto a match
If you be willing that it shall be so.

MOSBY: Ah, Master Clarke, it resteth at my grant;
You see my sister's yet at my dispose,
But so you'll grant me one thing I shall ask
I am content my sister shall be yours.

CLARKE: What is it, Master Mosby?

MOSBY: I do remember once in secret talk

580 *open* revealed.
601 *It . . . grant* It lies in your power to grant.
602 *haply* perhaps.
605 *dispose* disposal.

You told me how you could compound by art
610　A crucifix impoisoned,
That whoso look upon it should wax blind,
And with the scent be stifled, that ere long
He should die poison'd that did view it well.
I would have you make me such a crucifix,
And then I'll grant my sister shall be yours.

CLARKE: Though I am loth, because it toucheth life,
Yet rather or I'll leave sweet Susan's love,
I'll do it, and with all the haste I may.
620　But for whom is it?

ALICE: Leave that to us. Why, Clarke, is it possible
That you should paint and draw it out yourself,
The colours being baleful and impoisoned,
And no ways prejudice yourself withal?

MOSBY: Well questioned, Alice; Clarke, how answer
　　you that?

CLARKE: Very easily; I'll tell you straight
How I do work of these impoisoned drugs:
I fasten on my spectacles so close
630　As nothing can any way offend my sight;
Then, as I put a leaf within my nose,
So put I rhubarb to avoid the smell,
And softly as another work I paint.

MOSBY: 'Tis very well, but against when shall I have it?

CLARKE: Within this ten days.

MOSBY: 'Twill serve the turn.
Now, Alice, let's in and see what cheer you keep.
I hope now Master Arden is from home,
You'll give me leave to play your husband's part.

ALICE: Mosby, you know who's master of my heart;
640　He may well be the master of the house. *Exeunt.*

623 *baleful* harmful.
624 *prejudice* injure.
633 *softly* easily, comfortably. *as* as with.

SCENE TWO

Here enters GREENE *and* BRADSHAW.

BRADSHAW: See you them that comes yonder, Master
  Greene?

GREENE: Ay, very well. Do you know them?

Here enters BLACK WILL *and* SHAKEBAG.

BRADSHAW: The one I know not, but he seems a knave,
  Chiefly for bearing the other company;
  For such a slave, so vile a rogue as he,
  Lives not again upon the earth.
  Black Will is his name, I tell you, Master Greene.
  At Boulogne he and I were fellow soldiers
  Where he played such pranks
  As all the camp fear'd him for his villainy.   10
  I warrant you he bears so bad a mind
  That for a crown he'll murder any man.

GREENE [*aside*]: The fitter is he for my purpose, marry!

BLACK WILL: How now, fellow Bradshaw! Whither
  away so early?

BRADSHAW: Oh, Will, times are changed; no fellows
  now,
  Though we were once together in the field;
  Yet thy friend to do thee any good I can.

BLACK WILL: Why, Bradshaw, was not thou and I fellow soldiers at Boulogne where I was a corporal and   20
thou but a base, mercenary groom? No fellows now
because you are a goldsmith, and have a little plate in
your shop? You were glad to call me 'fellow Will' and
with a curtsey to the earth 'One snatch, good corporal'
when I stole the half ox from John the victualer, and
domineered with it amongst good fellows in one night.

26 *domineered* revelled.

BRADSHAW: Ay, Will, those days are past with me.

BLACK WILL: Ay, but they be not past with me, for I
keep that same honourable mind still. Good neighbour Bradshaw, you are too proud to be my fellow,
but were it not that I see more company coming down
the hill, I would be fellows with you once more, and
share crowns with you too. But let that pass and tell
me whither you go.

BRADSHAW: To London, Will, about a piece of service
Wherein haply thou may'st pleasure me.

BLACK WILL: What is it?

BRADSHAW: Of late, Lord Cheiny lost some plate,
Which one did bring and sold it at my shop
Saying he served Sir Antony Cooke.
A search was made, the plate was found with me,
And I am bound to answer at the 'size.
Now Lord Cheiny solemnly vows
If law will serve him he'll hang me for his plate.
Now I am going to London upon hope
To find the fellow. Now Will, I know
Thou art acquainted with such companions.

BLACK WILL: What manner of man was he?

BRADSHAW: A lean-faced, writhen knave,
Hawk-nos'd and very hollow-eyed,
With mighty furrows in his stormy brows,
Long hair down his shoulders curled;
His chin was bare, but on his upper lip
A mutchado which he wound about his ear.

BLACK WILL: What apparel had he?

BRADSHAW: A watchet satin doublet all to-torn
(The inner side did bear the greater show),

32–3 and . . . too i.e. rob you. 42 'size assize. 49 writhen twisted.
54 mutchado moustache. 56 watchet light blue. to-torn greatly torn.
57 The . . . show: The lining looked better than the outside, or
possibly, more lining than outside was visible.

A pair of threadbare velvet hose, seam rent,
A worsted stocking rent above the shoe,
A livery cloak, but all the lace was off; 60
'Twas bad, but yet it served to hide the plate.

BLACK WILL: Sirrah Shakebag, canst thou remember
since we trolled the bowl at Sittingburgh where I broke
the tapster's head of the Lion with a cudgel-stick?

SHAKEBAG: Ay, very well, Will.

BLACK WILL: Why, it was with the money that the plate
was sold for. Sirrah Bradshaw, what wilt thou give
him that can tell thee who sold thy plate?

BRADSHAW: Who, I pray thee, good Will?

BLACK WILL: Why, 'twas one Jack Fitten. He's now 70
in Newgate for stealing a horse, and shall be arraigned
the next 'size.

BRADSHAW: Why then, let Lord Cheiny seek Jack
    Fitten forth,
For I'll back and tell him who robbed him of his plate.
This cheers my heart. Master Greene, I'll leave you,
For I must to the Isle of Sheppey with speed.

GREENE: Before you go let me entreat you
To carry this letter to Mistress Arden of Faversham
And humbly recommend me to herself.

BRADSHAW: That will I, Master Greene, and so farewell. 80
Here, Will, there's a crown for thy good news.
    Exit BRADSHAW.

BLACK WILL: Farewell, Bradshaw; I'll drink no water
for thy sake whilst this lasts. Now, gentleman, shall
we have your company to London?

GREENE: Nay, stay, sirs,
A little more; I needs must use your help,
And in a matter of great consequence,

63–4 *trolled the bowl* passed round the drinking cup.
64 *the . . . Lion* the head of the tapster of the Lion.
71 *arraigned* indicted.

Wherein if you'll be secret and profound,
I'll give you twenty angels for your pains.

90 BLACK WILL: How? Twenty angels? Give my fellow
George Shakebag and me twenty angels, and if
thou'lt have thy own father slain that thou mayest
inherit his land we'll kill him.

SHAKEBAG: Ay, thy mother, thy sister, thy brother, or
all thy kin.

GREENE: Well, this is it: Arden of Faversham
Hath highly wrong'd me about the Abbey Land,
That no revenge but death will serve the turn.
Will you two kill him? Here's the angels down

100 And I will lay the platform of his death.

BLACK WILL: Plat me no platforms! Give me the money,
I'll stab him as he stands pissing against a wall, but I'll
kill him.

SHAKEBAG: Where is he?

GREENE: He is now at London, in Aldersgate Street.

SHAKEBAG: He's dead as if he had been condemned by
an Act of Parliament if once Black Will and I swear
his death.

GREENE: Here is ten pound, and when he is dead

110 Ye shall have twenty more.

BLACK WILL: My fingers itches to be at the peasant.
Ah, that I might be set a work thus through the year
and that murder would grow to an occupation, that a
man might without danger of law. Zounds! I warrant
I should be warden of the company. Come, let us be
going, and we'll bait at Rochester where I'll give thee a
gallon of sack to handsel the match withal. *Exeunt.*

89 *angels* gold coins, worth about 10s. each.
98 *That* so that. *serve the turn* serve my purpose.
100 *lay the platform* devise the plan.
114 *might* i.e. might do the job.   116 *bait* stop for food.
117 *sack* a class of white wines from Spain and the Canaries.
handsel inaugurate auspiciously.

SCENE THREE

Here enters MICHAEL.

MICHAEL: I have gotten such a letter as will touch the
painter and thus it is:

Here enters ARDEN *and* FRANKLIN *and hears* MICHAEL
read this letter

'My duty remembered, Mistress Susan, hoping in God
you be in good health, as I Michael was at the making
hereof. This is to certify you that, as the turtle true
when she hath lost her mate sitteth alone, so I, mourn-
ing for your absence, do walk up and down Paul's till
one day I fell asleep and lost my master's pantofles. Ah,
Mistress Susan, abolish that paltry painter, cut him off
by the shins with a frowning look of your crabbed   10
countenance, and think upon Michael who, drunk with
the dregs of your favour, will cleave as fast to your love
as a plaster of pitch to a galled horseback. Thus hoping
you will let my passions penetrate, or rather impetrate
mercy of your meek hands, I end.

              Yours, Michael, or else not Michael.'

ARDEN: Why, you paltry knave,
Stand you here loitering, knowing my affairs,
What haste my business craves to send to Kent?

FRANKLIN: 'Faith, friend Michael, this is very ill,   20
Knowing your master hath no more but you,
And do ye slack his business for your own?

ARDEN: Where is the letter, sirrah? Let me see it.

Then he [MICHAEL] *gives him the letter*.

See, Master Franklin, here's proper stuff:

5 *turtle* turtle-dove.
7 *Paul's* St Paul's Cathedral. See note.
8 *pantofles* slippers.   14 *impetrate* obtain by request.

Susan my maid, the painter and my man,
A crew of harlots, all in love, forsooth.
Sirrah, let me hear no more of this,
Nor, for thy life, once write to her a word.
 Here enters GREENE, BLACK WILL *and* SHAKEBAG.
Wilt thou be married to so base a trull?
30 'Tis Mosby's sister. Come I once at home
I'll rouse her from remaining in my house.
Now, Master Franklin, let us go walk in Paul's.
Come but a turn or two and then away.
 Exeunt [ARDEN, FRANKLIN *and* MICHAEL].
GREENE: The first is Arden, and that's his man.
 The other is Franklin, Arden's dearest friend.
BLACK WILL: Zounds, I'll kill them all three.
GREENE: Nay, sirs, touch not his man in any case,
 But stand close and take you fittest standing,
 And at his coming forth speed him.
40 To the Nag's Head, there is this coward's haunt.
 But now I'll leave you till the deed be done.
 Exit GREENE
SHAKEBAG: If he be not paid his own ne'er trust Shake-
 bag.
BLACK WILL: Sirrah Shakebag, at his coming forth I'll
 run him through and then to the Blackfriars and there
 take water and away.
SHAKEBAG: Why, that's the best; but see thou miss him
 not.
BLACK WILL: How can I miss him when I think on the
 forty angels I must have more?
 Here enters a PRENTICE.
PRENTICE: 'Tis very late; I were best shut up my stall,
50 for here will be old filching when the press comes forth
 of Paul's.

26 *harlots* lewd persons of either sex.
39 *speed* dispatch. 50 *old* plentiful.

Then lets he down his window and it breaks BLACK
WILL'S *head.*

BLACK WILL: Zounds, draw, Shakebag, draw! I am almost killed.

PRENTICE: We'll tame you, I warrant.

BLACK WILL: Zounds, I am tame enough already.

Here enters ARDEN, FRANKLIN *and* MICHAEL.

ARDEN: What troublesome fray or mutiny is this?

FRANKLIN: 'Tis nothing but some brabbling, paltry
fray,
Devised to pick men's pockets in the throng.

ARDEN: Is't nothing else? Come, Franklin, let us away.

Exeunt [ARDEN, FRANKLIN *and* MICHAEL].

BLACK WILL: What mends shall I have for my broken
head?

PRENTICE: Marry, this mends, that if you get you not   60
away all the sooner, you shall be well beaten and sent
to the Counter. *Exit* PRENTICE.

BLACK WILL: Well, I'll be gone. But look to your signs,
for I'll pull them down all. Shakebag, my broken head
grieves me not so much as by this means Arden hath
escaped. I had a glimpse of him and his companion.

Here enters GREENE.

GREENE: Why, sirs, Arden's as well as I; I met him and
Franklin going merrily to the ordinary again. What,
dare you not do it?

BLACK WILL: Yes, sir, we dare do it, but were my consent to give again we would not do it under ten pound
more. I value every drop of my blood at a French   70
crown. I have had ten pound to steal a dog, and we

56 *brabbling* brawling.
59 *mends* reparation.
62 *the Counter* a London prison.
65 *as* as the fact that.
68 *ordinary* tavern, or eating-room in a tavern.

have no more here to kill a man. But that a bargain
is a bargain and so forth you should do it yourself.

GREENE: I pray thee, how came thy head broke?

BLACK WILL: Why, thou seest it is broke, dost thou
    not?

SHAKEBAG: Standing against a stall watching Arden's
80   coming, a boy let down his shop window and broke
    his head. Whereupon arose a brawl, and in the tumult
    Arden escaped us, and passed by unthought on. But for-
    bearance is no acquittance; another time we'll do it,
    I warrant thee.

GREENE: I pray thee, Will, make clean thy bloody brow,
    And let us bethink us on some other place
    Where Arden may be met with handsomely.
    Remember how devoutly thou hast sworne
    To kill the villain; think upon thine oath.

90 BLACK WILL: Tush, I have broken five hundred oaths;
    But wouldst thou charm me to effect this deed,
    Tell me of gold, my resolution's fee;
    Say thou seest Mosby kneeling at my knees,
    Off'ring me service for my high attempt;
    And sweet Alice Arden with a lap of crowns
    Comes with a lowly curtsey to the earth,
    Saying 'Take this but for thy quarterage,
    Such yearly tribute will I answer thee'.
    Why, this would steel soft-mettled cowardice,
100   With which Black Will was never tainted with.
    I tell thee, Greene, the forlorn traveller,
    Whose lips are glued with summer's parching heat,
    Ne'er long'd so much to see a running brook
    As I to finish Arden's tragedy.
    Seest thou this gore that cleaveth to my face?
    From hence ne'er will I wash this bloody stain
    Till Arden's heart be panting in my hand.

97 *quarterage* quarterly payment.

GREENE: Why, that's well said; but what saith Shake-
　　　　bag?

SHAKEBAG: I cannot paint my valour out with words;
But, give me place and opportunity,　　　　　　　　　110
Such mercy as the starven lioness,
When she is dry-suck'd of her eager young,
Shows to the prey that next encounters her,
On Arden so much pity would I take.

GREENE: So should it fare with men of firm resolve.
And now, sirs, seeing this accident
Of meeting him in Paul's hath no success,
Let us bethink us on some other place,
Whose earth may swallow up this Arden's blood.

　　　Here enters MICHAEL.

See, yonder comes his man, and wot you what,　　　120
The foolish knave is in love with Mosby's sister,
And for her sake, whose love he cannot get
Unless Mosby solicit his suit,
The villain hath sworn the slaughter of his master.
We'll question him for he may stead us much.
How now, Michael, whither are you going?

MICHAEL: My master hath new supp'd
And I am going to prepare his chamber.

GREENE: Where supp'd Master Arden?

MICHAEL: At the Nag's Head, at the eighteen-pence　130
　　　　ordinary.
How now, Master Shakebag! What, Black Will!
God's dear lady, how chance your face is so bloody?

BLACK WILL: Go to, sirrah; there is a chance in it this
sauciness in you will make you be knocked.

---

120 *wot* know.　　　　　　125 *stead us much* be of great help to us.
127 *new* just, lately.
130 *eighteen-pence ordinary* room in an eating-house where the meal
cost eighteen-pence.
133 *Go to* exclamation expressing protest.

MICHAEL: Nay, and you be offended I'll be gone.

GREENE: Stay, Michael, you may not 'scape us so.
  Michael, I know you love your master well.

MICHAEL: Why, so I do; but wherefore urge you that?

GREENE: Because I think you love your mistress better.

140 MICHAEL: So think not I. But say, i'faith, what if I
      should?

SHAKEBAG: Come, to the purpose. Michael, we hear
  You have a pretty love in Faversham.

MICHAEL: Why, have I two or three, what's that to
      thee?

BLACK WILL: You deal too mildly with the peasant.
      Thus it is:
  'Tis known to us you love Mosby's sister;
  We know besides that you have ta'en your oath
  To further Mosby to your mistress' bed
  And kill your master for his sister's sake.
  Now sir, a poorer coward than yourself
150   Was never fostered in the coast of Kent.
  How comes it then that such a knave as you
  Dare swear a matter of such consequence?

GREENE: Ah, Will –

BLACK WILL: Tush, give me leave, there's no more
      but this:
  Sith thou hast sworn, we dare discover all,
  And hadst thou or shouldst thou utter it,
  We have devised a complot under hand –
  Whatever shall betide to any of us –
  To send thee roundly to the devil of hell.
160   And therefore thus: I am the very man,
  Mark'd in my birth-hour by the destinies,

138 *urge* bring up.
155 *Sith* since. *discover* reveal.
157 *complot* plot. *under hand* in secret.
159 *roundly* straightway.

To give an end to Arden's life on earth;
Thou but a member but to whet the knife
Whose edge must search the closet of his breast.
Thy office is but to appoint the place,
And train thy master to his tragedy;
Mine to perform it when occasion serves.
Then be not nice, but here devise with us
How and what way we may conclude his death.

SHAKEBAG: So shalt thou purchase Mosby for thy 170
    friend
And by his friendship gain his sister's love.

GREENE: So shall thy mistress be thy favourer
And thou disburdened of the oath thou made.

MICHAEL: Well, gentlemen, I cannot but confess,
Sith you have urged me so apparently,
That I have vowed my Master Arden's death,
And he whose kindly love and liberal hand
Doth challenge nought but good deserts of me
I will deliver over to your hands.
This night come to his house at Aldersgate. 180
The doors I'll leave unlock'd against you come.
No sooner shall ye enter through the latch,
Over the threshold to the inner court,
But on your left hand shall you see the stairs
That leads directly to my master's chamber.
There take him and dispose him as ye please.
Now it were good we parted company.
What I have promised I will perform.

BLACK WILL: Should you deceive us 'twould go wrong
    with you.

166 *train* lure.
168 *nice* coy, over-scrupulous.
175 *apparently* frankly.
178 *good deserts* good deeds in return.
181 *against you come* in preparation for your coming.

190 MICHAEL: I will accomplish all I have reveal'd.

BLACK WILL: Come, let's go drink. Choler makes me
as dry as a dog.

Exeunt BLACK WILL, GREENE *and* SHAKEBAG.
Manet MICHAEL.

MICHAEL: Thus feeds the lamb securely on the down
Whilst through the thicket of an arbour brake
The hunger-bitten wolf o'erpries his haunt
And takes advantage to eat him up.
Ah, harmless Arden, how, how hast thou misdone
That thus thy gentle life is levell'd at?
The many good turns that thou hast done to me
200 Now must I quittance with betraying thee.
I, that should take the weapon in my hand,
And buckler thee from ill-intending foes,
Do lead thee with a wicked, fraudful smile,
As unsuspected, to the slaughterhouse.
So have I sworn to Mosby and my mistress;
So have I promised to the slaughtermen.
And should I not deal currently with them
Their lawless rage would take revenge on me.
Tush, I will spurne at mercy for this once.
Let pity lodge where feeble women lie;
I am resolved, and Arden needs must die.

Exit MICHAEL.

192 *Manet* remains.   198 *levell'd* aimed.
200 *quittance* requite.
202 *buckler* shield.   207 *currently* honestly

SCENE FOUR

Here enters ARDEN *and* FRANKLIN.

ARDEN: No, Franklin, no. If fear or stormy threats,
  If love of me or care of womanhood,
  If fear of God or common speech of men,
  Who mangle credit with their wounding words
  And couch dishonour as dishonour buds,
  Might 'join repentance in her wanton thoughts,
  No question then but she would turn the leaf
  And sorrow for her dissolution.
  But she is rooted in her wickedness,
  Perverse and stubborn, not to be reclaim'd.   10
  Good counsel is to her as rain to weeds,
  And reprehension makes her vice to grow
  As Hydra's head that flourish'd by decay.
  Her faults, methink, are painted in my face
  For every searching eye to over-read,
  And Mosby's name, a scandal unto mine,
  Is deeply trenched in my blushing brow.
  Ah, Franklin, Franklin, when I think on this
  My heart's grief rends my other powers
  Worse than the conflict at the hour of death.   20
FRANKLIN: Gentle Arden, leave this sad lament.
  She will amend, and so your griefs will cease;
  Or else she'll die, and so your sorrows end.
  If neither of these two do haply fall,
  Yet let your comfort be that others bear
  Your woes twice doubled all with patience.

5 *couch* embroider. See note.
6 *'join* enjoin.
8 *dissolution* dissoluteness.   24 *fall* befall.

ARDEN: My house is irksome, there I cannot rest.

FRANKLIN: Then stay with me in London; go not home.

ARDEN: Then that base Mosby doth usurp my room
30   And makes his triumph of my being thence.
    At home or not at home, where'er I be,
    Here, here it lies, [*points to his heart*] ah Franklin, here it
        lies
    That will not out till wretched Arden dies.
        Here enters MICHAEL.

FRANKLIN: Forget your griefs awhile; here comes your
        man.

ARDEN: What o'clock is't, sirrah?

MICHAEL: Almost ten.

ARDEN: See, see how runs away the weary time.
    Come, Master Franklin, shall we go to bed?
        Exeunt ARDEN *and* MICHAEL.
        Manet FRANKLIN.

FRANKLIN: I pray you go before; I'll follow you.
40   Ah, what a hell is fretful jealousy!
    What pity-moving words, what deep-fetch'd sighs,
    What grievous groans and overlading woes
    Accompanies this gentle gentleman.
    Now will he shake his care-oppressed head,
    Then fix his sad eyes on the sullen earth,
    Ashamed to gaze upon the open world;
    Now will he cast his eyes up towards the Heavens,
    Looking that ways for redress of wrong.
    Sometimes he seeketh to beguile his grief
50   And tells a story with his careful tongue;
    Then comes his wife's dishonour in his thoughts
    And in the middle cutteth off his tale,
    Pouring fresh sorrow on his weary limbs.
    So woe-begone, so inly charged with woe

49 *beguile* divert attention away from.
50 *careful* full of care.

Was never any lived and bare it so.

   Here enters MICHAEL.

MICHAEL: My master would desire you come to bed.

FRANKLIN: Is he himself already in his bed?

   Exit FRANKLIN.

   Manet MICHAEL.

MICHAEL: He is and fain would have the light away.

  Conflicting thoughts encamped in my breast

  Awake me with the echo of their strokes;   60

  And I, a judge to censure either side,

  Can give to neither wished victory.

  My master's kindness pleads to me for life

  With just demand, and I must grant it him;

  My mistress, she hath forced me with an oath,

  For Susan's sake, the which I may not break,

  For that is nearer than a master's love;

  That grim-faced fellow, pitiless Black Will,

  And Shakebag, stern in bloody stratagem –

  Two rougher ruffians never lived in Kent –   70

  Have sworn my death if I infringe my vow,

  A dreadful thing to be consider'd of.

  Methinks I see them with their bolter'd hair,

  Staring and grinning in thy gentle face,

  And in their ruthless hands their daggers drawn,

  Insulting o'er thee with a peck of oaths,

  Whilst thou, submissive, pleading for relief,

  Art mangled by their ireful instruments.

  Methinks I hear them ask where Michael is,

  And pitiless Black Will cries 'Stab the slave!   80

  The peasant will detect the tragedy.'

55 *Was . . . lived* there was never anyone who lived.
61 *censure* pass sentence upon.
73 *bolter'd* tangled. See note.
76 *thee* i.e. Arden. *peck* heap (literally, fourth part of a bushel).
81 *detect* disclose.

The wrinkles in his foul, death-threat'ning face
Gapes open wide, like graves to swallow men.
My death to him is but a merriment,
And he will murder me to make him sport.
He comes, he comes! Ah, Master Franklin, help!
Call up the neighbours or we are but dead!

Here enters FRANKLIN *and* ARDEN.

FRANKLIN: What dismal outcry calls me from my rest?
ARDEN: What hath occasion'd such a fearful cry?
90   Speak Michael, hath any injur'd thee?
MICHAEL: Nothing, sir, but as I fell asleep
Upon the threshold, leaning to the stairs,
I had a fearful dream that troubled me,
And in my slumber thought I was beset
With murderer thieves that came to rifle me.
My trembling joints witness my inward fear.
I crave your pardons for disturbing you.
ARDEN: So great a cry for nothing I ne'er heard.
What, are the doors fast lock'd and all things safe?
100 MICHAEL: I cannot tell. I think I lock'd the doors.
ARDEN: I like not this but I'll go see myself.

[*He tries the doors.*]

Ne'er trust me but the doors were all unlock'd.
This negligence not half contenteth me.
Get you to bed, and if you love my favour
Let me have no more such pranks as these.
Come, Master Franklin, let us go to bed.
FRANKLIN: Ay, by my faith; the air is very cold.
Michael, farewell; I pray thee dream no more.

Exeunt.

---

92 *leaning to* (?)leaning against (referring to Michael; perhaps it should be 'leading to' referring to the threshold).

SCENE FIVE

Here enters BLACK WILL, GREENE *and* SHAKEBAG.

SHAKEBAG: Black night hath hid the pleasures of the
      day
  And sheeting darkness overhangs the earth,
  And with the black fold of her cloudy robe
  Obscures us from the eyesight of the world,
  In which sweet silence such as we triumph.
  The lazy minutes linger on their time,
  Loth to give due audit to the hour,
  Till in the watch our purpose be complete
  And Arden sent to everlasting night.
  Greene, get you gone and linger here about,   10
  And at some hour hence come to us again,
  Where we will give you instance of his death.
GREENE: Speed to my wish whose will soe'er says no;
  And so I'll leave you for an hour or two.
    Exit GREENE.
BLACK WILL: I tell thee, Shakebag, would this thing
      were done;
  I am so heavy that I can scarce go.
  This drowsiness in me bodes little good.
SHAKEBAG: How now, Will, become a precisian?
  Nay, then, let's go sleep when bugs and fears
  Shall kill our courages with their fancy's work.   20
BLACK WILL: Why, Shakebag, thou mistakes me much

8 *watch* time division of the night.
12 *instance* evidence.
13 *Speed . . . no* Success to my wish no matter who wills the contrary.
18 *precisian* Puritan.
19 *bugs* bugbears.

And wrongs me too in telling me of fear.
Wert not a serious thing we go about
It should be slipp'd till I had fought with thee.
To let thee know I am no coward, I,
I tell thee, Shakebag, thou abusest me.

SHAKEBAG: Why, thy speech bewrayed an inly kind of
fear,
And savour'd of a weak, relenting spirit.
Go forward now in that we have begun,
30   And afterwards attempt me when thou darest.

BLACK WILL: And if I do not, Heaven cut me off.
But let that pass, and show me to this house
Where thou shalt see I'll do as much as Shakebag.

SHAKEBAG: This is the door – but soft, methinks 'tis
shut.
The villain Michael hath deceived us.

BLACK WILL: Soft, let me see. Shakebag, 'tis shut indeed.
Knock with thy sword; perhaps the slave will hear.

SHAKEBAG: It will not be; the white-liver'd peasant
Is gone to bed and laughs us both to scorn.

40   BLACK WILL: And he shall buy his merriment as dear
As ever coistrel bought so little sport.
Ne'er let this sword assist me when I need,
But rust and canker after I have sworn,
If I, the next time that I meet the hind,
Lop not away his leg, his arm or both.

SHAKEBAG: And let me never draw a sword again,
Nor prosper in the twilight, cockshut light,

22 *telling me of* taxing me with.
24 *slipp'd* put off.   30 *attempt* attack.
41 *coistrel* varlet.
44 *hind* fellow.
47 *cockshut light* evening time when woodcocks (i.e. gulls) are
caught.

When I would fleece the wealthy passenger,
But lie and languish in a loathsome den,
Hated and spit at by the goers-by,   50
And in that death may die unpitied,
If I the next time that I meet the slave
Cut not the nose from off the coward's face,
And trample on it for this villainy.

BLACK WILL: Come, let's go seek out Greene; I know
    he'll swear.

SHAKEBAG: He were a villain and he would not swear.
'Twould make a peasant swear amongst his boys,
That ne'er durst say before but 'yea' and 'no',
To be thus flouted of a coist[e]rel.

BLACK WILL: Shakebag, let's seek out Greene and in the   60
    morning
At the alehouse 'butting Arden's house
Watch the out-coming of that prick-ear'd cur,
And then let me alone to handle him.   *Exeunt.*

SCENE SIX

Here enters ARDEN, FRANKLIN *and* MICHAEL.

ARDEN: Sirrah, get you back to Billingsgate
And learn what time the tide will serve our turn.
Come to us in Paul's. First go make the bed,
And afterwards go hearken for the flood.
    Exit MICHAEL.
Come, Master Franklin, you shall go with me.
This night I dream'd that being in a park,
A toil was pitch'd to overthrow the deer,
And I upon a little rising hill

56 *and* if.   62 *prick-ear'd* having erect ears.
4 *flood* flood-tide.   7 *toil* net, snare.

Stood whistly watching for the herd's approach.
10 Even there, methoughts, a gentle slumber took me,
And summon'd all my parts to sweet repose.
But in the pleasure of this golden rest
An ill-thew'd foster had removed the toil,
And rounded me with that beguilding home
Which late, methought, was pitch'd to cast the deer.
With that he blew an evil-sounding horn,
And at the noise another herdman came
With falchion drawn, and bent it at my breast,
Crying aloud, 'Thou art the game we seek.'
20 With this I wak'd and trembled every joint,
Like one obscured in a little bush
That sees a lion foraging about,
And when the dreadful forest king is gone,
He pries about with timorous suspect
Throughout the thorny casements of the brake,
And will not think his person dangerless,
But quakes and shivers though the cause be gone.
So trust me, Franklin, when I did awake
I stood in doubt whether I waked or no,
30 Such great impression took this fond surprise.
God grant this vision bedeem me any good.
FRANKLIN: This fantasy doth rise from Michael's fear
Who being awaked with the noise he made,
His troubled senses yet could take no rest;
And this, I warrant you, procured your dream.
ARDEN: It may be so; God frame it to the best;

9 *whistly* silently.
13 *ill-thew'd* unmannerly. *foster* forester.
15 *cast* overthrow.
18 *falchion* curved, broad sword. *bent* aim.
24 *suspect* suspicion.
30 *took . . . surprise* this foolish terror gave.
31 *bedeem . . . good* does not foretell evil for me.
36 *frame* bring to pass.

But oftentimes my dreams presage too true.
FRANKLIN: To such as note their nightly fantasies,
Some one in twenty may incur belief.
But use it not; 'tis but a mockery.   40
ARDEN: Come, Master Franklin, we'll now walk in
      Paul's,
And dine together at the ordinary,
And by my man's direction draw to the quay,
And with the tide go down to Faversham.
Say, Master Franklin, shall it not be so?
FRANKLIN: At your good pleasure, sir; I'll bear you
      company.   *Exeunt.*

SCENE SEVEN

Here enters MICHAEL *at one door* [*and*] GREENE,
  BLACK WILL *and* SHAKEBAG *at another door.*

BLACK WILL: Draw, Shakebag, for here's that villain
      Michael.
GREENE: First, Will, let's hear what he can say.
BLACK WILL: Speak, milksop slave, and never after
      speak.
MICHAEL: For God's sake, sirs, let me excuse myself,
For here I swear by Heaven and earth and all,
I did perform the utmost of my task,
And left the doors unbolted and unlock'd.
But see the chance: Franklin and my master
Were very late conferring in the porch,
And Franklin left his napkin where he sat,   10
With certain gold knit in it, as he said.
Being in bed he did bethink himself,

40 *use it not* don't practise it.
10 *napkin* handkerchief.

And coming down, he found the doors unshut.
He lock'd the gates and brought away the keys,
For which offence my master rated me.
But now I am going to see what flood it is,
For with the tide my master will away,
Where you may front him well on Rainham Down,
A place well fitting such a stratagem.

20 BLACK WILL: Your excuse hath somewhat mollified my
    choler.
Why now, Greene, 'tis better now nor e'er it was.

GREENE: But, Michael, is this true?

MICHAEL: As true as I report it to be true.

SHAKEBAG: Then, Michael, this shall be your penance,
To feast us all at the Salutation,
Where we will plot our purpose thoroughly.

GREENE: And, Michael, you shall bear no news of this
    tide
Because they two may be in Rainham Down
Before your master.

30 MICHAEL: Why, I'll agree to anything you'll have me,
So you will except of my company.　　　　*Exeunt.*

SCENE EIGHT

Here enters MOSBY.

MOSBY: Disturbed thoughts drives me from company
And dries my marrow with their watchfulness.
Continual trouble of my moody brain

15 *rated* berated.　　　18 *front* confront.
25 *Salutation* presumably an inn.
28 *Because* so that.
31 *except* See note.

'Feebles my body by excess of drink
And nips me, as the bitter north-east wind
Doth check the tender blossoms in the spring.
Well fares the man, howe'er his cates do taste,
That tables not with foul suspicion;
And he but pines amongst his delicates
Whose troubled mind is stuff'd with discontent.   10
My golden time was when I had no gold;
Though then I wanted yet I slept secure;
My daily toil begat me night's repose,
My night's repose made daylight fresh to me.
But since I climb'd the top bough of the tree
And sought to build my nest among the clouds,
Each gentlest airy gale doth shake my bed
And makes me dread my downfall to the earth.
But whither doth contemplation carry me?
The way I seek to find, where pleasure dwells,   20
Is hedged behind me that I cannot back
But needs must on, although to danger's gate.
Then, Arden, perish thou by that decree,
For Greene doth ear the land and weed thee up
To make my harvest nothing but pure corn.
And for his pains I'll heave him up awhile,
And after smother him to have his wax.
Such bees as Greene must never live to sting.
Then is there Michael and the painter, too,
Chief actors to Arden's overthrow,   30
Who, when they shall see me sit in Arden's seat,
They will insult upon me for my meed,

7 *cates* food.   8 *tables* dines.
9 *delicates* delicacies.
24 *ear* plough.
26 *heave him up* extol.
32 *meed* reward.

Or fright me by detecting of his end.
I'll none of that, for I can cast a bone
To make these curs pluck out each other's throat,
And then am I sole ruler of mine own.
Yet Mistress Arden lives; but she's myself,
And holy church rites makes us two but one.
But what for that I may not trust you, Alice?
40   You have supplanted Arden for my sake,
And will extirpen me to plant another.
'Tis fearful sleeping in a serpent's bed,
And I will cleanly rid my hands of her.
        Here enters ALICE [*with a prayerbook*].
But here she comes and I must flatter her. –
How now, Alice! What, sad and passionate?
Make me partaker of thy pensiveness:
Fire divided burns with lesser force.
ALICE: But I will dam that fire in my breast
Till by the force thereof my part consume.
50   Ah, Mosby!
MOSBY: Such deep pathaires, like to a cannon's burst
Discharg'd against a ruinated wall,
Breaks my relenting heart in thousand pieces.
Ungentle Alice, thy sorrow is my sore.
Thou know'st it well, and 'tis thy policy
To forge distressful looks to wound a breast
Where lies a heart that dies where thou art sad.
It is not love that loves to anger love.
ALICE: It is not love that loves to murder love.
60   MOSBY: How mean you that?
ALICE: Thou knowest how dearly Arden loved me.

33 *detecting* disclosing.   34 *a bone* i.e. Susan.
39 *But . . . that* but what about the fact that.
41 *extirpen* root out.
45 *passionate* sorrowful.
49 *part* share.
51 *pathaires* sad and passionate outbursts. See note.

MOSBY: And then?

ALICE: And then conceal the rest, for 'tis too bad,
Lest that my words be carried with the wind,
And publish'd in the world to both our shames.
I pray thee, Mosby, let our springtime wither,
Our harvest else will yield but loathsome weeds.
Forget, I pray thee, what hath past betwixt us,
For now I blush and tremble at the thoughts.

MOSBY: What, are you chang'd? 70

ALICE: Ay, to my former happy life again,
From title of an odious strumpet's name
To honest Arden's wife, not Arden's honest wife.
Ha, Mosby, 'tis thou hast rifled me of that,
And made me slanderous to all my kin.
Even in my forehead is thy name engraven,
A mean artificer, that low-born name.
I was bewitched; woe worth the hapless hour,
And all the causes that enchanted me.

MOSBY: Nay, if thou ban, let me breathe curses forth, 80
And if you stand so nicely at your fame
Let me repent the credit I have lost.
I have neglected matters of import
That would have stated me above thy state;
Forslow'd advantages, and spurn'd at time.
Ay, Fortune's right hand Mosby hath forsook
To take a wanton giglot by the left.
I left the marriage of an honest maid
Whose dowry would have weighed down all thy
    wealth,

73 second *honest* chaste.
78 *woe worth* may woe betide.
80 *ban* curse.
81 *if . . . fame* if you scruple so fastidiously at your reputation.
84 *stated* placed.
85 *Forslow'd* lost by sloth.
87 *giglot* worthless woman.

90 Whose beauty and deameanour far exceeded thee.
This certain good I lost for changing bad,
And wrapp'd my credit in thy company.
I was bewitch'd, – that is no theme of thine,
And thou unhallowed hast enchanted me.
But I will break thy spells and exorcisms,
And put another sight upon these eyes
That showed my heart a raven for a dove.
Thou art not fair, I view'd thee not till now;
Thou art not kind, till now I knew thee not.

100 And now the rain hath beaten off thy gilt
Thy worthless copper shows thee counterfeit.
It grieves me not to see how foul thou art
But mads me that ever I thought thee fair.
Go, get thee gone, a copesmate for thy hinds.
I am too good to be thy favourite.

ALICE: Ay, now I see, and too soon find it true,
Which often hath been told me by my friends,
That Mosby loves me not but for my wealth,
Which too incredulous I ne'er believed.

110 Nay, hear me speak, Mosby, a word or two;
I'll bite my tongue if it speak bitterly.
Look on me, Mosby, or I'll kill myself;
Nothing shall hide me from thy stormy look.
If thou cry war there is no peace for me;
I will do penance for offending thee,
And burn this prayerbook, where I here use
The holy word that had converted me.
See, Mosby, I will tear away the leaves,
And all the leaves, and in this golden cover

120 Shall thy sweet phrases and thy letters dwell,
And thereon will I chiefly meditate
And hold no other sect but such devotion.

93 *that . . . thine* cf. l. 78.   104 *copesmate* companion.
122 *hold . . . sect* keep no other religious faith.

Wilt thou not look? Is all thy love overwhelm'd?
Wilt thou not hear? What malice stops thine ears?
Why speaks thou not? What silence ties thy tongue?
Thou hast been sighted as the eagle is,
And heard as quickly as the fearful hare,
And spoke as smoothly as an orator,
When I have bid thee hear, or see, or speak.
And art thou sensible in none of these?   130
Weigh all thy good turns with this little fault
And I deserve not Mosby's muddy looks.
A fount once troubled is not thickened still;
Be clear again, I'll ne'er more trouble thee.

MOSBY: Oh no, I am a base artificer,
My wings are feather'd for a lowly flight.
Mosby? fie, no! not for a thousand pound.
Make love to you? why, 'tis unpardonable;
We beggars must not breathe where gentles are.

ALICE: Sweet Mosby is as gentle as a king,   140
And I too blind to judge him otherwise.
Flowers do sometimes spring in fallow lands,
Weeds in gardens, roses grow on thorns;
So whatsoe'er my Mosby's father was,
Himself is valued gentle by his worth.

MOSBY: Ah, how you women can insinuate
And clear a trespass with your sweet-set tongue.
I will forget this quarrel, gentle Alice,
Provided I'll be tempted so no more.
    Here enters BRADSHAW.

ALICE: Then with thy lips seal up this new-made match. 150
MOSBY: Soft, Alice, for here comes somebody.
ALICE: How now, Bradshaw, what's the news with you?

130 *sensible* capable of perceptions, feeling or expression.
131 *thy good turns* good turns done to you.
133 *still* always.
139 *gentles* gentlefolk.

BRADSHAW: I have little news but here's a letter,
That Master Greene importuned me to give you.
ALICE: Go in, Bradshaw; call for a cup of beer.
'Tis almost supper time; thou shalt stay with us.
Exit [BRADSHAW].
Then she reads the letter.
'We have missed of our purpose at London, but shall
perform it by the way. We thank our neighbour
Bradshaw.

160   Yours, Richard Greene.'
How likes my love the tenor of this letter?
MOSBY: Well, were his date complete and expired.
ALICE: Ah, would it were; then comes my happy hour.
Till then my bliss is mix'd with bitter gall.
Come, let us in to shun suspicion.
MOSBY: Ay, to the gates of death to follow thee.
Exeunt.

SCENE NINE

Here enters GREENE, BLACK WILL, *and* SHAKEBAG.
SHAKEBAG: Come, Will, see thy tools be in a readiness.
Is not thy powder dank, or will thy flint strike fire?
BLACK WILL: Then ask me if my nose be on my face,
Or whether my tongue be frozen in my mouth.
Zounds, here's a coil!
You were best swear me on the interrogatories
How many pistols I have took in hand,
Or whether I love the smell of gunpowder,
Or dare abide the noise the dag will make,

5 *coil* fuss.   6 *on the interrogatories* on oath.
9 *dag* pistol.

Or will not wink at flashing of the fire.   10
I pray thee, Shakebag, let this answer thee,
That I have took more purses in this Down
Than e'er thou handlest pistols in thy life.

SHAKEBAG: Ay, haply thou hast pick'd more in a throng;
But should I brag what booties I have took,
I think the overplus that's more than thine
Would mount to a greater sum of money
Than either thou or all thy kin are worth.
Zounds, I hate them as I hate a toad
That carry a muscado in their tongue,   20
And scarce a hurting weapon in their hand.

BLACK WILL: Oh Greene, intolerable!
It is not for mine honour to bear this.
Why, Shakebag, I did serve the king at Boulogne,
And thou canst brag of nothing that thou hast done.

SHAKEBAG: Why, so can Jack of Faversham,
That sounded for a fillip on the nose,
When he that gave it him hollaed in his ear,
And he supposed a cannon-bullet hit him.
    Then they fight.

GREENE: I pray you, sirs, list to Aesop's talk: 30
Whilst two stout dogs were striving for a bone,
There comes a cur and stole it from them both.
So while you stand striving on these terms of man-
    hood,
Arden escapes us and deceives us all.

SHAKEBAG: Why, he begun.

BLACK WILL: And thou shalt find I'll end.
I do but slip it until better time.
But if I do forget –
    Then he kneels down and holds up his hands to Heaven.

20 *muscado* (?) a musket.   27 *sounded* swooned.
31 *stout* valiant.
37 *slip* defer.

GREENE: Well, take your fittest standings, and once more
40   Lime your twigs to catch this weary bird.
        I'll leave you, and at your dag's discharge
        Make towards, like the longing water-dog
        That coucheth till the fowling-piece be off,
        Then seizeth on the prey with eager mood.
        Ah, might I see him stretching forth his limbs,
        As I have seen them beat their wings ere now.
SHAKEBAG: Why, that thou shalt see if he come this way.
GREENE: Yes, that he doth, Shakebag, I warrant thee.
        But brawl not when I am gone in any case,
50   But, sirs, be sure to speed him when he comes;
        And in that hope I'll leave you for an hour.
            Exit GREENE.
            [BLACK WILL *and* SHAKEBAG *take up their positions.*]
            Here enters ARDEN, FRANKLIN *and* MICHAEL.
MICHAEL: 'Twere best that I went back to Rochester.
        The horse halts downright; it were not good
        He travelled in such pain to Faversham.
        Removing of a shoe may haply help it.
ARDEN: Well, get you back to Rochester; but, sirrah, see
            ye
        Overtake us ere we come to Rainham Down,
        For it will be very late ere we get home.
MICHAEL [*aside*]: Ay, God he knows, and so doth Will
            and Shakebag,
60   That thou shalt never go further than that Down;
        And therefore have I prick'd the horse on purpose,
        Because I would not view the massacre.
            Exit MICHAEL.
ARDEN: Come, Master Franklin, onwards with your tale.

40 *weary* wearisome.
43 *coucheth* lies down.
53 *halts downright* is very lame.
61 *prick'd the horse* pierced the foot of the horse (to cause lameness).

FRANKLIN: I assure you, sir, you task me much.
  A heavy blood is gathered at my heart,
  And on the sudden is my wind so short
  As hindereth the passage of my speech.
  So fierce a qualm yet ne'er assailed me.
ARDEN: Come, Master Franklin, let us go on softly.
  The annoyance of the dust or else some meat   70
  You ate at dinner cannot brook you.
  I have been often so and soon amended.
FRANKLIN: Do you remember where my tale did leave?
ARDEN: Ay, where the gentleman did check his wife.
FRANKLIN: She being reprehended for the fact,
  Witness produced that took her with the deed,
  Her glove brought in which there she left behind,
  And many other assured arguments,
  Her husband ask'd her whether it were not so.
ARDEN: Her answer then? I wonder how she look'd,   80
  Having forsworn it with such vehement oaths,
  And at the instant so approved upon her.
FRANKLIN: First did she cast her eyes down to the earth,
  Watching the drops that fell amain from thence;
  Then softly draws she forth her handkerchief,
  And modestly she wipes her tear-stain'd face:
  Then hemm'd she out, to clear her voice should seem,
  And with a majesty address'd herself
  To encounter all their accusations. –
  Pardon me, Master Arden, I can no more;   90
  This fighting at my heart makes short my wind.
ARDEN: Come, we are almost now at Rainham Down;
  Your pretty tale beguiles the weary way.
  I would you were in state to tell it out.

71 *brook* agree with.   73 *leave* leave off.
74 *check* reprove.
75 *fact* deed.
82 *approved upon* proved against.

SHAKEBAG [*aside*]: Stand close, Will, I hear them com-
    ing.

    Here enters LORD CHEINY *with his* MEN.

BLACK WILL [*aside*]: Stand to it, Shakebag, and be re-
    solute.

LORD CHEINY: Is it so near night as it seems,
    Or will this black-faced evening have a shower?
    [*Seeing* ARDEN] What, Master Arden? you are well
      met.
100   I have long'd this fortnight's day to speak with you;
    You are a stranger, man, in the Isle of Sheppey.

ARDEN: Your honour's always! bound to do you service.

LORD CHEINY: Come you from London and ne'er a man
    with you?

ARDEN: My man's coming after,
    But here's my honest friend that came along with me.

LORD CHEINY: My Lord Protector's man I take you
    to be.

FRANKLIN: Ay, my good lord, and highly bound to you.

LORD CHEINY: You and your friend come home and
    sup with me.

ARDEN: I beseech your honour pardon me;
110   I have made a promise to a gentleman,
    My honest friend, to meet him at my house.
    The occasion is great, or else would I wait on you.

LORD CHEINY: Will you come tomorrow and dine with
    me
    And bring your honest friend along with you?
    I have divers matters to talk with you about.

ARDEN: Tomorrow we'll wait upon your honour.

LORD CHEINY: One of you stay my horse at the top of
    the hill.
    [*Seeing* BLACK WILL] What, Black Will! For whose
    purse wait you?
    Thou wilt be hanged in Kent when all is done.

BLACK WILL: Not hanged, God save your honour.   120
  I am your beadsman, bound to pray for you.
LORD CHEINY: I think thou ne'er saidest prayer in all thy
        life.
  One of you give him a crown; –
  And, sirrah, leave this kind of life.
  If thou beest 'tainted for a penny matter
  And come in question, surely thou wilt truss.
  Come, Master Arden, let us be going;
  Your way and mine lies four mile together.   *Exeunt.*
    Manet BLACK WILL *and* SHAKEBAG.
BLACK WILL: The Devil break all your necks at four
        miles' end!
  Zounds, I could kill myself for very anger.   130
  His lordship chops me in, even when
  My dag was levell'd at his heart.
  I would his crown were molten down his throat.
SHAKEBAG: Arden, thou hast wondrous holy luck.
  Did ever man escape as thou hast done?
  Well, I'll discharge my pistol at the sky,
  For by this bullet Arden might not die.
    Here enters GREENE.
GREENE: What, is he down? is he dispatch'd?
SHAKEBAG: Ay, in health towards Faversham to shame
    us all.
GREENE: The devil he is! Why, sirs, how escap'd he?   140
SHAKEBAG: When we were ready to shoot
  Comes my Lord Cheiny to prevent his death.
GREENE: The Lord of Heaven hath preserved him.
BLACK WILL: The Lord of Heaven a fig! The Lord
        Cheiny hath preserved him,

121 *beadsman* one paid to pray for others.
125 *'tainted* attainted, accused.
126 *in question* to trial. *truss* hang.
131 *chops me in* comes thrusting in.

And bids him to a feast, to his house at Shorlow.
But by the way once more I'll meet with him,
And if all the Cheinies in the world say no,
I'll have a bullet in his breast tomorrow.
Therefore come, Greene, and let us to Faversham.

150 GREENE: Ay, and excuse ourselves to Mistress Arden.
Oh, how she'll chafe when she hears of this.

SHAKEBAG: Why, I'll warrant you she'll think we dare
not do it.

BLACK WILL: Why, then let us go, and tell her all the
matter,
And plot the news to cut him off tomorrow. *Exeunt.*

SCENE TEN

Here enters ARDEN *and his wife* [ALICE], FRANKLIN
and MICHAEL.

ARDEN: See how the hours, the guardant of Heaven's
gate,
Have by their toil removed the darksome clouds,
That Sol may well discern the trampled pace
Wherein he wont to guide his golden car.
The season fits; come, Franklin, let's away.

ALICE: I thought you did pretend some special hunt
That made you thus cut short the time of rest.

ARDEN: It was no chase that made me rise so early,
But as I told thee yesternight, to go

10   To the Isle of Sheppey, there to dine with my Lord
Cheiny;
For so his honour late commanded me.

1 *guardant* guardian.   3 *pace* passage.
6 *pretend* intend.

ALICE: Ay, such kind husbands seldom want excuses.
Home is a wild cat to a wand'ring wit.
The time hath been – would God it were not past –
That honour's title, nor a lord's command
Could once have drawn you from these arms of mine.
But my deserts or your desires decay,
Or both; yet if true love may seem desert,
I merit still to have thy company.

FRANKLIN: Why, I pray you, sir, let her go along with   20
        us;
I am sure his honour will welcome her,
And us the more for bringing her along.

ARDEN: Content. [*To* MICHAEL] Sirrah, saddle your
        mistress' nag.

ALICE: No. Begg'd favour merits little thanks.
If I should go our house would run away
Or else be stol'n; therefore I'll stay behind.

ARDEN: Nay, see how mistaking you are. I pray thee, go.

ALICE: No, no, not now.

ARDEN: Then let me leave thee satisfied in this,
That time nor place nor persons alter me,   30
But that I hold thee dearer than my life.

ALICE: That will be seen by your quick return.

ARDEN: And that shall be ere night and if I live.
Farewell, sweet Alice; we mind to sup with thee.
        Exit ALICE.

FRANKLIN: Come, Michael, are our horses ready?

MICHAEL: Ay, your horse are ready but I am not ready
for I have lost my purse with six and thirty shillings in
it, with taking up of my master's nag.

FRANKLIN: Why, I pray you, let us go before,
Whilst he stays behind to seek his purse.   40

12 *want* lack.   18 *desert* deserving.
34 *mind* intend.
38 *taking up* ?catching.

ARDEN: Go to, sirrah; see you follow us to the Isle of
      Sheppey,
  To my Lord Cheiny's, where we mean to dine.
    Exeunt ARDEN *and* FRANKLIN.
    Manet MICHAEL.

MICHAEL: So, fair weather after you, for before you lies
  Black Will and Shakebag, in the broom close, too close
  for you. They'll be your ferrymen to long home.
    Here enters the Painter [CLARKE].
  But who is this? The painter, my co-rival, that would
  needs win Mistress Susan.

CLARKE: How now, Michael, how doth my mistress
  and all at home?

50 MICHAEL: Who, Susan Mosby? she is your mistress,
  too?

CLARKE: Ay, how doth she, and all the rest?

MICHAEL: All's well but Susan; she is sick.

CLARKE: Sick? of what disease?

MICHAEL: Of a great fear.

CLARKE: A fear of what?

MICHAEL: A great fever.

CLARKE: A fever? God forbid!

MICHAEL: Yes, faith, and of a lurdan, too, as big as
60 yourself.

CLARKE: Oh, Michael, the spleen prickles you. Go to;
  you carry an eye over Mistress Susan.

MICHAEL: Ay, faith, to keep her from the painter.

CLARKE: Why more from a painter than from a serving-
  creature like yourself?

MICHAEL: Because you painters make but a painting
  table of a pretty wench and spoil her beauty with
  blotting.

45 *long home* i.e. grave.
59 *lurdan* 1 vagabond; 2 fever of idleness.
62 *carry . . . over* keep an eye on.

CLARKE: What mean you by that?

MICHAEL: Why, that you painters paint lambs in the lin- 70
ing of wenches' petticoats, and we servingmen put
horns to them to make them become sheep.

CLARKE: Such another word will cost you a cuff or a
knock.

MICHAEL: What, with a dagger made of a pencil? Faith,
'tis too weak, and therefore thou too weak to win
Susan.

CLARKE: Would Susan's love lay upon this stroke.
Then he breaks MICHAEL'S *head.*
Here enters MOSBY, GREENE *and* ALICE.

ALICE: I'll lay my life, this is for Susan's love.
Stay'd you behind your master to this end?   80
Have you no other time to brabble in
But now when serious matters are in hand?
Say, Clarke, has thou done the thing thou promised?

CLARKE: Ay, here it is; the very touch is death.

ALICE: Then this, I hope, if all the rest do fail,
Will catch Master Arden,
And make him wise in death that lived a fool.
Why should he thrust his sickle in our corn,
Or what hath he to do with thee my love,
Or govern me that am to rule myself?   90
Forsooth, for credit sake I must leave thee!
Nay, he must leave to live that we may love,
May live, may love; for what is life but love?
And love shall last as long as life remains,
And life shall end before my love depart.

MOSBY: Why, what's love without true constancy?
Like to a pillar built of many stones,
Yet neither with good mortar well compact,

81 *brabble* quarrel noisily.
84 *it* i.e. the crucifix. See i, 608 ff.
92 *leave* cease.

Nor cement, to fasten it in the joints,
100   But that it shakes with every blast of wind,
And being touch'd, straight falls unto the earth,
And buries all his haughty pride in dust.
No, let our love be rocks of adamant,
Which time nor place nor tempest can asunder.
GREENE: Mosby, leave protestations now,
And let us bethink us what we have to do.
Black Will and Shakebag I have placed
In the broom close watching Arden's coming.
Let's to them and see what they have done.
    Exeunt.

SCENE ELEVEN

Here enters ARDEN *and* FRANKLIN.
ARDEN: Oh, ferryman, where art thou?
    Here enters the FERRYMAN.
FERRYMAN: Here, here! Go before to the boat,
And I will follow you.
ARDEN: We have great haste; I pray thee come away.
FERRYMAN: Fie, what a mist is here!
ARDEN: This mist, my friend, is mystical,
Like to a good companion's smoky brain,
That was half-drown'd with new ale over night.
FERRYMAN: 'Twere pity but his skull were opened
10   To make more chimney room.
FRANKLIN: Friend, what's thy opinion of this mist?
FERRYMAN: I think 'tis like to a curst wife in a little
house, that never leaves her husband till she have driven

---

7 *good companion*'s drinking fellow's.
9 *but if* . . . not.   12 *curst* shrewish.

him out at doors with a wet pair of eyes. Then looks
he as if his house were afire, or some of his friends dead.

ARDEN: Speaks thou this of thine own experience?

FERRYMAN: Perhaps ay, perhaps no: for my wife is as
other women are, that is to say, governed by the
moon.

FRANKLIN: By the moon? How, I pray thee? 20

FERRYMAN: Nay, thereby lies a bargain, and you shall
not have it fresh and fasting.

ARDEN: Yes, I pray thee, good ferryman.

FERRYMAN: Then for this once let it be midsummer
moon; but yet my wife has another moon.

FRANKLIN: Another moon?

FERRYMAN: Ay, and it hath influences and eclipses.

ARDEN: Why then, by this reckoning you sometimes
play the man in the moon.

FERRYMAN: Ay, but you had not best to meddle with 30
that moon lest I scratch you by the face with my
bramble-bush.

ARDEN: I am almost stifled with this fog; come let's
away.

FRANKLIN: And sirrah, as we go let us have some more
of your bold yeomanry.

FERRYMAN: Nay, by my faith, sir, but flat knavery.
Exeunt.

14 *at* of.
22 *fresh and fasting* (?)before breakfast, (?)for nothing.
34 *yeomanry* yeoman's talk.

SCENE TWELVE

Here enters BLACK WILL *at one door and* SHAKEBAG *at another.*

SHAKEBAG: Oh Will, where art thou?

BLACK WILL: Here, Shakebag, almost in hell's mouth, where I cannot see my way for smoke.

SHAKEBAG: I pray thee speak still that we may meet by the sound, for I shall fall into some ditch or other, unless my feet see better than my eyes.

BLACK WILL: Didst thou ever see better weather to run away with another man's wife, or play with a wench at potfinger.

10 SHAKEBAG: No, this were a fine world for chandlers, if this weather would last; for then a man should never dine nor sup without candle-light. But, sirrah Will, what horses are those that passed?

BLACK WILL: Why, didst thou hear any?

SHAKEBAG: Ay, that I did.

BLACK WILL: My life for thine, 'twas Arden and his companion, and then all our labour's lost.

SHAKEBAG: Nay, say not so; for if it be they, they may haply lose their way as we have done, and then we may

20 chance meet with them.

BLACK WILL: Come, let us go on like a couple of blind pilgrims.

Then SHAKEBAG *falls into a ditch.*

SHAKEBAG: Help, Will, help! I am almost drowned.

Here enters the FERRYMAN.

FERRYMAN: Who's that that calls for help?

BLACK WILL: 'Twas none here, 'twas thou thyself.

FERRYMAN: I came to help him that called for help.

9 *at potfinger* sexual allusion.

Why, how now? Who is this that's in the ditch? You
are well enough served to go without a guide, such
weather as this!

BLACK WILL: Sirrah, what companies hath passed your   30
ferry this morning?

FERRYMAN: None but a couple of gentlemen that went
to dine at my Lord Cheiny's.

BLACK WILL: Shakebag, did I not tell thee as much?

FERRYMAN: Why, sir, will you have any letters carried
to them?

BLACK WILL: No, sir; get you gone.

FERRYMAN: Did you ever see such a mist as this?

BLACK WILL: No, nor such a fool as will rather be
hocked than get his way.   40

FERRYMAN: Why, sir, this is no Hock Monday; you are
deceived.

What's his name, I pray you, sir?

SHAKEBAG: His name is Black Will.

FERRYMAN: I hope to see him one day hanged upon a
hill.

    Exit FERRYMAN.

SHAKEBAG: See how the sun hath clear'd the foggy mist,
Now we have miss'd the mark of our intent.

    Here enters GREENE, MOSBY *and* ALICE.

MOSBY: Black Will and Shakebag, what make you here?
What, is the deed done, is Arden dead?

BLACK WILL: What could a blinded man perform in
arms?

Saw you not how till now the sky was dark,   50
That neither horse nor man could be discerned?
Yet did we hear their horses as they pass'd.

GREENE: Have they escap'd you then and pass'd the
ferry?

28 *to go* for going.   40 *hocked* hamstrung.
41 *Hock Monday* Second Monday after Easter, a popular festival.

SHAKEBAG: Ay, for a while; but here we two will stay,
And at their coming back meet with them once more.
Zounds, I was ne'er so toil'd in all my life
In following so slight a task as this.
MOSBY: How cam'st thou so beray'd?
BLACK WILL: With making false footing in the dark;
60   He needs would follow them without a guide.
ALICE: Here's to pay for a fire and good cheer.
Get you to Faversham, to the Flower-de-Luce,
And rest yourselves until some other time.
GREENE: Let me alone; it most concerns my state.
BLACK WILL: Ay, Mistress Arden, this will serve the
turn
In case we fall into a second fog.
Exeunt GREENE, BLACK WILL *and* SHAKEBAG.
MOSBY: These knaves will never do it; let's give it over.
ALICE: First tell me how you like my new device:
Soon, when my husband is returning back,
70   You and I both marching arm in arm,
Like loving friends we'll meet him on the way,
And boldly beard and brave him to his teeth.
When words grow hot and blows begin to rise
I'll call those cutters forth your tenement,
Who, in a manner to take up the fray,
Shall wound my husband Hornsby to the death.
MOSBY: Ah, fine device; why, this deserves a kiss.
Exeunt.

56 *toil'd* fatigued.
58 *beray'd* covered with mud.
76 *Hornsby* evidently derisive name implying cuckold.

SCENE THIRTEEN

Here enters DICK REEDE *and a* SAILOR.

SAILOR: Faith, Dick Reede, it is to little end.
  His conscience is too liberal and he too niggardly
  To part with anything may do thee good.
REEDE: He is coming from Shorlow as I understand.
  Here I'll intercept him, for at his house
  He never will vouchsafe to speak with me.
  If prayers and fair entreaties will not serve
  Or make no batt'ry in his flinty breast
  I'll curse the carl and see what that will do.
    Here enters FRANKLIN, ARDEN *and* MICHAEL.
  See where he comes to further my intent. –   10
  Master Arden, I am now bound to the sea.
  My coming to you was about the plot of ground
  Which wrongfully you detain from me.
  Although the rent of it be very small,
  Yet will it help my wife and children,
  Which here I leave in Faversham, God knows,
  Needy and bare. For Christ's sake let them have it.
ARDEN: Franklin, hearest thou this fellow speak?
  That which he craves I dearly bought of him,
  Although the rent of it was ever mine.   20
  Sirrah, you that ask these questions,
  If with thy clamorous impeaching tongue
  Thou rail on me as I have heard thou dost,
  I'll lay thee up so close a twelve month's day
  As thou shalt neither see the sun nor moon.
  Look to it, for as surely as I live,
  I'll banish pity if thou use me thus.

9 *carl* fellow.   22 *impeaching* accusing.
24 *lay thee up* send you to prison.

REEDE: What, wilt thou do me wrong and threat me
      too?
  Nay then I'll tempt thee, Arden; do thy worst.
30 God, I beseech thee, show some miracle
  On thee or thine, in plaguing thee for this.
  That plot of ground, which thou detains from me,
  I speak it in an agony of spirit,
  Be ruinous and fatal unto thee.
  Either there be butcher'd by thy dearest friends,
  Or else be brought for men to wonder at,
  Or thou or thine miscarry in that place,
  Or there run mad and end thy cursed days.
FRANKLIN: Fie, bitter knave, bridle thine envious
      tongue,
40 For curses are like arrows shot upright,
  Which falling down light on the shooter's head.
REEDE: Light where they will; were I upon the sea
  As oft I have in many a bitter storm,
  And saw a dreadful southern flaw at hand,
  The pilot quaking at the doubtful storm,
  And all the sailors praying on their knees,
  Even in that fearful time would I fall down,
  And ask of God, whate'er betide of me,
  Vengeance on Arden, or some misevent,
50 To show the world what wrong the carl hath done.
  This charge I'll leave with my distressful wife;
  My children shall be taught such prayers as these.
  And thus I go but leave my curse with thee.
    Exeunt REEDE *and the* SAILOR.
ARDEN: It is the railingest knave in Christendom,
  And oftentimes the villain will be mad.
  It greatly matters not what he says,
  But I assure you I ne'er did him wrong.
FRANKLIN: I think so, Master Arden.

44 *flaw* squall.   49 *misevent* mischance.

ARDEN: Now that our horses are gone home before,
My wife may haply meet me on the way.   60
For God knows she is grown passing kind of late
And greatly changed from the old humour
Of her wonted frowardness,
And seeks by fair means to redeem old faults.
FRANKLIN: Happy the change that alters for the best.
But see in any case you make no speech
Of the cheer we had at my Lord Cheiny's
Although most bounteous and most liberal.
For that will make her think herself more wrong'd,
In that we did not carry her along;   70
For sure she grieved that she was left behind.
ARDEN: Come, Franklin, let us strain to mend our pace
And take her unawares, playing the cook,
    Here enters ALICE *and* MOSBY [*arm in arm*].
For I believe she'll strive to mend our cheer.
FRANKLIN: Why, there's no better creatures in the world
Than women are when they are in good humours.
ARDEN: Who is that? Mosby? What, so familiar?
Injurious strumpet and thou ribald knave,
Untwine those arms.
ALICE: Ay, with a sugar'd kiss let them untwine.   80
ARDEN: Ah, Mosby! perjur'd beast! bear this and all!
MOSBY: And yet no horned beast; the horns are thine.
FRANKLIN: Oh monstrous! Nay then, 'tis time to draw.
ALICE: Help, help, they murder my husband.
    Here enters BLACK WILL *and* SHAKEBAG.
SHAKEBAG: Zounds, who injures Master Mosby?
    [SHAKEBAG *and* MOSBY *are wounded in the struggle*].
Help, Will, I am hurt.

62 *humour* disposition.   63 *frowardness* ill-naturedness.
67 *cheer* hospitality.   72 *mend* improve.
After 85 *Shakebag . . . struggle* See Black Will's description, xiv,
58–72.

MOSBY: I may thank you, Mistress Arden, for this
    wound.

Exeunt MOSBY, BLACK WILL *and* SHAKEBAG.

ALICE: Ah, Arden, what folly blinded thee?
    Ah, jealous harebrain man what hast thou done?

90   When we, to welcome thee, intended sport,
    Came lovingly to meet thee on thy way,
    Thou drew'st thy sword, enraged with jealousy,
    And hurt thy friends whose thoughts were free from
        harm;
    All for a worthless kiss and joining arms,
    Both done but merely to try thy patience.
    And me unhappy that devised the jest,
    Which, though begun in sport, yet ends in blood!

FRANKLIN: Marry, God defend me from such a jest!

ALICE: Couldst thou not see us friendly smile on thee

100   When we join'd arms and when I kiss'd his cheek?
    Hast thou not lately found me over-kind?
    Didst thou not hear me cry they murder thee?
    Call'd I not help to set my husband free?
    No, ears and all were 'witch'd. Ah me accurs'd,
    To link in liking with a frantic man!
    Henceforth I'll be thy slave, no more thy wife;
    For with that name I never shall content thee.
    If I be merry, thou straightways thinks me light;
    If sad, thou sayest the sullens trouble me;

110   If well attired, thou thinks I will be gadding;
    If homely, I seem sluttish in thine eye.
    Thus am I still, and shall be while I die,
    Poor wench, abused by thy misgovernment.

ARDEN: But is it for truth that neither thou nor he
    Intendest malice in your misdemeanour?

ALICE: The Heavens can witness of our harmless
    thoughts.

109 *sullens* sulks.   112 *still* always. *while* till.

ARDEN: Then pardon me, sweet Alice, and forgive this
    fault;
  Forget but this and never see the like;
  Impose me penance and I will perform it;
  For in thy discontent I find a death,   120
  A death tormenting more than death itself.

ALICE: Nay, hadst thou loved me as thou dost pretend,
  Thou wouldst have mark'd the speeches of thy friend,
  Who going wounded from the place, he said
  His skin was pierc'd only through my device.
  And if sad sorrow taint thee for this fault
  Thou wouldst have followed him and seen him dress'd,
  And cried him mercy whom thou hast misdone;
  Ne'er shall my heart be eased till this be done.

ARDEN: Content thee, sweet Alice, thou shalt have thy 130
    will,
  Whate'er it be. For that I injur'd thee
  And wrong'd my friend, shame scourgeth my offence.
  Come thou thyself and go along with me,
  And be a mediator 'twixt us two.

FRANKLIN: Why, Master Arden, know you what you
    do?
  Will you follow him that hath dishonour'd you?

ALICE: Why, canst thou prove I have been disloyal?

FRANKLIN: Why, Mosby taunt your husband with the
    horn.

ALICE: Ay, after he had reviled him
  By the injurious name of perjur'd beast.   140
  He knew no wrong could spite an jealous man
  More than the hateful naming of the horn.

FRANKLIN: Suppose 'tis true, yet it is dangerous
  To follow him whom he hath lately hurt.

ALICE: A fault confessed is more than half amends:

---

131 *For that* because.   138 *taunt* taunted.

But men of such ill spirit as yourself
Work crosses and debates 'twixt man and wife.
ARDEN: I pray thee, gentle Franklin, hold thy peace;
I know my wife counsels me for the best.
150 I'll seek out Mosby where his wound is dress'd,
And salve his hapless quarrel if I may.
    Exeunt ARDEN *and* ALICE.
FRANKLIN: He whom the devil drives must go perforce.
Poor gentleman, how soon he is bewitch'd,
And yet, because his wife is the instrument,
His friends must not be lavish in their speech.
    Exit FRANKLIN.

SCENE FOURTEEN

Here enters BLACK WILL, SHAKEBAG *and* GREENE.
BLACK WILL: Sirrah Greene, when was I so long in killing a man?
GREENE: I think we shall never do it; let us give it over.
SHAKEBAG: Nay, zounds, we'll kill him, though we be hanged at his door for our labour.
BLACK WILL: Thou knowest, Greene, that I have lived in London this twelve years where I have made some go upon wooden legs for taking the wall on me; divers with silver noses for saying 'There goes Black
10 Will'. I have cracked as many blades as thou hast done nuts.
GREENE: Oh, monstrous lie!
BLACK WILL: Faith, in a manner I have. The bawdy-houses have paid me tribute; there durst not a whore set up unless she have agreed with me first for opening her shop-windows. For a cross word of a tapster I have

8 *taking . . . me* pushing me off the pavement.

pierced one barrel after another with my dagger and
held him by the ears till all his beer hath run out. In
Thames Street a brewer's cart was like to have run over
me; I made no more ado but went to the clerk and cut   20
all the notches off his tales and beat them about his
head. I and my company have taken the constable from
his watch and carried him about the fields on a coltstaff. I have broken a sergeant's head with his own mace,
and bailed whom I list with my sword and buckler.
All the tenpenny alehouses would stand every morning
with a quart pot in his hand saying 'Will it please your
worship drink?' He that had not done so had been sure
to have had his sign pulled down and his lattice borne
away the next night. To conclude, what have I not   30
done? yet cannot do this; doubtless, he is preserved by
miracle.

 Here enters ALICE *and* MICHAEL.

GREENE: Hence, Will; here comes Mistress Arden.

ALICE: Ah, gentle Michael, art thou sure they're friends?

MICHAEL: Why, I saw them when they both shook
   hands;
When Mosby bled he even wept for sorrow,
And rail'd on Franklin that was cause of all.
No sooner came the surgeon in at doors,
But my master took to his purse and gave him money,
And, to conclude, sent me to bring you word   40
That Mosby, Franklin, Bradshaw, Adam Fowle,
With divers of his neighbours and his friends,
Will come and sup with you at our house this night.

ALICE: Ah, gentle Michael, run thou back again,
And when my husband walks into the fair,
Bid Mosby steal from him and come to me,
And this night shall thou and Susan be made sure.

21 *tales* tallies (sticks on which the accounts were kept).
23–4 *coltstaff* cowlstaff, stick for carrying a cowl or tub.

MICHAEL: I'll go tell him.

ALICE: And as thou goest, tell John cook of our guests,
50   And bid him lay it on, spare for no cost.
    Exit MICHAEL.

BLACK WILL: Nay, and there be such cheer, we will bid
    ourselves.
    Mistress Arden, Dick Greene and I do mean to sup
    with you.

ALICE: And welcome shall you be. Ah, gentlemen,
    How miss'd you of your purpose yesternight?

GREENE: 'Twas long of Shakebag, that unlucky villain.

SHAKEBAG: Thou dost me wrong; I did as much as any.

BLACK WILL: Nay then, Mistress Alice, I'll tell you
    how it was. When he should have locked with both
60   his hilts, he in a bravery flourished over his head. With
    that comes Franklin at him lustily and hurts the slave;
    with that he slinks away. Now his way had been to
    have come hand and feet, one and two round at his
    costard. He like a fool bears his sword-point half a
    yard out of danger. I lie here for my life. [*Takes up a
    position of defence.*] If the devil come and he have no
    more strength than fence, he shall never beat me from
    this ward; I'll stand to it. A buckler in a skilful hand is
    as good as a castle; nay, 'tis better than a sconce, for I
70   have tried it. Mosby, perceiving this, began to faint.

51 *and if. bid* invite.
55 *miss'd . . . purpose* failed you in your intention.
56 *long of* on account of.
59 *locked* engaged in combat. *hilts* often used in plural to mean
'sword', though 'both his hilts' may mean 'sword and dagger'.
60 *bravery* bravado.
63 *round* roundly, without mincing matters.
64 *costard* head.   67 *fence* fencing skill.
68 *ward* posture of defence. *stand to it* See note.
69 *sconce* small fort or earthwork.
70 *this* i.e. Shakebag's wound.

With that comes Arden with his arming sword and
thrust him through the shoulder in a trice.

ALICE: Ay, but I wonder why you both stood still.

BLACK WILL: Faith, I was so amazed I could not strike.

ALICE: Ah, sirs, had he yesternight been slain,
For every drop of his detested blood,
I would have cramm'd in angels in thy fist,
And kiss'd thee too, and hugg'd thee in my arms.

BLACK WILL: Patient yourself; we cannot help it now.
Greene and we two will dog him through the fair,   80
And stab him in the crowd, and steal away.

    Here enters MOSBY [*his arm bandaged*].

ALICE: It is unpossible. But here comes he
That will, I hope, invent some surer means.
Sweet Mosby, hide thy arm; it kills my heart.

MOSBY: Ay, Mistress Arden, this is your favour.

ALICE: Ah, say not so, for when I saw thee hurt
I could have took the weapon thou let'st fall
And run at Arden, for I have sworn
That these mine eyes, offended with his sight,
Shall never close till Arden's be shut up.   90
This night I rose and walk'd about the chamber,
And twice or thrice I thought to have murder'd him.

MOSBY: What, in the night? Then we had been undone!

ALICE: Why, how long shall he live?

MOSBY: Faith, Alice, no longer than this night.
Black Will and Shakebag, will you two
Perform the complot that I have laid?

BLACK WILL: Ay, or else think me as a villain.

GREENE: And rather than you shall want, I'll help
    myself.

71 *arming sword* two-handed sword.
79 *Patient yourself* be patient.
85 *favour* 1 kindness; 2 token from a lover.
91 *This night* i.e. last night.

100 MOSBY: You, Master Greene, shall single Franklin forth
And hold him with a long tale of strange news,
That he may not come home till suppertime.
I'll fetch Master Arden home, and we, like friends,
Will play a game or two at tables here.
ALICE: But what of all this? How shall he be slain?
MOSBY: Why, Black Will and Shakebag, lock'd within
the countinghouse,
Shall, at a certain watchword given, rush forth.
BLACK WILL: What shall the watchword be?
MOSBY: 'Now I take you' – that shall be the word.
110 But come not forth before in any case.
BLACK WILL: I warrant you; but who shall lock me in?
ALICE: That will I do; thou'st keep the key thyself.
MOSBY: Come, Master Greene, go you along with me.
See all things ready, Alice, against we come.
ALICE: Take no care for that; send you him home.
         Exeunt MOSBY *and* GREENE.
And if he e'er go forth again blame me.
Come, Black Will, that in mine eyes art fair;
Next unto Mosby do I honour thee.
Instead of fair words and large promises
120 My hands shall play you golden harmony.
How like you this? Say, will you do it sirs?
BLACK WILL: Ay, and that bravely, too. Mark my
device;
Place Mosby, being a stranger, in a chair,
And let your husband sit upon a stool,
That I may come behind him cunningly
And with a towel pull him to the ground;
Then stab him till his flesh be as a seive.
That done, bear him behind the Abbey,

104 *tables* backgammon.
114 *against* in preparation for when.
120 *play . . . harmony* i.e. give you gold.

That those that find him murdered may suppose
Some slave or other kill'd him for his gold.   130
ALICE: A fine device! You shall have twenty pound,
And when he is dead you shall have forty more.
And lest you might be suspected staying here,
Michael shall saddle you two lusty geldings.
Ride whither you will, to Scotland or to Wales;
I'll see you shall not lack where'er you be.
BLACK WILL: Such words would make one kill a
          thousand men!
Give me the key; which is the countinghouse?
ALICE: Here would I stay and still encourage you
But that I know how resolute you are.   140
SHAKEBAG: Tush! You are too faint-hearted; we must
          do it.
ALICE: But Mosby will be there, whose very looks
Will add unwonted courage to my thought
And make me the first that shall adventure on him.
BLACK WILL: Tush, get you gone; 'tis we must do the
          deed.
When this door opens next, look for his death.
          [BLACK WILL and SHAKEBAG enter the countinghouse.]
ALICE: Ah, would he now were here, that it might open.
I shall no more be closed in Arden's arms,
That like the snakes of black Tisiphone
Sting me with their embracings. Mosby's arms   150
Shall compass me, and, were I made a star,
I would have none other spheres but those.
There is no nectar but in Mosby's lips;
Had chaste Diana kiss'd him, she like me
Would grow love-sick, and from her wat'ry bower
Fling down Endymion and snatch him up.
Then blame not me that slay a silly man
Not half so lovely as Endymion.
          Here enters MICHAEL.

MICHAEL: Mistress, my master is coming hard by.

160 ALICE: Who comes with him?

MICHAEL: Nobody but Mosby.

ALICE: That's well, Michael. Fetch in the tables,
  And when thou hast done,
  Stand before the countinghouse door.

MICHAEL: Why so?

ALICE: Black Will is lock'd within to do the deed.

MICHAEL: What, shall he die tonight?

ALICE: Ay, Michael.

MICHAEL: But shall not Susan know it?

170 ALICE: Yes, for she'll be as secret as ourselves.

MICHAEL: That's brave! I'll go fetch the tables.

ALICE: But Michael, hark to me a word or two:
  When my husband is come in lock the street door.
  He shall be murder'd ere the guests come in.
    Exit MICHAEL [*and re-enter shortly with the tables*].
    Here enters ARDEN *and* MOSBY.
  Husband, what mean you to bring Mosby home?
  Although I wish'd you to be reconciled,
  'Twas more for fear of you than love of him.
  Black Will and Greene are his companions,
  And they are cutters and may cut you short.

180 Therefore, I thought it good to make you friends.
  But wherefore do you bring him hither now?
  You have given me my supper with his sight.

MOSBY: Master Arden, methinks your wife would have
      me gone.

ARDEN: No, good Master Mosby; women will be
      prating.
  Alice, bid him welcome; he and I are friends.

ALICE: You may enforce me to it if you will,
  But I had rather die than bid him welcome.
  His company hath purchas'd me ill friends,

182 *given . . . supper* i.e. taken away my appetite.

And therefore will I ne'er frequent it more.

MOSBY [*aside*]: Oh how cunningly she can dissemble.   190

ARDEN: Now he is here you will not serve me so.

ALICE: I pray you be not angry or displeased;
I'll bid him welcome seeing you'll have it so.
You are welcome, Master Mosby; will you sit down?

MOSBY: I know I am welcome to your loving husband;
But for yourself, you speak not from your heart.

ALICE: And if I do not, sir, think I have cause.

MOSBY: Pardon me, Master Arden; I'll away.

ARDEN: No, good Master Mosby.

ALICE: We shall have guests enough, though you go   200
hence.

MOSBY: I pray you, Master Arden, let me go.

ARDEN: I pray thee, Mosby, let her prate her fill.

ALICE: The doors are open, sir; you may be gone.

MICHAEL [*aside*]: Nay, that's a lie, for I have lock'd the
doors.

ARDEN: Sirrah, fetch me a cup of wine; I'll make them
friends.

Exit MICHAEL *and returns with wine.*

And gentle Mistress Alice, seeing you are so stout,
You shall begin. Frown not; I'll have it so.

ALICE: I pray you meddle with that you have to do.

ARDEN: Why, Alice, how can I do too much for him
Whose life I have endangered without cause?   210

ALICE: 'Tis true, and seeing 'twas partly through my
means,
I am content to drink to him for this once.
Here, Master Mosby; and I pray you, henceforth
Be you as strange to me as I to you.
Your company hath purchased me ill friends,
And I for you, God knows, have undeserved
Been ill spoken of in every place.

206 *stout* stubborn.   207 *begin* drink first (to Mosby).

Therefore, henceforth frequent my house no more.

MOSBY: I'll see your husband in despite of you.

220   Yet, Arden, I protest to thee by Heaven,
Thou ne'er shalt see me more after this night.
I'll go to Rome rather than be forsworn.

ARDEN: Tush, I'll have no such vows made in my house.

ALICE: Yes, I pray you, husband, let him swear;
And on that condition, Mosby, pledge me here.

MOSBY: Ay, as willingly as I mean to live.

ARDEN: Come, Alice, is our supper ready yet?

ALICE: It will by then you have played a game at tables.

ARDEN: Come, Master Mosby, what shall we play for?

230 MOSBY: Three games for a French crown, sir, and please
    you.

ARDEN: Content.

    Then they play at the tables.

BLACK WILL [*looking out from the countinghouse*]: Can
    he not take him yet? What a spite is that!

ALICE [*aside*]: Not yet, Will. Take heed he see thee not.

BLACK WILL [*aside*]: I fear he will spy me as I am coming.

MICHAEL [*aside*]: To prevent that, creep betwixt my legs.

MOSBY: One ace, or else I lose the game.

    [*He throws the dice.*]

ARDEN: Marry, sir, there's two for failing.

MOSBY: Ay, Master Arden, 'Now I can take you'.

    Then BLACK WILL *pulls him down with a towel.*

ARDEN: Mosby, Michael, Alice, what will you do?

240 BLACK WILL: Nothing but take you up, sir, nothing else.

MOSBY: There's for the pressing iron you told me of.
    [*Stabs him.*]

---

225 *pledge* drink to.
230 *French crown* French coin called 'ecu'. *and* if it.
237 *for failing* in case one is not sufficient.
240 *take you up* deal with you (playing on the catchphrase).
241 *pressing iron* See i, 313.

SHAKEBAG: And there's for the ten pound in my sleeve.
    [*Stabs him.*]
ALICE: What, groans thou? Nay then, give me the
    weapon.
  Take this for hind'ring Mosby's love and mine.
    [*Stabs him*.]
MICHAEL: Oh, Mistress!
BLACK WILL: Ah, that villain will betray us all.
MOSBY: Tush, fear him not; he will be secret.
MICHAEL: Why, dost thou think I will betray myself?
SHAKEBAG: In Southwark dwells a bonny northern lass,
  The widow Chambley; I'll to her house now,   250
  And if she will not give me harborough,
  I'll make booty of the quean, even to her smock.
BLACK WILL: Shift for yourselves; we two will leave
    you now.
ALICE: First lay the body in the countinghouse.
  Then they lay the body in the countinghouse.
BLACK WILL: We have our gold; Mistress Alice, adieu;
  Mosby, farewell, and Michael, farewell too.
  Exeunt [BLACK WILL *and* SHAKEBAG].
  Enter SUSAN.
SUSAN: Mistress, the guests are at the doors.
  Hearken, they knock. What, shall I let them in?
ALICE: Mosby, go thou and bear them company.
  Exit MOSBY.
  And Susan, fetch water and wash away this blood.   260
  [*Exit* SUSAN, *returns with water, and washes the floor.*]
SUSAN: The blood cleaveth to the ground and will not
    out.
ALICE: But with my nails I'll scrape away the blood. –
  The more I strive the more the blood appears.
SUSAN: What's the reason, Mistress; can you tell?

251 *harborough* harbour.   252 *quean* wench.

ALICE: Because I blush not at my husband's death.
Here enters MOSBY.
MOSBY: How now, what's the matter? Is all well?
ALICE: Ay, well – if Arden were alive again!
In vain we strive for here his blood remains.
MOSBY: Why, strew rushes on it, can you not?
270 This wench doth nothing; fall unto the work.
ALICE: 'Twas thou that made me murder him.
MOSBY: What of that?
ALICE: Nay, nothing, Mosby, so it be not known.
MOSBY: Keep thou it close, and 'tis unpossible.
ALICE: Ah, but I cannot. Was he not slain by me?
My husband's death torments me at the heart.
MOSBY: It shall not long torment thee, gentle Alice;
I am thy husband; think no more of him.
Here enters ADAM FOWLE *and* BRADSHAW.
BRADSHAW: How now, Mistress Arden; what ail you
weep?
280 MOSBY: Because her husband is abroad so late.
A couple of ruffians threaten'd him yesternight,
And the poor soul is afraid he should be hurt.
ADAM: Is't nothing else? Tush, he'll be here anon.
Here enters GREENE.
GREENE: Now, Mistress Arden, lack you any guests?
ALICE: Ah, Master Greene, did you see my husband
lately?
GREENE: I saw him walking behind the Abbey even now.
Here enters FRANKLIN.
ALICE: I do not like this being out so late.
Master Franklin, where did you leave my husband?
FRANKLIN: Believe me, I saw him not since morning.
290 Fear you not, he'll come anon. Meantime,

269 *rushes* a normal floor covering.
274 *close* secret.
279 *what . . . weep* what ails you that you weep.

You may do well to bid his guests sit down.

ALICE: Ay, so they shall. Master Bradshaw, sit you there;
I pray you be content, I'll have my will.

Master Mosby, sit you in my husband's seat.

MICHAEL [aside]: Susan, shall thou and I wait on them?
Or, and thou say'st the word, let us sit down too.

SUSAN [aside]: Peace, we have other matters now in hand.
I fear me, Michael, all will be bewrayed.

MICHAEL [aside]: Tush, so it be known that I shall
marry thee in the morning I care not though I be 300
hanged ere night. But to prevent the worst I'll buy
some ratsbane.

SUSAN [aside]: Why, Michael, wilt thou poison thyself?

MICHAEL [aside]: No, but my mistress, for I fear she'll
tell.

SUSAN [aside]: Tush, Michael, fear not her, she's wise
enough.

MOSBY: Sirrah Michael, give's a cup of beer.
Mistress Arden, here's to your husband.

ALICE: My husband!

FRANKLIN: What ails you, woman, to cry so suddenly?

ALICE: Ah, neighbours, a sudden qualm came over my 310
heart.
My husband's being forth torments my mind.
I know something's amiss, he is not well;
Or else I should have heard of him ere now.

MOSBY [aside]: She will undo us through her foolishness.

GREENE: Fear not, Mistress Arden, he's well enough.

ALICE: Tell not me; I know he is not well.
He was not wont for to stay thus late.
Good Master Franklin, go and seek him forth,
And if you find him send him home to me,
And tell him what a fear he hath put me in.   320

FRANKLIN: I like not this; I pray God all be well.

298 *bewrayed* betrayed.

I'll seek him out and find him if I can.

Exeunt FRANKLIN, MOSBY *and* GREENE.

ALICE [*aside*]: Michael, how shall I do to rid the rest
    away?

MICHAEL [*aside*]: Leave that to my charge, let me alone. –
'Tis very late, Master Bradshaw,

And there are many false knaves abroad,

And you have many narrow lanes to pass.

BRADSHAW: Faith, friend Michael, and thou sayest true.

Therefore I pray thee light's forth and lend's a link.

Exeunt BRADSHAW, ADAM FOWLE *and* MICHAEL.

330 ALICE: Michael, bring them to the doors but do not stay.

You know I do not love to be alone.

Go, Susan, and bid thy brother come.

But wherefore should he come? Here is nought but
    fear.

Stay, Susan, stay, and help to counsel me.

SUSAN: Alas, I counsel! Fear frights away my wits.

Then they open the countinghouse door and look upon
ARDEN.

ALICE: See, Susan, where thy quondam master lies,

Sweet Arden, smear'd in blood and filthy gore.

SUSAN: My brother, you and I shall rue this deed.

ALICE: Come, Susan, help to lift this body forth,

340 And let our salt tears be his obsequies.

[*They bring him out of the countinghouse.*]

Here enters MOSBY *and* GREENE.

MOSBY: How now, Alice, whither will you bear him?

ALICE: Sweet Mosby, art thou come? Then weep that
    will;

I have my wish in that I joy thy sight.

GREENE: Well, it 'hoves us to be circumspect.

MOSBY: Ay, for Franklin thinks that we have murder'd
    him.

329 *link* torch.

ALICE: Ay, but he cannot prove it for his life.
  We'll spend this night in dalliance and in sport.
    Here enters MICHAEL.
MICHAEL: Oh mistress, the mayor and all the watch
  Are coming towards our house with glaives and bills.
ALICE: Make the door fast; let them not come in.   350
MOSBY: Tell me, sweet Alice, how shall I escape?
ALICE: Out at the back door, over the pile of wood,
  And for one night lie at the Flower-de-Luce.
MOSBY: That is the next way to betray myself.
GREENE: Alas, Mistress Arden, the watch will take me
      here,
  And cause suspicion where else would be none.
ALICE: Why, take that way that Master Mosby doth;
  But first convey the body to the fields.
    Then [MOSBY, GREENE, MICHAEL *and* SUSAN] *bear
    the body into the fields* [*and return*].
MOSBY: Until tomorrow, sweet Alice, now farewell,
  And see you confess nothing in any case.   360
GREENE: Be resolute, Mistress Alice, betray us not,
  But cleave to us as we will stick to you.
    Exeunt MOSBY *and* GREENE.
ALICE: Now let the judge and juries do their worst;
  My house is clear and now I fear them not.
SUSAN: As we went it snowed all the way,
  Which makes me fear our footsteps will be spied.
ALICE: Peace, fool; the snow will cover them again.
SUSAN: But it had done before we came back again.
ALICE: Hark, hark, they knock. Go, Michael, let them
      in.
    [*Exit* MICHAEL *and re-enters with*] *the* MAYOR *and the*
    WATCH.

347 *glaives and bills* spears and halberds carried by watchmen and
officers.
354 *next* quickest.   368 *done* i.e. stopped snowing.

370 How now, Master Mayor; have you brought my
    husband home?

MAYOR: I saw him come into your house an hour ago.

ALICE: You are deceived; it was a Londoner.

MAYOR: Mistress Arden, know you not one that is called
    Black Will?

ALICE: I know none such. What mean these questions?

MAYOR: I have the Council's warrant to apprehend him.

ALICE: I am glad it is no worse. Why, Master Mayor,
  Think you I harbour any such?

MAYOR: We are inform'd that here he is,
  And therefore pardon us for we must search.

380 ALICE: Ay, search and spare you not, through every
    room.
  Were my husband at home you would not offer this.
    Here enters FRANKLIN.
  Master Franklin, what mean you come so sad?

FRANKLIN: Arden, thy husband and my friend, is slain.

ALICE: Ah, by whom? Master Franklin, can you tell?

FRANKLIN: I know not; but behind the Abbey
  There he lies murder'd in most pitious case.

MAYOR: But Master Franklin, are you sure 'tis he?

FRANKLIN: I am too sure. Would God I were deceived.

ALICE: Find out the murderers; let them be known.

390 FRANKLIN: Ay, so they shall. Come you along with us.

ALICE: Wherefore?

FRANKLIN: Know you this hand-towel and this knife?

SUSAN [*aside*]: Ah, Michael, through this thy negligence
  Thou hast betrayed and undone us all.

MICHAEL [*aside*]: I was so afraid, I knew not what I did.
  I thought I had thrown them both into the well.

ALICE: It is the pig's blood we had to supper.
  But wherefore stay you? Find out the murderers.

386 *case* condition.   397 *to* at.

MAYOR: I fear me you'll prove one of them yourself.

ALICE: I one of them? What mean such questions? 400

FRANKLIN: I fear me he was murder'd in this house
And carried to the fields, for from that place
Backwards and forwards may you see
The print of many feet within the snow.
And look about the chamber where we are
And you shall find part of his guiltless blood;
For in his slipshoe did I find some rushes,
Which argueth he was murder'd in this room.

MAYOR: Look in the place where he was wont to sit.
See, see! His blood! It is too manifest. 410

ALICE: It is a cup of wine that Michael shed.

MICHAEL: Ay, truly.

FRANKLIN: It is his blood which, strumpet, thou hast
shed.
But if I live, thou and thy 'complices,
Which have conspired and wrought his death, shall
rue it.

ALICE: Ah, Master Franklin, God and Heaven can tell –
I loved him more than all the world beside.
But bring me to him; let me see his body.

FRANKLIN: Bring that villain and Mosby's sister too;
And one of you go to the Flower-de-Luce 420
And seek for Mosby, and apprehend him too. *Exeunt.*

SCENE FIFTEEN

Here enters SHAKEBAG *solus.*

SHAKEBAG: The widow Chambley in her husband's
days I kept;

---

407 *slipshoe* slipper.   419 *that villain* i.e. Michael.

And now he's dead she is grown so stout
She will not know her old companions.
I came hither thinking to have had
Harbour as I was wont,
And she was ready to thrust me out at doors.
But whether she would or no I got me up,
And as she followed me I spurn'd her down the stairs
And broke her neck, and cut her tapster's throat;
And now I am going to fling them in the Thames.
I have the gold; what care I though it be known?
I'll cross the water and take sanctuary.

      Exit SHAKEBAG.

SCENE SIXTEEN

Here enters the MAYOR, MOSBY, ALICE, FRANKLIN,
MICHAEL *and* SUSAN.

MAYOR: See, Mistress Arden, where your husband lies.
  Confess this foul fault and be penitent.
ALICE: Arden, sweet husband, what shall I say?
  The more I sound his name the more he bleeds.
  This blood condemns me and in gushing forth
  Speaks as it falls and asks me why I did it.
  Forgive me, Arden; I repent me now;
  And would my death save thine thou shouldst not die.
  Rise up, sweet Arden, and enjoy thy love,
  And frown not on me when we meet in Heaven:
  In Heaven I love thee though on earth I did not.
MAYOR: Say, Mosby, what made thee murder him?
FRANKLIN: Study not for an answer, look not down;
  His purse and girdle found at thy bed's head
  Witness sufficiently thou didst the deed.

2 *stout* proud.

It bootless is to swear thou didst it not.

MOSBY: I hired Black Will and Shakebag, ruffians both,
And they and I have done this murd'rous deed.
But wherefore stay we? Come and bear me hence.

FRANKLIN: Those ruffians shall not escape. I will up to   20
London
And get the Council's warrant to apprehend them.
Exeunt.

SCENE SEVENTEEN

Here enters BLACK WILL.

BLACK WILL: Shakebag, I hear, hath taken sanctuary.
But I am so pursued with hues and cries
For petty robberies that I have done
That I can come unto no sanctuary.
Therefore must I in some oyster-boat
At last be fain to go aboard some hoy,
And so to Flushing. There is no staying here.
At Sittinburgh the watch was like to take me,
And, had I not with my buckler cover'd my head
And run full blank at all adventures,   10
I am sure I had ne'er gone further than that place;
For the constable had twenty warrants to apprehend
me,
Besides that I robbed him and his man once at Gads-
hill.
Farewell, England; I'll to Flushing now.
Exit BLACK WILL.

16 *bootless* unavailing.
6 *hoy* small vessel, coaster.   7 *Sittinburgh* Sittingbourne.
10 *at all adventures* whatever might be the consequences.

SCENE EIGHTEEN

Here enters the MAYOR, MOSBY, ALICE, MICHAEL,
SUSAN *and* BRADSHAW.

MAYOR: Come, make haste, and bring away the prisoners.

BRADSHAW: Mistress Arden, you are now going to God.
And I am by the law condemned to die
About a letter I brought from Master Greene.
I pray you, Mistress Arden, speak the truth:
Was I ever privy to your intent or no?

ALICE: What should I say? You brought me such a letter,
But I dare swear thou knewest not the contents.
Leave now to trouble me with wordly things

10   And let me meditate upon my Saviour Christ
Whose blood must save me for the blood I shed.

MOSBY: How long shall I live in this hell of grief?
Convey me from the presence of that strumpet.

ALICE: Ah, but for thee I had never been strumpet.
What cannot oaths and protestations do
When men have opportunity to woo?
I was too young to sound thy villainies,
But now I find it, and repent too late.

SUSAN: Ah, gentle brother, wherefore should I die?

20   I knew not of it till the deed was done.

MOSBY: For thee I mourn more than for myself,
But let it suffice I cannot save thee now.

MICHAEL: And if your brother and my mistress
Had not promised me you in marriage,
I had ne'er given consent to this foul deed.

MAYOR: Leave to accuse each other now,

4 *About* on account of.
9 *Leave* cease.   17 *sound* plumb.

And listen to the sentence I shall give:
Bear Mosby and his sister to London straight
Where they in Smithfield must be executed;
Bear Mistress Arden unto Canterbury   30
Where her sentence is she must be burnt;
Michael and Bradshaw in Faversham must suffer death.

ALICE: Let my death make amends for all my sins.

MOSBY: Fie upon women! this shall be my song;
But bear me hence for I have lived too long.

SUSAN: Seeing no hope on earth in Heaven is my hope.

MICHAEL: Faith, I care not seeing I die with Susan.

BRADSHAW: My blood be on his head that gave the
sentence.

MAYOR: To speedy execution with them all.   *Exeunt.*

Epilogue

Here enters FRANKLIN.

FRANKLIN: Thus have you seen the truth of Arden's
   death.
As for the ruffians, Shakebag and Black Will,
The one took sanctuary and being sent for out
Was murdered in Southwark as he passed
To Greenwich where the Lord Protector lay.
Black Will was burnt in Flushing on a stage.
Greene was hanged at Osbridge in Kent.
The painter fled and how he died we know not.
But this above the rest is to be noted:
Arden lay murder'd in that plot of ground
Which he by force and violence held from Reede;
And in the grass his body's print was seen
Two years and more after the deed was done.
Gentlemen, we hope you'll pardon this naked tragedy
Wherein no filed points are foisted in
To make it gracious to the ear or eye;
For simple truth is gracious enough,
And needs no other points of glozing stuff.

10

6 *stage* scaffold.
15 *filed* polished, refined. *points* tagged laces for attaching hose to
doublet.
18 *glozing* specious.

Facsimile title page of the first edition of
A Yorkshire Tragedy

A

YORKSHIRE

Tragedy.

Not so New as Lamentable
and true.

Acted by his Maiesties Players at
the Globe.

VVritten by VV. Shakspeare.

At London
Printed by *R. B.* for *Thomas Pauier* and are to bee sold at his
shop on Cornhill, neere to the exchange.
1608.

Dramatis Personae

HUSBAND
MASTER OF A COLLEGE
KNIGHT, *a Magistrate*
OLIVER ⎫
RALPH ⎬ *Servingmen*
SAM ⎭
FOUR GENTLEMEN
SON
SERVANTS, OFFICERS, *other* GENTLEMEN
WIFE
MAID

SCENE ONE

Enter OLIVER *and* RALPH, *two servingmen.*

OLIVER: Sirrah Rafe, my young mistress is in such a
pitiful, passionate humour for the long absence of her
love.

RALPH: Why, can you blame her? Why, apples hanging
longer on the tree than when they are ripe makes so
many fallings; viz., mad wenches because they are not
gathered in time are fain to drop of themselves, and
then 'tis common you know for every man to take 'em
up.

OLIVER: Mass, thou sayest true; 'tis common indeed.   10
But sirrah, is neither our young master returned, nor
our fellow Sam come from London?

RALPH: Neither of either, as the Puritan bawd says. 'Slid,
I hear Sam, Sam's come; here's! Tarry! Come, i'faith,
now my nose itches for news.

OLIVER: And so does mine elbow.

SAM *calls within*: Where are you there?

    [*Enter* SAM] *furnished with things from London.*

SAM [*addressing offstage*]: Boy, look you walk my horse
with discretion. I have rid him simply; I warrant his
skin sticks to his back with very heat. If 'a should catch   20
cold and get the cough of the lungs I were well served,
were I not? What, Rafe and Oliver!

BOTH: Honest fellow Sam, welcome i'faith! What tricks
hast thou brought from London?

SAM: You see I am hanged after the truest fashion: three

2 *humour* state of mind.
13 *'Slid* an oath (=by God's lid).
19 *simply* foolishly.   23 *tricks* knick-knacks.

hats and two glasses bobbing upon 'em, two rebato
wires upon my breast, a capcase by my side, a brush at
my back, an almanac in my pocket, and three ballads
in my codpiece. Nay, I am the true picture of a com-
30   mon servingman.

OLIVER: I'll swear thou art. Thou may'st set up when
thou wilt. There's many a one begins with less, I can
tell thee, that proves a rich man ere he dies. But what's
the news from London, Sam?

RALPH: Ay, that's well said; what's the news from London, sirrah? My young mistress keeps such a puling for
her love.

SAM: Why, the more fool she; ay, the more ninny-
hammer she!

40   OLIVER: Why, Sam, why?

SAM: Why, he's married to another long ago.

BOTH: I'faith, ye jest!

SAM: Why, did you not know that till now? Why, he's
married, beats his wife, and has two or three children
by her: for you must note that any woman bears the
more when she is beaten.

RALPH: Ay, that's true, for she bears the blows.

OLIVER: Sirrah Sam, I would not for two years' wages
my young mistress knew so much. She'd run upon the
50   left hand of her wit, and ne'er be her own woman
again.

SAM: And I think she was blessed in her cradle, that he
never came in her bed. Why, he has consumed all,
pawned his lands, and made his university brother

26 *glasses* mirrors. *rebato wires* See note.
27 *capcase* hand-bag.   36 *puling* plaintive crying.
38–9 *ninny-hammer* simpleton.
49–50 *run . . . wit* go out of her mind.
50 *her own woman* herself.

stand in wax for him. (There's a fine phrase for a
scrivener!) Puh! He owes more than his skin's worth.

OLIVER: Is't possible?

SAM: Nay, I'll tell you moreover, he calls his wife
'whore' as familiarly as one would call Moll and Doll,
and his children 'bastards' as naturally as can be. But   60
what have we here? I thought 'twas somewhat pulled
down my breeches. I quite forgot my two poting-
sticks. These came from London. Now anything is
good here that comes from London.

OLIVER: Ay, far-fetched, you know.

SAM: But speak in your conscience, i'faith, have not we
as good poting-sticks i'the country as need to be put
i'the fire. The mind of a thing is all, the mind of a
thing's all. And as thou said'st e'en now, far-fetched is
the best things for ladies.   70

OLIVER: Ay, and for waiting gentlewomen, too.

SAM: But Ralph, what, is our beer sour this thunder?

RALPH: No, no, it holds countenance yet.

SAM: Why then, follow me. I'll teach you the finest
humour to be drunk in; I learnt it at London last week.

BOTH: I'faith, let's hear it, let's hear it.

SAM: The bravest humour! 'twould do a man good to be
drunk in't; they call it knighting in London, when they
drink upon their knees.

BOTH: Faith, that's excellent.   80

SAM: Come follow me; I'll give you all the degrees on't
in order. *Exeunt.*

---

55 *in wax* in legal bond.   56 *scrivener* notary.
72 *this thunder* i.e. on account of this thunder.
73 *holds countenance* retains its composure (punning on Sam's
'sour' = 1 bitter-tasting; 2 sullen-looking).
81 *degrees* stages.

SCENE TWO

Enter WIFE.

WIFE: What will become of us? All will away;
  My husband never ceases in expense,
  Both to consume his credit and his house;
  And 'tis set down by Heaven's just decree
  That riot's child must needs be beggary.
  Are these the virtues that his youth did promise,
  Dice, and voluptuous meetings, midnight revels,
  Taking his bed with surfeits? – ill beseeming
  The ancient honour of his house and name.
10 And this not all, but that which kills me most,
  When he recounts his losses and false fortunes,
  The weakness of his state so much dejected,
  Not as a man repentant, but half mad
  His fortunes cannot answer his expense.
  He sits and sullenly locks up his arms;
  Forgetting Heaven, looks downward, which makes him
  Appear so dreadful that he frights my heart;
  Walks heavily, as if his soul were earth;
  Not penitent for those his sins are past,
20 But vext his money cannot make them last:
  A fearful melancholy, ungodly sorrow.
  Oh, yonder he comes. Now in despite of ills
  I'll speak to him, and I will hear him speak,
  And do my best best to drive it from his heart.

  Enter HUSBAND.

HUSBAND: Pox o'th' last throw; it made
  Five hundred angels vanish from my sight.
  I'm damn'd, I'm damn'd: the angels have forsook me.
  Nay, 'tis certainly true, for he that has no coin

26 *angels* gold coins and obvious pun on heavenly angels.

Is damn'd in this world; he's gone, he's gone.

WIFE: Dear husband –

HUSBAND: Oh, most punishment of all, I have a wife.   30

WIFE: I do entreat you as you love your soul,

Tell me the cause of this your discontent.

HUSBAND: A vegeance strip thee naked, thou art cause,

Effect, quality, property; thou, thou, thou! *Exit.*

WIFE: Bad turned to worse!

Both beggary of the soul as of the body;

And so much unlike himself at first

As if some vexed spirit had got his form upon him.

He comes again.

    Enter HUSBAND *again.*

He says I am the cause. I never yet   40

Spoke less than words of duty and of love.

HUSBAND: If marriage be honourable, then cuckolds are
honourable, for they cannot be made without marriage. Fool! What meant I to marry to get beggars?
Now must my eldest son be a knave or nothing; he
cannot live upo'the fool, for he will have no land to
maintain him. That mortgage sits like a snaffle upon
mine inheritance and makes me chew upon iron. My
second son must be a promoter, and my third a thief,
or an underputter, a slave pander.   50

Oh beggary, beggary

To what base uses dost thou put a man!

I think the Devil scorns to be a bawd;

He bears himself more proudly, has more care on's
      credit.

Base, slavish, abject, filthy poverty!

WIFE: Good sir, by all our vows I do beseech you,

---

46 *live upo'the fool* live a life of riot.

47 *snaffle* bridle-bit.   49 *promoter* professional informer.

50 *underputter* procurer.

Show me the true cause of your discontent.

HUSBAND: Money, money, money, and thou must
    supply me.

WIFE: Alas, I am the least cause of your discontent;

60   Yet what is mine, either in rings or jewels,
Use to your own desire. But I beseech you,
As y'are a gentleman by many bloods,
Though I myself be out of your respect,
Think on the state of these three lovely boys
You have been father to.

HUSBAND: Puh! Bastards, bastards,
Bastards begot in tricks, begot in tricks.

WIFE: Heavens knows how those words wrong me. But
    I may
Endure these griefs among a thousand more.
Oh, call to mind your lands already mortgag'd,

70   Yourself wound into debts, your hopeful brother,
At the university, in bonds for you,
Like to be seized upon. And –

HUSBAND: Ha' done thou harlot,
Whom though for fashion sake I married
I never could abide. Think'st thou thy words
Shall kill my pleasures? Fall off to thy friends;
Thou and thy bastards beg; I will not bate
A whit in humour. Midnight, still I love you,
And revel in your company. Curb'd in,
Shall it be said in all societies

80   That I broke custom, that I flagg'd in money?
No, those thy jewels I will play as freely
As when my state was fullest.

WIFE: Be it so.

---

62 *by many bloods* of noble descent.
76 *bate* lessen.   77 *humour* wonted disposition.
80 *flagg'd in money* became hard up.

HUSBAND: Nay, I protest – and take that for an earnest –
　　Spurns her.
　I will for ever hold thee in contempt,
　And never touch the sheets that cover thee,
　But be divorc'd in bed till thou consent
　Thy dowry shall be sold to give new life
　Unto those pleasures which I most affect.
WIFE: Sir, do but turn a gentle eye on me,
　And what the law shall give me leave to do　　　　90
　You shall command.
HUSBAND: 　　　　　Look it be done. Shall I want dust
　And like a slave wear nothing in my pockets
　But my hands, to fill them up with nails?
　　Holding his hands in his pockets.
　Oh, much against my blood! Let it be done.
　I was never made to be a looker-on,
　A bawd to dice. I'll shake the drabs myself
　And make 'em yield. I say, look it be done.
WIFE: I take my leave. It shall. 　　　　　*Exit.*
HUSBAND: 　　　　　Speedily, speedily.
　I hate the very hour I chose a wife.
　A true trouble, three children like three evils　　100
　Hang upon me. Fie, fie, fie!
　Strumpet and bastards, strumpet and bastards!
　　Enter three GENTLEMEN *hearing him.*
FIRST GENTLEMAN: Still do those loathsome thoughts
　　　　jar on your tongue.
　Yourself to stain the honour of your wife
　Nobly descended! Those whom men call mad
　Endanger others, but he's more than mad
　That wounds himself; whose own words do proclaim
　Scandals unjust to soil his better name.

---

91 *dust* slang for money.
94 *blood* disposition. 　　　96 *drabs* prostitutes.

It is not fit, I pray forsake it.

110 SECOND GENTLEMAN: Good sir, let modesty reprove
       you.

THIRD GENTLEMAN: Let honest kindness sway so much
       with you.

HUSBAND: God den, I thank you sir, how do you, adieu;
    I'm glad to see you; farewell instructions,
    Admonitions.
       Exeunt GENTLEMEN.
       Enter a SERVANT.
               How now, sirrah, what would you?

SERVANT: Only to certify you, sir, that my mistress was
    met by the way by them who were sent for her up to
    London by her honourable uncle, your worship's late
    guardian.

120 HUSBAND: So sir, then she is gone and so may you be;
    But let her look that the thing be done she wots of,
    Or hell will stand more pleasant than her house at home
       [*Exit* SERVANT.]
       Enter a GENTLEMAN.

GENTLEMAN: Well or ill met I care not.

HUSBAND: No, nor I.

GENTLEMAN: I am come with confidence to chide you.

HUSBAND: Who me?
    Chide me? Do't finely then; let it not move me;
    For if thou chid'st me angry I shall strike.

GENTLEMAN: Strike thine own follies, for it is they
    Deserve to be well beaten. We are now in private,
    There's none but thou and I. Thou'rt fond and peevish,
    An unclean rioter; thy lands and credit

112 *God den* abbreviation of 'God give you good even'.
116 *certify* to inform.
117–18 *were . . . London* sent to fetch her up to London.
121 *wots* knows.
128 *fond* foolish. *peevish* perverse.

Lie now both sick of a consumption.   130
I am sorry for thee; that man spends with shame
That with his riches does consume his name.
And such art thou.

HUSBAND: Peace.

GENTLEMAN: No, thou shalt hear me further.
Thy father's and forefathers' worthy honours,
Which were our country monuments, our grace,
Follies in thee begin now to deface;
The springtime of thy youth did fairly promise
Such a most fruitful summer to thy friends
It scarce can enter into men's beliefs
Such dearth should hang on thee; we that see it   140
Are sorry to believe it. In thy change,
This voice into all places will be hurled:
Thou and the devil has deceived the world.

HUSBAND: I'll not endure thee.

GENTLEMAN: But of all the worst,
Thy virtuous wife right honourably allied
Thou hast proclaimed a strumpet.

HUSBAND: Nay then, I know thee;
Thou art her champion, thou, her private friend,
The party you wot on.

GENTLEMAN: Oh, ignoble thought!
I am past my patient blood. Shall I stand idle
And see my reputation touched to death?   150

HUSBAND: 'T'as galled you, this, has it?

GENTLEMAN: No, monster, I will prove
My thoughts did only tend to virtuous love.

HUSBAND: Love of her virtues? There it goes.

132 *name* good reputation.
135 *our country monuments* embellishments of our district.
142 *voice* opinion or rumour.
148 *The . . . on* euphemistic way of expressing an obscene idea.
151 *galled* annoyed.

GENTLEMAN: Base spirit,
   To lay thy hate upon the fruitful honour
   Of thine own bed.
       They fight and the HUSBAND *is hurt.*
HUSBAND: Oh!
GENTLEMAN: Wilt thou yield it yet?
HUSBAND: Sir, sir, I have not done with you.
GENTLEMAN: I hope nor ne'er shall do.
       Fight again.
HUSBAND: Have you got tricks,
   Are you in cunning with me?
GENTLEMAN: No, plain and right;
   He needs no cunning that for truth doth fight.
       HUSBAND *falls down.*
160 HUSBAND: Hard fortune! Am I levelled with the
               ground?
GENTLEMAN: Now, sir, you lie at mercy.
HUSBAND: Ay, you slave.
GENTLEMAN: Alas that hate should bring us to our grave.
   You see my sword's not thirsty for your life.
   I am sorrier for your wound than yourself.
   Y'are of a virtuous house, show virtuous deeds;
   'Tis not your honour, 'tis your folly bleeds.
   Much good has been expected in your life;
   Cancel not all men's hopes. You have a wife
   Kind and obedient; heap not wrongful shame
170   On your posterity; let only sin be sore,
   And by this fall, rise, never to fall more.
   And so I leave you.   *Exit.*
HUSBAND: Has the dog left me then
   After his tooth hath left me? Oh my heart
   Would fain leap after him. Revenge, I say,
   I'm mad to be revenged. My strumpet wife,

157 *I . . . do* Pun on 'finished with' and 'killed off'.
158 *tricks* underhand devices.

It is thy quarrel that rips thus my flesh
And makes my breast spit blood, but thou shalt bleed.
Vanquished? Got down? Unable e'en to speak?
Surely, 'tis want of money makes men weak.
Ay, 'twas that o'erthrew me; I'd ne'er been down else.   180
   Exit.

SCENE THREE

Enter WIFE *in a riding-suit, with a* SERVINGMAN.
SERVANT: Faith mistress, if it might not be presumption
  In me to tell you so, for his excuse
  You had small reason knowing his abuse.
WIFE: I grant I had, but alas,
  Why should our faults at home be spread abroad?
  'Tis grief enough within doors. At first sight
  Mine uncle could run o'er his prodigal life
  As perfectly as if his serious eye
  Had numbered all his follies;
  Knew of his mortgaged lands, his friends in bonds,   10
  Himself withered with debts; and in that minute,
  Had I added his usage and unkindness,
  'Twould have confounded every thought of good;
  Where now, fathering his riots on his youth,
  Which time and tame experience will shake off,
  Guessing his kindness to me (as I smoothed him
  With all the skill I had, though his defects
  Are in form uglier than an unshaped bear)
  He's ready to prefer him to some office
  And place at court, a good and sure relief   20
  To all his stooping fortunes. 'Twill be a means I hope

9 *numbered* reckoned up.   15 *tame* taming.
16 *smoothed him* glossed over his faults.

      To make new league between us, and redeem
      His virtues with his lands.

SERVANT: I should think so, mistress. If he should not
    now be kind to you and love you and cherish you up,
    I should think the devil himself kept open house in
    him.

WIFE: I doubt not but he will. Now prithee leave me:
    I think I hear him coming.

SERVANT: I am gone.   *Exit.*

30 WIFE: By this good means I shall preserve my lands,
      And free my husband out of usurers' hands;
      Now there is no need of sale; my uncle's kind.
      I hope, if ought, this will content his mind.
      Here comes my husband.

      Enter HUSBAND.

HUSBAND: Now, are you come? Where's the money?
    Let's see the money. Is the rubbish sold, those wise-
    acres, your lands? Why, when? The money, where
    is't? Pour't down, down with it, down with it, I say,
    pour't o'the ground. Let's see't, let's see't!

40 WIFE: Good sir, keep but in patience and I hope
      My words shall like you well; I bring you better com-
         fort
      Than the sale of my dowry.

HUSBAND: Ha! What's that?

WIFE: Pray do not fright me sir, but vouchsafe me hear-
        ing.
      My uncle, glad of your kindness to me and mild usage,
      For so I made it to him, has in pity
      Of your declining fortunes provided
      A place for you at court of worth and credit,
      Which so much overjoyed me –

36–7 *wiseacres* contemptuous reference to the wife's land (usual
meaning: 'pretender to wisdom').
41 *like* please.

HUSBAND: Out on thee filth!
    Spurns her.
Over and overjoyed when I'm in torments?
The politic whore, subtler than nine devils,   50
Was this thy journey to Nunk, to set down
The history of me, of my estate and fortunes?
Shall I that dedicated myself to pleasure be now con-
fined in service, to crouch and stand like an old man
i'the hams, my hat off, I that never could abide to
uncover my head i'the church? Base slut, this fruit
bears thy complaints.
WIFE: Oh Heaven knows
That my complaints were praises and best words
Of you and your estate; only my friends   60
Knew of your mortgaged lands, and were possessed
Of every accident before I came.
If thou suspect it but a plot in me
To keep my dowry, or for mine own good,
Or my poor children's (though it suits a mother
To show a natural care in their reliefs),
Yet I'll forget myself to calm your blood.
Consume it, as your pleasure counsels you,
And all I wish, e'en clemency affords:
Give me but comely looks and modest words.   70
HUSBAND: Money, whore, money, or I'll – [*Draws
    his dagger.*]
    Enter a SERVANT *very hastily.*
What the devil! How now? Thy hasty news? *To his*
    MANSERVANT [*who is*] *in a fear.*

50 *politic* scheming.
54–5 *to crouch . . . hams* i.e. to take up a deferential attitude.
56–7 *this . . . complaints* this is the fruit of your complaints.
61 *possessed* aware of.
62 *accident* event or outward symptom of the husband's troubles.
67 *blood* passion.

SERVANT: May it please you, sir –

HUSBAND: What! May I not look upon my dagger?
Speak villain, or I will execute the point on thee:
quick short!

SERVANT: Why sir, a gentleman from the university
stays below to speak with you.

HUSBAND: From the university? So, university – that
80 long word runs through me.   *Exeunt.*
  WIFE *alone.*

WIFE: Was ever wife so wretchedly beset?
Had not this news stept in between, the point
Had offered violence to my breast.
That which some women call great misery
Would show but little here, would scarce be seen
Amongst my miseries. I may compare
For wretched fortunes with all wives that are.
Nothing will please him until all be nothing;
He calls it slavery to be preferred;
90 A place of credit, a base servitude.
What shall become of me and my poor children,
Two here and one at nurse, my pretty beggars?
I see how ruin with a palsy hand
Begins to shake the ancient seat to dust.
The heavy weight of sorrow draws my lids
Over my dankish eyes; I can scarce see.
Thus grief will last, it wakes and sleeps with me. [*Exit.*]

75 *execute* use. 81 *beset* assailed.

SCENE FOUR

Enter the HUSBAND *with the* MASTER OF THE
COLLEGE.

HUSBAND: Please you draw near, sir; y'are exceeding
welcome.

MASTER: That's my doubt; I fear, I come not to be
welcome.

HUSBAND: Yes, howsoever.

MASTER: 'Tis not my fashion, sir, to dwell in long circumstance, but to be plain and effectual: therefore to
the purpose. The cause of my setting forth was pitious
and lamentable. That hopeful, young gentleman, your
brother, whose virtues we all love dearly, through your
default and unnatural negligence lies in bond executed
for your debt, a prisoner, all his studies amazed, his   10
hope struck dead, and the pride of his youth muffled
in these dark clouds of oppression.

HUSBAND: Hum, um, um.

MASTER: Oh, you have killed the towardest hope of all
our university: wherefore, without repentance and
amends, expect ponderous and sudden judgements to
fall grievously upon you; your brother a man who pro-
fited in his divine employments and might have made
ten thousand souls fit for Heaven, now by your careless courses cast in prison, which you must answer for;   20
and assure your spirit, it will come home at length.

HUSBAND: Oh God, oh!

MASTER: Wise men think ill of you, others speak ill of
you, no man loves you; nay, even those whom honesty

5 *effectual* to the point.
9–10 *executed for* put into effect on account of.
21 *come home* i.e. return to you.

condemns, condemn you. And take this from the virtuous affection I bear your brother: never look for
prosperous hour, good thought, quiet sleeps, contented walks, nor anything that makes man perfect, till
you redeem him. What is your answer? How will you
bestow him, upon desperate misery or better hopes?
I suffer till I hear your answer.

HUSBAND: Sir, you have much wrought with me; I feel
you in my soul; you are your art's master. I never had
sense till now; your syllables have cleft me. Both for
your words and pains I thank you. I cannot but acknow-
ledge grievous wrongs done to my brother, mighty,
mighty, mighty wrongs.

[*Addressing off-stage*] Within there!

    Enter a SERVINGMAN.

HUSBAND: Fill me a bowl of wine.

    Exit SERVANT *for wine*.

                              Alas, poor brother,
Bruis'd with an execution for my sake.

MASTER: A bruise indeed makes many a mortal sore
Till the grave cure 'em.

    Enter [SERVANT] *with wine* [*and exit*].

HUSBAND: Sir, I begin to you; y'ave chid your welcome.

MASTER: I could have wished it better for your sake.
I pledge you, sir, to the kind man in prison.

HUSBAND: Let it be so.

    Drink both.

                    Now, sir, if you so please
To spend but a few minutes in a walk
About my grounds below, my man here
Shall attend you. I doubt not but by that time
To be furnished of a sufficient answer,

28 *perfect* contented.   33 *art's master* pun on Master of Arts.
43 *begin to you* drink first to you.
45 *pledge* drink the health.

And therein my brother fully satisfied.

MASTER: Good sir, in that the angels would be pleased,
And the world's murmurs calmed, and I should say,
I set forth then upon a lucky day.　　　*Exit.*

HUSBAND: Oh thou confused man! Thy pleasant sins
have undone thee, thy damnation has beggared thee.
That Heaven should say we must not sin and yet made
women; gives our senses way to find pleasure which
being found confounds us! Why should we know
those things so much misuse us? Oh, would virtue had　60
been forbidden; we should then have proved all virtuous, for 'tis our blood to love what we are forbidden.
Had not drunkenness been forbidden what man would
have been fool to a beast and zany to a swine, to show
tricks in the mire? What is there in three dice to make
a man draw thrice three thousand acres into the compass of a round, little table, and with the gentleman's
palsy in the hand shake out his posterity thieves or
beggars? 'Tis done; I ha' don't i' faith: terrible, horrible
misery! How well was I left? Very well, very well.　70
My lands showed like a full moon about me, but now
the moon's i' the last quarter, waning, waning; and I
am mad to think that moon was mine. Mine and my
father's, and my forefathers': generations, generations!
Down goes the house of us, down, down it sinks. Now
is the name a beggar, begs in me; that name, which
hundreds of years has made this shire famous, in me
and my posterity runs out. In my seed five are made
miserable besides myself: my riot is now my brother's
gaoler, my wife's sighing, my three boys' penury, and　80
mine own confusion.
Why sit my hairs upon my cursed head?
　　　Tears his hair.

62 *blood* natural disposition.
64 *fool to* inferior to. *zany to* buffooning imitation of.

Will not this poison scatter them? Oh!
My brother's in execution among devils
That stretch him and make him give, and I in want
Not able to deliver, nor to redeem him.
Divines and dying men may talk of hell
But in my heart her several torments dwell.
Slavery and misery! Who in this case
90 Would not take up money upon his soul,
Pawn his salvation, live at interest?
I that did ever in abundance dwell,
For me to want exceeds the throes of hell.

 Enter his little SON *with a top and a scourge.*

SON: What ails you father, are you not well? I cannot
scourge my top as long as you stand so; you take up all
the room with your wide legs. Puh! you cannot make
me afeared with this; I fear no vizards nor bugbears.

 HUSBAND *takes up the* CHILD *by the skirts of his long
coat in one hand and draws his dagger with the other.*

HUSBAND: Up sir, for here thou hast no inheritance left.
SON: Oh, what will you do, father? I am your white boy.
100 HUSBAND: Thou shalt be my red boy; take that.

 Strikes him.

SON: Oh, you hurt me, father.
HUSBAND: My eldest beggar, thou shalt not live to ask
an usurer bread, to cry at a great man's gate, or follow
'Good your Honour' by a couch. No, nor your
brother; 'tis charity to brain you.
SON: How shall I learn now my head's broke?
HUSBAND: Bleed, bleed, rather than beg, beg!

 Stabs him.

85 *give* pun on 'stretch' and 'give money'.
90 *take up money* obtain credit.
97 *vizards* masks (i.e. Husband's angry faces). *bugbears* hobgoblins
(supposed to devour naughty children).
99 *white boy* term of endearment.
104 *couch* low bow. See note.

Be not thy name's disgrace;
Spurn thou thy fortunes first if they be base.
Come view thy second brother. Fates,   110
My children's blood shall spin into your faces.
You shall see
How confidently we scorn beggary.

    Exit with his SON.

SCENE FIVE

    Enter a MAID *with a* CHILD *in her arms, the* MOTHER
    [*discovered*] *by her asleep.*

MAID: Sleep, sweet babe; sorrow makes thy mother
    sleep;
It bodes small good when heaviness falls so deep.
Hush pretty boy, thy hopes might have been better.
'Tis lost at dice what ancient honour won:
Hard, when the father plays away the son.
Nothing but misery serves in this house,
Ruin and desolation – Oh!

    Enter HUSBAND *with the boy bleeding.*

HUSBAND: Whore, give me that boy! *Strives with her for*
    the CHILD.
MAID: Oh! help, help! Out, alas! murder, murder!
HUSBAND: Are you gossiping, prating, sturdy quean?   10
I'll break your clamour with your neck downstairs;
Tumble, tumble headlong.   *Throws her down.*
So, the surest way to charm a woman's tongue
Is break her neck; a politician did it.
SON: Mother, mother! I am killed, mother!

    WIFE *wakes.*

10 *quean* whore, hussy.
13 *charm a woman's tongue* silence a woman.

WIFE: Ha, who's that cried? Oh me, my children!
  Both, both, both; bloody, bloody.
    Catches up the YOUNGEST.
HUSBAND: Strumpet, let go the boy, let go the beggar.
WIFE: Oh my sweet husband!
20 HUSBAND: Filth, harlot!
WIFE: Oh, what will you do, dear husband?
HUSBAND: Give me the bastard.
WIFE: Your own sweet boy!
HUSBAND: There are too many beggars.
WIFE: Good my husband –
HUSBAND: Dost thou prevent me still?
WIFE: Oh God!
HUSBAND: Have at his heart.
    Stabs at the CHILD *in her arms.*
WIFE: Oh, my dear boy!
    [*He*] *gets it from her.*
30 HUSBAND: Brat, thou shalt not live to shame thy house.
WIFE: Oh, heaven!
    She is hurt and sinks down.
HUSBAND: And perish! Now, begone!
  There's whores enough, and want would make you one.
    Enter a lusty SERVANT.
SERVANT: Oh sir, what deeds are these?
HUSBAND: Base slave, my vassal:
  Com'st thou between my fury to question me?
SERVANT: Were you the devil I would hold you, sir.
HUSBAND: Hold me? Presumption! I'll undo thee for't.
SERVANT: 'Sblood! you have undone us all, sir.
40 HUSBAND: Tug at thy master?
SERVANT: Tug at a monster.
HUSBAND: Have I no power; shall my slave fetter me?
SERVANT: Nay, then the devil wrestles; I am thrown.
HUSBAND: Oh villain! now I'll tug thee, now I'll tear
        thee;

Overcomes him.

Set quick spurs to my vassal, bruise him, trample him.
So! I think thou wilt not follow me in haste.
My horse stands ready saddled, away, away!
Now to my brat at nurse, my sucking beggar.
Fates, I'll not leave you one to trample on.
   The MASTER [*enters and*] *meets him.*

MASTER: How is't with you, sir? Methinks you look of   50
  a distracted colour.

HUSBAND: Who I, sir? 'Tis but your fancy.
  Please you walk in, sir, and I'll soon resolve you.
  I want one small part to make up the sum,
  And then my brother shall rest satisfied.

MASTER: I shall be glad to see it; sir, I'll attend you.
  Exeunt.

SERVANT: Oh, I am scarce able to heave up myself;
  H'as so bruised me with his devilish weight
  And torn my flesh with his blood-hasty spur;
  A man before of easy constitution,   60
  Till now hell's power supplied to his soul's wrong.
  Oh, how damnation can make weak men strong!
  Enter MASTER *and two* SERVANTS.

SERVANT: Oh, the most piteous deed, sir, since you came.

MASTER: A deadly greeting! Has he summed up these
  To satisfy his brother? Here's another:
  And by the bleeding infants the dead mother.

WIFE: Oh! Oh!

MASTER: Surgeons, surgeons! She recovers life. –
  One of his men all faint and bloodied!

FIRST SERVANT: Follow; our murderous master has took   70
      horse
  To kill his child at nurse. Oh, follow quickly.

MASTER: I am the readiest; it shall be my charge

61 *hell's* (?) hell has. See note.
64 *summed up* referring to l. 54.

    To raise the town upon him.

FIRST SERVANT: Good sir, do follow him.

    Exeunt MASTER *and* SERVANTS.

WIFE: Oh, my children!

FIRST SERVANT: How is it with my most afflicted
       mistress?

WIFE: Why do I now recover? Why half live,
    To see my children bleed before mine eyes?
    A sight able to kill a mother's breast
80   Without an executioner. What!
    Art thou mangled, too?

FIRST SERVANT: I, thinking to prevent what his quick
       mischiefs
    Had so soon acted, came and rushed upon him.
    We struggled, but a fouler strength than his
    O'erthrew me with his arms. Then did he bruise me,
    And rent my flesh, and robbed me of my hair,
    Like a man mad in execution;
    Made me unfit to rise and follow him.

WIFE: What is it has beguiled him of all grace,
90   And stole away humanity from his breast? –
    To slay his children, kill his wife,
    And spoil his servants.

    Enter two SERVANTS.

BOTH SERVANTS: Please you leave this most accursed
       place;
    A surgeon waits within.

WIFE: Willing to leave it!
    'Tis guilty of sweet blood, innocent blood.
    Murder has took this chamber with full hands
    And will ne'er out as long as the house stands.

    Exeunt.

87 *execution* giving effect to a passion.

SCENE SIX

Enter HUSBAND *as being thrown off his horse, and falls.*

HUSBAND: Oh stumbling jade, the spavin overtake thee,
  The fifty diseases stop thee!
  Oh, I am sorely bruis'd. Plague founder thee!
  Thou run'st at ease and pleasure. Heart of chance!
  To throw me now, within a flight o'th'town,
  In such plain, even ground,
  'Sfoot, a man may dice upon't,
  And throw away the meadows. Filthy beast!

CRY WITHIN: Follow, follow, follow!

HUSBAND: Ha! I hear sounds of men, like hue and cry.   10
  Up, up and struggle to thy horse, make on:
  Dispatch that little beggar and all's done.

CRY WITHIN: Here, this way, this way!

HUSBAND: At my back? Oh!
  What fate have I? My limbs deny me go.
  My will is bated; beggary claims a part.
  Oh, could I here reach to the infant's heart!

    Enter MASTER OF THE COLLEGE, *three* GENTLE-
    MEN, *and others with halberds.* [*They*] *find him.*

ALL: Here, here! Yonder, yonder!

MASTER: Unnatural, flinty, more than barbarous!
  The Scithians, e'en the marble-hearted fates,
  Could not have acted more remorseless deeds   20
  In their relentless natures than these of thine.
  Was this the answer I long waited on,

---

1 *spavin* cartilage tumour in horses.
3 *founder* cause to go lame.   5 *flight* the reach of a bow-shot.
8 *throw away* lose at the throw of a dice.
15 *will is bated* purpose is foiled.

The satisfaction for thy prison'd brother?

HUSBAND: Why, he can have no more on's than our
skins,

And some of 'em want but flaying.

FIRST GENTLEMAN: Great sins have made him impudent.

MASTER: H'as shed so much blood that he cannot blush.

SECOND GENTLEMAN: Away with him, bear him along
to the justices.

A gentleman of worship dwells at hand:

30   There shall his deeds be blaz'd.

HUSBAND: Why, all the better

My glory 'tis to have my action known;

I grieve for nothing but I miss'd of one.

MASTER: There's little of a father in that grief.

Bear him away.   *Exeunt.*

SCENE SEVEN

Enter a KNIGHT *with two or three* GENTLEMEN.

KNIGHT: Endanger'd so his wife? Murdered his children?

FOURTH GENTLEMAN: So the cry comes.

KNIGHT: I am sorry I e'er knew him,

That ever he took life and natural being

From such an honoured stock and fair descent,

Till this black minute without stain or blemish.

FOURTH GENTLEMAN: Here come the men.

Enter the MASTER OF THE COLLEGE *and the rest, with
the* PRISONER.

KNIGHT: The serpent of his house!

I'm sorry for this time that I am in place of justice.

29 *of worship* respected.   30 *blaz'd* made known.

MASTER: Please you, sir –

KNIGHT: Do not repeat it twice;
I know too much. Would it had ne'er been thought
on. –
Sir, I bleed for you. 10

FOURTH GENTLEMAN: Your father's sorrows are alive
in me.
What made you show such monstrous cruelty?

HUSBAND: In a word, sir:
I have consumed all, played away long acre,
And I thought it the charitablest deed I could do
To cozen beggary, and knock my house o'the head.

KNIGHT: Oh, in a cooler blood you will repent it.

HUSBAND: I repent now that one's left unkilled,
My brat at nurse. Oh, I would full fain have weaned
him.

KNIGHT: Well, I do not think but in tomorrow's 20
judgement
The terror will sit closer to your soul,
When the dread thought of death remembers you;
To further which, take this sad voice from me:
Never was act played more unnaturally.

HUSBAND: I thank you, sir.

KNIGHT: Go lead him to the gaol.
Where justice claims all, there must pity fail.

HUSBAND: Come, come; away with me.
    Exit PRISONER [*and others*].

MASTER: Sir, you deserve the worship of your place;
Would all did so: in you the law is grace.

KNIGHT: It is my wish it should be so. 30
Ruinous man, the desolation of his house, the blot
Upon his predecessor's honoured name!
That man is nearest shame that is past shame.
    Exeunt.

16 *cozen* cheat.   23 *sad voice* earnest opinion.

SCENE EIGHT

Enter HUSBAND *with the officers, the* MASTER *and*
GENTLEMEN, *as going by his house.*

HUSBAND: I am right against my house, seat of my
        ancestors.

I hear my wife's alive but much endangered.

Let me entreat to speak with her

Before the prison gripe me.

    Enter his WIFE *brought in a chair.*

GENTLEMAN: See, here she comes of herself.

WIFE: Oh, my sweet husband, my dear distressed
        husband,

Now in the hands of unrelenting laws!

My greatest sorrow, my extremest bleeding;

Now my soul bleeds.

HUSBAND: How now? Kind to me?

10   Did I not wound thee, left thee for dead?

WIFE: Tut! Far greater wounds did my breast feel;

Unkindness strikes a deeper wound than steel.

You have been still unkind to me.

HUSBAND: Faith, and so I think I have.

I did my murders roughly out of hand,

Desperate and sudden; but thou has devised

A fine way now to kill me: thou has given mine eyes

Seven wounds apiece. Now glides the devil from me,

Departs at every joint, heaves up my nails.

20   Oh, catch him new torments that were ne'er invented;

Bind him one thousand more, you blessed angels,

In that pit bottomless; let him not rise

To make men act unnatural tragedies;

13 *still* always.
21 *one thousand* 'years' understood. See note.

To spread into a father, and in fury
Make him his children's executioners;
Murder his wife, his servants, and who not?
For that man's dark, where Heaven is quite forgot.

WIFE: Oh my repentant husband!

HUSBAND: My dear soul, whom I too much have wronged,
For death I die, and for this have I longed. 30

WIFE: Thou should'st not (be assured) for these faults die
If the law could forgive as soon as I.

HUSBAND: What sight is yonder?

    CHILDREN *laid out.*

WIFE: Oh, our two bleeding boys, laid forth upon the threshold.

HUSBAND: Here's weight enough to make a heart-string crack. –
Oh, were it lawful that your pretty souls
Might look from Heaven into your father's eyes,
Then should you see the penitent glasses melt,
And both your murders shoot upon my cheeks.
But you are playing in the angels' laps 40
And will not look on me
Who void of grace killed you in beggary.
Oh, that I might my wishes now attain,
I should then wish you living were again,
Though I did beg with you, which thing I feared.
Oh, 'twas the enemy my eyes so bleared.
Oh, would you could pray Heaven me to forgive
That will unto my end repentant live!

WIFE: It makes me e'en forget all other sorrows
And live apart with this.

OFFICER: Come, will you go? 50

30 *For death* for having caused death.
34 *threshold* of the family burial vault.
46 *the enemy* i.e. Satan.

HUSBAND: I'll kiss the blood I spilt and then I go:
My soul is bloodied; well may my lips be so.
Farewell, dear wife; now thou and I must part;
I of thy wrongs repent me with my heart.
WIFE: Oh, stay! Thou shalt not go.
HUSBAND: That's but in vain; you see it must be so.
Farewell ye bloody ashes of my boys;
My punishments are their eternal joys.
Let every father look into my deeds,
60   And then their heirs may prosper while mine bleeds.
WIFE: More wretched am I now in this distress
Than former sorrows made me.
    Exeunt HUSBAND *with* [*those with*] *halberds.*
MASTER: Oh kind wife,
Be comforted; one joy is yet unmurdered:
You have a boy at nurse; your joy's in him.
WIFE: Dearer than all is my poor husband's life.
Heaven give my body strength, which yet is faint
With much expense of blood, and I will kneel,
Sue for his life, number up all my friends
To plead for pardon for my dear husband's life.
70   MASTER: Was it in man to wound so kind a creature?
I'll ever praise a woman for thy sake.
I must return with grief; my answer's set;
I shall bring news weighs heavier than the debt:
Two brothers – one in bond lies overthrown,
This on a deadlier execution.   [*Exeunt.*]

54 *thy wrongs* my wrongs to you.
75 *execution* pun on legal writ and criminal's death.

Facsimile title page of the first edition of
A Woman Killed with Kindness

A
WOMAN
KILDE
with Kindneſſe.

Written by Tho: Heywood .

PRV
DEN
TIA

LONDON
Printed by William Iaggard dwelling in Barbican, and
are to be ſold in Paules Church-yard.
by Iohn Hodgets. 1607.

Dramatis Personae

SIR FRANCIS ACTON

SIR CHARLES MOUNTFORD

JOHN FRANKFORD

WENDOLL ⎫
CRANWELL ⎭ *his friends*

MALBY, *friend to Sir Francis*

OLD MOUNTFORD, *uncle to Sir Charles*

TYDY, *cousin to Sir Charles*

SANDY, *former friend to Sir Charles*

RODER, *former tenant to Sir Charles*

SHAFTON, *false friend to Sir Charles*

NICHOLAS ⎫
JENKIN ⎭ *servants to Frankford*

SPIGGOT, *butler to Frankford*

ROGER BRICKBAT ⎫
JACK SLIME ⎭ *country fellows*

SHERIFF

KEEPER OF THE PRISON

SERGEANT

OFFICERS, FALCONERS, HUNTSMEN, COACHMAN, CARTERS, MUSICIANS, SERVANTS, CHILDREN

ANNE, *wife to Frankford and sister to Sir Francis*

SUSAN, *sister to Sir Charles*

SISLY MILK-PAIL, *servingwoman to Anne*

JOAN MINIVER ⎫
JANE TRUBKIN ⎬ *country wenches*
ISBEL MOTLEY ⎭

SERVINGWOMEN

The Prologue

I come but like a harbinger, being sent
To tell you what these preparations mean:
Look for no glorious state, our Muse is bent
Upon a barren subject, a bare scene.
We could afford this twig a timber tree,
Whose strength might boldly on your favours build;
Our russet, tissue; drone, a honey bee;
Our barren plot, a large and spacious field;
Our coarse fare, banquets; our thin water, wine;
Our brook, a sea; our bat's eyes, eagle's sight;   10
Our poets dull and earthy, Muse divine;
Our ravens, doves; our crow's black feathers, white.
   But gentle thoughts, when they may give the foil,
    Save them that yield, and spare where they may spoil.

3 *glorious state* ostentatious pomp.
5 *afford . . . tree* wish this twig were a timber tree.
7 *russet* coarse homespun cloth. *tissue* finespun cloth.
8 *plot* place of action (?with pun on scheme of play).
13 *give the foil* defeat (wrestling term).

Act One

SCENE ONE

Enter MASTER JOHN FRANKFORD, MISTRESS
ANNE, SIR FRANCIS ACTON, SIR CHARLES
MOUNTFORD, MASTER MALBY, MASTER WEN-
DOLL, *and* MASTER CRANWELL.

SIR FRANCIS: Some music, there! None lead the bride a
    dance?

SIR CHARLES: Yes, would she dance 'The Shaking of
    the Sheets':

But that's the dance her husband means to lead her!

WENDOLL: That's not the dance that every man must
    dance,

According to the ballad.

SIR FRANCIS: Music ho!

By your leave, sister – by your husband's leave

I should have said – the hand that but this day

Was given you in the church I'll borrow. Sound!

This marriage music hoists me from the ground.

10 FRANKFORD: Ay, you may caper, you are light and
    free;

Marriage hath yok'd my heels, pray then pardon me.

SIR FRANCIS: I'll have you dance too, brother.

SIR CHARLES: Master Frankford,

You are a happy man, sir, and much joy

Succeed your marriage mirth; you have a wife

So qualified and with such ornaments

Both of the mind and body. First, her birth

---

2 '*The* . . . *Sheets*' popular tune and ballad, with sexual allusion.
4–5 *That's* . . . *ballad* i.e. the dance of death.
15 *qualified* of such qualities.

Is noble, and her education such
As might become the daughter of a prince;
Her own tongue speaks all tongues, and her own hand
Can teach all strings to speak in their best grace,   20
From the shrill treble to the hoarsest base.
To end her praises in one word:
She's beauty and perfection's eldest daughter,
Only found by yours, though many a heart hath
    sought her.

FRANKFORD: But that I know your virtues and chaste
    thoughts,
I should be jealous of your praise, Sir Charles.

CRANWELL: He speaks no more than you approve.

MALBY: Nor flatters he that gives to her her due.

ANNE: I would your praise could find a fitter theme
Than my imperfect beauties to speak on.   30
Such as they be, if they my husband please,
They suffice me now I am married.
His sweet content is like a flattering glass
To make my face seem fairer to mine eye;
But the least wrinkle from his stormy brow
Will blast the roses in my cheeks that grow.

SIR FRANCIS: A perfect wife already, meek and patient!
How strangely the word 'husband' fits your mouth,
Not married three hours since; sister, 'tis good.
You that begin betimes thus, must needs prove   40
Pliant and dutious in your husband's love.
Godamercies, brother, wrought her to it already! –
'Sweet husband' and a curtsy the first day.
Mark this, mark this, you that are bachelors,
And never took the grace of honest man;

---

20 *strings* i.e. string instruments.
27 *approve* confirm.
42 *Godamercies* exclamation of approval (= 'God have mercy').
45 *took . . . man* 'assumed the honourable state of husband' (Bates).

Mark this against you marry, this one phrase:
'In a good time that man both wins and woos,
That takes his wife down in her wedding shoes'.

FRANKFORD: Your sister takes not after you, Sir
    Francis;

50 All his wild blood your father spent on you.
He got her in his age when he grew civil.
All his mad tricks were to his land entailed
And you are heir to all. Your sister, she
Hath to her dower her mother's modesty.

SIR CHARLES: Lord, sir, in what a happy state live you;
This morning, which to many seems a burden
Too heavy to bear, is unto you a pleasure.
This lady is no clog as many are.
She doth become you like a well-made suit

60 In which the tailor hath used all his art;
Not like a thick coat of unseason'd frieze,
Forc'd on your back in Summer; she's no chain
To tie your neck, and curb you to the yoke:
But she's a chain of gold to adorn your neck.
You both adorn each other, and your hands
Methinks are matches. There's equality
In this fair combination; you are both scholars,
Both young, both being descended nobly.
There's music in this sympathy, it carries

70 Consort and expectation of much joy,
Which God bestow on you from this first day

46 *against* in expectation of the time when.
47 *In . . . time* at the right moment.
48 *takes . . . shoes* straightway makes his wife subservient.
51 *civil* i.e. milder, more respectable.
54 *to her dower* as her dowry.
61 *unseason'd* unseasonable.
61 *frieze* coarse woollen cloth (and pun).
65–6 *your . . . matches* you are a well-matched pair.
70 *Consort* 1 harmonious music; 2 companionship.

Until your dissolution – that's for aye.

SIR FRANCIS: We keep you here too long, good brother
    Frankford.
Into the hall! Away, go cheer your guests!
What, bride and bridegroom both withdrawn at once?
If you be miss'd, the guests will doubt their welcome,
And charge you with unkindness.

FRANKFORD: To prevent it,
I'll leave you here, to see the dance within.

ANNE: And so will I.

    [*Exeunt* FRANKFORD *and* ANNE.]

SIR FRANCIS: To part you it were sin.
Now gallants, while the town musicians   80
Finger their frets within, and the mad lads
And country lasses, every mother's child
With nosegays and bride-laces in their hats,
Dance all their country measures, rounds, and jigs,
What shall we do? Hark, they are all on the hoigh;
They toil like mill-horses and turn as round, –
Marry, not on the toe! Ay, and they caper
But without cutting. You shall see tomorrow
The hall floor peck'd and dinted like a millstone,
Made with their high shoes; though their skill be 90
    small,
Yet they tread heavy where their hobnails fall.

SIR CHARLES: Well, leave them to their sports. Sir
    Francis Acton,
I'll make a match with you: meet me tomorrow
At Chevy Chase; I'll fly my hawk with yours.

SIR FRANCIS: For what, for what?

---

81 *frets* divisions on fingerboard of lute.
83 *bride-laces* pieces of lace used to bind up sprigs of rosemary worn
at weddings.   84 *measures. . . jigs* three sorts of dance.
85 *on the hoigh* in high excitement.
86 *as round* with as easy motion.   88 *cutting* twirling the feet.

SIR CHARLES: Why, for a hundred pound.

SIR FRANCIS: Pawn me some gold of that.

SIR CHARLES: Here are ten angels;
I'll make them good a hundred pound tomorrow
Upon my hawk's wing.

SIR FRANCIS: 'Tis a match, 'tis done.
Another hundred pound upon your dogs,
Dare you Sir Charles?

100 SIR CHARLES: I dare. Were I sure to lose
I durst do more than that. Here's my hand,
The first course for a hundred pound.

SIR FRANCIS: A match.

WENDOLL: Ten angels on Sir Francis Acton's hawk;
As much upon his dogs.

CRANWELL: I am for Sir Charles Mountford; I have seen
His hawk and dog both tried. What, clap your hands?
Or is't no bargain?

WENDOLL: Yes, and stake them down;
Were they five hundred they were all my own.

SIR FRANCIS: Be stirring early with the lark tomorrow;
110 I'll rise into my saddle ere the sun
Rise from his bed.

SIR CHARLES: If there you miss me, say
I am no gentleman; I'll hold my day.

SIR FRANCIS: It holds on all sides. Come, tonight let's
                    dance.
Early tomorrow let's prepare to ride:
We had need be three hours up before the bride.
    [*Exeunt.*]

96 *Pawn* pledge.   *angels* gold coins.
102 *course* matching of two dogs.
106 *clap your hands* shake hands on the agreement.
107 *stake them down* put down stake-money.
112 *hold my day* keep the appointment.
113 *holds* is valid.

SCENE TWO

Enter NICHOLAS *and* JENKIN, JACK SLIME, ROGER
BRICKBAT, *with country wenches, and two or three
Musicians.*

JENKIN: Come Nick, take you Joan Miniver to trace
withal; Jack Slime, traverse you with Sisly Milk-pail;
I will take Jane Trubkin; and Roger Brickbat shall have
Isbel Motley; and now that they are busy in the parlour, come strike up, we'll have a crash here in the
yard.

NICHOLAS: My humour is not compendious; dancing I
possess not, though I can foot it; yet since I am fallen
into the hands of Sisly Milk-pail I assent.

JACK: Truly, Nick, though we were never brought up   10
like serving courtiers, yet we have been brought up
with serving creatures, ay, and God's creatures too,
for we have been brought up to serve sheep, oxen,
horses, and hogs, and such like; and though we be but
country fellows, it may be in the way of dancing we
can do the horse-trick as well as servingmen.

ROGER: Ay, and the cross-point, too.

JENKIN: Oh Slime! Oh Brickbat! Do not you know that
comparisons are odious? Now we are odious ourselves,
too; therefore there are no comparisons to be made be-   20
twixt us.

NICHOLAS: I am sudden, and not superfluous;

1 *trace* dance.   2 *traverse* dance.
5 *crash* frolic.
7 *humour* disposition. *compendious* evidently an error for 'compre-
hensive'.
8 *possess not* am not master of.
16, 17 *horse-trick, cross-point* dances, with sexual implication.

I am quarrelsome, and not seditious;
I am peaceable and not contentious;
I am brief, and not compendious.
Slime, foot it quickly. If the music overcome not my
melancholy I shall quarrel, and if they suddenly do not
strike up, I shall presently strike thee down.

JENKIN: No quarrelling, for God's sake! Truly, if you
do I shall set a knave between you.

SLIME: I come to dance, not to quarrel. Come, what shall
it be? 'Rogero'?

JENKIN: 'Rogero'? No, we will dance 'The Beginning
of the World'.

SISLY: I love no dance so well as 'John Come Kiss Me
Now'.

NICHOLAS: I, that have ere now deserved a cushion, call
for 'The Cushion Dance'.

ROGER: For my part I like nothing so well as 'Tom
Tyler'.

JENKIN: No, we'll have 'The Hunting of the Fox'.

SLIME: 'The Hay', 'The Hay', there's nothing like 'The
Hay'.

NICHOLAS: I have said, I do say, and I will say again –

JENKIN: Every man agree to have it as Nick says.

ALL: Content.

NICHOLAS: It hath been, it now is, and it shall be –

SISLY: What master Nich'las, what?

NICHOLAS: 'Put on Your Smock a Monday'.

JENKIN: So the dance will come cleanly off. Come for

30 *knave* menial (i.e. himself).

32–53 'Rogero', 'The . . . World', 'John . . . Now', 'Tom Tyler',
'The . . . Fox', 'Put . . . Monday', 'Sellenger's Round' popular tunes
('Sellenger's Round' alternative title for 'The . . . World').

37 *deserved a cushion* 'earned the right to some luxury' (Van
Fossen).

38, 42 'The Cushion Dance', 'The Hay' dances.

49 *Smock* woman's shift.

God's sake, agree of something; if you like not that put it to the musicians or let me speak for all, and we'll have 'Sellenger's Round'.

ALL: That, that, that!

NICHOLAS: No, I am resolv'd thus it shall be:
First take hands, then take you to your heels.

JENKIN: Why, would you have us run away?

NICHOLAS: No, but I would have you shake your heels.
Music strike up!

They dance; NICHOLAS *dancing speaks stately and scurvily, the rest after the country fashion.*

JENKIN: Hey, lively my lasses! Here's a turn for thee!   60
[*Exeunt.*]

SCENE THREE

Wind horns. Enter SIR CHARLES, SIR FRANCIS, CRANWELL, WENDOLL, *Falconers, and Huntsmen.*

SIR CHARLES: So! well cast off. Aloft, aloft! Well flown!
Oh, now she takes her at the souse, and strikes her
Down to the earth, like a swift thunderclap.

WENDOLL: She hath struck ten angels out of my way.

SIR FRANCIS: A hundred pound from me.

SIR CHARLES: What, falconer?

FALCONER: At hand, sir.

SIR CHARLES: Now she hath seiz'd the fowl and 'gins to
plume her.
Rebeck her not; rather stand still and check her.

After 59 S.D. *speaks* looks. *stately and scurvily* with dignity and sourly. See note.
2 *at the souse* on the swoop.
8 *rebeck* call back. See note.

So! seize her gets, her jesses, and her bells.
10   Away!
SIR FRANCIS: My hawk kill'd too.
SIR CHARLES: Ay, but'twas at the querre,
Not at the mount like mine.
SIR FRANCIS: Judgement my masters.
CRANWELL: Yours miss'd her at the ferre.
WENDOLL: Ay, but our merlin first hath plum'd the
      fowl,
And twice renewed her from the river, too.
Her bells, Sir Francis, had not both one weight,
Nor was one semitone above the other;
Methinks these Milan bells do sound too full,
And spoil the mounting of your hawk.
SIR CHARLES: 'Tis lost.
20 SIR FRANCIS: I grant it not; mine likewise seiz'd a fowl
Within her talents, and you saw her paws
Full of the feathers; both her petty singles
And her long singles gripp'd her more than other.
The terrials of her legs were stain'd with blood;
Not of the fowl only she did discomfit
Some of her feathers, but she brake away.
SIR CHARLES: Come, come, your hawk is but a rifler.

9 *gets* unidentified parts of hawk's harness.   *jesses* leg straps.
11 *at the querre* before prey rises from the ground.
12 *at the mount* from above.
13 *at the ferre* at close proximity. See note.
14 *merlin* type of hawk.   15 *renewed* driven back.
21 *talents* talons.
22, 3 *petty singles*, *long singles* outer and middle claws.
23 *other* i.e. the other hawk.
24 *terrials* probably error for 'terrets', part of a hawk's harness.
25 *discomfit* tear out.
26 *she* i.e. the quarry.
27 *rifler* hawk which seizes feathers without capturing its prey.

SIR FRANCIS: How?

SIR CHARLES: Ay, and your dogs are trindle-tails and
    curs.

SIR FRANCIS: You stir my blood.

SIR CHARLES: You keep not a good hound in all your   30
    kennel,

Nor one good hawk upon your perch.

SIR FRANCIS: How, knight?

SIR CHARLES: So, knight? You will not swagger, sir?

SIR FRANCIS: Why, say I did?

SIR CHARLES: Why, sir, I say you would gain as much
    by swagg'ring

As you have got by wagers on your dogs:

You will come short in all things.

SIR FRANCIS: Not in this.

Now I'll strike home.

SIR CHARLES: Thou shalt to thy long home

Or I will want my will.

SIR FRANCIS: All they that love Sir Francis follow me.

SIR CHARLES: All that affect Sir Charles draw on my   40
    part.

CRANWELL: On this side heaves my hand.

WENDOLL: Here goes my heart.

> *They divide themselves.* SIR CHARLES, CRANWELL,
> *the Falconer and Huntsman fight against* SIR FRANCIS,
> WENDOLL, *his Falconer and Huntsman; and* SIR
> CHARLES *hath the better and beats them away, killing
> both of* SIR FRANCIS *his men.*
>
> [*Exeunt all but* SIR CHARLES.]

28 *trindle-tails* curly-tailed dogs (hence low-bred).

32 *swagger* bluster.

37 *long home* grave.

40 *affect* love.   40 *part* side.

41 *heaves* strives.

SIR CHARLES: My God! What have I done? what have I
      done?
My rage hath plung'd into a sea of blood,
In which my soul lies drown'd. Poor innocents,
For whom we are to answer. Well, 'tis done,
And I remain the victor. A great conquest,
When I would give this right hand, nay this head,
To breathe in them new life whom I have slain.
Forgive me, God, 'twas in the heat of blood,
50 And anger quite removes me from myself.
It was not I but rage did this vile murder;
Yet I, and not my rage, must answer it.
Sir Francis Acton, he is fled the field,
With him, all those that did partake his quarrel,
And I am left alone, with sorrow dumb,
And in my height of conquest overcome.
    Enter SUSAN.
SUSAN: Oh God! My brother wounded among the dead;
Unhappy jest that in such earnest ends.
The rumour of this fear stretch'd to my ears
60 And I am come to know if you be wounded.
SIR CHARLES: Oh sister, sister, wounded at the heart.
SUSAN: May God forbid!
SIR CHARLES: In doing that thing which he forbade,
I am wounded sister.
SUSAN: I hope not at the heart.
SIR CHARLES: Yes, at the heart.
SUSAN: Oh God! a surgeon there!
SIR CHARLES: Call me a surgeon, sister, for my soul;
The sin of murder, it hath pierc'd my heart,
And made a wide wound there; but for these scratches,
They are nothing, nothing.

54 *partake his quarrel* take his part.
58 *jest* 1 notable deed; 2 joke.
59 *fear* something to be feared.

SUSAN: Charles, what have you done?
Sir Francis hath great friends, and will pursue you 70
Unto the utmost danger of the law.

SIR CHARLES: My conscience is become my enemy,
And will pursue me more than Acton can.

SUSAN: Oh fly, sweet brother.

SIR CHARLES: Shall I fly from thee?
What, Sue, art weary of my company?

SUSAN: Fly from your foe.

SIR CHARLES: You, sister, are my friend,
And flying you I shall pursue my end.

SUSAN: Your company is as my eyeball dear;
Being far from you no comfort can be near.
Yet fly to save your life. What would I care 80
To spend my future age in black despair,
So you were safe? And yet to live one week
Without my brother Charles, through every cheek
My streaming tears would downward run so rank
Till they could set on either side a bank,
And in the midst a channel; so my face
For two salt water brooks shall still find place.

SIR CHARLES: Thou shalt not weep so much, for I will
  stay
In spite of danger's teeth. I'll live with thee
Or I'll not live at all; I will not sell 90
My country, and my father's patrimony,
Nor thy sweet sight, for a vain hope of life.
  Enter SHERIFF *with Officers.*

SHERIFF: Sir Charles, I am made the unwilling instrument
Of your attach and apprehension.

71 *danger* power, jurisdiction.　　83 *every* either.
84 *so rank* in such quantity.
87 *still* always.
94 *attach* capture.

I am sorry that the blood of innocent men
Should be of you exacted. It was told me
That you were guarded with a troop of friends,
And therefore I come arm'd.

SIR CHARLES: Oh, master Sheriff,
I came into the field with many friends,
100   But see they all have left me; only one
Clings to my sad misfortune, my dear sister.
I know you for an honest gentleman;
I yield my weapons and submit to you.
Convey me where you please.

SHERIFF: To prison then,
To answer for the lives of these dead men.

SUSAN: Oh God! oh God!

SIR CHARLES: Sweet sister, every strain
Of sorrow from your heart augments my pain.
Your grief abounds and hits against my breast.

SHERIFF: Sir, will you go?

SIR CHARLES: Even where it likes you best.
     [*Exeunt.*]

108 *abounds* overflows.   109 *likes* pleases.

Act Two

SCENE ONE

Enter MASTER FRANKFORD *in a study.*

FRANKFORD: How happy am I amongst other men,
That in my mean estate embrace content.
I am a gentleman, and by my birth
Companion with a king; a king's no more.
I am possess'd of many fair revenues,
Sufficient to maintain a gentleman.
Touching my mind, I am studied in all arts,
The riches of my thoughts, and of my time
Have been a good proficient. But the chief
Of all the sweet felicities on earth,   10
I have a fair, a chaste, and loving wife,
Perfection all, all truth, all ornament.
If man on earth may truly happy be,
Of these at once possess'd, sure I am he.

    Enter NICHOLAS.

NICHOLAS: Sir, there's a gentleman attends without
To speak with you.

FRANKFORD: On horseback?

NICHOLAS: Ay, on horseback.

FRANKFORD: Entreat him to alight; I will attend him.
Knowest thou him, Nick?

NICHOLAS: I know him; his name's Wendoll.
It seems he comes in haste: his horse is booted
Up to the flank in mire, himself all spotted   20
And stain'd with plashing. Sure he rid in fear

s.d. *in a study* in deep contemplation. 2 *mean* moderate.
8–9 *and . . . proficient* have made full use of my time.
14 *at once* at the same time.

Or for a wager; horse and man both sweat.
I ne'er saw two in such a smoking heat.

FRANKFORD: Entreat him in; about it instantly.

    [*Exit* NICHOLAS.]

This Wendoll I have noted, and his carriage
Hath pleas'd me much by observation.
I have noted many good deserts in him:
He's affable and seen in many things,
Discourses well, a good companion:
30 And though of small means, yet a gentleman
Of a good house, somewhat press'd by want.
I have preferr'd him to a second place
In my opinion, and my best regard.

    Enter WENDOLL, ANNE *and* NICHOLAS.

ANNE: Oh Master Frankford, Master Wendoll here
Brings you the strangest news that e'er you heard.

FRANKFORD: What news, sweet wife? What news, good
    Master Wendoll?

WENDOLL: You knew the match made twixt Sir Francis
    Acton
And Sir Charles Mountford?

FRANKFORD: True, with their hounds and hawks.

WENDOLL: The matches were both play'd.

FRANKFORD: Ha! and which won?

40 WENDOLL: Sir Francis, your wife's brother, had the
    worst,
And lost the wager.

FRANKFORD: Why, the worse his chance.
Perhaps the fortune of some other day
Will change his luck.

WENDOLL: Oh, but you hear not all!

25 *carriage* habitual conduct.
27 *deserts* qualities.
28 *seen* accomplished.
32 *second place* i.e. after that held by Anne.

Sir Francis lost and yet was loth to yield.
In brief, the two knights grew to difference,
From words to blows, and so to banding sides,
Where valorous Sir Charles slew in his spleen
Two of your brother's men, his falconer
And his good huntsman, whom he lov'd so well.
More men were wounded, no more slain outright.   50

FRANKFORD: Now trust me, I am sorry for the knight.
But is my brother safe?

WENDOLL: All whole and sound,
His body not being blemish'd with one wound.
But poor Sir Charles is to the prison led
To answer at th'assize for them that's dead.

FRANKFORD: I thank your pains, sir. Had the news been
                    better
Your will was to have brought it, Master Wendoll.
Sir Charles will find hard friends; his case is heinous
And will be most severly censur'd on.
I am sorry for him. Sir, a word with you: 60
I know you, sir, to be a gentleman
In all things, your possibilities but mean;
Please you to use my table and my purse;
They are yours.

WENDOLL: Oh Lord, sir, I shall never deserve it!

FRANKFORD: Oh sir, disparage not your worth too
                    much;
You are full of quality and fair desert.
Choose of my men which shall attend on you
And he is yours. I will allow you, sir,
Your man, your gelding, and your table,
All at my own charge; be my companion.   70

46 *banding sides* forming factions.
47 *Where* at which.
58 *find hard friends* find friends with difficulty.
62 *possibilities* resources.

WENDOLL: Master Frankford, I have oft been bound to
    you
By many favours. This exceeds them all
That I shall never merit your least favour.
But when your last remembrance I forget,
Heaven at my soul exact that weighty debt.

FRANKFORD: There needs no protestation, for I know
    you
Virtuous, and therefore grateful. Prithee, Nan,
Use him with all thy loving'st courtesy.

ANNE: As far as modesty may well extend,
80   It is my duty to receive your friend.

FRANKFORD: To dinner; come, sir. From this present
    day
Welcome to me for ever; come away.

    [*Exeunt* FRANKFORD, ANNE *and* WENDOLL.]

NICHOLAS: I do not like this fellow by no means.
I never see him but my heart still earns.
Zounds, I could fight with him, yet know not why;
The Devil and he are all one in my eye.

    Enter JENKIN.

JENKIN: Oh Nicholas, what gentleman is that comes to
lie at our house? My master allows him one to wait on
him, and I believe it will fall to thy lot.

90 NICHOLAS: I love my master; by these hilts I do!
But rather than I'll ever come to serve him,
I'll turn away my master.

    Enter SISLY.

SISLY: Nich'las, where are you, Nich'las? You must
come in, Nich'las, and help the young gentleman off
with his boots.

NICHOLAS: If I pluck off his boots, I'll eat the spurs,
And they shall stick fast in my throat like burrs.   *Exit.*

73 *That* i.e. so much that.   84 *still earns* always grieves.
90 *hilts* hilt of dagger.

SISLY: Then Jenkin, come you.

JENKIN: 'Tis no boot for me to deny it. My master hath
given me a coat here, but he takes pains himself to   100
brush it once or twice a day with a holly wand.

SISLY: Come, come, make haste, that you may wash
your hands again, and help to serve in dinner. [*Exit.*]

JENKIN [*to the audience*]: You may see, my masters,
though it be afternoon with you, 'tis but early days
with us, for we have not dined yet. Stay but a little,
I'll but go in and help to bear up the first course and
come to you again presently.   [*Exit.*]

SCENE TWO

Enter MALBY *and* CRANWELL.

MALBY: This is the sessions day; pray, can you tell me
How young Sir Charles hath sped? Is he acquit,
Or must he try the law's strict penalty?

CRANWELL: He's clear'd of all, 'spite of his enemies
Whose earnest labours was to take his life.
But in this suit of pardon, he hath spent
All the revenues that his father left him,
And he is now turn'd a plain countryman,
Reform'd in all things. See, sir, here he comes.

Enter SIR CHARLES *and his* KEEPER.

KEEPER: Discharge your fees and you are then at free-   10
        dom.

98 *'Tis no boot* it avails not (with pun).

104–6 *though . . . yet* Performances began about 2.00 p.m. Dinner
at midday.   3 *try* undergo.

6 *in this suit of pardon* in conducting his defence.

9 *Reform'd* changed.

SIR CHARLES: Here, master Keeper, take the poor
    remainder
Of all the wealth I have. My heavy foes
Have made my purse light, but, alas, to me
'Tis wealth enough that you have set me free.
MALBY: God give you joy of your delivery;
I am glad to see you abroad, Sir Charles.
SIR CHARLES: The poorest knight in England, Master
    Malby.
My life hath cost me all the patrimony
My father left his son. Well, God forgive them
20   That are the authors of my penury.
    Enter SHAFTON.
SHAFTON: Sir Charles, a hand, a hand! At liberty!
Now by the faith I owe, I am glad to see it.
What want you? Wherein may I pleasure you?
SIR CHARLES: Oh me! Oh most unhappy gentleman!
I am not worthy to have friends stirr'd up,
Whose hands may help me in this plunge of want.
I would I were in Heaven to inherit there
Th'immortal birthright which my Saviour keeps,
And by no unthrift can be bought and sold;
30   For here on earth what pleasures should we trust?
SHAFTON: To rid you from these contemplations,
Three hundred pounds you shall receive of me –
Nay, five for fail. Come, sir, the sight of gold
Is the most sweet receipt for melancholy,
And will revive your spirits. You shall hold law
With your proud adversaries. Tush! Let Frank Acton

16 *abroad* at large.
22 *owe* own.   23 *want* lack.
26 *plunge* crisis.
33 *for fail* to be on the safe side.
34 *receipt* remedy.
35 *hold law* engage in litigation.

Wage with knighthood-like expense with me,
And he will sink, he will! Nay, good Sir Charles,
Applaud your Fortune, and your fair escape
From all these perils.

SIR CHARLES: Oh sir, they have undone me.   40
Two thousand and five hundred pound a year
My father at his death possess'd me of,
All which the envious Acton made me spend.
And notwithstanding all this large expense,
I had much ado to gain my liberty.
And I have now only a house of pleasure
With some five hundred pounds, reserved
Both to maintain me and my loving sister.

SHAFTON [aside]: That must I have; it lies convenient for
          me.
If I can fasten but one finger on him,   50
With my full hand I'll gripe him to the heart.
'Tis not for love I proffer'd him this coin,
But for my gain and pleasure. – Come, Sir Charles,
I know you have need of money; take my offer.

SIR CHARLES: Sir, I accept it, and remain indebted
Even to the best of my unable power.
Come, gentlemen, and see it tender'd down.
          Exeunt.

SCENE THREE

Enter WENDOLL *melancholy.*

WENDOLL: I am a villain if I apprehend
But such a thought; then, to attempt the deed!

37 *Wage* contend.   43 *envious* malicious.
46 *house of pleasure* summer cottage.
57 *tender'd down* paid.

Slave, thou art damn'd without redemption.
I'll drive away this passion with a song.
A song! Ha, ha! A song, as if, fond man,
Thy eyes could swim in laughter, when thy soul
Lies drench'd and drown'd in red tears of blood.
I'll pray, and see if God within my heart
Plant better thoughts. Why, prayers are meditations,
And when I meditate, oh God forgive me,
It is on her divine perfections.
I will forget her, I will arm myself
Not to entertain a thought of love to her;
And when I come by chance into her presence,
I'll hale these balls until my eye-strings crack
From being pull'd and drawn to look that way.

    Enter over the stage FRANKFORD, ANNE *and*
    NICHOLAS.

Oh God! Oh God! with what a violence
I am hurried to my own destruction.
There goest thou, the most perfect'st man
That ever England bred a gentleman.
And shall I wrong his bed? Thou God of thunder
Stay, in Thy thoughts of vengeance and of wrath,
Thy great, almighty and all-judging hand
From speedy execution on a villain,
A villain, and a traitor to his friend.

    Enter JENKIN.

JENKIN: Did your worship call?
WENDOLL [*not noticing him*]: He doth maintain me, he
    allows me largely
  Money to spend –
JENKIN [*aside*]: By my faith, so do not you me; I cannot
    get a cross of you.

5 *fond* foolish.
15 *hale* pull away forcibly. *balls* eye-balls.
27 *largely* generously.   30 *cross* coin.

WENDOLL: My gelding and my man.

JENKIN [*aside*]: That's Sorrel and I.

WENDOLL: This kindness grows of no alliance betwixt us.

JENKIN [*aside*]: Nor is my service of any great acquaintance.

WENDOLL: I never bound him to me by desert.
Of a mere stranger, a poor gentleman,
A man by whom in no kind he could gain,
He hath plac'd me in the height of all his thoughts,
Made me companion with the best and chiefest
In Yorkshire. He cannot eat without me,   40
Nor laugh without me; I am to his body
As necessary as his digestion,
And equally do make him whole or sick.
And shall I wrong this man? Base man, ingrate!
Hast thou the power straight with thy gory hands
To rip thy image from his bleeding heart?
To scratch thy name from out the holy book
Of his remembrance, and to wound his name,
That holds thy name so dear? Or rend his heart
To whom thy heart was join'd and knit together?   50
And yet I must. Then, Wendoll, be content;
Thus villains when they would cannot repent.

JENKIN [*aside*]: What a strange humour is my new master
in. Pray God he be not mad. If he should be so, I
should never have any mind to serve him in Bedlam.
It may be he is mad for missing of me.

WENDOLL: What, Jenkin! Where's your mistress?

JENKIN: Is your worship married?

WENDOLL: Why dost thou ask?

33 *alliance* kinship.
34 *great acquaintance* close relationship.
37 *kind* way.   45 *straight* directly.
47 *name* reputation.
55 *Bedlam* Bethlehem, the London lunatic asylum.

60 JENKIN: Because you are my master and if I have a mistress I would be glad like a good servant to do my duty
to her.

WENDOLL: I mean where's Mistress Frankford?

JENKIN: Marry sir, her husband is riding out of town,
and she went very lovingly to bring him on his way to
horse. Do you see, sir, here she comes, and here I go.

WENDOLL: Vanish!   [*Exit* JENKIN.]

Enter ANNE.

ANNE: You are well met, sir. Now in troth my husband,
Before he took horse, had a great desire

70 To speak with you. We sought about the house,
Halloo'd into the fields, sent every way
But could not meet you. Therefore, he enjoined me
To do unto you his most kind commends.
Nay more, he wills you as you prize his love,
Or hold in estimation his kind friendship,
To make bold in his absence and command
Even as himself were present in the house.
For you must keep his table, use his servants,
And be a present Frankford in his absence.

80 WENDOLL: I thank him for his love.
[*Aside*] Give me a name, you whose infectious tongues
Are tipp'd with gall and poison, as you would
Think on a man that had your father slain,
Murdered thy children, made your wives base strum-
pets;
So call me, call me so! Print in my face
The most stigmatic title of a villain
For hatching treason to so true a friend.

ANNE: Sir, you are much beholding to my husband;
You are a man most dear in his regard.

90 WENDOLL: I am bound unto your husband and you too.

73 *do . . . commends* convey to you his kindest regards.
86 *stigmatic* infamous.

[*Aside*] I will not speak to wrong a gentleman
Of that good estimation, my kind friend.
I will not. Zounds, I will not! I may choose,
And I will choose! Shall I be so misled,
Or shall I purchase to my father's crest
The motto of a villain? If I say
I will not do it, what thing can enforce me?
Who can compel me? What sad destiny
Hath such command upon my yielding thoughts?
I will not. Ha! some fury pricks me on,   100
The swift fates drag me at their chariot wheel
And hurry me to mischief. Speak I must;
Injure myself, wrong her, deceive his trust.

ANNE: Are you not well, sir, that you seem thus troubled?
  There is sedition in your countenance.

WENDOLL: And in my heart, fair angel, chaste and wise;
  I love you. Start not, speak not, answer not.
  I love you – nay, let me speak the rest.
  Bid me to swear, and I will call to record
  The host of Heaven.   110

ANNE: The host of Heaven forbid
  Wendoll should hatch such a disloyal thought.

WENDOLL: Such is my fate; to this suit was I born:
  To wear rich Pleasure's crown or Fortune's scorn.

ANNE: My husband loves you.

WENDOLL: I know it.

ANNE: He esteems you
  Even as his brain, his eye-ball, or his heart.

WENDOLL: I have tried it.

ANNE: His purse is your exchequer, and his table
  Doth freely serve you.

95 *purchase* acquire otherwise than by inheritance.
98 *sad* unyielding.
105 *sedition* rebellion (i.e. Wendoll's inner strife).
116 *tried* made test of.

WENDOLL: So I have found it.

ANNE: Oh, with what face of brass, what bow of steel,
120   Can you unblushing speak this to the face
    Of the espoused wife of so dear a friend?
    It is my husband that maintains your state.
    Will you dishonour him? I am his wife
    That in your power hath left his whole affairs.
    It is to me you speak!

WENDOLL: Oh, speak no more,
    For more than this I know and have recorded
    Within the red-leav'd table of my heart.
    Fair, and of all belov'd, I was not fearful
    Bluntly to give my life into your hands,
130   And at one hazard all my earthly means.
    Go, tell your husband; he will turn me off,
    And I am then undone. I care not, I;
    'Twas for your sake. Perchance in rage he'll kill me.
    I care not; 'twas for you. Say I incur
    The general name of villain through the world,
    Of traitor to my friend; I care not, I.
    Beggary, shame, death, scandal, and reproach:
    For you I'll hazard all. What care I?
    For you I'll live and in your love I'll die.

140 ANNE: You move me, sir, to passion and to pity.
    The love I bear my husband is as precious
    As my soul's health.

WENDOLL: I love your husband, too,
    And for his love I will engage my life.
    Mistake me not; the augmentation
    Of my sincere affection borne to you
    Doth no whit lessen my regard of him.
    I will be secret, lady, close as night,

127 *table* notebook.   140 *passion* sorrow. See note.
147 *close* secret.

And not the light of one small glorious star
Shall shine here in my forhead to bewray
That act of night.   150

ANNE: What shall I say?
My soul is wand'ring and hath lost her way.
Oh Master Wendoll, oh!

WENDOLL: Sigh not, sweet saint,
For every sigh you breathe draws from my heart
A drop of blood.

ANNE: I ne'er offended yet.
 My fault, I fear, will in my brow be writ;
Women that fall not quite bereft of grace
Have their offences noted in their face.
I blush and am asham'd. Oh Master Wendoll,
Pray God I be not born to curse your tongue
That hath enchanted me! This maze I am in   160
I fear will prove the labyrinth of sin.

    Enter NICHOLAS [*unobserved*].

WENDOLL: The path of pleasure and the gate to bliss,
Which on your lips I knock at with a kiss.

NICHOLAS [*aside*]: I'll kill the rogue.

WENDOLL: Your husband is from home, your bed's no
    blab –
Nay, look not down and blush.

    [*Exeunt* WENDOLL *and* ANNE.]

NICHOLAS: Zounds, I'll stab.
Ay, Nick, was it thy chance to come just in the
    nick?
I love my master, and I hate that slave;
I love my mistress, but these tricks I like not.
My master shall not pocket up this wrong;   170

---

148 *glorious* boastful.   149 *bewray* betray.
156 *not . . . grace* i.e. not utterly hardened to sin.
167 *in the nick* at the right moment (with pun).

I'll eat my fingers first. [*Drawing his dagger.*] What
    say'st thou, metal?
Does not the rascal Wendoll go on legs
That thou must cut off? Hath he not hamstrings
That thou must hock? Nay, metal, thou shalt stand
To all I say. I'll henceforth turn a spy
And watch them in their close conveyances.
I never look'd for better of that rascal
Since he came miching first into our house.
It is that Satan hath corrupted her,
For she was fair and chaste. I'll have an eye
In all their gestures. Thus I think of them:
If they proceed as they have done before,
Wendoll's a knave, my mistress is a —.   *Exit.*

171 *metal* i.e. his dagger (possibly with reference to 'mettle' =
courage. Similarly, l. 174).
176 *close conveyances* underhand dealings.
178 *miching* sneaking.

Act Three

SCENE ONE

Enter SIR CHARLES *and* SUSAN.

SIR CHARLES: Sister, you see we are driven to hard shift
  To keep this poor house we have left unsold.
  I am now enforc'd to follow husbandry,
  And you to milk; and do we not live well?
  Well, I thank God!

SUSAN: Oh brother, here's a change
  Since old Sir Charles died, in our father's house.

SIR CHARLES: All things on earth thus change, some up, some down;
  Content's a kingdom, and I wear that crown.

    Enter SHAFTON *with a Sergeant.*

SHAFTON: Good morrow, good morrow, Sir Charles.
    What, with your sister
  Plying your husbandry? – Sergeant, stand off. –   10
  You have a pretty house, here, and a garden,
  And goodly ground about it; since it lies
  So near a lordship that I lately bought
  I would fain buy it of you. I will give you –

SIR CHARLES: Oh, pardon me; this house successively
  Hath 'long'd to me and my progenitors
  Three hundred year. My great great grandfather,
  He in whom first our gentle style began,
  Dwelt here, and in this ground increas'd this molehill
  Unto that mountain which my father left me.   20

After 8 S.D. *Sergeant* sheriff's officer.
13 *lordship* estate.   18 *gentle style* title to gentility.

Where he the first of all our house begun,
I now the last will end and keep this house,
This virgin title never yet deflower'd
By any unthrift of the Mountford's line.
In brief, I will not sell it for more gold
Than you could hide or pave the ground withal.

SHAFTON: Ha, ha! A proud mind and a beggar's purse.
Where's my three hundred pounds beside the use?
I have brought it to an execution
30   By course of law. What, is my money ready?

SIR CHARLES: An execution, sir, and never tell me?
You put my bond in suit? You deal extremely.

SHAFTON: Sell me the land and I'll acquit you straight.

SIR CHARLES: Alas, alas! 'Tis all trouble hath left me,
To cherish me and my poor sister's life.
If this were sold our names should then be quite
Raz'd from the bead-roll of gentility.
You see what hard shift we have made to keep it
Allied still to our own name. This palm you see
40   Labour hath gall'd within; her silver brow,
That never tasted a rough winter's blast
Without a mask or fan, doth with a grace
Defy cold Winter and his storms outface.

SUSAN: Sir, we feed sparing and we labour hard,
We lie uneasy to reserve to us
And our succession this small plot of ground.

SIR CHARLES: I have so bent my thoughts to husbandry
That I protest I scarcely can remember
What a new fashion is, how silk or satin

28 *use* interest.
29 *have ... execution* have had prepared a warrant of seizure.
32 *put ... suit* put my bond in force in a court of law.
35 *cherish* support, harbour.
37 *bead-roll* list (of names to be prayed for).
40 *her* i.e. Susan's.
46 *succession* descendants.

Feels in my hand. Why, pride is grown to us   50
A mere, mere stranger. I have quite forgot
The names of all that ever waited on me;
I cannot name ye any of my hounds,
Once from whose echoing mouths I heard all the
          music
That e'er my heart desired. What should I say?
To keep this place I have chang'd myself away.

SHAFTON: Arrest him at my suit! – Actions and actions
Shall keep thee in perpetual bondage fast.
Nay more: I'll sue thee by a late appeal,
And call thy former life in question.   60
The keeper is my friend; thou shalt have irons,
And usage such as I'll deny to dogs. Away with him!

SIR CHARLES: You are too timorous; but trouble is my
          master,
And I will serve him truly. My kind sister,
Thy tears are of no force to mollify
This flinty man. Go to my father's brother,
My kinsmen and allies; entreat them from me
To ransom me from this injurious man
That seeks my ruin.

SHAFTON: Come, irons, irons, away!
I'll see thee lodg'd far from the sight of day.   70
          Exeunt [except SUSAN].
          Enter SIR FRANCIS *and* MALBY.

SUSAN: My heart's so harden'd with the frost of grief
Death cannot pierce it through. Tyrant too fell!

51 *mere* absolute.
56 *chang'd . . . away* transformed my way of life.
59 *sue . . . appeal* prosecute you on an accusation undertaken after
the usual time.
60 *former life* i.e. judgement which had granted him his life.
63 *timorous* dreadful.
67 *allies* relatives.
72 *fell* cruel.

So lead the fiends condemned souls to hell.

SIR FRANCIS: Again to prison! Malby, hast thou seen
A poor slave better tortur'd? Shall we hear
The music of his voice cry from the grate
'Meat for the Lord's sake'? No, no. Yet I am not
Throughly reveng'd. They say he hath a pretty
  wench
Unto his sister; shall I, in mercy sake
To him and to his kindred, bribe the fool
To shame herself by lewd, dishonest lust?
I'll proffer largely, but the deed being done
I'll smile to see her base confusion.

MALBY: Methinks, Sir Francis, you are full reveng'd
For greater wrongs than he can proffer you.
See where the poor, sad gentlewoman stands.

SIR FRANCIS: Ha, ha! Now I will flout her poverty,
Deride her fortunes, scoff her base estate;
My very soul the name of Mountford hates.
But stay, my heart! Oh, what a look did fly
To strike my soul through with thy piercing eye!
I am enchanted, all my spirits are fled,
And with one glance my envious spleen struck dead.

SUSAN: Acton, that seeks our blood!   *Runs away.*

SIR FRANCIS: Oh, chaste and fair.

MALBY: Sir Francis, why Sir Francis! Zounds, in a
  trance!
Sir Francis, what cheer, man? Come, come, how is't?

SIR FRANCIS: Was she not fair? Or else this judging eye
Cannot distinguish beauty.

MALBY: She was fair.

SIR FRANCIS: She was an angel in a mortal's shape
And ne'er descended from old Mountford's line.

---

76 *grate* grating of prison.
83 *base confusion* degrading ruin.
92 *spirits* senses.   93 *envious spleen* malicious anger.

But soft, soft, let me call my wits together.
A poor, poor wench, to my great adversary
Sister, whose very souls denounce stern war,
One against other. How now, Frank, turn'd fool
Or madman, whether? But no! master of
My perfect senses and directest wits.
Then why should I be in this violent humour
Of passion and of love, and with a person
So different every way, and so oppos'd
In all contractions and still-warring actions?   110
Fie, fie, how I dispute against my soul!
Come, come, I'll gain her, or in her fair quest
Purchase my soul free and immortal rest.   *Exeunt*.

SCENE TWO

Enter three or four SERVINGMEN [*including* SPIGGOT
the Butler and NICHOLAS], *one with a voider and a
wooden knife, to take away all, another the salt and
bread, another the tablecloth and napkins, another the
carpet;* JENKIN *with two lights after them.*

JENKIN: So, march in order and retire in battle 'ray. My
master and the guests have supped already; all's taken
away. Here, now spread for the servingmen in the hall.
Butler, it belongs to your office.

103 *denounce* proclaim.
104 *One against other* i.e. his against mine.
105 *whether*? which?
110 *contractions* dealings.
112 *her fair quest* fair quest of her.
S.D. *voider* tray or basket for clearing the table. *salt* salt-cellar.
carpet table cover of tapestry work.

SPIGGOT: I know it, Jenkin. What do you call the
gentleman that supped there tonight?

JENKIN: Who? My master?

SPIGGOT: No, no, Master Wendoll, he is a daily guest.
I mean the gentleman that came but this afternoon.

10 JENKIN: His name is Master Cranwell. God's light!
Hark within there, my master calls to lay more billets
on the fire. Come, come. Lord, how we that are in
office here in the house are troubled! One spread
the carpet in the parlour and stand ready to snuff the
lights; the rest be ready to prepare their stomachs.
More lights in the hall there. Come, Nich'las.

[*Exeunt all except* NICHOLAS.]

NICHOLAS: I cannot eat; but had I Wendoll's heart
I would eat that; the rogue grows impudent.
Oh, I have seen such vild, notorious tricks,
20 Ready to make my eyes dart from my head.
I'll tell my master, by this air I will;
Fall what may fall, I'll tell him. Here he comes.

Enter FRANKFORD, *as it were brushing the crumbs from*
his clothes with a napkin, and newly risen from supper.

FRANKFORD: Nich'las, what make you here? Why are
not you
At supper in the hall there with your fellows?

NICHOLAS: Master, I stay'd your rising from the board
To speak with you.

FRANKFORD: Be brief then, gentle Nich'las;
My wife and guests attend me in the parlour.
Why dost thou pause? Now Nich'las, you want money
And unthrift-like would eat into your wages
30 Ere you have earn'd it. Here's half-a-crown.
Play the good husband, and away to supper.

13 *office* service.   19 *vild* vile.
25 *stay'd* waited for.
31 *husband* thrifty man.

NICHOLAS [*aside*]: By this hand an honourable gentleman; I will not see him wronged. [*To* FRANKFORD]
Sir, I have served you long; you entertained me seven
years before your beard; you knew me sir before you
knew my mistress.

FRANKFORD: What of this, good Nich'las?

NICHOLAS: I never was a make-bate or a knave.
I have no fault but one: I am given to quarrel,
But not with women. I will tell you, master,   40
That which will make your heart leap from your breast.
Your hair to startle from your head, your ears to
      tingle.

FRANKFORD: What preparation's this to dismal news?

NICHOLAS: 'Sblood, sir, I love you better than your wife.
I'll make it good.

FRANKFORD: Thou art a knave, and I have much ado
With wonted patience to contain my rage
And not to break thy pate. Thou art a knave;
I'll turn you with your base comparisons
Out of my doors.   50

NICHOLAS: Do, do!
There's not room for Wendoll and me too
Both in one house. Oh master, master,
That Wendoll is a villain.

FRANKFORD: Ay, saucy!

NICHOLAS: Strike, strike, do strike; yet hear me, I am
      no fool,
I know a villain when I see him act
Deeds of a villain. Master, master, that base slave
Enjoys my mistress and dishonours you.

FRANKFORD: Thou hast kill'd me with a weapon whose
      sharpen'd point

---

34 *entertained* took into service.
35 *before your beard* before you grew a beard.
36 *make-bate* trouble-causer.

       Hath prick'd quite through and through my shivering
          heart.
60   Drops of cold sweat sit dangling on my hairs
       Like morning's dew upon the golden flowers,
       And I am plung'd into a strange agony.
       What didst thou say? If any word that touch'd
       His credit or her reputation,
       It is as hard to enter my belief,
       As Dives into Heaven.

NICHOLAS: I can gain nothing;
       They are two that never wrong'd me. I knew before
       'Twas but a thankless office, and perhaps
       As much as my service or my life is worth.
70   All this I know; but this and more,
       More by a thousand dangers, could not hire me
       To smother such a heinous wrong from you.
       I saw, and I have said.

FRANKFORD [*aside*]: 'Tis probable. Though blunt, yet
          he is honest.
       Though I durst pawn my life, and on their faith
       Hazard the dear salvation of my soul,
       Yet in my trust I may be too secure.
       May this be true? Oh may it? Can it be?
       Is it by any wonder possible?
80   Man, woman, what thing mortal may we trust
       When friends and bosom wives prove so unjust?
       [*To* NICHOLAS.] What instance hast thou of this
          strange report?

NICHOLAS: Eyes, eyes.

FRANKFORD: Thy eyes may be deceiv'd I tell thee,
       For should an angel from the heavens drop down
       And preach this to me that thyself hast told,
       He should have much ado to win belief,

77 *secure* trusting.   82 *instance* evidence.

In both their loves I am so confident.

NICHOLAS: Shall I discourse the same by circumstance?

FRANKFORD: No more; to supper. And command your   90
    fellows
  To attend us and the strangers. Not a word;
  I charge thee on thy life, be secret then,
  For I know nothing.

NICHOLAS: I am dumb, and now that I have eas'd my
    stomach,
  I will go fill my stomach.   *Exit.*

FRANKFORD: Away, begone!
  She is well born, descended nobly,
  Virtuous her education; her repute
  Is in the general voice of all the country
  Honest and fair; her carriage, her demeanour
  In all her actions that concern the love   100
  To me her husband, modest, chaste, and godly.
  Is all this seeming gold plain copper?
  But he, that Judas that hath borne my purse
  And sold me for a sin – oh God, oh God,
  Shall I put up these wrongs? No! Shall I trust
  The bare report of this suspicious groom
  Before the double gilt, the well-hatch'd ore
  Of their two hearts? No, I will lose these thoughts,
  Distraction I will banish from my brow,
  And from my looks exile sad discontent.   110
  Their wonted favours in my tongue shall flow;
  Till I know all, I'll nothing seem to know.
  Lights and a table there! Wife, Master Wendoll and
    gentle Master Cranwell!

89 *by circumstance* in detail.   91 *strangers* visitors.
105 *put up* submit quietly to.
107 *double gilt* 1 refined gold; 2 double guilt. *well-hatch'd* richly
    inlaid.
111 *their wonted favours* accustomed kindnesses to them.

Enter ANNE, MASTER WENDOLL, MASTER CRAN-
WELL, NICHOLAS *and* JENKIN, *with cards, carpet,*
stools and other necessaries.

FRANKFORD: Oh, you are a stranger, Master Cranwell,
   you,
And often balk my house; faith you are a churl.
Now we have supp'd, a table and to cards.

JENKIN: A pair of cards, Nich'las, and a carpet to cover
   the table. Where's Sisly with her counters and her
120   box? Candles and candlesticks there! [*Enter* SISLY *and*
   a servingman with counters and candles.]
Fie, we have such a household of serving creatures.
Unless it be Nick and I, there's not one amongst them
all can say 'boo' to a goose. Well said, Nick.
   They spread a carpet and set down lights and cards.
   [*Exeunt all the servants except* NICHOLAS.]

ANNE: Come, Master Frankford, who shall take my part?

FRANKFORD: Marry, that will I, sweet wife.

WENDOLL: No, by my faith, sir; when you are together
   I sit out. It must be Mistress Frankford and I, or else
   it is no match.

FRANKFORD: I do not like that match.

130 NICHOLAS [*aside*]: You have no reason, marry, knowing
   all.

FRANKFORD: 'Tis no great matter, neither. Come,
   Master Cranwell, shall you and I take them up?

CRANWELL: At your pleasure, sir.

FRANKFORD: I must look to you, Master Wendoll, for
   you will be playing false; nay, so will my wife, too.

NICHOLAS [*aside*]: Ay, I will be sworn she will.

ANNE: Let them that are taken playing false forfeit the
   sct.

116 *balk* avoid.   118 *pair* pack.
123 *Well said* Well done.
124 *take my part* partner me.

FRANKFORD: Content. It shall go hard, but I'll take you.

CRANWELL: Gentlemen, what shall our game be?   140

WENDOLL: Master Frankford, you play best at Noddy.

FRANKFORD: You shall not find it so; indeed you shall not!

ANNE: I can play at nothing so well as Double-ruff.

FRANKFORD: If Master Wendoll and my wife be together, there's no playing against them at Double-hand.

NICHOLAS: I can tell you, sir, the game that Master Wendoll is best at.

WENDOLL: What game is that, Nick?

NICHOLAS: Marry sir, Knave-out-of-doors.   150

WENDOLL: She and I will take you at Lodam.

ANNE: Husband, shall we play at Saint?

FRANKFORD [*aside*]: My saint's turned devil. – No, we'll none of Saint. You're best at New-cut, wife; you'll play at that.

WENDOLL: If you play at New-cut, I am soonest hitter of any here for a wager.

FRANKFORD [*aside*]: 'Tis me they play on. Well, you may draw out;

For all your cunning, 'twill be to your shame.

I'll teach you at your New-cut a new game. –   160
Come, come!

---

141 *Noddy* 1 game like cribbage; 2 booby.

143 *Double-ruff* 1 variant of ruff, game like whist; 2 play on ruff = excitement, passion.

145 *Double-hand* (?)another name for Double-ruff, with same innuendo.

150 *Knave-out-of-doors* card game, with innuendo.

151 *Lodam* card game.

152 *Saint* game like Picquet.

154 *New-cut* card game with sexual implication.

156 *hitter* point-maker.

158 *draw out* so pick your cards as to lose the game.

CRANWELL: If you cannot agree upon the game, to
  Post-and-pair.

WENDOLL: We shall be soonest pairs, and my good host,
  When he comes late home, he must kiss the post.

FRANKFORD: Whoever wins, it shall be to thy cost.

CRANWELL: Faith, let it be Vide-ruff, and let's make
    honours.

FRANKFORD: If you make honours, one thing let me
    crave:

Honour the king and queen, except the knave.

170 WENDOLL: Well, as you please for that. Lift who shall
    deal.

ANNE: The least in sight. What are you, Master Wen-
    doll?

WENDOLL: I am a knave.

NICHOLAS [aside]:   I'll swear it.

ANNE: I a queen.

FRANKFORD[aside]: A quean, thou should'st say! – Well,
    the cards are mine;

They are the grossest pair that e'er I felt.

ANNE: Shuffle, I'll cut. [Aside] Would I had never dealt!

FRANKFORD: I have lost my dealing.

WENDOLL: Sir, the fault's in me;

This queen I have more than my own, you see.

Give me the stock.

163 Post-and-pair game like poker.
165 kiss the post i.e. be shut out.
167 Vide-ruff another variant of Ruff.
168 make honours ?name the highest cards.
170 lift . . . deal cut for the deal.
171 least lowest.   173 quean whore.
174 grossest pair 1 thickest pack; 2 lewdest couple.
175 dealt (here) had sexual dealings.
176 lost my dealing made a mistake in my dealing.
177 This queen 1 the card; 2 Anne.
178 stock stack.

FRANKFORD: My mind's not on the game.

   [*Aside*] Many a deal I have lost, the more's your
      shame. –

   You have serv'd me a bad trick, Master Wendoll.   180

WENDOLL: Sir, you must take your lot. To end this
      strife,

   I know I have dealt better with your wife.

FRANKFORD [*aside*]: Thou has dealt falsely, then.

ANNE: What's trumps?

WENDOLL: Hearts. Partner, I rub.

FRANKFORD [*aside*]: Thou rob'st me of my soul, of her
      chaste love,

   In thy false dealing; thou hast robb'd my heart.

   Booty you play; I like a loser stand,

   Having no heart, or here or in my hand. –

   I will give o'er the set, I am not well;   190

   Come, who will hold my cards?

ANNE: Not well, sweet Master Frankford?

   Alas, what ail you. 'Tis some sudden qualm.

WENDOLL: How long have you been so, Master Frank-
      ford?

FRANKFORD: Sir, I was lusty and I had my health,

   But I grew ill when you began to deal.

   Take hence this table.

     [*The Servants enter and remove the table, etc.*]
                Gentle Master Cranwell,

   You are welcome; see your chamber at your pleasure.

   I am sorry that this megrim takes me so;

   I cannot sit and bear you company.   200

   Jenkin, some lights, and show him to his chamber.

180 *trick* 1 hand of cards; 2 piece of roguery.
185 *rub* take all the cards of one suit.
188 *Booty you play* you join together to plunder a third.
195 *lusty* healthy.
199 *megrim* migraine.

[*Exeunt* CRANWELL *and* JENKIN.]

ANNE: A night-gown for my husband, quickly there.

[*Enter a Servant with a gown, and exit.*]

It is some rheum or cold.

WENDOLL: Now, in good faith,
This illness you have got by sitting late
Without your gown.

FRANKFORD: I know it, Master Wendoll.
Go, go to bed, lest you complain like me.
Wife, prithee wife, into my bed-chamber.
The night is raw, and cold, and rheumatic.
Leave me my gown and light; I'll walk away my fit.

210 WENDOLL: Sweet sir, good night.

FRANKFORD: Myself, good night. [*Exit* WENDOLL.]

ANNE: Shall I attend, you, husband?

FRANKFORD: No, gentle wife, thou'lt catch cold in thy
              head.
Prithee, begone, sweet; I'll make haste to bed.

ANNE: No sleep will fasten on mine eyes, you know,
Until you come.

FRANKFORD: Sweet Nan, I prithee, go.

    [*Exit* ANNE.]

[*To* NICHOLAS] I have bethought me: get me by de-
        grees
The keys of all my doors which I will mould
In wax, and take their fair impression,
To have by them new keys. This being compass'd,
220 At a set hour a letter shall be brought me,
And when they think they may securely play,
They are nearest to danger. Nick, I must rely
Upon thy trust and faithful secrecy.

NICHOLAS: Build on my faith.

---

203 *rheum* cold.   208 *rheumatic* rheum inducing.
211 *Myself* my own.

FRANKFORD: To bed then, not to rest;
  Care lodges in my brain, grief in my breast.
    Exeunt.

SCENE THREE

  Enter SUSAN, OLD MOUNTFORD, SANDY, RODER,
  and TYDY.

OLD MOUNTFORD: You say my nephew is in great
      distress:
  Who brought it to him but his own lewd life?
  I cannot spare a cross. I must confess
  He was my brother's son; why, niece, what then?
  This is no world in which to pity men.
SUSAN: I was not born a beggar, though his extremes
  Enforce this language from me; I protest
  No fortune of mine could lead my tongue
  To this base key. I do beseech you, uncle,
  For the name's sake, for Christianity,   10
  Nay, for God's sake, to pity his distress.
  He is denied the freedom of the prison
  And in the hole is laid with men condemn'd;
  Plenty he hath of nothing but of irons,
  And it remains in you to free him thence.
OLD MOUNTFORD: Money I cannot spare. Men should
      take heed;
  He lost my kindred when he fell to need.   *Exit.*
SUSAN: Gold is but earth; thou earth enough shalt have
  When thou hast once took measure of thy grave.

3 *cross* coin.
6 *extremes* extreme circumstances.
10 *For the name's sake* for the sake of the family reputation.
13 *the hole* the worst sort of cell.

20   You know me, Master Sandy, and my suit.

SANDY: I knew you, lady, when the old man liv'd;
  I knew you ere your brother sold his land.
  Then you were Mistress Sue trick'd up in jewels,
  Then you sung well, play'd sweetly on the flute;
  But now I neither know you nor your suit. [*Exit.*]

SUSAN: You, Master Roder, was my brother's tenant;
  Rent-free he plac'd you in that wealthy farm
  Of which you are possess'd.

RODER: True, he did,
  And have I not there dwelt still for his sake?
  I have some business now, but without doubt
30   They that have hurl'd him in will help him out.
    Exit.

SUSAN: Cold comfort still. What say you, cousin Tydy?

TYDY: I say this comes of roisting, swagg'ring.
  Call me not 'cousin'; each man for himself.
  Some men are born to mirth and some to sorrow;
  I am no cousin unto them that borrow.   *Exit.*

SUSAN: Oh charity, why art thou fled to Heaven,
  And left all things on this earth uneven?
  Their scoffing answers I will ne'er return,
40   But to myself his grief in silence mourn.
    Enter SIR FRANCIS *and* MALBY.

SIR FRANCIS: She is poor; I'll therefore tempt her with
    this gold.
  Go, Malby, in my name deliver it.
  And I will stay thy answer.

MALBY: Fair Mistress, as I understand, your grief
  Doth grow from want; so I have here in store
  A means to furnish you, a bag of gold
  Which to your hands I freely tender you.

---

33 *roisting* rudely revelling.
38 *uneven* unjust.   43 *stay* await.

SUSAN: I thank you, Heavens; I thank you, gentle sir.
  God make me able to requite this favour.
MALBY: This gold Sir Francis Acton sends by me, 50
  And prays you –
SUSAN: Acton! Oh God, that name I am born to curse.
  Hence bawd! Hence broker! See, I spurn his gold;
  My honour never shall for gain be sold.
SIR FRANCIS: Stay, lady, stay.
SUSAN: From you I'll posting hie,
  Even as the doves from feathered eagles fly. [Exit.]
SIR FRANCIS: She hates my name, my face; how
        should I woo?
  I am disgrac'd in everything I do.
  The more she hates me and disdains my love,
  The more I am rapt in admiration 60
  Of her divine and chaste perfections.
  Woo her with gifts I cannot, for all gifts
  Sent in my name she spurns. With looks I cannot,
  For she abhors my sight. Nor yet with letters,
  For none she will receive. How then? How then?
  Well, I will fasten such a kindness on her,
  As shall o'ercome her hate and conquer it.
  Sir Charles, her brother, lies in execution
  For a great sum of money; and besides,
  The appeal is sued still for my huntsmen's death, 70
  Which only I have power to reverse.
  In her I'll bury all my hate of him.
  Go seek the keeper, Malby, bring me to him.
  To save his body I his debts will pay;
  To save his life, I his appeal will stay.
    [Exeunt.]

53 *broker* procurer.   55 *posting* hurriedly.
68 *in execution* in the power of the law.
70 *appeal is sued* prosecution is in hand.

Act Four

SCENE ONE

Enter SIR CHARLES *in prison with irons, his feet bare,
his garments all ragged and torn.*

SIR CHARLES: Oh, fall on the earth's face most miser-
  able!
Breathe in the hellish dungeon thy laments,
Thus, like a slave ragg'd, like a fellon gyv'd!
What hurls thee headlong to this base estate?
Oh, unkind uncle! Oh, my friends ingrate!
Unthankful kinsmen! Mountfords all too base,
To let thy name lie fettered in disgrace.
A thousand deaths here in this grave I die;
Fear, hunger, sorrow, cold – all threat my death,
10 And join together to deprive my breath.
But that which most torments me, my dear sister
Hath left to visit me, and from my friends
Hath brought no hopeful answer; therefore I
Divine they will not help my misery.
If it be so, shame, scandal and contempt
Attend their covetous thoughts, need make their
  graves;
Usurers they live, and may they die like slaves.
 Enter KEEPER.
KEEPER: Knight, be of comfort, for I bring thee freedom
From all thy troubles.
SIR CHARLES: Then am I doom'd to die;
20 Death is th'end of all calamity.

3 *gyv'd* shackled. 5 *ingrate* ungrateful.
10 *deprive* deprive me of. 12 *left to visit* ceased visiting.
14 *Divine* conjecture.

KEEPER: Live! your appeal is stayed, the execution
  Of all your debts discharg'd, your creditors
  Even to the utmost penny satisfied;
  In sign whereof, your shackles I knock off.
  You are not left so much indebted to us
  As for your fees; all is discharg'd, all paid.
  Go freely to your house or where you please;
  After long miseries, embrace your ease.
SIR CHARLES: Thou grumblest out the sweetest music to
      me,
  That ever organ play'd. Is this a dream,   30
  Or do my waking senses apprehend
  The pleasing taste of these applausive news?
  Slave that I was, to wrong such honest friends,
  My loving kinsmen, and my near allies!
  Tongue, I will bite thee for the scandal breath'd
  Against such faithful kinsmen. They are all
  Compos'd of pity and compassion,
  Of melting charity, and of moving ruth.
  That which I spake before was in my rage;
  They are my friends, the mirrors of this age,   40
  Bounteous and free. The noble Mountford's race
  Ne'er bred a covetous thought or humour base.
    Enter SUSAN.
SUSAN: I can no longer stay from visiting
  My woeful brother. While I could, I kept
  My hapless tidings from his hopeful ear.
SIR CHARLES: Sister, how much am I indebted to thee
  And to thy travail!
SUSAN: What, at liberty?

21 *your appeal is stayed* the charge has been withdrawn.
21–2 *the execution . . . debts* all judgement for debt.
32 *applausive* agreeable.   38 *ruth* pity.
40 *mirrors* exemplars.
42 *humour* disposition.

SIR CHARLES: Thou seest I am, thanks to thy industry.
 Oh, unto which of all my courteous friends
50 Am I thus bound? My uncle Mountford, he,
 Even of an infant lov'd me. Was it he?
 So did my cousin Tydy. Was it he?
 So Master Roder; Master Sandy too.
 Which of all these did this high kindness do?
SUSAN: Charles, can you mock me in your poverty,
 Knowing your friends deride your misery?
 Now I protest I stand so much amaz'd
 To see your bonds free and your irons knock'd off
 That I am rapt into a maze of wonder,
60 The rather for I know not by what means
 This happiness hath chanc'd.
SIR CHARLES: Why, by my uncle,
 My cousins, and my friends; who else, I pray,
 Would take upon them all my debts to pay?
SUSAN: Oh brother, they are men all of flint,
 Pictures of marble, and as void of pity
 As chased bears. I begg'd, I sued, I kneel'd,
 Laid open all your griefs and miseries,
 Which they derided; more than that, denied us
 A part in their alliance, but in pride
70 Said that our kindred with our plenty died.
SIR CHARLES: Drudges too much! What, did they? Oh,
    known evil:
 Rich fly the poor, as good men shun the devil.
 Whence should my freedom come? Of whom alive,
 Saving of those, have I deserv'd so well?
 Guess, sister, call to mind, remember me.
 These I have rais'd, these follow the world's guise:

65 *pictures* statues. 66 *chased* harassed (in bear-baiting).
71 *drudges too much* slaves too base.
75 *remember* remind.

Whom rich they honour, they in woe despise.

SUSAN: My wits have lost themselves. Let's ask the
    keeper.

SIR CHARLES: Gaoler!

KEEPER: At hand, sir.   80

SIR CHARLES: Of courtesy, resolve me one demand:
What was he took the burden of my debts
From off my back, stay'd my appeal to death,
Discharg'd my fees, and brought me liberty?

KEEPER: A courteous knight, one call'd Sir Francis
    Acton.

SUSAN: Acton!

SIR CHARLES: Ha, Acton! Oh me, more distress'd in
    this
Than all my troubles. Hale me back,
Double my irons, and my sparing meals
Put into halves, and lodge me in a dungeon   90
More deep, more dark, more cold, more comfortless.
By Acton freed! Not all thy manacles
Could fetter so my heels as this one word
Hath thrall'd my heart; and it must now lie bound
In more strict prison than thy stony gaol;
I am not free, I go but under bail.

KEEPER: My charge is done, sir, now I have my fees;
As we get little, we will nothing leese.   *Exit.*

SIR CHARLES: By Acton freed, my dangerous opposite!
Why, to what end? or what occasion? ha!   100
Let me forget the name of enemy,
And with indifference balance this high favour. Ha!

SUSAN [*aside*]: His love to me, upon my soul 'tis so;

76 *rais'd* mentioned. *guise* fashion.
81 *resolve . . . demand* answer me one question.
98 *leese* lose.   99 *opposite* opponent.
102 *with indifference* impartially. *balance* weigh.

That is the root from whence these strange things
    grow.
SIR CHARLES: Had this proceeded from my father, he
That by the law of nature is most bound
In offices of love, it had deserv'd
My best employment to requite that grace.
Had it proceeded from my friends or him,
From them this action had deserv'd my life;
And from a stranger more, because from such
There is less expectation of good deeds.
But he, nor father, nor ally, nor friend,
More than a stranger, both remote in blood
And in his heart oppos'd my enemy,
That this high bounty should proceed from him!
Oh there I lose myself. What should I say,
What think, what do, his bounty to repay?
SUSAN: You wonder, I am sure, whence this strange
    kindness
Proceeds in Acton. I will tell you, brother:
He dotes on me, and oft hath sent me gifts,
Letters and tokens; I refus'd them all.
SIR CHARLES: I have enough. Though poor, my heart
    is set
In one rich gift to pay back all my debt.   *Exeunt.*

110

120

SCENE TWO

Enter FRANKFORD *with a letter in his hand, and*
NICHOLAS *with keys.*
FRANKFORD: This is the night, and I must play the
    touch

1 *play the touch* i.e. make a test (alchemical metaphor of using a
touchstone to test gold).

To try two seeming angels. Where's my keys?

NICHOLAS: They are made according to your mould in
  wax;
  I bade the smith be secret, gave him money,
  And there they are. The letter, sir.

FRANKFORD: True, take it; there it is.
  And when thou seest me in my pleasant'st vein,
  Ready to sit to supper, bring it me.

NICHOLAS: I'll do't; make no more question but I'll
  do't.   *Exit.*

  Enter ANNE, CRANWELL, WENDOLL, *and* JENKIN.

ANNE: Sirrah, 'tis six o'clock already struck;   10
  Go bid them spread the cloth and serve in supper.

JENKIN: It shall be done, forsooth, mistress. Where is
  Spiggot, the butler, to give us our salt and trenchers?
  [*Exit.*]

WENDOLL: We that have been a-hunting all the day
  Come with prepar'd stomachs, Master Frankford.
  We wish'd you at our sport.

FRANKFORD: My heart was with you, and my mind was
        on you.
  Fie, Master Cranwell, you are still thus sad.
  A stool, a stool! Where's Jenkin, and where's Nick?
  'Tis supper time at least an hour ago.   20
  What's the best news abroad?

WENDOLL: I know none good.

FRANKFORD [*aside*]: But I know too much bad.

  Enter [SPIGGOT] *the Butler and* JENKIN *with a tablecloth, bread, trenchers, and salt.*

CRANWELL: Methinks, sir, you might have that interest
  In your wife's brother to be more remiss

---

2 *angels* with pun on 'gold coins'.
21 *abroad* in the outside world.
After 22 S.D. *trenchers* plates.
23–4 *interest In* influence with.   24 *remiss* lenient.

In this hard dealing against poor Sir Charles,
Who, as I hear, lies in York castle, needy,
And in great want.

FRANKFORD: Did not more weighty business of my own
Hold me away, I would have labour'd peace
Betwixt them with all care; indeed I would, sir.

ANNE: I'll write unto my brother earnestly
In that behalf.

WENDOLL: A charitable deed,
And will beget the good opinion
Of all your friends that love you, Mistress Frankford.

FRANKFORD: That's you for one; I know you love Sir
      Charles,
And my wife too well.

WENDOLL: He deserves the love
Of all true gentlemen; be yourselves judge.

FRANKFORD: But supper, ho! Now as thou lovest me,
      Wendoll,
Which I am sure thou dost, be merry, pleasant,
And frolic it tonight. Sweet Master Cranwell,
Do you the like. Wife, I protest my heart
Was ne'er more bent on sweet alacrity.
Where be those lazy knaves to serve in supper?
      Enter NICHOLAS.

NICHOLAS: Sir, here's a letter.

FRANKFORD: Whence comes it and who
      brought it?

NICHOLAS: A stripling that below attends your answer,
And as he tells me it is sent from York.

FRANKFORD: Have him into the cellar. Let him taste a
      cup
Of our March beer; go, make him drink.

36 *too* very. See note.   42 *alacrity* cheerfulness.
48 *March beer* a strong beer brewed in March.

NICHOLAS: I'll make him drunk if he be a Trojan.
    [*Exit*.]
FRANKFORD: My boots and spurs! Where's Jenkin?   50
        God forgive me;
  How I neglect my business. Wife, look here;
  I have a matter to be tried tomorrow
  By eight o'clock, and my attorney writes me
  I must be there betimes with evidence
  Or it will go against me. Where's my boots?
    Enter JENKIN *with boots and spurs*.
ANNE: I hope your business craves no such dispatch
  That you must ride tonight.
WENDOLL [*aside*]:   I hope it doth.
FRANKFORD: God's me! No such dispatch?
  Jenkin, my boots. Where's Nick? Saddle my roan,
  And the grey dapple for himself. Content ye,   60
  It much concerns me. [*Exit* JENKIN.] Gentle Master
      Cranwell
  And Master Wendoll, in my absence use
  The very ripest pleasure of my house.
WENDOLL: Lord, Master Frankford, will you ride to-
      night?
  The ways are dangerous.
FRANKFORD: Therefore will I ride
  Appointed well, and so shall Nick my man.
ANNE: I'll call you up by five o'clock tomorrow.
FRANKFORD: No, by my faith, wife, I'll not trust to
      that;
  'Tis not such easy rising in a morning
  From one I love so dearly. No, by my faith,   70
  I shall not leave so sweet a bedfellow

49 *Trojan* good fellow, drunkard.   56 *dispatch* speed.
60 *Content ye* you may be sure.
66 *Appointed* equipped.

But with much pain. You have made me a sluggard
Since I first knew you.

ANNE: Then if you needs will go
This dangerous evening, Master Wendoll,
Let me entreat you bear him company.

WENDOLL: With all my heart, sweet mistress. My boots
                there!

FRANKFORD: Fie, fie, that for my private business
I should disease my friend and be a trouble
To the whole house. Nick!

NICHOLAS [*off-stage*]:   Anon, sir.

80 FRANKFORD: Bring forth my gelding. [*To* WENDOLL]
                As you love me, sir,
Use no more words. A hand, good Master Cranwell.

CRANWELL: Sir, God be your good speed.

FRANKFORD: Goodnight, sweet Nan. Nay, nay, a kiss
                and part.
[*Aside*] Dissembling lips, you suit not with my heart.
[*Exit*.]

WENDOLL: How business, time and hours all gracious
                proves
And are the furtherers to my newborn love.
I am the husband now in Master Frankford's place
And must command the house. My pleasure is
We will not sup abroad so publicly
90   But in your private chamber, Mistress Frankford.

ANNE: Oh sir, you are too public in your love,
And Master Frankford's wise.

CRANWELL: Might I crave favour,
I would entreat you I might see my chamber.
I am on the sudden grown exceeding ill
And would be spar'd from supper.

WENDOLL: Light there, ho!
See you want nothing, sir, for if you do

78 *disease* put to inconvenience.

You injury that good man and wrong me too.

CRANWELL: I will make bold. Goodnight.   [*Exit.*]

WENDOLL: How all conspire
To make our bosom sweet and full entire.
Come, Nan, I prithee let us sup within.   100

ANNE: Oh, what a clog unto the soul is sin.
We pale offenders are still full of fear;
Every suspicious eye brings danger near,
When they whose clear heart from offence are free,
Despise report, base scandals to outface,
And stand at mere defiance with disgrace.

WENDOLL: Fie, fie, you talk too like a Puritan.

ANNE: You have tempted me to mischief, Master
       Wendoll.
I have done I know not what. Well, you plead custom;
That which for want of wit I granted erst,   110
I now must yield through fear. Come, come, let's in;
Once o'er shoes, we are straight o'er head in sin.

WENDOLL: My jocund soul is joyful above measure;
I'll be profuse in Frankford's richest treasure.

    Exeunt.

97 *injury* sometimes used as verb.
99 *bosom* inward desires.
104 *When* whereas.   105 *report* gossip.
106 *mere* complete.   108 *mischief* wickedness.
110 *erst* formerly.

SCENE THREE

Enter SISLY, JENKIN, [SPIGGOT *the*] *Butler, and other Servingmen.*

JENKIN: My mistress and Master Wendoll, my master, sup in her chamber tonight. Sisly, you are preferred from being the cook to be chambermaid. Of all the loves betwixt thee and me, tell me what thou thinkest of this?

SISLY: Mum; there's an old proverb: 'when the cat's away the mouse may play'.

JENKIN: Now you talk of a cat, Sisly, I smell a rat.

SISLY: Good words, Jenkin, lest you be called to answer
10   them.

JENKIN: Why, God make my mistress an honest woman! Are not these good words? Pray God my new master play not the knave with my old master! Is there any hurt in this? God send no villainy intended, and if they do sup together, pray God they do not lie together! God keep my mistress chaste, and make us all His servants! What harm is there in all this? Nay more, here is my hand; thou shalt never have my heart unless thou say 'Amen'.

20   SISLY: 'Amen, I pray God', I say.
        Enter SERVINGMEN.

SERVINGMAN: My mistress sends that you should make less noise, to lock up the doors, and see the household all got to bed. You, Jenkin, for this night are made the porter, to see the gates shut in.

JENKIN: Thus by little and little I creep into office.

9 *lest* unless.
25 *creep into office* slyly get promotion. Van Fossen glosses 'office' as 'office of a bawd or pander'.

Come to kennel, my masters, to kennel. 'Tis eleven
o'clock already.

SERVINGMAN: When you have locked the gates in, you
must send up the keys to my mistress.

SISLY: Quickly, for God's sake, Jenkin; for I must carry   30
them. I am neither pillow nor bolster, but I know
more than both.

JENKIN: To bed, good Spiggot, to bed, good honest
serving creatures, and let us sleep as snug as pigs in
pease-straw.   *Exeunt.*

SCENE FOUR

Enter FRANKFORD *and* NICHOLAS.

FRANKFORD: Soft, soft. We have tied our geldings to a
    tree
Two flight-shoot off, lest by their thund'ring hooves
They blab our coming back. Hear'st thou no noise?

NICHOLAS: Hear? I hear nothing but the owl and you.

FRANKFORD: So, now my watch's hand points upon
    twelve,
And it is dead midnight. Where are my keys?

NICHOLAS: Here, sir.

FRANKFORD: This is the key that opes my outward gate,
This is the hall door, this my withdrawing chamber.
But this, that door that's bawd unto my shame,   10
Fountain and spring of all my bleeding thoughts,
Where the most hallowed order and true knot
Of nuptial sanctity hath been profan'd.

35 *pease-straw* fodder from pea plants.
2 *Two flight-shoot off* two bow-shots away ('flight-arrow' feathered
for long range).

It leads to my polluted bedchamber,
 Once my terrestrial heaven, now my earth's hell,
The place where sins in all their ripeness dwell.
But I forget myself; now to my gate.

NICHOLAS: It must ope with far less noise than Cripple-
gate, or your plot's dashed.

20 FRANKFORD: So, reach me my dark-lantern to the rest.
Tread softly, softly.

NICHOLAS: I will walk on eggs this pace.

FRANKFORD: A general silence hath surpris'd the house,
And this is the last door. Astonishment,
Fear and amazement play against my heart
Even as a madman beats upon a drum.
Oh, keep my eyes, you Heavens, before I enter,
From any sight that may transfix my soul;
Or if there be so black a spectacle,
Oh, strike mine eyes stark blind; or if not so,
30 Lend me such patience to digest my grief,
That I may keep this white and virgin hand
From any violent outrage or red murder.
And with that prayer I enter.   [*Exit.*]

NICHOLAS: Here's a circumstance!
A man may be made cuckold in the time
That he's about it. And the case were mine,
As 'tis my master's – 'sblood, that he makes me swear –
I would have plac'd his action, enter'd there;
I would, I would.

    [*Enter* FRANKFORD.]

40 FRANKFORD: Oh, oh!

---

18 *Cripple-gate* one of the northern gates of London.
20 *dark-lantern* lantern with slide for concealing the light. *to the
rest* ?i.e. of the gates.
21 *I . . . pace* I could walk on eggs at this pace (proverbial).
34 *circumstance* roundabout behaviour.
36 *And* if.   38 *plac'd his action* 'Established his case' (Ward).

NICHOLAS: Master, 'sblood, master, master!

FRANKFORD: Oh me unhappy, I have found them
    lying
  Close in each other's arms, and fast asleep.
  But that I would not damn two precious souls
  Bought with my Saviour's blood, and send them
    laden
  With all their scarlet sins upon their backs
  Unto a fearful judgement, their two lives
  Had met upon my rapier.

NICHOLAS: 'Sblood, master, have you left them sleeping
    still?
  Let me go wake them.

FRANKFORD: Stay, let me pause awhile.   50
  Oh God, oh God, that it were possible
  To undo things done, to call back yesterday;
  That time could turn up his swift sandy glass,
  To untell the days, and to redeem these hours;
  Or that the sun
  Could, rising from the West, draw his coach backward,
  Take from the account of time so many minutes
  Till he had all these seasons call'd again,
  Those minutes and those actions done in them,
  Even from her first offence, that I might take her   60
  As spotless as an angel in my arms.
  But oh, I talk of things impossible
  And cast beyond the moon. God give me patience,
  For I will in to wake them.   *Exit.*

NICHOLAS: Here's patience perforce;
  He needs must trot afoot that tires his horse.

---

47 *fearful judgement* i.e. if they have not opportunity to repent.
54 *untell* count backwards.
63 *cast . . . moon* impossible, translunary.
64 *perforce* of necessity.

Enter WENDOLL, *running over the stage in a night gown, he* [FRANKFORD] *after him with his sword drawn;* [*followed by*] *the* MAID *in her smock* [*who*] *stays his hand, and clasps hold on him. He pauses awhile.*

FRANKFORD: I thank thee, maid; thou like the angel's hand

Hast stay'd me from a bloody sacrifice.

Go, villain, and my wrongs sit on thy soul

As heavy as this grief doth upon mine.

70 When thou record'st my many courtesies,

And shalt compare them with thy treacherous heart,

Lay them together, weigh them equally,

'Twill be revenge enough. Go, to thy friend

A Judas; pray, pray, lest I live to see

Thee Judas-like hang'd on an elder tree.

Enter ANNE *in her smock, night gown, and night attire.*

ANNE: Oh, by what word, what title, or what name

Shall I entreat your pardon? Pardon? Oh,

I am as far from hoping such sweet grace

As Lucifer from Heaven. To call you 'husband'!

80 Oh me most wretched; I have lost that name,

I am no more your wife.

NICHOLAS:　　　　　　　　'Sblood, sir, she swoons.

FRANKFORD: Spare thou thy tears, for I will weep for thee;

And keep thy countenance, for I'll blush for thee.

Now I protest, I think 'tis I am tainted,

For I am most asham'd, and 'tis more hard

For me to look upon thy guilty face

Than on the sun's clear brow. What would'st thou speak?

ANNE: I would I had no tongue, no ears, no eyes,

No apprehension, no capacity.

89 *apprehension, capacity* active and passive powers of the mind.

When do you spurn me like a dog? When tread me   90
Under your feet? When drag me by the hair?
Though I deserve a thousand, thousandfold
More than you can inflict, yet, once my husband,
For womanhood, to which I am a shame
Though once an ornament, even for His sake
That hath redeem'd our souls, mark not my face,
Nor hack me with your sword, but let me go
Perfect and undeformed to my tomb.
I am not worthy that I should prevail
In the least suit, no, not to speak to you,   100
Nor look on you, nor to be in your presence.
Yet, as an abject, this one suit I crave;
This granted, I am ready for my grave.

FRANKFORD: May God with patience arm me. Rise,
        nay rise,
  And I'll debate with thee. Was it for want
  Thou play'dst the strumpet? Wast thou not supplied
  With every pleasure, fashion, and new toy,
  Nay, even beyond my calling?

ANNE: I was.

FRANKFORD: Was it then disability in me,
  Or in thine eye seem'd he a properer man?   110

ANNE: Oh, no.

FRANKFORD: Did I not lodge thee in my bosom?
  Wear thee here in my heart?

ANNE: You did.

FRANKFORD: I did indeed; witness my tears I did.
  Go bring my infants hither.

    [*Exit* MAID *and returns with two* CHILDREN.]
                    Oh Nan, oh Nan!
  If either fear of shame, regard of honour,

102 *abject* outcast.   107 *toy* trinket.
108 *calling* rank.
110 *properer* more attractive.

The blemish of my house, nor my dear love,
Could have withheld thee from so lewd a fact,
Yet for these infants, these young, harmless souls,
On whose white brows thy shame is character'd,
120 And grows in greatness as they wax in years –
Look but on them, and melt away in tears.
Away with them, lest as her spotted body
Hath stain'd their name with stripes of bastardy,
So her adult'rous breath may blast their spirits
With her infectious thoughts. Away with them!
[*Exeunt* MAID *and* CHILDREN.]
ANNE: In this one life I die ten thousand deaths.
FRANKFORD: Stand up, stand up; I will do nothing
rashly.
I will retire awhile into my study,
And thou shalt hear thy sentence presently.   *Exit.*
130 ANNE: 'Tis welcome be it death. Oh me, base strumpet,
That having such a husband, such sweet children,
Must enjoy neither! Oh, to redeem my honour,
I would have this hand cut off, these my breasts sear'd,
Be rack'd, strappado'd, put to any torment;
Nay, to whip but this scandal out, I would hazard
The rich and dear redemption of my soul.
He cannot be so base as to forgive me,
Nor I so shameless to accept his pardon.
Oh, women, women, you that have yet kept
140 Your holy matrimonial vow unstain'd,
Make me your instance when you tread awry;
Your sins like mine will on your conscience lie.
Enter SISLY, SPIGGOT, *all the Servingmen, and*
JENKIN, *as newly come out of bed.*
ALL: Oh mistress, mistress, what have you done, mistress?

117 *fact* deed.   124 *blast* blight.
141 *instance* example.

NICHOLAS: 'Sblood, what a caterwauling keep you
    here!

JENKIN: Oh Lord, mistress, how comes this to pass?
  My master is run away in his shirt, and never so much
  as called me to bring his clothes after him.

ANNE: See what guilt is; here stand I in this place,
  Asham'd to look my servants in the face.

> *Enter* MASTER FRANKFORD *and* CRANWELL, *whom*
> *seeing she falls on her knees.*

FRANKFORD: My words are register'd in Heaven already; 150
  With patience hear me. I'll not martyr thee,
  Nor mark thee for a strumpet, but with usage
  Of more humility torment thy soul,
  And kill thee, even with kindness.

CRANWELL: Master Frankford –

FRANKFORD: Good Master Cranwell. – Woman, hear
        thy judgement:
  Go make thee ready in thy best attire,
  Take with thee all thy gowns, all thy apparel;
  Leave nothing that did ever call thee mistress,
  Or by whose sight being left here in the house
  I may remember such a woman by.   160
  Choose thee a bed and hangings for a chamber,
  Take with thee everything that hath thy mark,
  And get thee to my manor seven mile off,
  Where live; 'tis thine; I freely give it thee.
  My tenants by shall furnish thee with wains
  To carry all thy stuff within two hours;
  No longer will I limit thee my sight.
  Choose which of all my servants thou likest best
  And they are thine to attend thee.

ANNE: A mild sentence.

FRANKFORD: But as thou hop'st for Heaven, as thou 170
        believ'st

165 *by* near by. *wains* carts.

Thy name's recorded in the Book of Life,
I charge thee never after this sad day
To see me, or to meet me, or to send
By word, or writing, gift, or otherwise
To move me, by thyself or by thy friends,
Nor challenge any part in my two children.
So, farewell Nan, for we will henceforth be
As we had never seen, ne'er more shall see.

ANNE: How full my heart is in my eyes appears;
180   What wants in words, I will supply in tears.

FRANKFORD: Come take your coach, your stuff, all must
    along.
Servants and all make ready, all be gone.
It was thy hand cut two hearts out of one.

  [*Exeunt.*]

Act Five

SCENE ONE

Enter SIR CHARLES, *gentleman-like, and* [SUSAN] *his*
Sister, gentlewomanlike.

SUSAN: Brother, why have you trick'd me like a bride,
Bought me this gay attire, these ornaments?
Forget you our estate, our poverty?

SIR CHARLES: Call me not brother, but imagine me
Some barbarous outlaw, or uncivil kern;
For if thou shut'st thy eye and only hear'st
The words that I shall utter, thou shalt judge me
Some staring ruffian, not thy brother Charles.
Oh Susan!

SUSAN: Oh brother, what doth this strange language   10
    mean?

SIR CHARLES: Dost love me, sister? Wouldst thou see
    me live
A bankrupt beggar in the world's disgrace
And die indebted to my enemies?
Wouldst thou behold me stand like a huge beam
In the world's eye, a byword and a scorn?
It lies in thee of these to acquit me free,
And all my debt I may outstrip by thee.

SUSAN: By me? Why, I have nothing, nothing left.
I owe even for the clothes upon my back.
I am not worth –

SIR CHARLES: Oh sister, say not so.   20
It lies in you my downcast state to raise,

1 *trick'd* decked.   5 *uncivil kern* barbarous peasant.
8 *staring* wild.

To make me stand on even points with the world.
Come, sister, you are rich! Indeed you are.
And in your power you have, without delay,
Acton's five hundred pound back to repay.

SUSAN: Till now I had thought you lov'd me. By mine
    honour,
Which I had kept as spotless as the moon,
I ne'er was mistress of that single doit
Which I reserv'd not to supply your wants.

30   And do you think that I would hoard from you?
Now, by my hopes in Heaven, knew I the means
To buy you from the slavery of your debts,
Especially from Acton whom I hate,
I would redeem it with my life or blood.

SIR CHARLES: I challenge it, and kindred set apart
Thus Russian-like I lay siege to your heart.
What do I owe to Acton?

SUSAN: Why, some five hundred pounds, toward which
    I swear
In all the world I have not one denier.

40 SIR CHARLES: It will not prove so. Sister, now resolve
    me,
What do you think, and speak your conscience,
Would Acton give might he enjoy your bed?

SUSAN: He would not shrink to spend a thousand pound
To give the Mountford's name so deep a wound.

SIR CHARLES: A thousand pound! I but five hundred
    owe:
Grant him your bed, he's paid with interest so.

SUSAN: Oh brother!

SIR CHARLES: Oh sister, only this one way,

22 *on even points* on even terms.
28 *doit* i.e. half a farthing (actually, Dutch coin of little worth).
39 *denier* another low-value coin (French).
40 *resolve* inform.

With that rich jewel you my debts may pay.
In speaking this my cold heart shakes with shame,
Nor do I woo you in a brother's name   50
But in a stranger's. Shall I die in debt
To Acton my grand foe, and you still wear
The precious jewel that he holds so dear?

SUSAN: My honour I esteem as dear and precious
  As my redemption.

SIR CHARLES: I esteem you, sister,
  As dear for so dear prizing it.

SUSAN: Will Charles
  Have me cut off my hands, and send them Acton?
  Rip up my breast, and with my bleeding heart
  Present him as a token?

SIR CHARLES: Neither, sister;
  But hear me in my strange assertion: 60
  Thy honour and my soul are equal in my regard;
  Nor will thy brother Charles survive the shame.
  His kindness like a burden hath surcharged me
  And under his good deeds I stooping go,
  Not with an upright soul. Had I remain'd
  In prison still, there doubtless I had died;
  Then unto him that freed me from that prison
  Still do I owe that life. What mov'd my foe
  To enfranchise me? 'Twas, sister, for your love.
  With full five hundred pounds he bought your love,   70
  And shall he not enjoy it? Shall the weight
  Of all this heavy burden lean on me,
  And will not you bear part? You did partake
  The joy of my release; will you not stand
  In joint-bond bound to satisfy the debt?
  Shall I be only charg'd?

SUSAN: But that I know

69 *enfranchise* free.
75 *In . . . bound* bound with me jointly.

These arguments come from an honor'd mind,
As in your most extremity of need,
Scorning to stand in debt to one you hate,
80   Nay, rather would engage your unstain'd honour
Than to be held ingrate, I should condemn you.
I see your resolution, and assent;
So Charles will have me, and I am content.

SIR CHARLES: For this I trick'd you up.

SUSAN: But here's a knife,
To save mine honour, shall slice out my life.

SIR CHARLES: I know thou pleasest me a thousand
               times
More in that resolution than thy grant.
[*Aside*] Observe her love: to soothe them in my suit
Her honour she will hazard though not lose
90   To bring me out of debt, her rigorous hand
Will pierce her heart. Oh wonder, that will choose,
Rather than stain her blood, her life to lose. –
Come, you sad sister to a woeful brother,
This is the gate. I'll bear him such a present,
Such an acquittance for the knight to seal,
As will amaze his senses, and surprise
With admiration all his fantasies.

          Enter ACTON *and* MALBY.

SUSAN: Before his unchaste thoughts shall seize on me,
'Tis here shall my imprisoned soul set free.

100 SIR FRANCIS: How! Mountford with his sister hand in
               hand?
What miracle's afoot?

MALBY: It is a sight
Begets in me much admiration.

80 *engage* compromise.
95 *acquittance* document of release.
97 *admiration* wonder.   99 '*Tis here* i.e. the knife.

SIR CHARLES: Stand not amaz'd to see me thus attended.
　　Acton, I owe thee money, and being unable
　　To bring thee the full sum in ready coin,
　　Lo! for thy more assurance here's a pawn,
　　My sister, my dear sister, whose chaste honour
　　I prize above a million. Here – nay, take her,
　　She's worth your money, man; do not forsake her.
SIR FRANCIS: I would he were in earnest.   110
SUSAN: Impute it not to my immodesty.
　　My brother being rich in nothing else
　　But in his interest that he hath in me,
　　According to his poverty hath brought you
　　Me, all his store, whom howsoe'er you prize
　　As forfeit to your hand, he values highly,
　　And would not sell, but to acquit your debt,
　　For any Emperor's ransom.
SIR FRANCIS [aside]:   Stern heart, relent;
　　Thy former cruelty at length repent;
　　Was ever known in any former age   120
　　Such honourable wrested courtesy?
　　Lands, honours, lives, and all the world forgo,
　　Rather than stand engag'd to such a foe!
SIR CHARLES: Acton, she is too poor to be thy bride,
　　And I too much oppos'd to be thy brother.
　　There, take her to thee; if thou hast the heart
　　To seize her as a rape or lustful prey,
　　To blur our house that never yet was stain'd,
　　To murder her that never meant thee harm,
　　To kill me now whom once thou savedst from death, 130
　　Do them at once on her; all these rely
　　And perish with her spotted chastity.

106 *pawn* pledge.　　121 *wrested* achieved by struggle.
127 *lustful prey* prey to your lust.
131 *at once* at one stroke. *rely* depend on.

SIR FRANCIS: You overcome me in your love, Sir
        Charles.
    I cannot be so cruel to a lady
    I love so dearly. Since you have not spar'd
    To engage your reputation to the world,
    Your sister's honour which you prize so dear,
    Nay, all the comforts which you hold on earth,
    To grow out of my debt being your foe,
140   Your honoured thoughts, lo, thus I recompense:
    Your metamorphos'd foe receives your gift
    In satisfaction of all former wrongs.
    This jewel I will wear here in my heart,
    And where before I thought her for her wants
    Too base to be my bride, to end all strife
    I seal you my dear brother, her my wife.
SIR CHARLES: You still exceed us. I will yield to fate
    And learn to love where I till now did hate.
SUSAN: With that enchantment you have charm'd my
        soul,
150   And make me rich even in those very words.
    I pay no debt but am indebted more;
    Rich in your love, I never can be poor.
SIR FRANCIS: All's mine is yours; we are alike in state.
    Let's knit in love what was oppos'd in hate.
    Come, for our nuptials we will straight provide,
    Bless'd only in our brother and fair bride.
        [*Exeunt.*]

144 *wants* circumstances of want.
155 *straight* immediately.

SCENE TWO

Enter CRANWELL, FRANKFORD, *and* NICHOLAS.

CRANWELL: Why do you search each room about your
    house,
Now that you have dispatch'd your wife away?
FRANKFORD: Oh, sir, to see that nothing may be left
That ever was my wife's. I loved her dearly,
And when I do but think of her unkindness,
My thoughts are all in hell; to avoid which torment
I would not have a bodkin or a cuff,
A bracelet, necklace, or rebato wire,
Nor anything that ever was hers
Left me, by which I might remember her.   10
Seek round about!
NICHOLAS: 'Sblood, master, here's her lute flung in a
    corner.
FRANKFORD: Her lute! Oh God, upon this instrument
Her fingers have run quick division,
Sweeter than that which now divides our hearts.
These frets have made me pleasant, that have now
Frets of my heart-strings made. Oh master Cranwell,
Oft hath she made this melancholy wood,
Now mute and dumb for her disastrous chance,
Speak sweetly many a note, sound many a strain   20
To her own ravishing voice, which being well strung,
What pleasant strange airs have they jointly sung.

7 *bodkin* pin for fastening hair.
8 *rebato wire* see note to *A Yorkshire Tragedy*, i, 26–7.
14 *run quick division* executed a rapid melodic passage.
16 *frets* as at I, i, 81, with pun.   *pleasant* merry.
19 *for . . . chance* because of her misfortune.

Post with it after her. Now nothing's left;
Of her and hers I am at once bereft.

NICHOLAS: I'll ride and overtake her, do my message,
And come back again.   [*Exit.*]

CRANWELL: Meantime, sir, if you please,
I'll to Sir Francis Acton, and inform him
Of what hath pass'd betwixt you and his sister.

FRANKFORD: Do as you please. How ill am I bestead
30   To be a widower ere my wife be dead.
    [*Exeunt.*]

SCENE THREE

Enter ANNE, *with* JENKIN, *her maid* SISLY, *her*
COACHMAN, *and three* CARTERS.

ANNE: Bid my coach stay. Why should I ride in state
Being hurl'd so low down by the hand of fate?
A seat like to my fortunes let me have;
Earth for my chair, and for my bed a grave.

JENKIN: Comfort, good mistress, you have watered
your coach with tears already. You have but two mile
now to go to your manor. A man cannot say by my old
Master Frankford as he may say by me, that he wants
manners, for he hath three or four, of which this is one
10   that we are going to.

SISLY: Good mistress, be of good cheer. Sorrow you see
hurts you, but helps you not. We all mourn to see you
so sad.

CARTER: Mistress, I spy one of my landlord's men
Come riding post; 'tis like he brings some news.

ANNE: Comes he from Master Frankford he is welcome;

23 *Post* hurry.   9 *manners* obvious pun.

So are his news, because they come from him.
    Enter NICHOLAS.
NICHOLAS [*handing her the lute*]: There!
ANNE: I know the lute. Oft have I sung to thee.
We both are out of tune, both out of time.   20
NICHOLAS: Would that had been the worst instrument
that e'er you played on. My master commends him to ye.
There's all he can find that was ever yours. He hath
nothing left that ever you could lay claim to but his
own heart, and he could afford you that. All that I have
to deliver you is this: he prays you to forget him, and
so he bids you farewell.
ANNE: I thank him; he is kind and ever was.
All you that have true feeling of my grief,
That know my loss, and have relenting hearts,   30
Gird me about and help me with your tears,
To wash my spotted sins. My lute shall groan:
It cannot weep but shall lament my moan.
    Enter WENDOLL [*unobserved*].
WENDOLL: Pursued with horror of a guilty soul,
And with the sharp scourge of repentance lash'd,
I fly from my own shadow. Oh my stars,
What have my parents in their lives deserv'd
That you should lay this penance on their son?
When I but think of Master Frankford's love,
And lay it to my treason, or compare   40
My murd'ring him for his relieving me,
It strikes a terror like a lightning's flash
To scorch my blood up. Thus I, like the owl
Asham'd of day, live in these shadowy woods
Afraid of every leaf or murmuring blast,
Yet longing to receive some perfect knowledge

17 *news* a plural concept.
21 *instrument* sexual pun.
40 *lay* compare.   46 *perfect* correct.

How he hath dealt with her. [*Seeing* ANNE] Oh my sad
    fate,
Here, and so far from home, and thus attended.
Oh God, I have divorc'd the truest turtles

50   That ever liv'd together, and being divided
In several places, make their several moan;
She in the fields laments and he at home.
So poets write that Orpheus made the trees
And stones to dance to his melodious harp,
Meaning the rustic and the barbarous hinds
That had no understanding part in them;
So she from these rude carters tears extracts,
Making their flinty hearts with grief to rise,
And draw down rivers from their rocky eyes.

60 ANNE [*to* NICHOLAS]: If you return unto your master,
    say –
Though not from me, for I am all unworthy
To blast his name with a strumpet's tongue –
That you have seen me weep, wish myself dead.
Nay, you may say too, for my vow is pass'd,
Last night you saw me eat and drink my last.
This to your master you may say and swear,
For it is writ in Heaven and decreed here.

NICHOLAS: I'll say you wept, I'll swear you made me
    sad.

70   Why, how now, eyes? What now, what's here to do?
I am gone, or I shall straight turn baby too.

WENDOLL [*aside*]: I cannot weep, my heart is all on
    fire;
Curs'd be the fruits of my unchaste desire.

ANNE: Go break this lute upon my coach's wheel,

---

49 *turtles* turtle-doves.
51 *several* separate.   55 *hinds* rustics.
64 *pass'd* made.

As the last music that I e'er shall make,
Not as my husband's gift but my farewell
To all earth's joy; and so your master tell.

NICHOLAS: If I can for crying.

WENDOLL [*aside*]:   Grief have done,
Or like a madman I shall frantic run.

ANNE: You have beheld the woefullest wretch on earth,
A woman made of tears. Would you had words   80
To express but what you see. My inward grief
No tongue can utter, yet unto your power
You may describe my sorrow, and disclose
To thy sad master my abundant woes.

NICHOLAS: I'll do your commendations.

ANNE: Oh no,
I dare not so presume; nor to my children.
I am disclaim'd in both; alas, I am.
Oh, never teach them when they come to speak
To name the name of mother; chide their tongue
If they by chance light on that hated word;   90
Tell them tis naught. For when that word they name,
Poor pretty souls, they harp on their own shame.

WENDOLL [*aside*]: To recompense her wrongs what canst
          thou do?
Thou hast made her husbandless and childless too.

ANNE: I have no more to say. Speak not for me;
Yet you may tell your master what you see.

NICHOLAS: I'll do't.   *Exit.*

WENDOLL [*aside*]: I'll speak to her and comfort her in
          grief.
Oh, but her wound cannot be cur'd with words.
No matter, though, I'll do my best goodwill   100
To work a cure on her whom I did kill.

82 *unto your power* to the best of your ability.
85 *do your commendations* present your remembrances.
91 *naught* wicked. See note.

ANNE: So, now unto my coach, then to my home
  So to my deathbed, for from this sad hour
  I never will nor eat, nor drink, nor taste
  Of any cates that may preserve my life.
  I never will nor smile, nor sleep, nor rest;
  But when my tears have wash'd my black soul white,
  Sweet Saviour, to Thy hands I yield my sprite.
WENDOLL: Oh, Mistress Frankford –
ANNE: Oh, for God's sake fly!
110 The devil doth come to tempt me ere I die.
  My coach! This fiend that with an angel's face
  Courted mine honour till he sought my wrack
  In my repentant eyes seems ugly black.
      Exeunt all [except WENDOLL *and* JENKIN], *the*
      CARTERS *whistling.*
JENKIN: What, my young master that fled in his shirt?
  How come you by your clothes again? You have made
  our house in a sweet pickle, have you not, think you?
  What, shall I serve you still, or cleave to the old
  house?
WENDOLL: Hence slave, away with thy unseasoned
        mirth.
120 Unless thou canst shed tears, and sigh, and howl,
  Curse thy sad fortunes, and exclaim on fate,
  Thou art not for my turn.
JENKIN: Marry, and you will not another will. Farewell
  and be hanged! Would you had never come to have
  kept this coil within our doors. We shall ha' you run
  away like a sprite again.   [*Exit.*]
WENDOLL: She's gone to death, I live to want and woe.

---

105 *cates* food.   108 *sprite* spirit.
112 *wrack* ruin.
119 *unseasoned* unseasonable.
122 *for my turn* suitable for me.
125 *kept this coil* made this trouble.

Her life, her sins and all upon my head,
And I must now go wander like a Cain
In foreign countries and remoted climes, 130
Where the report of my ingratitude
Cannot be heard. I'll over, first, to France,
And so to Germany, and Italy,
Where when I have recovered, and by travel
Gotten those perfect tongues, and that these rumours
May in their height abate, I will return.
And I divine, how ever now dejected,
My worth and parts being by some great man prais'd,
At my return I may in court be rais'd. *Exit.*

SCENE FOUR

Enter SIR FRANCIS, SIR CHARLES, CRANWELL, MALBY *and* SUSAN.

SIR FRANCIS: Brother, and now my wife, I think these troubles
Fall on my head by justice of the Heavens,
For being so strict to you in your extremities,
But we are now aton'd. I would my sister
Could with like happiness o'ercome her griefs
As we have ours.

SUSAN: You tell us, Master Cranwell, wondrous things
Touching the patience of that gentleman,
With what strange virtue he demeans his grief.

CRANWELL: I told you what I was witness of; 10
It was my fortune to lodge there that night.

135 *Gotten those perfect tongues* learnt the languages perfectly.
4 *aton'd* reconciled.
9 *demeans his grief* bears himself in his grief.

SIR FRANCIS: Oh that same villain Wendoll, 'twas his
    tongue
  That did corrupt her. She was of herself
  Chaste and devoted well. Is this the house?

CRANWELL: Yes, sir, I take it here your sister lies.

SIR FRANCIS: My brother Frankford show'd too mild a
    spirit
  In the revenge of such a loathed crime;
  Less than he did no man of spirit could do.
  I am so far from blaming his revenge
20 That I commend it. Had it been my case
  Their souls at once had from their breasts been freed;
  Death to such deeds of shame is the due meed.
    Enter JENKIN *and* SISLY.

JENKIN: Oh my mistress, my mistress, my poor mistress!

SISLY: Alas that ever I was born! What shall I do for my
    poor mistress?

SIR CHARLES: Why, what of her?

JENKIN: O Lord, sir, she no sooner heard that her
  brother and his friends were come to see how she did,
  but she for very shame of her guilty conscience, fell
30 into a swoon, and we had much ado to get life into her.

SUSAN: Alas, that she should bear so hard a fate;
  Pity it is repentance comes so late.

SIR FRANCIS: Is she so weak in body?

JENKIN: Oh, sir, I can assure you there's no help of life
  in her, for she will take no sustenance. She hath plainly
  starved herself, that now she is as lean as a lath. She ever
  looks for the good hour. Many gentlemen and gentlewomen of the country are come to comfort her.
    Enter ANNE *in her bed.*

MALBY: How fare you, Mistress Frankford?

40 ANNE: Sick, sick, oh sick! Give me some air, I pray you.

14 *devoted well* faithful.   15 *lies* lives.
37 *the good hour* i.e. of death.

Tell me, oh tell me, where's Master Frankford?
Will he not deign to see me ere I die?
MALBY: Yes, Mistress Frankford. Divers gentlemen,
  Your loving neighbours, with that just request
  Have mov'd and told him of your weak estate,
  Who, though with much ado to get belief,
  Examining of the general circumstance,
  Seeing your sorrow and your penitence
  And hearing therewithal the great desire
  You have to see him ere you left the world,   50
  He gave to us his faith to follow us,
  And sure he will be here immediately.
ANNE: You half reviv'd me with those pleasing news.
  Raise me a little higher in my bed.
  Blush I not, brother Acton, blush I not Sir Charles?
  Can you not read my fault writ in my cheek?
  Is not my crime there? Tell me, gentlemen.
SIR CHARLES: Alas, good mistress, sickness hath not left
        you
  Blood in your face enough to make you blush.
ANNE: Then sickness like a friend my fault would hide.   60
  Is my husband come? My soul but tarries
  His arrive and I am fit for Heaven.
SIR FRANCIS: I came to chide you, but my words of
        hate
  Are turn'd to pity and compassionate grief.
  I came to rate you, but my brawls, you see,
  Melt into tears, and I must weep by thee.
      Enter FRANKFORD.
  Here's Master Frankford now.
FRANKFORD: Good morrow, brother, good morrow,
        gentlemen.
  God that hath laid this cross upon our heads

45 *mov'd* informed.   51 *faith* promise.
65 *rate* reproach. *brawls* chidings.

70 Might, had He pleas'd, have made our cause of meeting
On a more fair and a more contented ground;
But He that made us made us to this woe.

ANNE: And is he come? Methinks that voice I know.

FRANKFORD: How do you, woman?

ANNE: Well, Master Frankford, well, but shall be better
I hope within this hour. Will you vouchsafe,
Out of your grace and your humanity,
To take a spotted strumpet by the hand?

FRANKFORD: That hand that once held my heart in
faster bonds
80 Than now 'tis gripp'd by me. God pardon them
That made us first break hold.

ANNE: Amen, amen.
Out of my zeal to Heaven wither I am now bound,
I was so impudent to wish you here,
And once more beg your pardon. Oh good man,
And father to my children, pardon me.
Pardon, oh pardon me! My fault so heinous is,
That if you in this world forgive it not,
Heaven will not clear it in the world to come.
Faintness hath so usurp'd upon my knees,
90 That kneel I cannot; but on my heart's knees
My prostrate soul lies thrown down at your feet
To beg your gracious pardon. Pardon, oh pardon me!

FRANKFORD: As freely from the low depth of my soul
As my Redeemer hath forgiven His death,
I pardon thee. I will shed tears for thee,
Pray with thee, and in mere pity
Of thy weak state, I'll wish to die with thee.

ALL: So do we all.

NICHOLAS [aside]: So will not I;
I'll sigh and sob, but, by my faith, not die.

100 SIR FRANCIS: Oh Master Frankford, all the near alliance

100 *alliance* kinship.

I lose by her shall be supplied in thee;
You are my brother by the nearest way;
Her kindred hath fallen off but yours doth stay.

FRANKFORD: Even as I hope for pardon at that day,
When the great Judge of Heaven in scarlet sits,
So be thou pardoned; though thy rash offence
Divorc'd our bodies, thy repentant tears
Unite our souls.

SIR CHARLES: Then comfort, Mistress Frankford;
You see your husband hath forgiven your fall;
Then rouse your spirits and cheer your fainting soul.   110

SUSAN: How is it with you?

SIR FRANCIS: How do you feel yourself?

ANNE: Not of this world.

FRANKFORD: I see you are not and I weep to see it.
My wife, the mother to my pretty babes,
Both those lost names I do restore thee back,
And with this kiss I wed thee once again.
Though thou art wounded in thy honor'd name,
And with that grief upon thy deathbed liest,
Honest in heart, upon my soul, thou diest.

ANNE: Pardon'd on earth, soul, thou in Heaven art free.   120
Once more thy wife, dies thus embracing thee.

FRANKFORD: New married and new widowed! Oh, she's
          dead,
And a cold grave must be our nuptial bed.

SIR CHARLES: Sir, be of good comfort, and your heavy
          sorrow
Part equally amongst us; storms divided
Abate their force, and with less rage are guided.

CRANWELL: Do, Master Frankford. He that hath the
          least part
Will find enough to drown one troubled heart.

119 *Honest* chaste.
121 *thy wife, dies* i.e. thy wife, I die.

SIR FRANCIS: Peace with thee, Nan. Brothers and
    gentlemen,
130   All we that can plead interest in her grief,
    Bestow upon her body funeral tears.
    Brother, had you with threats and usage bad
    Punish'd her sin, the grief of her offence
    Had not with such true sorrow touch'd her heart.
FRANKFORD: I see it had not. Therefore, on her grave,
    I will bestow this funeral epitaph,
    Which on her marble tomb shall be engrav'd;
    In golden letters shall these words be fil'd:
    'Here lies she whom her husband's kindness kill'd'.

138 *fil'd* arranged in order. See note.

FINIS

The Epilogue

An honest crew, disposed to be merry,
Came to a tavern by and call'd for wine.
The drawer brought it, smiling like a cherry,
And told them it was pleasant, neat, and fine.
  'Taste it,' quoth one. He did so. 'Fie!' quoth he,
  'This wine was good; now 't runs too near the lee.'

Another sipp'd, to give the wine his due,
And said unto the rest it drunk too flat.
The third said it was old, the fourth too new,
'Nay,' quoth the fifth, 'the sharpness likes me not.'
  Thus gentlemen, you see how in one hour
  The wine was new, old, flat, sharp, sweet, and sour.

Unto this wine we do allude our play,
Which some will judge too trivial, some too grave.
You as our guests we entertain this day,
And bid you welcome to the best we have.
  Excuse us, then; good wine may be disgrac'd
  When every several mouth hath sundry taste.

2 *by* nearby.   4 *neat* pure.
6 *lee* lees, sediment.   13 *allude* compare.

Additional Notes

The references are to line numbers.

S.D. = Stage direction. S.P. = Speech prefix.
Q1, Q2, etc. = First, second quarto. Qq = Quartos.

ARDEN OF FAVERSHAM

SCENE ONE

2, 7, 34. *Duke of Somerset, the king, the Lord Protector*: In 1551, the year of the murder, the king was Edward VI, a minor, for whom the Duke of Somerset acted as Lord Protector.

60. *Ovid-like*: Ovid, the first-century Roman love-poet and author of the favourite Elizabethan book, *Metamorphoses*, was widely known and translated in the Tudor period. It has been suggested that the Ovidian lines which follow smack strongly of Marlowe.

116. *raving Hercules*: Hercules' wife, Deianira, gave him a shirt to wear which, unknown to her, was poisoned by the blood of the centaur, Nessus, whom Hercules had killed. Hercules suffered great pain before bringing about his own death.

135. *narrow-prying*: Q2, 3. Q1 reads 'marrow prying'.

159. *she*: omitted in Qq.

166-7. *Susan . . . sheriff*: It was a popular belief that a virgin could save a criminal from the gallows if she offered him marriage.

173. *Bolton*: Assumed to be Boughton under Blean, between Canterbury and Faversham. Tucker Brooke points out that Boughton is mentioned by Chaucer at the beginning of the *Canon's Yeoman's Prologue*. See Map, Appendix A.

213, 14. *mermaid, basilisk*: Two types of mythical danger for the unwary traveller. The mermaid was equated with the siren of classical mythology who lured sailors to destruction with its song; the basilisk was a fabulous serpent whose very look was death.

231. A contemporary theory of sight held that the eye sent forth beams to the object sighted. Cf. ll. 609–12.

291. *Master ... yourself*: This is for Arden's ears, and Mosby responds skilfully to Alice's cue.

353. *By ... sir*: Qq read 'By faith my sir'.

382. *Mithridate*: So called from Mithridates VI, King of Pontus, who is said to have taken poison in ever-increasing doses to immunize himself.

468. *Chancery seal*: The Court of Chancery supplemented the Common Law in civil matters and was the highest court of judicature next to the House of Lords.

617–20. *Though ... it*: Clarke's scruples and his question are blatantly inconsistent with what has passed earlier in the scene. Perhaps the business of the crucifix, independent of the source, is a late addition.

SCENE TWO

105. *Aldersgate Street*: A street running south from Aldersgate to Cheapside.

SCENE THREE

7. *Paul's*: The nave and portico of St Paul's Cathedral formed an accepted meeting-place for businessmen and merchants in the city. The central aisle was commonly known as 'Paul's Walk' and 'Duke Humphrey's Walk'.

28. *Nor*: Jacob (noted in Tucker Brooke). Qq read 'New'.

49–62. The apprentice is in charge of a book-stall. St Paul's churchyard was the centre of the book trade, the vaults of the cathedral being used as storeplaces for the booksellers' stocks. The stationers or booksellers who had larger shops elsewhere had stalls in the churchyard placed against the walls of the cathedral.

140. S.P. *Michael*: Q2, 3. Q1 gives the line to Greene.

SCENE FOUR

5. *couch*: Q3. Q1, 2 read 'cooch', explained by Tucker Brooke as 'cause to germinate'. In *OED*, 'couch' (4¹, 4, b) is glossed 'To embroider with gold thread or the like laid flat on the

surface'. The second example, in *OED*, uses 'couch' metaphorically, as here.

13. *Hydra's head*: The Hydra was a many-headed, mythical monster. As each head was cut off two more grew in its place. The killing of the Hydra was the second labour of Hercules.

13. *flourish'd*: Tucker Brooke. Qq's reading, 'perisht', makes no sense at all.

41. *pity-moving*: Q2, 3. Q1 reads 'pitty moning'.

73. *bolter'd*: All editions read 'bolster'd'. See 'balter', *OED*, v, 3, 'To tangle, "mat" (the hair)'; and compare 'blood-bolter'd' of *Macbeth*, IV, i.

76. *thee*: Q3. Q1, 2 read 'there'.

SCENE FIVE

4. *Obscures*: Q3. Q1, 2 read 'Obscure'.

57. *'Twould . . . boys*: All editions. The line seems feeble and I am tempted to read 'pedant' (= schoolteacher) for 'peasant' (Qq read 'pesant').

SCENE SIX

1. *Billingsgate*: Not just a fishmarket but an important wharf and landing-place on the north side of the Thames.

SCENE SEVEN

31. *except*: This is ambiguous. Baskervill explains the whole line: 'Excuse me from accompanying you'; McIlwraith suggests the opposite by glossing 'except' as 'accept'. *OED* records 'except' as an error for 'accept' (1635). From the context Baskervill's reading appears the likelier. The timorous Michael is hardly likely to choose to accompany the would-be murderers.

SCENE EIGHT

17. *Each . . . gale*: Reading proposed by P. A. McElwaine, *Notes and Queries*, 11th series, II, 1910, p. 226. Qq read 'Each gentle stary gaile'.

51. *pathaires*: The authenticity of the word is now accepted. P. Simpson, *Modern Language Review*, i, 1906, pp. 326–7, cites another usage of it (in W. Smith's *The Hector of Germany*).

133. *A ... troubled*: The reading is supplied by W. Headlam, *The Athenaeum*, 26 December 1903. Qq read 'A fence of trouble'. Headlam explains that the text arose from writing or printing 'A fonce troubled' instead of 'A fon[t on]ce troubled'.

145. *is*: Not in Qq.

157–9. *We ... Greene*: The letter must be the one entrusted to Bradshaw by Greene in scene ii, but the failure to kill Arden in London, of course, occurs after this. This is an error by the playwright; but the letter is mentioned in Holinshed and functions importantly in the last scene of the play.

166. S.P. *Mosby*: Q3. Q1, 2 give this splendidly proleptic line to Alice.

SCENE NINE

30. *Aesop's talk*: One of the collection of fables attributed to the semi-legendary Greek of the sixth century B.C. There is a similar reference at viii, 34–5.

34. *deceives*: Qq read 'deceive'.

40. *Lime ... bird*: Birdlime, a sticky substance, was spread on twigs to catch birds.

144. *The ... Heaven*: All editions read 'Preserved'. Suggestion for the emendation by M. P. Jackson.

SCENE TEN

3. *discern*: Tucker Brooke. Qq read 'deserue'.

17. *desires*: Tucker Brooke. Qq read 'deserues'.

99. *cement*: Q3. Q1, 2 read 'semell'.

SCENE ELEVEN

24–5. *midsummer moon*: A time associated with lunacy.

32. *bramble-bush*: By tradition the Man in the Moon had a lantern, a dog, and a bush of thorn. See *A Midsummer Night's Dream*, V, i. ll. 24–30 carry a bawdy joke.

SCENE THIRTEEN

90. *thee*: Baskervill. Qq read 'thy'.

96. *And*: Qq Perhaps this should read 'Ah'.

SCENE FOURTEEN

29. A red- or green-painted lattice was the sign of an alehouse.

68. *I'll stand to it*: Qq's punctuation allows an ambiguity. If the phrase is taken with the previous clause, as here, it means 'I'll fight resolutely', 'I'll maintain my position'; if with the next sentence, 'I maintain that . . .'

127. *seive*: Q3 ('sive'); Q1, 2 read 'sine'. 'Seine', a fishing-net, is marginally possible.

149. *black Tisiphone*: One of the Furies, the avenging deities who tortured the guilty with the stings of conscience; represented as having snakes about her arms and in her hair.

154–6. *Had . . . up*: Diana, the moon-goddess, fell in love with Endymion, a mortal.

178. *Greene*: One would expect 'Shakebag', not 'Greene', at this point. Greene is not a 'cutter', and it was Shakebag, not Greene, involved with Mosby and Black Will in the scuffle of scene xiii. However, 'Greene' better suits the rhythm of the line.

241. *There's . . . of*: See i, 313. In Holinshed, Mosby actually uses a pressing-iron in his attack and perhaps he is intended to do the same in the play. There is no S.D. in Q1 at this point. The 'weapon' of l. 243 is presumably Shakebag's.

SCENE FIFTEEN

The insertion of this scene and scene xvii in the continuous narrative of Mosby's apprehension and Alice's repentance involves at this point a double time-scheme. In the theatre, the effect is barely noticeable, and the licence allows the playwright to tie up the loose ends without creating anti-climax.

SCENE SIXTEEN

4. *The . . . bleeds*: It was a common superstition that a murdered corpse bled when confronted with the murderer.

17. *I . . . both*: It was in fact Greene who hired the murderers (scene ii). Greene is only briefly mentioned in the Epilogue, and his fade-out from the play is one of the few unsatisfactory elements in the dramatization of the Holinshed material.

Mosby's assumption of extra guilt, here, is either an error of the playwright or a device by the playwright to cover Greene's absence. It is hardly likely to be a generous gesture on Mosby's part.

A YORKSHIRE TRAGEDY

SCENE ONE

For the relation of this scene to the rest of the play, see Introduction, pp. 34–5.

13. *Neither . . . says*: 'This is designed as a ridicule on the circumstantiality of expression by the *saints* of Shakespeare's age.' Steevens (in Malone's edition).

16. *And . . . elbow*: In anticipation of a drinking session.

26–7. *rebato wires*: The rebato was a stiff collar, fashionable among both sexes *c.* 1590–1630. The wires were used as supports.

29. *codpiece*: An appendage, sometimes conspicuous and ornamental, to the front of the close-fitting hose or breeches, worn by men from the fifteenth to the seventeenth century. Often with sexual connotations.

29–30. *any . . . blows*: Allusion to the proverb that 'A woman and a walnut-tree bear the better for being thrashed'.

31–3. *Thou . . . dies*: Oliver's statement appears to imply that Sam could set up in business. If so, 'common servingman', l. 29–30, ought to mean a pedlar, but I know of no parallel use of 'servingman'. The 'tricks' Sam has brought, together with the poting-sticks of l. 62 ff., were the traditional wares of a pedlar (compare those of Autolycus in *The Winter's Tale*).

59. *Moll and Doll*: Evidently common names for prostitutes.

62–3. *poting-sticks*: A poting-stick (or poking-stick or putting-stick) was a metal rod which was heated and used to stiffen the starched ruff. Made of iron, steel, brass and even silver, poting-sticks were often of great value. Probably the references here have a ribald connotation.

69–70. *far-fetched . . . ladies*: A proverbial expression, usually in the extended form of 'far-fetched and dear bought is good for ladies'.

71. *Ay ... too*: The companion-play, *The Miseries of Enforced Marriage*, appears to contain an expansion of this joke. A character, queried about the sort of woman he is to marry, replies: 'No lady, no widow, nor no waiting gentlewoman, for under protection –

> Ladies may lard their husband's heads,
> Widows will woodcocks make,
> And chambermaids of servingmen
> Learn that they'll ne'er forsake.'

73. S.P. *Ralph*: Q2. Q1 reads *Oli*. Ralph, who has not spoken for some time, has been directly addressed by Sam.

78–9. *they ... knees*: This is an allusion to a favourite tavern game involving the 'knighting' of boon companions.

SCENE TWO

16. *Heaven, looks*: Q2. Q1 omits the comma, but the parallel passage in *Two Unnatural Murders* (see p. 305) makes it clear that Q2 is correct.

33–4. *cause ... property*: Either 'effect', 'quality' and 'property' are synonymous with 'cause'; or the four words form two pairs of opposites – 'cause' and 'effect'; and 'quality' (= nature) and 'property' (= attribute).

100. *A true trouble:* Different copies of Q1 read 'A true troubled' and 'trouble trouble', the latter being the reading of all subsequent editions. The corrector of Q1 who produced 'trouble trouble' was evidently over-zealous.

170. *On your posterity*: Q1 reads 'On her your posterity'; Q2 and all subsequent editions read 'On her and your posterity'.

172–3. *left ... left*:The repetition of 'left' appears to be too feeble to be correct. The second 'left' has been variously emended to 'gor'd', 'ript', and 'cleft'. 'Reft' (*OED*, Reave, v.²2) is also possible, and 'cleft' appears again at iv, 31. But there is no clear guidance for the emender.

SCENE THREE

17. *defects*: All editions read 'deserts'. The two words were very similar in Elizabethan hand.

18. *unshaped bear*: It was a common belief that the mother-bear literally licked her new-born cubs into shape. The image is clearly related to 'smoothed' of two lines earlier.

52. *estate*: All editions read 'state'. 'Estate' makes a marginally better rhythm and is in the corresponding passage of *Two Unnatural Murders* (see p. 309). Compare the Wife's repetition of the word at l. 60.

SCENE FOUR

4 ff. *Tis not my fashion . . .*: Despite the Master's disclaimer, there is an attempt here and elsewhere in the scene to reproduce the prolix and ponderous speech evidently expected of a university teacher.

83. *Will . . . them*: 'Alluding to the effects of some kind of poison' (Steevens in Malone's edition).

86. *to deliver*: All editions read 'for to live' except Simmes (*Supplement to the plays of W. Shakespeare*, 1848) who has 'to relieve'. 'Deliver' is in the parallel passage of *Two Unnatural Murders* (see p. 311).

87–8. *Divines . . . dwell*: The couplet comes from Nashe's *Pierce Penniless: His Supplication to the Devil* (1592). It appears also in Nicholson's *Acolastus his Afterwit* (1600) and Marston's *Insatiate Countess* (1613).

103–4. *or . . . couch*: The sense is – Follow the obsequious form of address ('Good your Honour') by a low bow. Q2's substitution of 'coach' for 'couch' obscured the sense for all subsequent editions.

SCENE FIVE

S.D. *Enter . . . asleep*: For the staging of this see *A Note on Staging*, pp. 50–51.

13–14. *So . . . it*: The politician is assumed to be Robert Dudley, Earl of Leicester, favourite of Queen Elizabeth. His wife, Amy Robsart, fell downstairs at her house at Cumnor and broke

her neck, and it was rumoured that Leicester was respon-
sible.

61. *Till . . . wrong*: The sense is obvious though the construction
is not. Qq's spelling is retained here, and 'hell's' = 'hell has'.
Malone reads 'Till now Hell power supplied . . .'

70. S.P. *First Servant*: Qq (1. *Seru.*). This distinguishes the
injured servant from those who enter after l. 62. It is not clear
which servant speaks l. 63, but l. 69 suggests that it is probably a newly entered one.

96–7. *Murder . . . stands*: Legend bears out the Wife's prophecy.
Ghost-stories became connected with the Calverley family and
house, retold by Steevens in Malone's edition and at greater
length by J. H. Ingram, *The Haunted Homes and Family Legends
of Great Britain*, 2nd ed., 1886, pp. 394–400.

SCENE SIX

S.D. *Enter . . . falls*: See 'A Note on Staging', p. 50.

15 *My . . . bated*: For 'bated' Steevens (Malone's edition) con-
jectured 'barred' and Simmes 'baited' (i.e. 'tormented'). The
sense of the line is that the Husband's intention to kill his third
child has been thwarted by circumstances. We retain the sense
of 'bate' as to 'hem in' or 'pent up' in 'to bate one's breath'.

19. *e'en the*: Qq read 'in their', Malone 'even the'.

24–5. *Why . . . flaying*: Proverbial: 'You can have no more of a
cat than her skin'.

SCENE SEVEN

2. S.P. *Fourth Gentleman*: Qq (4. *Gen.*). So designated because
of the three Gentlemen of the previous scene. He may be the
single Gentleman of scene ii. Similarly, the three Gentlemen
of scene vi may be those of scene ii.

22. *When . . . you*: Either 'When you are reminded of the dread
thought of death' or 'When the proximity of death reminds
you [of what you have done]'. *Two Unnatural Murders* (see
p. 315) shows the latter to be correct.

33. *That . . . shame*: Presumably means 'That man is most shameful who has lost all sense of shame'. Malone suggested that
the first 'shame' should be 'sin'.

SCENE EIGHT

21–2. *Bind . . . bottomless*: The allusion is to Revalation, xx, verses
1–3: 'And I saw an angel come down from heaven, having the
key of the bottomless pit and a great chain in his hand. / And
he laid hold on the dragon, the serpent, which is the Devil,
and Satan, and bound him a thousand years. / And cast him
into the bottomless pit, and shut him up, and set a seal upon
him, that he should deceive the nations no more, till the thousand years should be fulfilled: and after that he must be loosed
a little season.'

50. *And . . . this*: Malone. Qq. read 'And leave part with this'.
The emendation is not satisfactory but none better has been
proposed.

S.P. *Officer*: Q2. Q1 gives 'Come will you go?' to the Wife.

A WOMAN KILLED WITH KINDNESS

THE PROLOGUE

13–14. *But . . . spoil*: The playwright asks for mercy for his play.
The 'gentle thoughts' are those of the audience.

ACT ONE

SCENE ONE

30. *beauties*: Dodsley (cited by Van Fossen). Qq read 'beauty'.
65. *adorn*: Q2. Q1 reads 'adore'.

SCENE TWO

1–3. *Miniver, Trubkin, Motley*: The surnames mean respectively –
a kind of fur used as a trimming in a ceremonial costume; a
small, squat woman; a cloth of mixed colour (especially as
worn by a professional fool).

26. *Slime*: Q1. Printed as S.P. by Q2.

After 59. S.D. NICHOLAS . . . *fashion*: I take this to mean –
'Nicholas in his dancing assumes a dignified aloofness [in char-

acter with his mood throughout the scene]; the rest dance after the country fashion [less inhibitedly, as described at I, i, 80–91]. *OED* gives no example of 'speak' in exactly this construction, but see IV, 29, and 'bespeak', 7. Oliphant emended 'speaks' to 'moves'. Van Fossen explains the S.D. thus: 'The actors speak ad. lib. during the dancing, Jenkin's final line only being established to serve as a cue.' This line obviously does serve as a cue, but it is rather late in the scene to indicate how the characters speak.

SCENE THREE

S.D. *Enter . . . Huntsmen*: All editions, including Qq, include Malby in the entry, but he never speaks in the scene, he is not mentioned in the S.D. after l. 41, when the characters take sides in the quarrel, and in the first scene of the play he takes no part in the wagering.

1–27. The presentation of the hawking match rests heavily, for its technical language, on a famous treatise on hunting, hawking and heraldry called *The Book of St Albans*. The situation of the scene is described by Bates: 'Apparently the scene opens in the midst of the trial, when the hawk of Sir Francis has been flown, and the falconer of Sir Charles has just cast off the rival bird. Sir Francis' merlin had struck the quarry, which escaped to the river. Thence it was driven out into the fields by its pursuer, until finally the merlin, hiding in the stubble, caught it on the ground and killed it there.'

8. *Rebeck . . . her*: Bates emends 'Rebeck' to 'Rebuke' and 'check' to 'cherk', translating the line: 'Don't startle her. Stand still a minute if she seems likely to take flight and re-assure her by chirping to her.'

13. *at the ferre*: The Book of St Albans states: 'If yowre hawk nym the fowle at the fer side of the Ryver . . . from you then she sleeth the fowle at the fer Jutty and if she slee it upon that side that ye ben on . . . ye shall say she hath sleen the fowle at the Jutty ferry' (cited in *OED*). 'At the ferre' evidently means 'at the nearer side'.

16–19. *Her . . . hawk*: Hawks' bells were supposed to be of equal weight and a semitone apart in pitch. Their function was to frighten the prey and help the huntsman to trace the birds. Milan bells were made of silver and were regarded as the best quality. The lines appear to be mis-assigned. Wendoll has replied to Cranwell's criticism of l. 13, but as the text stands he then goes on to criticize Sir Francis's bird which is the one he has wagered on and is supporting. Notice how 'our merlin' (l. 14) changes to 'your hawk' (l. 19). Probably Cranwell speaks ll. 16–19.

27. S.P. *Sir Charles*: All editions make this the last line of Sir Francis's previous speech. Q2, followed by all later editions, emends S.P. *Sir Francis* of l.27. to *Sir Charles*, making further reorganization necessary so that ll. 39–40 can be assigned to their rightful owners. Obviously, at l. 22 Sir Charles briefly refutes all Sir Francis's claims for his hawk in ll. 20–26.

After 41. S.D. *killing . . . men*: Q2. Q1 reads 'killing one of Sir Francis his huntsmen', but Heywood evidently had second thoughts as l. 105 of this scene and II, i, 48–9 indicate.

After 56. S.D. *Susan*: Q2. Throughout the scene and once again in V, i, Susan is called 'Jane' in Q1, evidence of another second thought by Heywood.

62. *May*: Oliphant (cited by Van Fossen). Qq read 'My'. Heywood frequently omitted vowels before 'y'.

92. *Nor*: Dodsley (cited by Van Fossen). Qq read 'No'.

ACT TWO

SCENE ONE

43. S.P. *Wendoll*: Baskervill. Qq read *'Anne'*, unlikely because Anne as the dutiful wife would not interrupt like this, the circumstantial detail suggests considerable knowledge of the incident, and 'your brother' (l. 48) would come sooner from Wendoll than from Sir Francis's sister.

74. *But . . . remembrance*: Ambiguous, meaning either 'But when I forget your latest favour to me' or 'But when I lose my last memory of you'. Probably the former.

SCENE THREE

138. *live*: Q1. Q2 gives 'love', a possible reading.

139. *passion*: Van Fossen glosses 'anger (not amorousness)', but

in this context, when Wendoll's suit is already half-successful, the meaning is closer to 'compassion'. Pity was the reward requested by the courtly lover; in pity lay the seeds of acceptance.

ACT THREE

SCENE ONE

36. *names*: Pearson. Qq read 'meanes'.

40. *gall'd*: Q1 reads 'gloud', Q2 and subsequent editions read 'glow'd'. Van Fossen interprets 'Labour hath glow'd within' as 'has been made red by labour'. But Q1 evidently intended the word 'gloved', the compositor being influenced by 'palm' and the succeeding reference to 'mask' for Susan's brow. 'Glow'd' I believe to be Q2's interpretation of Q1's misreading of 'gald'. Heywood's own *Pleasant Dialogues and Dramas* supplies a parallel situation with a similar use of 'galled': Dialogue Four includes the vision of the labouring Timon (a sort of Mountford) surrounded by personifications: 'Poverty by him fast stands, / And the rough fellow Labour, with galled hands.'

42. *mask*: Masks, made of velvet or silk, were a common item of outdoor dress for women. The context supplies their purpose.

90. *Oh*: Van Fossen. Qq read 'Or'.

SCENE TWO

44. *I . . . wife*: Presumably, 'I love you better than your wife loves you'.

66. *Dives*: Allusion to the parable of Dives and Lazarus, Luke, xvi.

108. *lose*: Dodsley (cited by Van Fossen). Qq read 'loose' (twice elsewhere in the play the spelling for 'lose'). Van Fossen retains 'loose' and glosses it 'let loose, rid myself of'.

124 ff.: The card game presents the ambiguity of the relationships of the main characters by means of a series of puns. See Introduction, p. 45. It is not always clear which comments are '*asides*'.

SCENE THREE

51. *And prays you* –: Qq read 'And prays you &c.' Van Fossen interprets '&c.' as 'indicating whispering', but more probably Malby is simply interrupted at this point. Compare V, i, 19, where Qq again read '&c.' and here the interruption is certain.

ACT FOUR

SCENE ONE

S.D. *feet*: Q2. Q1 reads 'face', presumably picked up from l. 1.

1. *Oh, fall*: All editions read 'Of all'. The emendation produces a gain in clarity at the same time as it creates a typical visual accompaniment to Mountford's formal lament. Compare l. 4.

4. *What*: Verity (cited by Van Fossen). Qq read 'That'.

35. *breath'd*: Pearson. Qq read 'breath'. Van Fossen glosses 'scandal breath' as 'scandalous talk', but Mountford is remembering his lament in which (l. 2) he had used 'breathe' as a verb and then gone on to castigate his kinsmen.

77. *they*: Neilson. Qq read 'in'.

112. *expectation*: Dodsley (cited by Van Fossen). Qq read 'execution'.

SCENE TWO

5. *And . . . sir*: Q2. Two lines in Q1, the second ('The letter sir') prefixed by a second *Nick*. Something may be lost here in view of the second S.P., the corrected lines' irregularity, the brusqueness of the second sentence, and the fact that the second sentence makes a pentameter with Frankford's following half-line.

23–7. *Methinks . . want*: Mountford was released in the previous scene, IV, i, which I suspect was originally intended to come between IV, ii, and IV, iv.

36. *And . . . well*: Neilson, followed by Van Fossen, makes this an aside. But if we take 'too' to be an intensive (= 'very'), Frankford's half-line, though full of hidden menace, would be fit hearing for Wendoll.

92. *wise*: Qq read 'wife' followed by a full-stop. Van Fossen retains 'wife' and indicates that the speech is interrupted: 'And Master Frankford's wife –.' I assume that Anne makes a simple contrast between Wendoll's lack of discretion and Frankford's good sense. Q1's reading of 'wife' for 'wise' is an easy error.

SCENE FOUR

1–129. For the staging of Frankford's secret entry into his own house G. F. Reynolds (in *Staging of Elizabethan Plays at the Red Bull Theatre*) has suggested a complicated series of exits and entrances to enact the negotiation of the various doors. But it is as likely that till l. 128 Frankford only leaves the stage at ll. 33 and 64. Passage through the doors is represented symbolically by mention of the keys, ll. 8–16.

66–7. *like . . . sacrifice*: Allusion to the sacrifice of Isaac, *Genesis*, xxii.

74–5. *A Judas . . . elder tree*: See Matthew, xxvii, 5. It was a tradition that Judas hanged himself on an elder tree.

94. *a shame*: Van Fossen. Qq read 'ashamd'.

114. *my infants*: The detail of the children is the only one which indicates that the main plot occupies several years. The apparent foreshortening is a typical effect of Elizabethan drama.

134. *strappado'd*: The strappado was a form of torture in which the victim's hands were tied across his back and secured to a pulley. The victim was then hoisted from the ground and allowed to fall half way back with a jerk.

139–42. *Oh . . . lie*: This is addressed to the audience. Anne steps out of the play to point up the moral message.

ACT FIVE

SCENE ONE

14. *Wouldst . . . eye*: Allusion to a passage in the Sermon on the Mount, Matthew, vii, 3: 'And why seest thou the mote in thy brother's eye, and perceivest not the beam that is in thine own eye?'

36. *Russian-like*: Q1. Q2 and all subsequent editions read 'ruffian-
   like'. Q1's reading does not seem to have been noticed, and it
   may be a misprint; but Russians were synonymous with
   uncivil roughness. Earlier, at l. 8, Q1 spells 'ruffian' 'ruffin'.

88. *to . . . suit*: Q1. Q2 reads 'to soothe it to my suit', accepted
   by Van Fossen and glossed 'to make her honour comply with
   my suit'. Q1 may mean 'to soothe those people [like Acton]
   involved in my legal struggle', but perhaps more radical
   emendation is needed. Possibly the line should read: 'Observe
   her love too sooth when in my suit . . .' = 'Observe her very
   genuine love when at my request . . .'

147, 9. S.P.s. SIR CHARLES, SUSAN: In all editions these S.P.s are
   in reverse order, but Mountford has been addressed in the
   speech previous to l. 147 and the reference to fate in l. 147 suits
   his character. Furthermore, the magical arrival of romantic love
   between the sexes has twice already in the play been expressed
   through the idea of charm and enchantment in l. 149 (II, iii,
   159–60, and III, i, 92). Susan's two-line response to Acton
   (i.e. ll. 147–8) is rather lame while ll. 149–52, though not
   fulsome, are at least more positive. Acton's first two lines of
   reply, ll. 153–4, are surely addressed to his future wife.

SCENE THREE

53–6. The allegorization of the Orpheus myth was a common
   one. A famous example occurs in Sidney's *Defence of Poesy*:
   'Orpheus [was said] to be listened to by beasts – indeed stony
   and beastly people – . . .'

59. *down*: Q2. Omitted by Q1.

91. *naught*: Qq read 'nought' and the two words were often
   confused. 'Naught' meaning 'wicked' seems preferable to
   'nought' meaning 'nothing'.

111. *fiend*: Dodsley (cited by Van Fossen). Qq read 'sinne', an
   easy misreading for 'fiend'.

After 113. S.D. *the Carters whistling*: Van Fossen, after Bates,
   draws attention to the fact that Carters were famous for their
   whistling. However, these are not professional carters or
   carmen (see IV, iv, 165–6) and their action seems both dramatically meaningless and tactless. I suspect they are taking action

to ward off the devil in view of Anne's speech at ll. 109–13, music being considered efficacious for such a purpose. Compare next note.

125–6. *We . . . again*: Jenkin is presumably thinking of Wendoll as an evil spirit and may be referring to Frankford's pursuing Wendoll with sword drawn (IV, iv, after l. 65). The brandishing of a sword was thought to be a defence against the devil. (That Jenkin was not present is not highly relevant.)

129. *wander like a Cain*: An allusion to Cain's punishment. See Genesis, iv, 12.

SCENE FOUR

1–38. During these lines, by a convention of Elizabethan staging, the opening characters pass from outside Anne's house to her bed-chamber. See 'A Note on Staging', pp. 50–51.

After 38. S.D. *Enter . . . bed*: Typical stage direction in Elizabethan drama. It indicates a discovery or the thrusting out of a bed on to stage. Compare the opening of scene v of *A Yorkshire Tragedy*. See 'A Note of Staging', pp. 50–51.

55. *brother Acton*: Q2. Q1 reads 'maister Frankford'. If Q2's reading is a printing-house emendation of Q1 the correct reading may be 'Master Malby', a reply to the preceding speech. Sir Francis, meanwhile, may not be pressing round the bed with the same concern as the others. He is undergoing a change of mind (see ll. 63–6) if we accept Q2's S.P. for l. 63.

63. S.P. SIR FRANCIS: Q2. Q1 reads 'SIR CHARLES' but see ll. 16–22.

89. *knees*: All editions. I suspect Q1 picked up the word from the next line and the copy text read 'strength' or something equally obvious.

138. *fil'd*: Q1 reads 'fild' (rhyming with 'kild'), Q2 reads 'fill'd' (and 'kill'd'). Van Fossen quotes Spencer's explanation of Q2's reading: 'The engraved letters shall be filled in with gold.' But see *OED* 'file', $v^3 2$: 'to arrange in consecutive order', which seems to suit Frankford's emphasis on the words.

Appendix A   Part of the North Kent coast, from Philip Symonson's *Map of Kent*, 1596.*

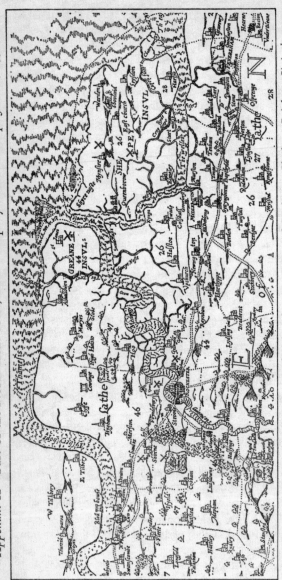

Places mentioned in *Arden* and Holinshed can be found on this map. Gravesend, Rochester, Chatham, Sittingbourne, Shorlow (Shouland), the ferry, Faversham, Ospring (Osyrenge), Preston, and Boughton against Faversham (Borton under Bleane) are on or near the London-Canterbury-Dover road. Arden, Bradshaw and Greene in the play (Arden and Greene in the prose narrative) travel to and from London, by horse between Faversham and Gravesend and by boat between Gravesend and London (see *Arden*, vi, 1-2, 43-4; and Holinshed, pp. 292-4). At the end of the sixteenth century the fare for the river journey was 2d. by barge or 6d. by the more salubrious tilt-boat. Lidsing might be 'Leedes', referred to by Holinshed, p. 292. ('Lydsing' = 'Little Leedes'?) Leeds is about ten miles south of the road and would hardly serve as a good, local direction-finder.

* I am grateful to Miss G. M. Maxted for drawing my attention to this map.

Appendix B.

From Holinshed's Chronicles, 1577, II, 1703–8.

ABOUT this time there was, at Faversham in Kent, a gentleman named Arden most cruelly murdered and slain by the procurement of his own wife. The which murder, for the horribleness thereof (although otherwise it may seem to be but a private matter, and therefore, as it were, impertinent to this history) I have thought good to set it forth somewhat at large, having the instructions delivered to me by them that have used some diligence to gather the true understanding of the circumstances.

This Arden was a man of a tall and comely personage, and matched in marriage with a gentlewoman young, tall, and well-favoured of shape and countenance; who chancing to fall in familiarity with one Mosby (a tailor by occupation, a black, swart man, servant to the Lord North) it happened this Mosby, upon some misliking, to fall out with her. But she, being desirous to be in favour with him again, sent him a pair of silver dice by one Adam Fowle, dwelling at the Flour-de-lys in Faversham. After which he resorted to her again, and oftentimes lay in Arden's house, insomuch that within two years after he obtained such favour at her hands that he lay with her, or, as they term it, kept her, in abusing her body. And although, as it was said, Master Arden perceived right well their mutual familiarity to be much greater than their honesty, yet because he would not offend her and so lose the benefit which he hoped to gain at some of her friends' hands in bearing with her lewdness, which he might have lost if he should have fallen out with her, he was contented to wink at her filthy disorder, and both permitted and also invited Mosby very often to lodge in his house. And thus it continued a good space before any practice was begun by them against Master Arden. She, at length, inflamed in love with Mosby and loathing her husband, wished and after practised the mean how to hasten his end.

There was a painter dwelling in Faversham who had skill of poisons, as was reported. She therefore demanded of him, whether it were true that he had such skill in that feat or not; and he denied not but that he had indeed. 'Yea,' said she, 'but I would have such a one made as should have most vehement and speedy operation to dispatch the eater thereof.' 'That can I do,' quoth he, and forthwith made her such a one, and willed her to put it into the bottom of a porringer, and then after to pour milk upon it; which circumstance she forgetting, did clean contrary, putting in the milk first and afterward the poison.

Now Master Arden purposing that day to ride to Canterbury, his wife brought him his breakfast, which was wont to be milk and butter. He, having received a spoonful or two of the milk, misliked the taste and colour thereof and said to his wife, 'Mistress Alice, what milk have you given me here?' Wherewithal she tilted it over with her hand, saying, 'I ween nothing can please you'. Then he took horse and rode towards Canterbury, and by the way fell into extreme purging upwards and downwards, and so escaped for that time.

After this, his wife fell in acquaintance with one Greene of Faversham, servant to Sir Anthony Ager, from which Greene Master Arden had wrested a piece of ground on the backside of the Abbey of Faversham, and there had blows and great threats passed betwixt them about that matter. Therefore she, knowing that Greene hated her husband, began to practise with him how to make him away, and concluded that if he could get any that would kill him, he should have ten pounds for a reward. This Greene, having doings for his master, Sir Anthony Ager, had occasion to go up to London where his master then lay, and having some charge up with him, desired one Bradshaw, a goldsmith of Faversham that was his neighbour, to accompany him to Gravesend, and he would content him for his pains. This Bradshaw, being a very honest man, was content and rode with him. And when they came to Rainham Down they chanced to see three or four servingmen that were coming from Leeds, and therewith Bradshaw spied coming up the hill from Rochester one Black Will, a terrible cruel ruffian with a sword and a buckler, and another with a great staff on his neck. Then said Bradshaw to Greene, 'We are happy that here cometh some company from Leeds, for here cometh up against us as murdering a knave as any is in England. If it were not for them, we might chance hardly to escape without loss of our money and lives.' 'Yea,' thought Greene (as he after confessed) 'such a one is for my purpose,' and therefore asked, 'Which is he?' 'Yonder is he,' quoth Bradshaw, 'the same that hath the sword and buckler. His name is Black Will.' 'How know you that?' said Greene. Bradshaw answered, 'I knew him at Boulogne where we both served. He was a soldier and I was Sir Richard Cavendish's man. And there he committed many robberies and heinous murders on such as travelled betwixt Boulogne and France.' By this time the other company of servingmen came to them, and they going all together met with Black Will and his fellow. The servingmen knew Black Will, and saluting him demanded of him whither he went. He answered, 'By his blood!' (for his use was to swear almost at every word) 'I know not nor care not, but set up my staff and even as it falleth I go'. 'If thou,' quoth they, 'wilt go back again to Gravesend, we will give thee thy supper.' 'By his blood!' said he, 'I care not; I am content. Have with you.' And so he returned again with them. Then Black Will took acquaintance of Bradshaw saying, 'Fellow Bradshaw, how dost thou?' Bradshaw, unwilling to revive acquaintance or to have ought to do with so shameless a ruffian, said, 'Why, do you know me?' 'Yea, that I do,' quoth he, 'did we not serve in Boulogne together?' 'But ye must pardon me,' quoth Bradshaw, 'for I have forgotten you.' Then Greene talked with Black Will and said, 'When ye have supped, come to my hostess' house at such a sign, and I will give you the sack and sugar'. 'By his blood!' said he, 'I thank you. I will come and take it, I warrant you.' According to his promise he came, and there they made good cheer. Then Black Will and Greene went and talked apart from Bradshaw and there concluded together that if he would kill Master Arden, he should have ten pound for his labour. Then he answered, 'By his wounds! That I will if I may know him'. 'Marry, tomorrow in Paul's I will show him thee,' said Greene. Then they left their talk, and Green bade him go home to his hostess' house.

Then Greene wrote a letter to Mistress Arden, and among other things put in these words: 'We have got a man for our purpose, we may thank my brother Bradshaw'. Now Bradshaw, not knowing anything of this, took the letter of him and in the morning departed home again, and delivered the letter to Mistress Arden. And Greene and Black Will went up to London at the tide.

At the time appointed, Greene showed Black Will Master Arden walking in Paul's. Then said Black Will, 'What is he that goeth after him?' 'Marry,' said Greene, 'one of his men.' 'By his blood!' said Black Will, 'I will kill them both.' 'Nay,' said Greene, 'do not so, for he is of counsel with us in this matter.' 'By his blood!' said he, 'I care not for that. I will kill them both!' 'Nay,' said Greene, 'in any wise do not so.' Then Black Will thought to have killed Master Arden in Paul's Churchyard, but there were so many gentlemen that accompanied him to dinner that he missed of his purpose. Greene showed all this talk to Master Arden's man, whose name was Michael, which ever after stood in doubt of Black Will lest he should kill him. The cause that this Michael conspired with the rest against his master was for that it was determined that he should marry a kinswoman of Mosby's. After this, Master Arden lay at a certain parsonage which he held in London, and therefore his man Michael and Greene agreed, that Black Will should come in the night to the parsonage where he should find the doors left open that he might come in and murder Master Arden. This Michael, having his master to bed, left open the doors according to the appointment. His master, then being in bed, asked him if he had shut fast the doors, and he said 'yea'. But yet afterwards, fearing lest Black Will would kill him as well as his master, after he was in bed himself, he rose again and shut the doors, bolting them fast, so that Black Will, coming thither and finding the doors shut, departed, being disappointed at that time. The next day Black Will came to Greene in a great chafe, swearing and staring because he was so deceived, and with many terrible oaths threatened to kill Master Arden's man first, wheresoever he met him. 'No,' said Greene, 'do not so. I will first know the cause of shutting the doors.' Then Greene met and talked with Arden's man and asked of him why he did not leave open the doors according to his promise. 'Marry,' said Michael, 'I will show you the cause.

My master yesternight did that he never did before, for after I was abed he rose up and shut the doors, and in the morning rated me for leaving them unshut.' And herewith Greene and Black Will were pacified. Arden being ready to go homewards, his maid came to Greene and said, 'This night will my master go down'. Whereupon it was agreed that Black Will should kill him on Rainham Down. When Master Arden came to Rochester his man, still fearing that Black Will would kill him with his master, pricked his horse of purpose and made him to halt, to the end he might protract the time and tarry behind. His master asked him why his horse halted. He said, 'I know not'. 'Well,' quoth his master, 'when ye come at the smith herebefore, between Rochester and the hill-foot over against Cheetham, remove his shoe and search him and then come after me.' So Master Arden rode on, and ere he came at the place where Black Will lay in wait for him there overtook him divers gentlemen of his acquaintance who kept him company; so that Black Will missed here also of his purpose. After that Master Arden was come home, he sent, as he usually did, his man to Sheppey to Sir Thomas Cheiny, then Lord Warden of the cinque ports, about certain business; and at his coming away he had a letter delivered, sent by Sir Thomas Cheiny to his master. When he came home, his mistress took the letter and kept it, willing her man to tell his master that he had a letter delivered him by Sir Thomas Cheiny, and that he had lost it, adding that he thought it best that his master should go the next morning to Sir Thomas because he knew not the matter. He said he would, and therefore he willed his man to be stirring betimes. In this meanwhile, Black Will and one George Shakebag his companion were kept in a store-house of Sir Anthony Ager's at Preston, by Greene's appointment; and thither came Mistress Arden to see him, bringing and sending him meat and drink many times. He, therefore, lurking there and watching some opportunity for his purpose, was willed in any wise to be up early in the morning to lie in wait for Master Arden in a certain broom close betwixt Faversham and the ferry (which close he must needs pass) and there to do his feat. Now Black Will stirred in the morning betimes, but he missed the way and tarried in a wrong place.

Master Arden and his man coming on their way early in the morning towards Shornelan [=Shorlow] where Sir Thomas Cheiny lay, as they were almost come to the broom close, his man, always fearing that Black Will would kill him with his master, feigned that he had lost his purse. 'Why,' said his master, 'thou foolish knave, couldst thou not look to thy purse but lose it? What was in it?' 'Three pound,' said he. 'Why then, go thy ways back again like a knave,' said his master, 'and seek it; for being so early as it is there is no man stirring, and therefore thou mayest be sure to find it; and then come and overtake me at the ferry.' But nevertheless, by reason that Black Will lost his way, Master Arden escaped yet once again. At that time Black Will yet thought he should have been sure to have met him homewards, but whether that some of the Lord Warden's men accompanied him back to Faversham, or that being in doubt, for that it was late, to go through the broomy close, and therefore took another way, Black Will was disappointed then also. But now St Valentine's fair being at hand, the conspirators thought to dispatch their devilish intention at that time. Mosby minded to pick some quarrel to Master Arden at the fair to fight with him, for, he said, he could not find in his heart to murder a gentleman in that sort as his wife wished (although she had made a solemn promise to him and he again to her to be in all points as man and wife together, and thereupon they both received the sacrament one Sunday at London, openly in a church there). But this device to fight with him would not serve, for Master Arden, both then and at other times, had been greatly provoked by Mosby to fight with him but he would not. Now Mosby had a sister that dwelt in a tenement of Master Arden's, near to his house in Faversham, and on the fair even, Black Will was sent for to come thither; and Greene bringing him thither met there with Mistress Arden accompanied with Michael, his man, and one of her maids. There were also Mosby and George Shakebag, and there they devised to have him killed in manner as afterwards he was. But yet Mosby at the first would not agree to that cowardly murdering of him, but in a fury flung away, and went up the Abbey street towards the Flour-de-lys, the house of the afore-mentioned Adam Fowle's, where he did often host. But before he came thither now at this time, a messenger overtook him that was sent from Mistress Arden, desiring him of all loves to come back again to help to accomplish the matter he knew of. Hereupon he returned to her again, and at his coming back she fell down upon her knees to him and besought him to go through with the matter, as if he loved her he would be contented to do; sith, as she had divers times told him, he needed not to doubt, for there was not any that would care for his death nor make any great enquiry for them that should dispatch him. Thus, she being earnest with him, at length he was contented to agree unto that horrible device; and thereupon they conveyed Black Will into Master Arden's house, putting him into a closet at the end of his parlour. Before this they had sent out of the house all the servants, those excepted which were privy to the devised murder. Then went Mosby to the door and there stood in a nightgown of silk girded about him, and this was betwixt six and seven of the clock at night. Master Arden, having been at a neighbour's house of his named Dumpkin, and having cleared certain reckonings betwixt them, came home, and finding Mosby standing at the door asked him if it were suppertime. 'I think not,' quoth Mosby, 'it is not yet ready.' 'Then let us go and play a game at the tables in the mean season,' said Master Arden. And so they went straight into the parlour, and as they came by through the hall, his wife was walking there, and Master Arden said, 'How now, Mistress Alice?' But she made small answer to him. In the meantime, one chained the wicket door of the entry. When they came into the parlour, Mosby sat down on the bench, having his face toward the place where Black Will stood. Then Michael, Master Arden's man, stood at his master's back, holding a candle in his hand to shadow Black Will, that Arden might by no means perceive him coming forth. In their play, Mosby said thus (which seemed to be the watchword for Black Will's coming forth): 'Now may I take you, sir, if I will'. 'Take me?' quoth Master Arden, 'which way?' With that, Black Will stepped forth and cast a towel about his neck so to stop his breath and strangle him. Then Mosby, having at his girdle a pressing iron of 14 pound weight, struck him on the head with the same, so that he fell down and gave a great groan, insomuch that they thought he had been killed. Then they bare him away to lay him in the countinghouse, and as they were about to lay him down, the pangs of death coming on him, he gave a great groan and stretched himself. And then Black Will gave him a great gash in the face and so killed him out of hand, laid him along, took the money out of his purse and the rings from his fingers, and then coming out of the countinghouse said, 'Now this feat is done, give me my money'. So Mistress Arden gave him ten pounds, and he coming to Greene had a horse of him, and so rode his ways. After that Black Will was gone, Mistress Arden came into the countinghouse and with a knife gave him seven or eight pricks into the breast. Then they made clean the parlour, took a clout and wiped where it was bloody, and strewed again the rushes that were shuffled with struggling, and cast the clout with which they wiped the blood and the knife that was bloody, wherewith she had wounded her husband, into a tub by the well's side, where afterward both the same clout and knife were found. Thus this wicked woman, with her 'complices, most shamefully murdered her own husband who most entirely loved her all his life-time. Then she sent for two Londoners to supper, the one named Prune and the other Cole, that were grocers, which before the murder was committed were bidden to supper. When they came she said, 'I marvel where Master Arden is. Well, we will not tarry for him. Come ye and sit down, for he will not be long'. Then Mosby's sister was sent for. She came and sat down, and so they were merry.

After supper, Mistress Arden caused her daughter to play on the virginals; they danced, and she with them, and so seemed to protract time, as it were, till Master Arden should come. And she said, 'I marvel where he is so long. Well, he will come anon I am sure. I pray you in the meanwhile let us play a game at the tables.' But the Londoners said they must go to their hostess' house or else they should be shut out at doors, and so, taking their leave, departed. When they were gone, the servants that were not privy to the murder were sent abroad into the town, some to seek their master and some of other errands, all saving Michael and a maid, Mosby's sister, and one of Mistress Arden's own daughters. Then they took the dead body, and carried it out to lay it in a field next to the churchyard and joining to his garden wall, through the which he went to the church. In the meantime it began to snow, and when they came to the garden-gate, they remembered that they had forgotten the key, and one went in for it, and finding it, at length brought it, opened the gate, and carried the corpse into the same field, as it were ten paces from the garden-gate, and laid him down on his back straight in his nightgown, with his slippers on, and between one of his slippers and his foot a long rush or two remained. When they had thus laid him down, they returned the same way they came through the garden into the house. They being returned thus back again into the house, the doors were opened and the servants returned home that had been sent abroad, and being now very late, she sent forth her folks again to make enquiry for him in divers places, namely among the best in the town where he was wont to be, who made answer that they could tell nothing of him. Then she began to make an outcry and said, 'Never woman had such neighbours as I have,' and herewith wept, insomuch that her neighbours came in and found her making great lamentation, pretending to marvel what was become of her husband. Whereupon the mayor and others came to make search for him. The fair was wont to be kept partly in the town and partly in the Abbey, but Arden, for his own private lucre and covetous gain, had this present year procured it to be wholly kept within the Abbey ground which he had purchased, and so reaping all the gains to himself, and bereaving the town of that portion which was wont to come to the inhabitants, got many a bitter curse. The mayor, going about the fair in this search, at length came to the ground where Arden lay, and as it happened, Prune the grocer getting sight of him first said, 'Stay, for methink I see one lie here'. And so they, looking and beholding the body, found that it was Master Arden lying there thoroughly dead, and viewing diligently the manner of his body and hurts, found the rushes sticking in his slippers, and, marking further, espied certain footsteps, by reason of the snow, betwixt the place where he lay and the garden door. Then the mayor commanded every man to stay, and herewith appointed some to go about and to come in at the inner side of the house through the garden as the way lay, to the place where Master Arden's dead body did lie, who all the way as they came perceived footings still before them in the snow; and so it appeared plainly that he was brought along that way from the house through the garden and so into the field where he lay. Then the mayor and his company that were with him went into the house, and knowing her evil demeanour in times past examined her of the matter. But she defied them and said, 'I would you should know I am no such woman'. Then they examined her servants, and in the examination – by reason of a piece of his hair and blood found near to the house in the way by the which they carried him forth, and likewise by the knife with which she had thrust him into the breast, and the clout wherewith they wiped the blood away which they found in the tub into the which the same were thrown – they all confessed the matter, and herself beholding her husband's blood said, 'Oh, the blood of God help, for this blood have I shed'. Then were they all attached and committed to prison, and the mayor with others presently went to the Flour-de-lys where they found Mosby in bed. And as they came towards him they espied his hose and purse stained with some of Master Arden's blood, and when he asked what they meant by their coming in such sort they said, 'See, here ye may understand wherefore by these tokens,' showing him the blood on his hose and purse. Then he confessed the deed, and so he and all the other that had conspired the murder were apprehended and laid in prison, except Greene, Black Will and the painter, which painter and George Shakebag, that was also fled before, were never heard of. Shortly were the sessions kept at Faversham, where all the prisoners were arraigned and condemned. And thereupon being examined whether they had any other 'complices, Mistress Arden accused Bradshaw upon occasion of the letter sent by Greene from Gravesend (as before ye have heard) which words had none other meaning but only by Bradshaw's describing of Black Will's qualities, Greene judged him a meet instrument for the execution of their pretended murder. Whereunto, notwithstanding (as Greene confessed at his death certain years after) this Bradshaw was never made privy, howbeit, he was upon this accusation of Mistress Arden immediately sent for to the sessions and indicted, and declaration made against him as a procurer of Black Will to kill Master Arden, which proceeded wholly by misunderstanding of the words contained in the letter which he brought from Greene. Then he desired to talk with the persons condemned and his request was granted. He therefore demanded of them if they knew him or ever had any conversation with him, and they all said no. Then the letter being showed and read, he declared the very truth of the matter and upon what occasion he told Greene of Black Will.

Nevertheless, he was condemned and suffered. These condemned persons were diversely executed in sundry places; for Michael, Master Arden's man, was hanged in chains at Faversham, and one of the maids was brent [=burnt] there, pitifully bewailing her case, and cried out on her mistress that had brought her to this end, for the which she would never forgive her. Mosby and his sister were hanged in Smithfield at London. Mistress Arden was burned at Canterbury the 14. of March. Greene came again certain years after, was apprehended, condemned, and hanged in chains in the highway betwixt Ospring and Boughton against Faversham. Black Will was brent on a scaffold at Flushing in Zealand. Adam Fowle that dwelt at the Flour-de-lys in Faversham was brought into trouble about this matter, and carried up to London with his legs bound under the horse belly and committed to prison in the Marshalsea, for that Mosby was heard to say, 'Had it not been for Adam Fowle I had not come to this trouble'; – meaning that the bringing of the silver dice for a token to him from Mistress Arden, as ye have heard, occasioned him to renew familiarity with her again. But when the matter was thoroughly ripped up, and that Mosby had cleared him, protesting that he was never of knowledge in any behalf to the murder, the man's innocency preserved him. This one thing seemeth very strange and notable touching Master Arden, that in the place where he was laid, being dead, all the proportion of his body might be seen two years after and more so plain as could be, for the grass did not grow where his body had touched, but between his legs, between his arms, and about the hollowness of his neck and round about his body, and where his legs, arms, head or any part of his body had touched, no grass growed at all of all that time, so that many strangers came in that meantime, beside the townsmen, to see the print of his body there on the ground in that field; which field he had (as some have reported) cruelly taken from a woman that had been a widow to one Cooke, and after married to one Richard Reede, a mariner, to the great hindrance of her and her husband, the said Reede; for they had long enjoyed it by a lease which they had of it for many years, not then expired. Nevertheless, he got it from them, for the which the said Reede's wife not only exclaimed against him in shedding many a salt tear, but also cursed him most bitterly even to his face, wishing many a vengeance to light upon him and that all the world might wonder on him. Which was thought then to come to pass when he was thus murdered and lay in that field from midnight till the morning, and so all that day, being the fair day till night; all the which day there were many hundreds of people came wondering about him. And thus far touching this horrible and heinous murder of Master Arden.

Appendix C.

From *Two Unnatural Murders*, 1605.*

Master Calverley's unnatural and bloody murder, practised upon his wife and committed upon his children.

There hath happened of late within the county of York, not far from Wakefield, a murder so detestable, that were it not it desires record for example sake, humanity could wish it rather utterly forgot, than any Christian heart should tremble with the remembrance of it.

Within this county was bred a gentleman, one Master Calverley of Calverley, a man whose parents were such, as left him seven or eight hundred pound a year to enrich his hopes, cherish his content, and make him fortunate. His father dying before he had reached the years of privilege, during his nonage he was ward to a most noble and worthy gentleman in this land, in all which time his course of life did promise so much good that there was a commendable gravity appeared even in his youth. He being of this hope, virtuous in his life and worthy by his birth, was sought unto by many gallant gentlemen, and desired that he would unite his fortune into their families, by matching himself to one and the chief of their daughters.

Among which number it happened, being once invited for such a purpose – a welcome guest – to an ancient gentleman of chief note in his country, he came, where in short time was such an interchangeable affection, shot in by two pair of eyes to one pair of hearts, that this gentleman's best beloved daughter was by private assurance made Master Calverley's best beloved wife. Nor could it be kept so close between the pair of lovers (for love will discover itself in loving looks) but it came to the father's knowledge, who with a natural joy was contented with the contract. Yet in regard Master Calverley's years could not discharge the charge his honourable guardian had over him, the father thought it meet (though the lovers could have wished it

* Throughout the account Calverley's name is spelt 'Caverly' or 'Caverley'.

otherways) to lengthen their desired haste till time should finish [sic; = ?furnish] a fit hour to solemnize their happy wedlock. Master Calverley having spent some time there in decent recreation, much abroad and more at home with his new mistress, at last he bethought himself that his long stay made him looked for at London. And having published his intended departure, the father thought it convenient, though the virtuous gentlewoman danced a loth-to-depart upon his contracted lips. Master Calverley came to London; and whether concealing his late contract from his honourable guardian, or forgetting his private and public vows, or both – I know not – but time, mother of alterations, had not fanned over many days, but he had made a new bargain, knit a new marriage knot, and was husband by all matrimonial rites to a courteous gentlewoman, and near by marriage to that honourable personage to whom he was ward.

Rumour with his thousand tongues and ten thousand feet was not long in travel before he had delivered this distasted message to his first mistress' ears, who looking for a more lovely commendations [sic] and having heard but part of that, such as truly it was, the wind of her sighs had so raised up the tide of her tears that she clipped the report, ere it could be told out, into many pieces. And as she would still fain have asked this question: 'Is it so indeed?' she was fain to make up her distracted syllables with the letters of her eyes. This gentlewoman, Master Calverley's wife (if vows may make a wife) took, with an inward consideration, so to heart this unjust wrong, that exercising her hours only in continual sorrow she brought herself to a consumption; who so played the insulting tyrant over her unblemished beauty that the civil contention dwelt in ['her,' omitted?] face of white and red was turned to a death-like paleness, and all her arteries, wherein the spirit of life mixed with blood doth run, like giddy subjects in the empire of her body, greedy of innovation, took such ungentle part with this foreign usurper that where health before was her peaceable sovereign, now distracted sickness and feeble weakness were her untimely conquerors. Yet under this yoke of grief, she so patiently endured that though she had great reason, a foundation whereon she might have built arguments to have cursed his proceedings, and where others would have contrasted [? contracted] syllables both of reproach and reproof against him, she only married these letters together: 'I entreat of God to grant both prosperous health and fruitful wealth to him and his, though I am sick for his sake'.

But to Master Calverley, who having finished this wrong to this gentlewoman and begun too much distress to her that he married (as too soon appeared) for though the former, conquered by the gentleness of her nature, forgave his fault, yet revenge being always in God's hand, thus it fell.

This gentleman had not lived many months with his wife but he was so altered in disposition from that which he was, and so short from the perfection which he had, as a body dying is of a life flourishing; and where before his thoughts only studied the relish of virtue and her effects, his actions did now altogether practise the unprofitable taste of vice and her fruits. For though he were a man of so good revenue as before, he continued his expense in such exceeding riot that he was forced to mortgage his lands, run in great debts, entangle his friends by being bound for him, and in short time so weakened his estate that, having not wherewithal to carry that port which before he did, he grew into a discontent which so swayed in him he would sit sullenly, walk melancholy, bethinking continually, and, with steady looks nailed to the ground, seem astonished, that when his wife would come to desire the cause of his sadness, and entreat to be a willing partner in his sorrow – for

> Consortium rerum omnium inter nos
> Facit amicitia –

he would either sit still without giving her an answer, or rising up, depart from her with these words: 'A plague on thee! Thou art the cause of my sadness'. The gentlewoman, which without question this report is true of, never so much as in thought offended him, and having been sundry times cursed without cause once came to him and making her tears parley with her words she thus entreated him: 'Sir, Master Calverley, I beseech you by the mutual league of love which should be betwixt us, by the vows we made together both before and at our marriage, and by that God that registers our thoughts, tell me what I have done, the remembrance of which should afflict you, or what I may do that might content you. As you desire the three lovely boys you have been father unto should grow up and make your name live in your country, acquaint me with your griefs, and what a wife can show to manifest her love to her husband shall be perfected in me.' Master Calverley, fixing himself with a steady eye on her, at last delivered this: 'I now want money, and thou must help me'.

'Oh Master Calverley,' quoth she, 'though God and yourself know I am no cause of your want, yet what I have to supply you, either in jewels or rings, I pray you take; and I beseech you, as you are a gentleman, and by the love you should bear to your children, although you care not for me, look back a little into your estate and restrain this great flood of your expense before your house be utterly overthrown. You know, sir,' quoth she, 'your land is mortgaged already, yourself otherwise greatly in debt, some friends of yours that are bound for you like to be undone.' But as she would have gone forward, he cut her off with these words: 'Base strumpet, whom though I married I never loved, shall my pleasure be confined by your will? If you and your bastards be in want, either beg, or retire to your friends. My humour shall have the ancient scope. Thy rings and jewels I will sell, and as voluntary spend them as when I was in the best of my estate.' The good gentlewoman's eyes being drawn full of water with these words made him no other reply but this: 'Sir, your will be done'. But he fled on in this vehemency of blood: 'I protest by Heaven, I will ever hereafter loathe thee and never lie with thee, till thou give thy consent thy dowry shall be sold to maintain my pleasure, and leave thyself and children destitute of maintenance'. 'Sir', answered she, 'in all this I will be a wife. What in all this the law will allow me to do you shall command.' 'See thou dost it,' quoth he, 'for no longer than I am full of money shalt thou partake from me a taste of kindness.'

Mistress Calverley, going forward with this intent to sell away her dowry, was sent for up to London by that honourable friend whose niece she was and whose ward he had been, who, having heard of her husband's prodigal course, at her coming up began to question her about her estate and whether he bore himself as a husband should do in familiar love to her. The gentlewoman, though she knew how desperate his estate was and her tongue could too well have told his unkindness, she answered both thus: 'For my husband's estate, I make no doubt but it is in the same height his father left it to him; but for our love one to another, I am assured, and I praise God for it, we live like Abraham and Sarah, he loving to me, I obedient to him'.

'Howsoever,' answered this honourable friend, 'your words are an ornament a good wife should have and you seek to shadow the blemishes his actions have cast upon his life, let this suffice you: I know of his prodigal course; I know how his land is all, or the most part of it mortgaged, himself in debt to many. Yet censuring these infirmities to proceed of no other cause but from the rash heat of youth, which will in time no doubt be suppressed by experience; and for that I believe your words be true and am glad to hear of his kindness toward you, I will take such order for him as he shall continue still Master Calverley, in the same degree or better than e'er his ancestors were in Yorkshire, and at your return to [sic] certify him withal that he hasten up to court. Nor let the fear of his creditors abridge his coming up, for I will protect him both from them and also provide some place in court for him; wherein he shall find I am his honourable kinsman.'

The good gentlewoman was so struck with joy at this comfortable promise that she was scarce able to speak out her dutiful thanks. And thinking her husband would be satisfied with this preferment, hoping that kindness would be contracted again betwixt them, and assuring herself there would be now no need to make sale of her dowry (for that was also a part of her business), having taken leave of her honourable kinsmen she returned toward Calverley.

During this her absence, Master Calverley maintained his accustomed habit and indeed grew from bad to worse. For mischief is of that nature, that it cannot stand but by strengthening of one evil with another, and so multiply in itself until it come unto the highest and then falls with his own weight. So Master Calverley, being given to excess rioting as dicing, drinking, revelling, and, it is thought, etc. [=whoring], fed one evil with another and in such continual use that his body was not in temper without the exercise of sin; for who knows not *sine Cerere & Baccho friget Venus?* So, without money pleasure will hardly be maintained.

And this gentleman, having now made wrack of his estate and finding himself not able to maintain his pleasure when his desire was as great as before (for pleasure being once delightful unto the memory is as hard to be resisted as madness), first he fell into a hatred with his wife, and in this her absence to such a loathing of his children that in what company soever he had happened he could not contain his rage but would openly proclaim his wife was a strumpet, his children were bastards; and although their marriage was made by honourable personages, herself nobly descended, from the first hour he embraced her to that very minute he did loathe her. Some would mildly persuade him from this frenzy; others would courteously reprove him, saying it was not fit; and all whose modesty thought it unmeet to meddle betwixt man and wife, knowing her virtuous life, did utterly condemn him.

But he continued this publication in all places where he came, and at one among the number, there happened a gentleman to be who, having known the discreetness of his wife from her very cradle, and hearing him so wild in his abuses, prepared himself confidently to correct him. And having begun his speech of chastisement, the other not enduring to be detected, both being soon inflamed fell to quarrelous terms, and in such heat that Master Calverley did not spare to say that he might well be his wife's friend for aught that he knew; nay, there was great presumption for it since he so easily should be stirred up in his wife's excuse. The gentleman, not enduring to hear her reputation but especially his own to be touched, so answered Master Calverley and again Master Calverley him, that they both agreed to purge themselves in the field. Both met, and after some thrusts changed between them Master Calverley was hurt. Yet would he not give over, so that after he became at the gentleman's mercy. But he, of that humane condition not to desire his life, nor so much blood as was had he not been urged, bade him rise and left him with these words: 'Master Calverley, you are a gentleman of an ancient house; there hath been much good expected from you. Deceive not men's hopes. You have a virtuous wife; be kind to her. I forget my wrong and continue your friend'.

But Master Calverley, unsatisfied with this, his heart flew to his mouth as it would have leapt out after him for revenge; yet knowing he could get little by following him but hurts such as he had already, prepared to turn his wrath another way. Then looking upon his wounds and seeing them bleed, said to himself, 'Strumpet, thou art the cause that I bleed now, but I will be the cause that thou shalt bleed hereafter'. So taking his horse, rode presently home, where, before his wounds were thoroughly cured, his wife was come from London; and the first greeting was [sic] given her by her husband, was: 'What? Hast thou brought the money? Is the land sold?' She answered, 'Sir, I hope I have made a journey shall redound both to your comfort and mine'. So, acquainting him with the precedency, which was his promised preferment by her kinsman, and expecting a loving acceptance, the first thanks he gave her was a spurn. And looking upon her as if his eyes would have shot fire into her face: 'Have you been at London to make your complaint of me, you damnable strumpet,' quoth he, 'that the greatness of your friends might oversway the weakness of my estate? And I that have lived in that rank of will which I have done, that freedom of pleasure, should forsake it now? Shall I, being a Calverley of Calverley, stoop my thoughts so low to attend on the countenance of your alliance, to order my life by their direction, and neither do nor undo anything but what they list? Which if I refuse to do, your complaints have so wrought with them, and you have so possessed them of my estate, they will enforce me forsooth for your good and the good of my children. Was this your trick to save your dowry, the which I swore you should sell? Was this your going to London?'

The good gentlewoman, being almost blown to death with this vehemency of his wrath, fell at his feet and desired him to hear her, when (poor soul) she was so full of grief she had not the power to speak. Yet, having eased the way with a few of sorrow's drops, she began to plead this true excuse to him, that like one had lost all his senses had scarce patience to hear: 'Sir,' said she, 'God knows the words I speak have no fashion of untruth. My friends are fully possessed your land is mortgaged; they know to whom and for what. But not by me, I beseech you believe. And for any difference betwixt yourself and me, which I doubt would offend more than the mortgaging of your land, I protest yet there is no occasion of suspect. If you think I have published anything to him with desire to keep the sale of my dowry from you, either for mine own good or my children's (though it fits I should have a motherly care of them), you being my husband, pass it away how you please, spend it how you will, so I may enjoy but welcome looks and kind words from you. And when all which you call yours is gone, ere you or yours shall want, I will work for your maintenance. Neither of which extremities, sir, need [sic], if you please, if you will but accept preferment in England's court, being offered you *gratis*, which many men would purchase with cost and cannot compass it'.

At which words, though thus mildly uttered and on her humble knees, he was so without cause enraged, that had not one of his men come up in the instant, and told him there was a gentleman from one of the universities stayed to speak with him, he had offered her present violence.

Master Calverley went down to talk with this gentleman, leaving his wife stuffed with grief up to the eye-lids; and she, good soul, having eased her heart with a long-fetched sigh or two, laid her down upon her bed, where in her careful slumbers we will leave her and attend the conference between Master Calverley and this gentleman.

Master Calverley had a second brother, who at this present was of good standing in the university, who upon some extremity Master Calverley was in (for so he would plead himself to be to his friends when he would have them bound for him) had passed his bond with his brother for a thousand pound. This bond was by Master Calverley forfeited; and this young gentleman, being reputed of staid government, the execution was served upon him, and he at this instant prisoner for his brother's debt.

About this business came this gentleman to Master Calverley, who being master of the college wherein his brother had his

instruction and having ever noted his forward will to the exercise of virtue, in pity of his estate, being moved thereunto by the
young student, came purposely thither; who without long circumstance told Master Calverley that the cause of his coming
was to stir up his conscience to have regard of his brother, for he
heard he was careless; and, indeed, dealt so sharply and forcibly,
in laying open to him what scandal the world would throw upon
him, what judgement by God should fall upon him, for suffering
his brother to spend the glory of his youth, which is the time
young men of hope should seek for preferment, in prison by his
means; and did so harrow up his soul with his invincible arguments, that in that minute he made him look back into the error
of his life, which scarce ever in his life he had done before this
instant.

The gentleman, having spoke his mind, asketh him what he
meant to do with his brother, for he now waited his answer.
Master Calverley made him this mild reply: 'Sir, I thank you,
both for your pains and good instructions to me in my brother's
behalf. And I must confess I have done him much wrong'. So
calling for a cup of beer, drank to him and bade him welcome.
'Now, sir,' quoth Master Calverley, 'if you please but to walk
down and see the grounds about my house, one of my men shall
go along with you. At your return I will give so sufficient answer
that my brother by you shall be satisfied, and he a prisoner but
few hours.' The gentleman thanked him, and told him, in
performing that natural office he should both glorify God, satisfy
the world, and he himself account his pains profitable.

This stranger is gone to walk with one of Master Calverley's
men to over-view his ground, and Master Calverley retires
himself into a gallery, where, being alone, he presently fell into
a deep consideration of his state, how his prodigal course of life
had wronged his brother, abused his wife, and undone his
children. Then was presented before the eyes of his imagination
the wealth his father left him, and the misery he should leave his
children in. Then he saw what an unnatural part it was, his brother
to lie in prison for his debt, and he not able to deliver him. Then
he saw that his wife being nobly descended, unless her own friends
took pity upon her, should with his children be driven to beg

remorse of the world, which is composed all of flint. Then saw he the extirpation of his family, the ruin of his ancient house, which hundreds of years together had been gentlemen of the best reputation in Yorkshire. And every one of these, out of their several objects, did create a several distraction in him. Sometimes he would tear his hair; by and by the tears would flush into his eyes; straight break out into this exclamation: 'Oh, I am the most wretched man that ever mother received the seed of! Oh, would I had been slain in my [sic] womb, and that my mother had been my sepulchre! I have begot my children to eat their bread in bitterness, made a wife to be nothing but lamentation, and a brother to die in care'. And as he was thus tormented in the remembrance of his own folly, his eldest son, being a child of four years old, came into the gallery to scourge his top; and, seeing his father stand in a study, looked prettily up to him, saying, 'How do you, father?' Which lovely look and gentle question of the child raised again the remembrance of the distress that he should leave him in. And as the sea, being hurled into hideous billows by the fury of the wind, hideth both Heaven and earth from the eye of man; so he being overwhelmed by the violence of his passion, all natural love was forgot in his remembrance; caught his child up by the neck, and striking at him with his dagger, the child lent him such a look, would have driven a hand, seven years prentice unto murder, to an ague. Yet he - oh, would it had never been done, it might never have been told! - though his arm seemed twice to remember him of the monstrousness of the fact, he struck the lovely infant into the head. And holding the bleeding child at his arm's length, that the blood might not sprinkle his clothes which had stained his heart and honour, he so carried it into a near chamber, where his wife lay asleep upon a bed, and the maid was dressing another child by the fire. (Here is to be noted, his third was at nurse abroad.) But the woman, seeing him come in in that cruel sort – his child in one hand, his reeking dagger in the other; the child bleeding, he staring – started from the fire, and with the child in her arms cried out. But he, letting go the boy he had wounded, caught violently the other out of her arms, and this chamber door being at the top of a high pair of stairs, carried her forth by main strength, and threw the poor woman down to the bottom, who in tender pity by precedent of the one would have preserved the other. The child that was wounded was all this while crying in the chamber and with his woeful noise waked as woeful a mother, who, seeing one child bleeding, the other lie on the ground (for he had laid the younger down while he strove to throw the maid downstairs), she caught up the youngest, and going to take the elder which was going toward the door, her husband, coming back, met her and came to struggle with her for the child which she sought to preserve – with words, tears, and all what a mother could do – from so tragical an end. And when he saw he could not get it from her, most remorseless, stabbed at it some three or four times, all which she saved the child from by taking it on herself. And having a pair of whale-bone bodice on, it pleased God his dagger so glanced on them that she had yet but one wound in the shoulder. But he, more cruel by this resistance, caught fast hold upon the child and in the mother's arms stabbed it to the heart. And after giving his wife two or three mortal wounds she fell backward, and the child dead at her feet. The maid that was thrown down the stairs by him, with the greatness of the fall, the stairs being high, lay for dead at the bottom. The noise of this had brought the servants (not knowing of that which was more tyrannous) to help the maid, thinking she had fell by mischance, and did their best to comfort her beneath, while the father and the mother were striving, one to preserve the infant, the other to kill it. The child which was first wounded sought to get to the door, and having recovered the top of the stairs, by expense of blood and the greatness of the wound, having nobody to comfort it, fell also downstairs, that the arms of the servants helping the maid at the stair foot were fain to let her go to receive him. Some caught up the dead infant, some helped at the maid; all, amazed at this tragic alteration, knew not what to think. Yet one of the men, more hardy than the rest, ran up and met his master in the chamber where he saw his mistress lie on the ground and her dead child at her feet. And saying to him, 'Oh Sir, what have you done?'–'That which I repent not, knave,' answered he; and having still his dagger in his hand came to stab at him. But the fellow seeking to save himself as also to attach his master, they both fell to struggling. Master Calverley, which was known before a man of weak constitution, was in the strife too hard for the fellow who was reputed of a very able body; and in the wrestling together did so tear him with the rowels of his spurs, both on the face and legs, that there he left him not being able to follow him. Master Calverley went downstairs and presently took toward the stable. By the way he met the gentleman who before was walking to view his grounds, who, wondering to see him in such a heat, asked, 'What ail you, sir?' He answered, 'No great matter; but sir, I will resolve you within, where I have taken order for my brother's business'. So the gentleman walked in, and Master Calverley hasted to the stable, where finding a gelding ready saddled, backed him and fled away presently. The gentleman coming in was entertained with outcries and shrieks, the mother for the children (for by this time she was almost recovered), the menservants at this doleful mischance, and all lamenting a father should be so unnatural. The gentleman, doubting that which was of Master Calverley's escape, left all the house making elegies of sorrow, and betook himself to his pursuit, and having forthwith raised the town and heard which way he rode, followed him with the swiftest haste. Master Calverley again being well horsed spurred as fast as they, not earnest to escape but thirsty after more blood. For having an infant of half a year old at nurse some twelve mile off, he, pricked by his preposterous fate, had a desire to root out all his own generation; and only intending to murder it, was careless what became of himself. He rode hard for an act of sin, and they pursued for the execution of justice. But God, that ordereth the life of a wren, hath then a care of his reasonable creatures; and though Cain was suffered to kill his brother Abel, God bound him not to destroy himself. So for Master Calverley, though God permitted the sun to blush at his unnatural acts, yet he suffered him not escape without his revenge. For when he was at the town's end, within a bow-shot where his child sucked that he came to murder, and his heart had made sharp the knife to cut his own infant's throat – oh God, how just thou art! – his horse that flew with him from his former tragedies, as appointed by God to tie him from any more guilt and to preserve the infant's life, in a plain ground where there was scarce a pebble to resist his haste, the horse fell down and Master Calverley under him. The horse got up, and breaking from the hold his master had to stay him, ran violently toward the town, leaving Master Calverley not able to stir from thence, where he was soon overtaken by the pursuit; and indeed seized on by those did both lament his fall and pity his folly. From thence he was carried to a worshipful gentleman's, one Sir John Savile, who, having heard the tempest of this evil and knowing from what ancestors he was descended, did bewail his fate. Yet being in the place of justice, he was enforced to ask him the cause that had made him so monstrous. He, being like a strumpet made impudent by her continuance in sin, made this answer: 'I have done that, sir, I rejoice at, and repent this, that I had not killed the other. I had brought them to beggary and am resolved I could not have pleased God better than by freeing them from it'. 'Oh sir,' answered that worshipful knight, 'you have done so much that when you shall yourself but think upon the terror of death, the remembrance of this will make you wish you had never been born.' But his heart being for that instant hardened, was from thence committed to one Master Key's house, a gaol but lately built up in Wakefield, for at this time the infection of the plague was violent in York.

The way to Wakefield from Sir John Savile's lay direct by Master Calverley's house, against which, when he came, he entreated of the multitude that were his conduct he might speak with his wife before he came to prison, who, he heard, was alive though in great danger. That liberty was granted him. The distressed gentlewoman, when she saw him, forgot both her own wounds and the death of her two children, and did as lovingly kiss him and tenderly embrace him as he had never done her wrong. Which strange kindness so struck to his heart, remembering the misery he had heaped on her, that, embracing one another, there was so pitiful lamentation between them that had flint had ears it would have melted into water. And could either words or tears have persuaded his keepers to have left him in her arms, she, Mistress Calverley, before the blood was washed off from her clothes which he pierced out of her and her infants' bodies, gave occasion, [sic] would have altered them. But here they were divorced, she unable to rise to follow him, and he enforced to leave her. And by the way he should pass from his house the grave chamber of his ancestors, which he never should see again. Even on the threshold lay his two children to take their farewell with bleeding tongues, which when he beheld his eyes were scarce able to bear up their covers. Nor was he distracted with the sight, but all like a pillar of salt; and the remembrance of their lively shape reflected such a natural heat upon him, that he was melted into water and had not power to take any farewell of them but only in tears.

He was not long before he came to Key's house. He was not long there, but the memory of his children sat in his eyes, so that for the one he repented all the day, and for the other lamented all the night. Nor can the pen of the divinest poet express half the grief in words that he conceives in heart. For whereas before he told Sir John Savile he was glad he had rid the world of beggars, he now employs his hours in these words: 'I would I had those beggars, either I to beg with them, or they to ask Heaven's alms for me'.

FINIS

EXAMINATION OF CALVERLEY BY
SIR JOHN SAVILE, MAGISTRATE,
DATED 24 APRIL 1605*

Being examined whether he did kill two of his own children, the name of the one thereof was William and the other Walter, saith, that he did kill them both at his own house in Calverley yesterday, being the 23rd. of April aforesaid. Being further examined what moved him to wound his wife yesterday, to that he said, that one Carver coming into the chamber where he was with his said wife, he commanded her to will the said Carver to go and fetch another son of his, whose name is Henry Calverley, who was nursed by the said Carver's wife, which she accordingly did; whereupon the said Carver went down into the court, and stayed there about a quarter of an hour, and returned again, but brought not the said child with him; and being commanded to go down again, he refused so to do, and that therefore he did wound his wife if she be wounded. And being further examined whether at any time he had any intention to kill his said children, to that he said, that he hath had an intention to kill them for the whole space of two years past, and the reasons that moved him thereunto was, for that his said wife had many times theretofore uttered speeches and given signs and tokens unto him, whereby he might easily perceive and conjecture, that the said children were not by him begotten, and that he hath found himself to be in danger of his life sundry times by his wife.

WALTER CALVERLEY
Capt' Coram JOHN SAVILE
THO. BLAND

*Printed by T. D. Whitaker, *Loidis and Elmete*, 1816, p. 228. Steevens, in Malone's edition of the play, records an oral tradition in Yorkshire: 'Mr Calverley is represented to have been of a passionate disposition, and to have struck one of his children in the presence of his wife, who pertly told him to correct children of his own when he could produce any. On this single provocation

POSTSCRIPT

Philippa Calverley, the injured wife, later remarried, to Sir Thomas Burton of Leicester. The surviving son, Henry, lived on at Calverley Hall till his death in 1661. Calverley Hall still stands, divided now into several houses.

———————

he is said to have immediately committed all the bloody facts that furnish matter for the tragedy before us'.

MORE ABOUT PENGUINS, PELICANS
AND PUFFINS

For further information about books available from Penguins please write to Dept EP, Penguin Books Ltd, Harmondsworth, Middlesex UB7 0DA.

In the U.S.A.: For a complete list of books available from Penguins in the United States write to Dept DG, Penguin Books, 299 Murray Hill Parkway, East Rutherford, New Jersey 07073.

In Canada: For a complete list of books available from Penguins in Canada write to Penguin Books Canada Ltd, 2801 John Street, Markham, Ontario L3R 1B4.

In Australia: For a complete list of books available from Penguins in Australia write to the Marketing Department, Penguin Books Australia Ltd, P.O. Box 257, Ringwood, Victoria 3134.

In New Zealand: For a complete list of books available from Penguins in New Zealand write to the Marketing Department, Penguin Books (N.Z.) Ltd, Private Bag, Takapuna, Auckland 9.

In India: For a complete list of books available from Penguins in India write to Penguin Overseas Ltd, 706 Eros Apartments, 56 Nehru Place, New Delhi 110019.